Jules:
Hope you enjoy
Kimberly

Comfort Foods

~ A Novel by Kimberly Fish ~

Comfort Foods

Published by Fish Tales
Fish Tales Publishing
303 W. Loop 281 STE 110
PMB 316
Longview, Texas 75605

Cover Design: Holly Forbes, Forbes and Butler Graphics
Photo Credit: Bryan Boyd
Formatted by Enterprise Book Services, LLC

ISBN—9781732338661

Other books by Kimberly Fish

Comfort Songs
Comfort Plans
Emeralds Mark the Spot
The Big Inch
Harmon General

Praise for Kimberly Fish's novel *Comfort Songs*, Blogger's Choice Awards 2019 Best Texas Book and Best Romance:

"A satisfying romance for gardeners and music lovers alike." -Kirkus Reviews

"When I read books, my brain tends to turn the story into a cinematic experience. *Comfort Songs* by Kimberly Fish very easily converted into a movie in my mind because of its vivid imagery (and lovely smells!) and natural dialogue. I wasn't surprised to read that several of the characters from the companion book, *Comfort Plans*, reappear in this novel. Fish obviously has a clear picture of each character and effortlessly translates that image onto the page so that we can see it as well." -Lorilei Gonzales, book reviewer

"Kimberly! Kimberly! Here I go again, I am crying. Another book that had me in tears by the end. I am not complaining in the least." -Christena Stephens, book reviewer

"This book has so much going for it from dramatic scenes to those that will make you laugh. And then the ending … you'll have to read the book to see how it turns out!" -- Leslie Storey, book reviewer

"*Comfort Songs* is a wonderful story! Kimberly Fish is a seasoned professional when it comes to crafting stories that cling to your heart yet provide enough action (and other stuff) to keep all readers interested and entertained. With that mindset, I can say this novel did not disappoint me." -- Michael O'Connor, book reviewer

Praise for Fish's WWII historical fiction *The Big Inch*:

"With an eye for detail, Kimberly Fish weaves a compelling story of a war widow who finds herself in Longview, Texas, in 1942. Reading Kimberly's novel was a bit like going back to a cloak-and-dagger time, and I enjoyed the local references. Longview was an amazing place to be during WWII." --Van Craddock, *Longview News-Journal*

"Kimberly Fish has a gift for combining conflict, emotion, and characterization to create a compelling story. Readers will enjoy her books from start to finish." --Louise M. Gouge, author of Love Inspired Historical/Four Stones Ranch series

"If you enjoy suspenseful stories infused with historical facts and intrigue, then this is one novel you won't want to miss." -Susan Sewell, Reader's Favorite book reviews

Readers,

If you're a fan of second chances, small towns, families, and characters discovering their grit then find a comfy chair and dive into these pages. *Comfort Foods* is the third full-length novel I've set in the Hill Country community of Comfort, Texas, and though I take liberty with fictional characters and their environments, the rugged, hills are real. I'm grateful for residents of Comfort who've shown hospitality over the years and welcome me back with my books.

To read the backstory on these novels, buy the books, and receive the free e-book that began the series, *Emeralds Mark the Spot,* visit kimberlyfish.com. Like the characters in this novel, I post to social media. You can follow me on Instagram at fish_writer or on Facebook at Kimberly Fish, author. On Pinterest, I create inspiration boards for the stories, so consider yourself invited to peek around and see what helped craft these stories.

An element of this story deals with the issue of human trafficking. I respect Dr. Claire Renzetti's expertise in this matter and appreciated her willingness to consult on the details. A huge debt of gratitude goes to Zonta International for their effort to educate and bring awareness to those of us oblivious to human exploitation.

These past months, I've had so much fun thinking about food and imagining great meals, all for research, of course, that I plan to include some of the recipes to the back pages of this novel. Big thanks to Nan and Chris Tomboni of Tomboni's Bistro for reading an early draft of the manuscript to make sure I gave credibility to the hardworking folks in a restaurant's "front and back of the house." The real fun of being in the kitchen, for me, is cooking with my husband, son, and daughter, on those weekends we're all together, and the laughter that inevitably follows. Hope you, too, get pleasure from enjoying comfort foods with those you love.

Thanks for choosing this book and reading through the pages,

Kimberly

To my brother Jay who has long thought he'd make a great character for a novel.

"When someone cooks for you, they are saying something. They are telling you about themselves; where they come from, who they are, and what makes them happy." —Anthony Bourdain

Comfort Foods

~ A Novel by Kimberly Fish ~

Prologue

Lacy Cavanaugh twirled a goblet between her hands and listened as an attorney deconstructed her world. She'd have preferred this moment to have never occurred, but some place more private would at least allow her to cry, scream at the injustice, maybe even kick something to release the strain of having to endure surgery on her character; but no, when the tap pouring unbelievable goodness dried up, the resulting hiss happened in one of Dallas' finest restaurants.

Clinking silverware and noise from a distant kitchen provided an undertone to the bossa nova tunes drifting over the heads of diners, but none of that detracted from the man's Texas accent rolling syllables over her despair. Every word sliced off a layer of her life, and she doubted he knew the shambles this left.

"You're not eating." Christopher Woodley waved away the server and picked up his knife. "Which is unfortunate because this beef lives up to the chef's reputation."

True to habit, she'd investigated social media regarding City Café the moment she'd heard Woodley wanted to celebrate the legal compromise. The photos needed a food stylist, but she'd guessed that when customers paid this much for a meal, they didn't worry about marketing.

"I'm not hungry." Glancing at her plate, the scallops floated like islands in a bay of wine sauce. Normally, she'd dive in, savoring every bite, relentlessly greedy when presented with well-cooked food. Grilled polenta acted as the mainland in the dish, with stalks of parsley and sprinkles of paprika giving color. The presentation nudged her to snap a photo, but her phone with the photoshop apps had been confiscated during mediation, and she doubted the flip phone she'd received in exchange even had a camera. She'd not bothered looking.

"You should, at least, eat something. It's a long drive in the morning."

Gritting her molars, she said, "I know the way to Comfort."

"Stubborn." He slid the knife through the oven-roasted tenderloin. "I'll add that to the qualities I've discovered about you."

"You're keeping a list?"

He picked up his glass. "To represent your best interests and prepare you to survive this hiccup, I needed to know your behaviors."

When Christopher Woodley first approached her, he had raved about her beauty, insisting that she'd be forgiven because her followers saw her as living their rags-to-riches dream. Once he found out how uncooperative she could be, he'd focused on her personality.

"My behaviors?"

"Well, isn't that why your brother-in-law called me? To rescue you from yourself?"

She had no idea why Jake Hamilton had called this man. If she had to guess, it was because the law firm's website listed that he once represented an heiress who'd created an international incident. The difference being that Lacy was not an heiress.

In her brief dance with celebrity, she'd acquired advertisers who wanted exposure on her social-media accounts, and, the last time she'd checked, she'd collected over three million followers on Instagram and YouTube. With the advertising income, she'd rented an apartment at the W, indulged an expensive Highland Park fashion bug, hired a virtual assistant, and bought a car worthy of a country-music fashionista. She'd opted out of traveling with the band about a million followers ago.

Woodley nudged the basket of rolls toward her. "What will people do if they can't peek into the world of the Blonde Goddess?"

Bristling as she always did when people taunted her DNA, she blinked away the countless photos featuring the looks that won her a Miss Texas crown. "That was my nickname in the band, not my social-media tagline."

Ire wrestled with disgrace, and she'd march out of the restaurant if she didn't need her attorney to explain the details of the legal agreement she'd signed this afternoon. Pinching a piece of bread, she nibbled on the sourdough, hoping an ulcer wouldn't erupt.

Woodley savored his wine. "Well, Blonde Goddess or not, you're a has-been. And you'd better stay that way too. The Marsh family will watch you like hawks. One iota of smear and they'll charge in with a full slander suit, instead of this mediated effort. Killing off your income stream satisfied them as a penalty, but I can't promise they won't return with stronger measures if they think you're taunting Amy on social media again. If you invent some alias, they will discover it. Amy's father is in the IT business."

Another wave of shame rolled in, and waterworks popped from her eyes. She'd seen none of this coming and couldn't explain how unfair it all was without sounding like a child. The guys she'd thought were lifelong friends had turned on her as the role of lifestyle influencer outgrew her position as a member of a red-dirt band from the Hill Country. When her video camera focused on Amy Marsh, lead singer and new fan-favorite on *America's Got Talent,* Lacy's life turned to dust in an instant.

There was a $3000 Neiman Marcus bill on her desk. How in the world was she going to meet her minimum? Remembering a friend's story, she guessed she could apply to shine boots at Country 2000. Tip money might cover a payment.

Lacy wiped her lips with the napkin. "You had mentioned there was a silver lining?"

A question mark hovered over his gaze.

Swallowing her humiliations, she said, "Today, as we walked to the car, you mentioned that, though I'll never be taken seriously by anyone ever again, you had something positive to offer."

Woodley leaned back in his chair, his gaze fixed on the autumn scarf she'd looped around her throat.

She squirmed.

Up until today, she'd not minded people staring because she knew it was something she could use to further exposure. *The band's exposure,* she corrected. This journey into social-media branding had begun to help college friends get into the conversation about notable musicians. Telling their story had changed her life within weeks: photos and texts about the van breakdowns, the lightning strikes at private parties, behind-the-scene dramas, and the fashion mistakes. The photos featured uncertain attempts at finding the right look for the guys—and herself—as they'd approached various venues.

The posts revealed how people devoured the insider content and pushed her to create even more. Before long, people wanted to know more about *her* looks and ideas and less about the guys. The attention spawned a regular gig for them at The Rustic in Uptown. From those weekend concerts came opening acts for bigger stars and the addition last year of local nobody, Amy Marsh. With Amy's arrival, Lacy was moved off microphone and assigned to bang a tambourine, but she still supplied images to the ever-starving group of online followers.

"I watched the You Tube videos and Instagram posts. Once I got past the makeup tips and how to wear boots in the in-between seasons, I saw a nugget of something that resonated. It took me a while to figure out what it was, and I almost thought I imagined it."

She'd worked deep into the midnight hours perfecting that content. Eventually, she thought in soundbites and captions. "With praise like that, you can imagine I'm sitting here hanging on for your next words."

"See, you still have your sense of humor." His grin revealed the excellent work of an orthodontist. He was a manicured man with a certain flair for style, but he was also the type to prefer people to stay in their boxes. "You're a survivor, Lacy Cavanaugh."

"I'm bitter." She'd seen herself in the mirror this afternoon. Survivors didn't have tear-swollen eyes and hollows under their cheeks. "I believe that was how you described it as we left the conference room."

"I have faith that you're going to turn things around." He reached for his cell phone and scrolled through contacts. "That's why I'm doing you a big favor."

"I'll be in Comfort by mid-afternoon tomorrow. My sister will assign me to work at her goat farm." Acid flared in her stomach. "Favors are welcomed."

He leaned out of the way, as the waiter served a slice of chocolate-covered cheesecake and followed it with an individual French press of coffee. The aroma of roasted grounds enveloped the table on a waft of indulgence.

The scandal of being slammed on social media these past few weeks burned into her shoulders, and exhaustion made it hard to breathe. She had no idea what Woodley would suggest, but if he didn't end this soon, she'd bolt.

"Despite everything, Lacy, I think you have the instincts of a journalist." He poured coffee into the fine china and hesitated. "You created a brand for your followers and gave more than lip service to what life was like building a band's credibility. Your videos—save the ones exposing Amy's bulimia—were insightful."

The downward spiral paused as she processed his words. She'd watched this man negotiate with the Marsh family attorneys, reminding them how Amy's ratings soared with the exposure surrounding this fiasco. Maybe he would offer a way to redeem herself—could she leverage this into a move to Los Angeles? Could she keep the Audi?

"When Jake told me you'd be moving home, I made a phone call."

Lacy placed her palm on the linen tablecloth. Her brother-in-law raised Thoroughbred horses and sold them on the international market. As the only heir of a family that would never notice one more legal fee in a roster of thousands, he'd thought nothing of solving this problem for his wife's sister. "I may be broke, but Jake doesn't dictate my life."

Woodley's eyes narrowed. "Hamilton has covered my bill, so I wouldn't snap at him."

Chagrined, she swallowed the fantasy that she'd created something successful, something that put her on every list that mattered. In a few headline-laced weeks, she'd been reduced to the awkward teenager who'd been the caboose in a strange family pieced together by a late-in-life marriage. The notion that she'd finally escaped the stigma of being related to "Cousin Olivia" evaporated. She was back to being another one of those odd girls who lived in the house at the top of the hill in Alamo Heights. The neighbors gossiped so loudly that their scorn would seep through the open windows on mild nights. Ten years she'd been searching for a way out and in the snap of a finger, she was right back on the radar for people who needed a scapegoat to make them feel better about themselves.

She glanced at the man who just celebrated a thirtieth birthday. She wasn't sure how Jake knew this guy, but either they'd met at a summer camp for the super-rich or Jake and Kali had developed a secret friend group. "Your phone calls?"

"My father has a colleague who owns newspapers in Central Texas. He offices in Kerrville, but he does a lot of the work on the *Comfort News* because he can't seem to recruit anyone to stay in the area."

A qualm twisted her gut. She hadn't seen an edition of *Comfort News* in years and doubted anyone else had either.

"And when I told him I had a candidate to be his intern, he was mildly interested."

No. No. No.

"He refused to hire you when I told him you had no experience."

Lacy's relief was short lived when she realized she'd been deemed unreliable to broadcast coyote sightings and ranch sales. "I have a degree in marketing. I know how to write."

"But I doubt you know anything about running newspapers."

"And you do?"

He paused as if waiting on a new wave of patience, and then his eyes softened, gazing upon on the desperation of a woman still resisting her penance. "You show up at the office of the *Comfort News* Monday morning at nine. Maybe Mr. Bachman will take you on."

The last imaginings that she was getting out of this mess with any shred of pride burned to ash. "Maybe?"

"He won't put you on salary, but he needs the help. And you can prove to the Marsh family that you've learned your lesson." Christopher grinned. "Welcome to your new life."

Chapter One

Lacy set a digital camera on the desk and waited while Frank Bachman leaned back in his leather chair and rolled a cigar between his fingers, searching for some defect in the pacifier he'd chew throughout this wintry day. She'd watched the pattern for months. Every morning he worked in Comfort, he'd park his pickup truck within spitting distance of the office door, walk in at 9:00 a.m. sharp, and prepare a caffeine-like substance in an archaic machine. While it brewed, he'd unwrap a cigar and size it up before going through the performance of lighting.

Lacy learned that she was not invited to interrupt or comment on this process, as she found out the week she'd finally drug herself through the paint-peeling doors of the *Comfort News* and submitted herself to the sullenness of a man who'd lost faith in humanity.

Even though Frank didn't like to communicate, he loved an audience. He'd thump his fist on the stack of statewide newspapers delivered to this address and speculate on why publishers even bothered to report the news when readers cared more about cat pictures on Facebook than they did the hypocrisy of the electorate.

Drawing in a breath, Lacy braced for his mood.

She'd already seen the headlines on Twitter and had a list of potential stories to develop, but those ideas were ignored until he'd gone through the wire-service reports and drank his first cup of coffee.

Coffee, as if the brown ilk could go by such a name. She was no expert in the kitchen arts, but even she knew recycling grounds day after day was the stuff of nightmares. She'd wondered if she was the first to bring dish soap onto this hallowed ground. The day she walked in with a broom, he'd bellowed that she'd become domestic help, and he wasn't paying her to clean.

She'd reminded him he wasn't paying her at all.

Over the last four months, she'd felt a margin of success that the office no longer reeked of indistinguishable fumes. It also had a dedicated area for the rare customer who stopped in to purchase an ad. The storage closet, crammed with old newspapers, had been cataloged and boxed by decade. Though he'd never thanked her, she'd also disinfected his collection of campaign mugs and performed a minor miracle on the bathroom. She was forbidden from moving the stash of papers on his desk, and, as a result, she'd questioned the nature of the colonies living underneath the out-of-date message book. All of this he endured with irritated grousing.

The hollering came when she tried to update his computer's operating system.

Now, she sat at her small desk, propped underneath a wall calendar that Frank had kept because it had phone numbers penciled in the margins, and waited. Woodley's sentencing for her crimes hadn't been as awful as she'd imagined in November. Her girlfriends were sure she would be forced into detox from the absence of Starbucks, not to mention the withdrawals she'd face by not parading around NorthPark Center. And it was true—the addictions of glamour had been hard to surrender, but not impossible.

Sipping a cream-topped espresso, she thought about her days: some painful, others intolerable, but—no, not entirely impossible. Not that she'd admit any of this was on her list of life goals. Living in the land time forgot smelled too much of farm animals, but at least there was a local coffee shop, her sister, a new friend group that actually knew about life beyond the hills, and—dare she admit it?—a boss she was beginning to think wasn't a complete idiot.

The wildly fresh air and relentless sunshine had allowed her to unwind from the noise of the city and recognize that there was a world beyond Uptown. Not that she didn't grieve the loss of stimulation, gorgeous people, and a checking account that grew with every post she'd made, but she'd eventually stopped crying. Sleeping nine hours every night helped too, but that was more or less a surrender to the local culture than anything she'd planned.

The hardest part was the quiet.

Few people drove around in vehicles that boomed bass notes, even fewer drove around after dark. For a woman inching toward the end of her twenties, being relegated to a town that cared more for a bargain than they did fashion was a bitter pill. And though no one forced her to stay inside the barbed-wire limits, watching her bank balance dwindle with every swipe of her debit card had put the brakes on trips to San Antonio and Austin.

Yes, if anyone from Dallas had bothered to ask how she was doing, she'd have to say she was surviving—barely.

Frank limped to the coffeemaker and poured himself a mug. He was about three years past needing a hip replacement, but he was too afraid of a surgeon's scalpel—her interpretation—to submit to the process.

"No, thank you," Lacy called out, as she watched him dump powdery milk substitute into his mug. She lifted her to-go cup from Cup of Joe's toward him. "I brought my own." She'd not offered to share the cranberry scone she'd snagged because he didn't need to know her weakness for baked goods. It was bad enough that he knew as much as he did, but that's because, despite the gruff exterior and horn-rimmed glasses that seemed in perpetual need of a cleaning, Frank was a remarkably observant man.

"It's a sign of your bad judgement that you spend an outrageous amount of money for what is basically a ten-cent beverage."

Argument number twenty-two on his regular playlist. He had a top forty of rants, but in the months she'd been dragging herself to this office, she'd condensed the complaints into categories. Once he started in on a familiar refrain, she knew she had about ten minutes to surf the internet while throwing out an occasional reply to fill in the spaces when he grabbed a wheezy breath.

"I watched the barista heat the beans yesterday at their new roasting facility, so I, at least, know the origins of what I'm consuming. Unlike you, who have put faith in the ingredient mumbo jumbo printed on a can that could survive the apocalypse."

She knew he was grinning, though any hint was disguised by the wiry gray beard that grew well below his chin.

"So, you covered that development even though I told you I'd not publish the story?" He settled into his chair behind the desk.

"I live in hope that you will see the value in local news appealing to local readers." Last month, Lacy had supplied him with features, from a grape stomp at a winery to the high school's UIL one-act-play competition, and he'd buried them all under the label of "fluff." "Besides, I sold my photos to the coffee shop, and that will pay for my suppers this week."

"You're as optimistic as a spring chicken." He propped his cigar between his teeth before he glanced at her, saying, "I thought your landlady included meals with her rent."

Frank knew exactly what her landlady provided.

His ex-wife, Gloria Bachman, made a point of saying it was easier to cook for two than it was for one, so Lacy's meager rent for the cottage behind the limestone bungalow on Seventh Street included breakfast and supper. Spending mornings and evenings in her pink-and-white kitchen, outfitted with an expensive gas stove and an Italian espresso machine, almost made up for the loss of living within walking distance of twenty restaurants near American Airlines Center. What Lacy was learning in the world of news production paled in comparison to the graduate-level course she was getting in cookery. Seriously, her proudest moment was when she learned the appropriate method to cut an onion.

Until the night when Gloria whispered the life-altering words, "Commit to the knife and let it slide with purpose," she'd had no idea that there was even a process to using knives, short of breaking into packaging or smearing cream cheese on a bagel. She was nowhere near ready to create a dinner-party menu, but she'd be lying if she kept telling people she didn't know how to boil an egg.

Gloria was a generous landlady and a fast friend, but she refused to talk about her ex-husband. One of these days Lacy would ferret the story between the retired Bank of the Hills president and the *Comfort News* publisher. For two people who went out of their way to avoid each other, they were incredibly aware of each other's movements.

"My landlady has taken off for Florida."

"Oh?" He sipped his mug. "Her sister's place, I'm sure—a crabby woman if there ever was one."

It takes one to know one, Lacy thought, but she wouldn't correct Frank's impression. Gloria was meeting an old flame in Miami, and the less Frank knew about that, the better.

Lacy sipped the espresso and thought about the conversation she'd overheard at Cup of Joe's this morning. She'd been waiting for her friends, Anna and AJ, to arrive for their weekly breakfast chat when she heard a man in line discussing the cost of upgrading electrical panels in a storefront farther near the park with the monument. Because she'd recently covered a city-council meeting, she knew that side of town was off the grid for most tourists, so it wouldn't appeal to investors wanting to slice into Comfort's shopping district. So, why would this man be working a dead-end prospect?

She tried to resist the pull of a potential story (because she really didn't want to care), but curiosity had always been her downfall.

Turning around, she'd spied an Asian guy, wearing designer sunglasses, camo gear, and Armani boots, talking into his cell phone. Taken aback by his fashion mistakes, she forgot to wonder about the location he discussed. Her brain still juiced with coffee and memories, she was stunned to realize Frank was standing near her chair.

"I'll throw you a bone today, Cavanaugh."

Startled away from her thoughts, she glanced up and noticed that Frank seemed thinner today, more like the bone he was willing to toss.

"I'm sending you on assignment," Frank announced.

Dread tickled her spine. He'd given her a lot of liberty for a publisher who thought she was nothing more than a vanity writer, but "assignment" was a term relegated for the big leagues. Or so he'd preached when reminiscing about his days on the *Austin American-Statesman* beat. "I thought you said I write with too much hyperbole to be credible."

"You do, but I can edit." He scribbled an address on a scrap of paper and tossed it on her desk. "Go visit Jesse Boerner and find out why the EPA is sniffing around his gas station."

Her hand stilled before snatching the directions. "That sounds like hard news."

"Could be."

"Last week you made me cover the chamber of commerce banquet."

He puffed his cigar. "You didn't entirely blow that piece."

Standing, she collected the camera. Photos were the one thing she could count on Frank printing when she turned in ideas during their meetings. Early on she realized that it wasn't due to her keen eye for lighting and details. It was that he resented supplying pictures instead of text to make folks buy issues of the *Comfort News*. Last week's coverage of the banquet had resulted in eight front-page photos, two paragraphs of summary, and a sellout at every location.

"What do you want me to ask him?" Lacy added a battery-operated voice recorder to her seasons-old designer bag because her flip phone didn't have a recording feature. Down in the recesses, it mingled with all the other tools she'd learned how to use since surrendering her iPhone: a calculator borrowed from Gloria, a dog-eared map she'd collected from the lady working the chamber offices, and a key-chain-sized compass she bought at the Bust-A-Gut gas station because she was dense with directions. To make room for the notepad and local phone book, which was almost more ads than it was addresses, she'd had to downsize her makeup bag and opt for just one pair of sunglasses at a time. She'd also stopped carrying her beloved shawl—the Neiman Marcus bargain she toted absolutely *everywher*e to ward off the cold in over-air-conditioned restaurants—because no one air-conditioned their places in Kendall County to the levels of Dallas.

Frank blew a puff of smoke then hacked a cough that sounded like it travelled from his toes. "I will not dignify that with an answer."

Pausing, she gauged his attitude—not good, but she would ask anyway. "Is there an angle you want me to take?"

"The truth." He leaned his shoulder into the bookshelf. "Just get the facts and assemble the words into some sort of coherent order."

On the scale of historic moments, this wouldn't rate, but for her, a writing assignment was epic. And terrifying. The hounds who'd chased her Instagram videos always seemed to breathe at her heels.

"Why are you still here?" He thumped his knuckles on an unopened package of computer paper. "Go on, get to the station before the testing equipment vanishes."

Throwing her bag over her shoulder, she paced her steps toward the door. It wouldn't do to let Frank see nerves. Reaching for the knob, she wondered . . . had months of subservience proved she wasn't a total flake? If she wrote this well, might she get paid for this story like the other freelancers who submitted articles?

She stepped into the sunshine radiating off Main Street and breathed disgustingly clean air.

Waiting at the curb, a late-model Ford, instead of the sexy Audi she'd once owned, gleamed like it was ready to take on any challenge. Could she—maybe, possibly—shuck off the mantle of social-media pariah and disgraced beauty queen? A million Instagram-worthy thoughts flew through her mind, but she had to focus. This was the break she'd been praying for. If she could take this baby step, she'd be a whole foot closer to reclaiming her future.

She glanced at her sneakers and wished she'd worn better shoes.

Chapter Two

Rudy Delgardo leaned over the sauté pan and ran a spoon through the bubbling béchamel sauce. Tasting the sample, he wrinkled his nose. "Too much salt. Try again."

"Again, Chef?" The twenty-year-old cook sighed. "That's the third time this morning."

"And if you fail next time, consider yourself unemployed." Rudy wiped his spoon on a dishcloth. "There are half a dozen cooks standing behind you waiting for you to fail. Either you have the desire to do this right, or you're wasting both our time."

An aroma of chicken stock and clatter from the worker stacking pans in the sink announced the hour. Rudy's kitchen ran on a synchronized system, and every member of the staff knew what they were doing and when. One false step and the evening's service was shot.

"Chef?"

He turned to see the general manager of Stella's, a fine-dining restaurant in the Clarksville neighborhood of Austin, scowling over his iPad.

"We have sold out seating for tonight, no surprise." Jay Tumlin tapped the stylus against the iPad. "But an eight o'clock reservation was claimed by Alan Gale—the food critic for *Vogue*. I thought you should know."

Curses skirted over Rudy's tongue. Gale wrote scathing articles that had more to do with his pomposity than they did the deliciousness of food. The man had dogged Rudy ever since they were students at the Culinary Institute of America. Both CIA dropouts, one stayed in the kitchen; one chased a skirt to a Los Angles publishing house. Neither of them stayed in California.

Rudy watched the delivery man set a box of white asparagus next to the vegetable cook and was distracted from history by the potential for tonight's menu. "Then I hope he's pleased with his order. Assign Terre to his table. She can coax the crankiest customer into leaving with a smile."

Jay nodded and double-checked the PAR-stock list thumbtacked to the board outside the chef's office. Rudy rubbed his thumb along his stubbled jawline. He had a capable kitchen staff, an outstanding general manager, and servers who could work any five-star restaurant. He didn't have to worry about Gale.

But he did.

Tossing a dishcloth over his shoulder, he walked behind the cooks prepping the ingredients. His head sous chef, Ken Lin, was in Comfort today inspecting the property Rudy had temporarily rented for an event in December. He wished Kenny were in the kitchen. He'd need his A team to combat any grenades Gale tossed.

"Chef?" Jay asked, maintaining the military order Rudy required in the kitchen. "I need a few minutes of your time to discuss the Comfort project. Kenny called this morning with a contractor's report."

Rudy tapped his pastry chef and left her in charge while he stepped into the dining room.

Following Jay through the swing doors, he let his eyes dim to the urban color scheme of Stella's. In this part of the house, purples, orange, and golds warmed the walls. A sloping, high ceiling with skylights evoked the Sonoma style he'd never been able to leave behind in California. He and Jay climbed onto leather stools at the bar.

"Can we bring Kenny back in time to make service tonight?" Rudy motioned to the bartender for his usual club soda and lime. "We've got newbies on the line."

"You've mentored them for months. They'll be fine." Jay read through his notes. "The contractor in the area, a guy named Beau Jefferson, sent a detailed analysis of that storefront you rented a few months back, and I have to say it sounds like a disaster."

Rudy scanned the printouts Jay slid over to him.

"Kenny said that, though you guys made it work for the Worthington wedding, the location will have to be gutted." Jay added a budget recap to the final option pages Rudy read. "There are even cracks in the foundation. And we'd have to buy the house next door, tear it down, and pave the space for parking."

Numbers swam before his eyes as Rudy remembered that crazy December when he and Kenny hustled to a little has-been town off the interstate and set up a makeshift kitchen and service area in what had been a hardware store. Of all the places he could have rented to prepare for that feast, it was the only space clean enough and with natural light to facilitate his staff.

And he'd relished every minute inside those limestone walls.

Unlike anything else he'd experienced in the last several years of building Stella's, he'd had creativity pouring from his fingertips. He could step outside, breathe air free of car emissions, and sit undisturbed under a tree for an entire hour. No one strutted around with a cell phone gripped in their palms or asked him pensive questions about the culture of his food. The locals barely acknowledged him.

The silence liberated his thinking, recharged his batteries, and brainwaves travelled to his fingertips. Nimble and inspired, he'd cooked better than he had in ages.

He craved that scenario like he needed coffee in the mornings.

The pace of running Stella's drove him into the ground, and he knew he was near a cracking point. Comfort had restored him. Since his daughter, Luna, had been with his ex-wife for Christmas during those weeks, he'd enjoyed days wandering that town, imaging how a bistro, in a fertile region of Texas, could be both a playground for an inventive chef and the simpler life he desired.

Kenny, never one to question a chef, had seconded the idea. Driving back to Austin, he threw out menu suggestions for a Hill-Country-meets-France bistro, an airy boutique venue for cuisine nerds.

Rudy had been obsessed ever since, hoping it was a dream he could explore—until right now. The numbers cut sharper than his best knife.

Jay hadn't seen the location, but he'd torpedoed the bistro from the first breath. Stella's had made it through the semi-final round of the James Beard Award for Restaurant of the Year in the Southwest. They had recovered from the financial chaos of Rudy's divorce and had reclaimed the bakery, Stella Too, that he'd lost in the settlement. They did not need a third property to manage.

Logically, Rudy agreed. As a former CPA, Jay's financial advice proved spot-on. But everyone knew Jay didn't have the soul of a poet, or a visionary, or whatever it was that drove Rudy.

"You can see this number is foolishness." Jay pointed to the recap. "I'll cut a check to Jefferson to cover his estimate, and we can call off the realtor."

Rudy placed a scarred hand over Jay's. "You didn't see the sunlight in that yard."

Jay shook his head. "There's an obscene amount of sunlight in Austin."

"There was an empty lot near the hardware store perfect for growing vegetables and herbs that could supply the bistro, and even Stella's."

"We have produce vendors already."

"No one grows apples here." Rudy accepted the soda from his bartender and wrapped his hands around the tall, cool glass. "The flavors in the fruit from Love Orchards are unique."

"So, we'll add them to our vendor list."

"That's not the point."

"It should be the point," Jay insisted. "You have enough to do here without starting a new venture."

Rudy sipped, hoping the seltzer burn would quell the urge to create. "Maybe."

"Have you forgotten what you went through to get to the top of your game?" Jay stood from the seat. "If you can't remember, I'll just say that you have been working countless hours to get the team ready for the James Beard, and you haven't seen your daughter in almost two months."

All thoughts of a bistro flew out of his brain as he remembered the challenges of trying to buy Christmas gifts for his precocious seven-year-old. She was in the sweetest phase of childhood, and he'd been arguing with his ex about having Luna for the summer this year. Driving back and forth to Abilene had put miles on his soul. He'd promised that nothing in his life meant more than being part of his daughter's life, and he was going to prove it.

Rudy set the glass on the bar and pushed the estimates toward Jay. "So, you're saying it's a pipe dream to think running a bistro would be less stressful and give me more time for Luna?" He knew the flavor of regret, and he swallowed. "Who knows, maybe you're right. But I do want Luna close and cooking with me in the kitchen, like I did with my grandmother."

"She can do that here just as easily as in Comfort," Jay said, although they both knew that running Stella's was an eighteen-hour day. "So, were you really thinking of being the one to run this fantasy bistro?"

"Of course," Rudy cut his gaze to the mirror behind the bar, seeing the senior wait-staff coordinator enter the dining room. "I can't create the culture I want to see without being the one to make it happen."

"I thought you would give the bistro over to Kenny. Let him be the chef and you be the benevolent executive chef."

"Kenny?" Rudy stood. "He's my right hand, but he's not head-chef material."

"Why not? He's trained under you for five years or more, and he's the most talented of all your cooks."

"Ken Lin is . . . well, he's too young. And he has no idea what goes into running a restaurant." His ego bruised that Jay thought his protégé was a stand-in. "He thinks what I tell him to think, he's a mini-me."

Jay chuckled because at six-foot-three, Rudy towered over his head sous chef. "Well, you need a reliable backup, and if I were in your shoes, I'd train Kenny to run the kitchen and make time for him to understand restaurant management too."

Rudy socked Jay's shoulder. "Next time I want your opinion, I'll ask someone else."

"And this is the thanks I get for saving you from making a life-altering mistake." Jay acted injured. "Now, on to better news. I had an email that the JBF judges will be in town next month. I really think that restaurant award is ours to lose. We've never had sharper and more consistent service than we've had the last six months."

Rudy pulled a notepad from his pocket and scribbled a reminder to call one of his friends who'd won the award and find out more details about the final round. The James Beard Award was the Oscars of the American food industry, and he wanted it so bad he could taste mile-high meringue.

Not only would a win raise Stella's to national attention, beyond the food journals and celebrity magazines that featured it as one of Austin's best restaurants, but he'd be able to prove to Luna that good guys finish first. All the crayon drawings taped to his office door featured him as a prince and she as a princess—he'd like to be worthy of her faith in him and leverage this distinction into making their life better.

Nanny. He scribbled that on his notepad too. If he were going to get Luna for the summer, he'd need someone who could consistently watch her while he worked. Four months ought to give him enough time to vet a suitable candidate.

"Chef?"

He looked up, seeing the woman who managed the waitstaff.

Concern shadowed her expression. "Your ex-wife is here. She's at the front door. She has your daughter with her. There's luggage."

Chapter Three

Dirt, dust, and the distinctive odor of goat urine encircling the barn proved hard to ignore, even as the skylights shined sunny hues onto the alfalfa hay. Lacy's skin itched every time she got near the brown-and-white beasts that her sister adored. And the flies. *Seriously,* she wondered, *how had her sister, who'd grown up in a house free of pets, turned into a self-taught goat guru?* It defied understanding. And, if anyone asked the obvious questions, she'd reply that she totally missed the gene.

Glancing at Kali in her rubber boots, skinny jeans, and a T-shirt stained with some mysterious gunk, was enough to make her run the opposite direction. But this strange farm, filled with a variety of breeds and expensive corrals, was not only a paradise for her sister, it was a lucrative enterprise that created a milk product she turned into gourmet cheese.

Lacy had been here at the beginning, when Kali chucked in her savings and an inheritance from Aunt Annalise to fund a "maker's project" in a quiet valley of the Hill Country on the outskirts of Comfort, Texas. Yes, the two-story farmhouse on the property had been darling, and, yes, there was something ethereal about the scrubby trees and hazy sun rises, but not enough to justify buying twenty goats and disappearing from society.

Lacy had stuck around for the first year or so, helping Kali start the business and get the cheese products perfected, and then she'd split.

The irony that she'd landed here—on this very same spot—after everything fell apart in Dallas was too much to digest. The goats braying at her confirmed it. They wondered why she'd returned too. They seemed to sense her disrespect and sneered.

Kali chuckled. "It's so funny to me how the goats don't hurry over to nuzzle you. They love people."

Lacy grimaced. "And after all I did for them too." She handed Kali her phone, opened already to the Instagram app, and received her nephew in exchange. "How's the cutest baby in the world?" she cooed, pecking kisses into the fat rolls circling his neck.

Smelling his baby soap, Lacy tried to forget the argument she'd had with Frank about how many features on the PRCA rodeo were too many for this week's issue. He'd hacked and coughed and then ultimately insisted she couldn't even recognize the varieties of horses involved, so why did she think anyone else would care. He'd been right, of course. She couldn't tell an American Quarter Horse from an American Paint Horse and had no idea why it mattered. But she'd not been able to look away from the bright expressions of those teenagers who won ribbons or were promoted to the next level of competition—*that* she related to, the thrill of winning. Sadly, Frank didn't think readers would buy papers littered with feel-good stories. He said Comfort-ites were freethinkers. Just give them the facts and let them make up their own minds.

Stepping out of the barn, she squinted against the light. The barn was new, built with modern amenities. Her sister had duplicated the old farmhouse style of the original 1940s homestead that was the brain center of Provence Farm, but Lacy wasn't fooled. It was just one of many metal buildings she'd walked through during the last few months, and there was no disguising animal odors with a sloped roof and trendy patio furniture.

Ignoring the current breeze of poop rolling in from the corral, she also disregarded the temptation to check Kali's followers on Instagram and see if the infusion of new content was bringing a rush of fans. It was one thing to post images for her sister's account, it was another to look at analytics. It was too easy to peek at her old site. She'd done that a few times since the quarantine, and she'd quickly learned that seeing the messages from fans wondering where she was felt like getting kicked in the gut. Again.

For someone making a form of peace with social isolation, getting close to fan mail was begging to be bit. She wouldn't put it past the Marsh family to catfish her site in order to prove she was still active.

Amy Marsh. A name she hoped to never hear again. Even though it had ripped through enough headlines this week, she didn't want to invite more temptations than necessary. Grappling with the unfairness of her punishment still felt like a one-sided story. Had anyone gotten Amy into rehab? Based on the talking heads of *Entertainment Tonight,* she'd say no.

Besides, playing with Charlie helped her put aside news. Being a part of his babyhood was a blessing she'd never have had living five hours away. She tickled him, and he laughed. Yes. Charlie was a good distraction.

"You did such a great job lighting the goat pens." Kali admired the Instagram post as she followed Lacy outside. "I love how you captioned me and Charlie—like he has a clue that he's inheriting knowledge about artisanal-cheese products."

Lacy hugged the infant. "I think it's wise to keep his face off-screen for now to protect your privacy, but I know your followers will eat up the idea of bringing your baby to work."

"It certainly is more interesting than watching me milking goats or salting the cheese." Kali placed Charlie's pacifier into her fanny pack. "But the images of the construction going on at the Lavender Hill party barn always get a reaction too. You've turned AJ, Beau, and Colette into internet sensations."

Lacy held her nephew out to study any changes in him during the last week. "They're doing all the hard work at Lavender Hill, I'm just updating business pages with photos."

"You're giving us all rock-star content."

Walking toward a stack of alfalfa, Lacy tucked Charlie under her chin and hurried past another barnyard distraction. She doubted she'd have many more months when he'd be content to rest in her arms without getting down to muck about with his mother. Between the goats, the dogs, the chickens, and the tractors, she was destined to drop in the ranks of people who could hold his attention. Maybe one day he'd want to hang with his super-cool Aunt Lacy, but that was about twenty years down the road and a million miles away from her current job status.

"So, I saw the news." Kali opened a gate to a pasture, letting goats roam into the wilds. "Amy Marsh got the sympathy vote on *America's Got Talent*."

Lacy turned back and watched her sister brush her hands on the backside of her jeans. "Thanks, I appreciate that."

"Well, it's true. Months ago, the media went haywire suggesting that you had something to do with outing her in mean-girls style, but she's the one who used deliberately gorging and purging to gain attention, and the judges fell for her story."

"Let's not discount her voice. She can sing."

Kali folded her arms. "Well, time will tell if she has the will to survive in that business. Meanwhile, you—the one who got her into the national spotlight—are slaving away for Frank Bachman, a man who doesn't even know the definition of 'mentor.'"

Lacy squeezed her sister's shoulder. "Your faith means the world to me."

"I'm not immune to the fact that you went too far in publishing those videos, but there is so much worse going on in the world, and I hate that you're suffering at the *Comfort News* as some sort of atonement."

The worst is never really the worst. If Gloria Bachman has said that once, she's said it hundreds of times. The mantra had wormed into Lacy's brain and popped up every time self-pity raised its head—which, truthfully, was a daily battle. Gloria had a way of mixing wisdom with her cooking lessons, and the end result was Lacy's thicker waistline and an evolving attitude adjustment. Or, as evidenced by her bolting away from the computer today, maybe just tighter clothes.

"Well, I'm nowhere near the end of my sentence, and the good news is I've learned a few things along the way, so maybe I could network this into an entry-level job in San Antonio—at the newspaper or a magazine."

"Once the media coverage of Amy Marsh goes away," Kali added, swatting a honeybee.

Bad press never dies. "Yeah, then."

They walked a few paces and stopped at the round pen that contained the kids—too rambunctious for the noisy baby pen but not yet big enough to fend off the males. Charlie squirmed and begged to get close. Lacy held him tight and turned away from the dust in the air.

"I ran into Anna today at the supermarket, and she said that you're making a name for yourself in town." Kali reached into her pocket and tossed pellet treats to her crop of four-legged babies. "She says everyone wants you to cover their events."

Anna Weber, a single mother of twins and independent music publisher, had no idea how the messages left at the

Comfort News had escalated in the last few weeks. Frank belittled the rush by suggesting she was paying people to be this annoying.

"To Frank's horror, the main requests are for weddings, memorials, high-school achievements, and every fundraiser in Kendall County."

"But you produced the news about the EPA's investigation into pollution seeping into the drinking water."

"That turned out to be nothing more than a neighbors' feud over property lines. The EPA called to complain that I'd played right into the hands of the instigator and that I needed to do more research before I used words like 'Superfund site' in print. But at least I was right about exposing the county commissioner." She'd developed an ally in Frank once she uncovered who had made the phone calls reporting groundwater leakage. "Turns out he's a land man with a stake in buying those corner properties."

"Oh."

There was a volume of dismay in those two letters. Kali didn't like discovering her neighbors could be complicit in underhanded dealings. Maybe Dallas had hardened Lacy, but fast talkers and manipulators wore overalls as easily as those who wore suits. She'd met a few of the type as she called to collect on ad revenue. Despite her eyes-wide-open approach to the Hill Country, it would be eons before Frank let her forget that she'd imposed her bias into an article that was supposed to be about facts. He cautioned, and wisely so, to listen first and jump to conclusions never. For the foreseeable future, she'd be covering birth announcements and obituaries. One thing she'd learned was that a bad death could wipe out a lifetime of good works. But she'd also discovered interesting, tongue-twisting names. There were a boatload of German descendants in these hills.

In an effort to change the topic and lighten the mood, Lacy handed the baby back to his mother and asked, "What was that cheese product on the cooling racks? I didn't recognize it."

"It's a recipe for mascarpone cheese." Kali rubbed a sunscreen stick over Charlie's nose and chin. "Do you remember that chef who catered AJ's wedding?"

Lacy dialed back her images to Christmas Eve, when AJ Worthington and Luke English rode to Lavender Hill in a rented sleigh for an over-the-top reception that popped up on the slab that was the foundation for Kali and AJ's new business venture, an event center. She'd snapped so many photos of celebrities who'd arrived that night, and the charm of a Christmas-themed reception, that the pictures were single-handedly responsible for every bride in the area wanting Lacy to document their weddings too. Lavender Hill dominated social media for a few weeks into the new year.

"I'm not sure I even ate that night," Lacy said, trying to remember the supper.

"Roger Worthington hired a hot-shot chef from Austin, apparently an old friend, and the guy whipped out a feast that was some of the best food we've ever eaten." Kali motioned for Lacy to follow her to the production house. "Jake and I drove to Austin last month to dine at his signature restaurant, Stella's, and it's as great as everyone raves."

Lacy wasn't sure how they'd made the leap to the Hamiltons' date night. "How does this have any bearing on mascarpone cheese?"

"Well, let me back up and say that when this chef was preparing the food for the reception, he'd hired local vendors to supply his ingredients, and he loved the cheeses I delivered. He'd rented an old storefront in town for food prep, and I saw all the best products laid out on folding tables. Things I didn't even know grew in this area." Kali stepped onto the back porch, kicking off her rubber boots and sliding her toes into clean sneakers. "I've been working with one of his sous chefs to make a mascarpone cheese that will hold up to his cooking standards."

"That's great, Kals. I had no idea. Do you want me to make a few posts about that, and we can schedule them to roll out later in the week?"

She shook her head. "It's hush-hush right now. There are no guarantees of a contract unless the chef says the cheese is reliable through multiple servings. I'm shipping them another batch tomorrow to see if they still like my quality."

Lacy ran her fingers through the handwashing station. "I'm really proud of you. You've worked hard."

Kali passed Charlie off to the nanny who babysat him in the playroom. "It's getting crazy between Provence Farm, the construction at the event center, and the new foals at Jake's ranch. I'm not sure what the next twelve months are going to look like."

Pausing at the doorway where three ladies worked the cheese-making stations, Lacy breathed in the tang of the heated curds. The stainless-steel counters, the straining cloths drying over a heater, the racks of different-sized chinois, and the industrial lighting making sure no flaw was overlooked were all key to her sister's organic label, but Lacy despised the aromas that had seeped into every surface. The only upside to working at the newspaper was that she didn't have to smell the heated goat milk or the special recipe Brie, a bloomy rind that burned a chloride stain she could never quite shake off.

"Do you need me to babysit more often?" Lacy's calendar had become a hollow excuse for a schedule. Outside of her hours at the *Comfort News*, she'd spent valuable daylight bingeing entire seasons of bygone television and long-forgotten movies. "Charlie adores me, and I'm itching to teach him how to wind people around his little finger."

With a smile, Kali led the way back to the small room that served as the shipping department. "Attempting to pass off your evil ways on an unsuspecting infant?"

"At this rate, I'm never going to have children of my own, so I need to give my wisdom to someone."

"Oh, please. When you're forty, then we'll cry. Until then, you've got potential right around the corner."

"There is hardly anyone to date in Comfort. I know—I was desperate enough to look online. And Deputy Mayne, the only credible candidate, thinks I'm shallow because I've worn a tiara."

Kali pouted. "Beautiful, street-smart, and downright pitiful. I can see why you're ready to give up."

She *had* given up on dating, not that she was ever asked out. When she complained about her lonely Valentine's Day, everyone consoled her by saying she was too beautiful, *too intimidating* for guys. That backhanded compliment did little to inspire putting up a profile on a dating app—no need to get rejected on a viral level. "I guess I could devote myself to my career. Do you think I could pitch a TV show called the 'Real Housewives of Comfort?'"

"Not enough bling or Botox in these hills."

Lacy propped her hip on the shipping desk. "The sooner I can get to a city, the sooner I can do something—anything—that feels like me again."

"Comfort must seem like the back of the moon to you after Dallas, but you lived here with me for that first year and seemed to have fun."

"I was twenty-two and coming off the pageant circuit. I was brain-dead."

Kali chuckled. "You *were* remarkably agreeable."

"After three years of dieting for those swimsuit competitions, I was starving. You fed me. So, I slowly came back to life."

"And once you got your attitude back, you ran off with the guys in that band."

"Hardly ran off . . . more like it was a summer lark that somehow worked." Lacy remembered the various disasters, manual labor, hours of boredom, and wild flirtations with more glow than she'd felt at the time. "But no one thought it would last. That was supposed to be a gap year for a few of them before starting grad school."

"And you were reinventing yourself or some such excuse for abandoning me."

"I didn't desert you. You had four employees and a college romance returning for round two. Besides, you were ready for me to leave. We hadn't spent that much time together since we were teenagers, and you were running out of patience."

Smiling, as if looking back at simpler times, Kali corrected the memory. "We made it work though, didn't we? Aunt Annalise would have been proud. That year that I lived with her in France, she was worried sick that we would drift apart when we needed each other the most."

"She was eaten up with cancer. I doubt she worried because she rarely called to check on me."

"She did worry, she just didn't know how to relate to your decision to go into pageants. Her ugly duckling had turned into a swan, and she didn't understand why you chased those sashes."

Lacy had never given the *why* much thought. Once she emerged from her awful high-school years with better looks than anyone would have guessed, she ran headlong into anything that would give her the affirmation she'd been denied. "It was how I paid for college."

"But Aunt Annalise worried it would—"

"Let's be honest, she let me sink or swim on my own merits. She said I was as stubborn as Mom."

Kali stayed silent as long as she could. "You *are* stubborn. But you've also got twice as much stick-to-it-iveness as anyone else I know. Look how you made it all the way to Miss Texas."

"And didn't even place in the top ten for Miss America."

Grimacing, Kali shaded her eyes. "You'd lost your drive for it by then."

Lacy both loved and hated those days. Discovering her power and poise felt like a survival contest on some lost planet, but it was over. She never wanted to go back.

"No more. Talking about those days is boring. You've got Provence Farm, Charlie, and Jake, and one day, I'm going to figure out what I was meant to do too. Until then, let's get through the next few months without dredging the past."

Kali picked up the clipboard with the current shipping schedule. "I don't know why you don't develop a business card as a media consultant. What you've done for me and AJ is priceless, and it would keep you busy doing what you're good at."

Sighing, Lacy stared at her nails. As a recovering social-media addict, she still ached to post. There were mornings she reached to the nightstand and grabbed her phone, forgetting that this model didn't include a screen full of messages indicating who'd left comments about her pictures. "That's skating close to the promise I made to the Marsh family about staying off social media for a year."

"Only if you were posting as yourself. But there's no rule against logging on to other people's accounts and helping them with exposure. Right?"

Lacy kicked her Sam Edelman boots and stared at a spot of mud that needed to be polished away. "I have thought about the idea, but I'm still in AA for Facebook. Doing occasional posts for you and the newspaper is one thing. Going whole hog onto the platform would tempt my pride. I'd see what others were blogging about, and I'd have ten better ideas for a look or a style. I don't think I can handle it."

Setting the clipboard onto the desk, Kali looked at her sister. "You're serious."

"As a heart attack."

"Who has been your confessor? I didn't know you were in counseling."

Lacy smiled and remembered the InstaPot chicken dish Gloria had set out for supper last night. It took both of them to shred the chicken breasts and return the meat to the cheese and bacon broth before eating every morsel of the juicy meat right off the chopping block. They spent hours in the kitchen, mastering everything from French toast to fried chicken. They cooked well together, and conversation always flowed. "Well, you don't know everything, now, do you?"

"Come on, don't leave me hanging. Are you really in counseling, or are you just watching Doctor Phil and calling that a twelve-step program?"

"Pure Doctor Phil."

Kali's eyebrow rose.

"I don't have the attention span for a counselor. Besides, that might require accountability, and you know me better than anyone—I'm the least reliable person on the planet."

"That is not true." Kali returned to the messages on the desk. "Most of the time."

Lacy had left jobs undone at Provence Farm when she lived here, which had prompted some heated arguments, but those days had faded. Lacy's foray into lifestyle blogging had taught her to be her own best employee.

Until she was fired, banished back to square one.

The only person from Dallas who'd called more than twice after she'd left the city had been the manager of one of the boutiques in West Village. She'd accidentally phoned Lacy to explore a release regarding a designer, and once Lacy explained why she wasn't the candidate to promote a rising star, they'd talked for an hour about the whims of life and how to hold steady in a world that was ever changing. They'd talked three times since. *On the phone.* A conversational skill that had gone dormant during her text-happy days in Dallas.

Since she had to do an archaic number punch to send messages with this phone, she'd learned that calling someone reduced carpal tunnel syndrome. She'd startled more than one of her old friends with a random ring. They'd delighted telling her who was seeing whom and the little dramas that consumed them, but no one asked what she was doing now that she couldn't include them in some hot post snapped from a rooftop bar.

Anna and AJ had dragged Lacy along with them to church events and—*God forbid*—an author talk at the library. She'd have died of monotony had they not been there to explain why people listened to someone read out loud.

"Are you staying for supper?" Kali asked, glancing at her watch.

"I can if you need me too, but I gain five pounds sitting at your table. The things you do to a potato are sinful."

"Jake insists on a carb-friendly diet since he's outdoors from dawn to dusk. I really think he asked me to marry him after he learned I could cook chicken-fried steak."

"And this is why I've never kept a boyfriend. They drop me as soon as they discover I'm inept in the kitchen."

"You're not inept, you just choose to let others cook for you."

Lacy cringed. Everyone always had a reason for why she was a failure. "Why work if I don't have to?"

"You landed in a bowl of cream with Gloria Bachman. I didn't know landladies still provided meals with rent."

"She's retired and likes to cook enough to have leftovers." Lacy thought about how Gloria had recently taken up painting, attempting to find the outlet she'd been denied while working in finance. "And she likes to experiment, so I'm her guinea pig."

"Well, Jake has one of his ranch hands riding in with him tonight, and I was hoping you'd stay and eat with us. This is not a setup, I promise. It's just that I don't know this guy, and you're the best person to welcome a stranger into the mix. I know you hate it when people say you're a natural networker, but it's true."

"It doesn't take rocket science to be friendly."

"And it doesn't hurt that you're easy on the eyes."

Like she had any control over her bone structure. "I thought you said this wasn't a setup."

"Compassionate hospitality. If this guy is like the others Jake brings home, he's more comfortable with horses than humans."

The only thing worse than the smell of cheese curdling was the fragrance of pity. "Thanks for the offer, but I really need to wash my hair."

Kali scanned the extra two inches that had grown on Lacy's head since she'd had to separate from her beloved stylist. "Too flimsy an excuse. You're staying, and I'll let you escape to bathe Charlie if this guy is dull."

There were a million things she'd rather do than meet a cowboy, but her sister would see right through the excuses. Since Jake wasn't allowing her to pay back Christopher Woodley's fees, she'd owed them. Probably forever. "When you make such a compelling offer, how can I refuse?"

Grinning, Kali hugged her sister. "I knew you loved being here more than you do that guesthouse packed to the roof with boxes."

She preferred her stacks and the furniture she'd hauled south from her high-rise apartment. The few things she owned clashed with the early-settler décor in the cottage, but rent was cheap, and for now, those boxes contained what was left from her brush with independence.

"This will be fun," Kali said, bustling around the cooling room. "Like a party."

Lacy's ulcer rumbled, reminding her how it was best to keep her sister busy if she wanted to remain under her radar. "Hey, have you and AJ discussed a grand opening for the event center? That's something to promote and maybe lure this whiz chef back to town to do the catering."

Chapter Four

Rudy stared at his daughter's sleeping form, tucked under a table in Stella's main dining room, and wondered how to make sense of the next two weeks.

He flipped his wrist and saw that it was almost two o'clock in the morning, and he'd lost track of the last fifteen hours. A team from the James Beard Foundation had almost escaped his notice this evening. If Jay hadn't recognized a panelist, they'd have never known about the blind tasting on a busy Friday night.

He and Kenny were due to fly to New York in ten days to cook for the JBF panel, and he was still fine-tuning his menu and gathering ingredients. Lists piled in his memory like pavers, but none of that justified why he'd let his seven-year-old spend the evening in his office, playing games on his computer.

Hannah called him irresponsible.

Hannah said he was not father material.

And this was why Hannah preferred to work at Paragon Ranch than stay with him.

He wiped his hand across the beard stubble.

Two more weeks. Hannah's mother had half a month of physical therapy left, and Hannah wasn't coming back to Texas until her mother could walk on her own. She knew full well what the James Beard Award would mean for his restaurant; the Paragons had won it for their steakhouse. But her loyalties were to her new employers and to her family. She had reduced her ex-husband to Luna's babysitter.

And he was doing a half-assed job at that.

The cleaning team pushed vacuums over the carpets. Bending to his knees, he tugged on her fluffy blanket, hoping the disturbance would wake her before the noise.

She slept as hard as he did, and it would require a shovel to move her from under the table. Embarrassed that staff would spread tales of him letting his daughter sleep on the floor, he had to suck that up with all the other complaints they'd tacked to his back.

"Honey, it's time to go home." He scooped her close and tried to pull her out. She curled trustingly into his arms, and it reminded him why she was the best thing in his world.

Laboring to stand, he hitched her against his chest, sorry that her nose was buried against grease-splattered fabric stained with sauces. Glancing over his shoulder, he double-checked that the lights were off in the kitchen.

Heading to the door, he ran through his checklist of procedures that confirmed the servers and bartenders had left the front of the house as sharp as the back of the house. With limited seating, he had considered opening Stella's for Saturday brunch to shore up weekend receipts. But times like this, he was glad he didn't have to rush back in the morning.

Damp, cool air blew over them as he set the security alarm. He wished he'd thought to throw a jacket over Luna. He was struggling to hold her as it was, and it was a good thing his car was parked close. Folding her onto the backseat, he watched the shadows consume her and, once again, it hit him how fast she was growing up—and away from him.

The only hours he didn't spend contemplating food service or escaping into the kitchen were the days he devoted to Luna.

That tiny, naïve heart danced and twirled behind her brown eyes, and he wanted to be the man she thought he was. He wondered how he'd gotten so lucky to have a daughter who was easygoing, creative, and imaginative. Nothing like her mother, save the eyes, yet seemingly a living incarnation of his grandmother, the original Stella.

He walked around to the driver's seat and climbed in, regretting that he'd run off the last babysitter, someone who could have put Luna to bed at a reasonable hour on the coziness of a mattress. No more hiring off-duty waitresses. He'd pay whatever a licensed caregiver cost because, despite her tears that she just wanted to be with him, bringing Luna to the restaurant was a no-win situation.

The drive to his condo didn't take long this late at night, but its location wasn't anywhere near an elementary school or a park. It had been the most convenient option after Hannah had insisted they sell their home, but the neighbors were odd and seemed to run an after-hours business. He overlooked the comings and goings because he was at the restaurant, but with Luna home he was on high alert that someone might take advantage of a sitter.

"Daddy?"

He braked as he pulled under the carport. "Hey, sleepyhead."

"Are we home?"

Through the rear-view mirror, he saw the tousled brown hair and a lopsided bow. "Safe and sound."

Yawning, she asked, "Is it breakfast time?"

He was hungry because he rarely ate until the end of service, when a cook would whip up a pan of spaghetti or baked eggs. Tonight, he'd worked on menu ideas and had nibbled. "No, but I could make you toast if you're hungry."

She waited until he opened her door, then crawled out, gathering her blanket close to her chest. "French toast? With jam and powdered sugar?"

"Sure, why not?"

Hugging his leg, she announced, "You're the best!"

He could hear Hannah in his head, ranting that he was creating a monster. He ignored the voice. He often did. Luna was with him, and he wouldn't deny her anything.

Scanning the neighbor's lights, he tugged Luna close and hurried her through the door before she asked questions about the electric scooters littering the yard next door.

Inside, he set the alarm and dropped his keys on the Formica counter. This space was a quarter of the gourmet kitchen he'd outfitted in their home, but it served his purposes. There was room for his Italian coffee machine, the chopping block he'd inherited from his grandmother, and the knife set he'd invested in with his first paycheck.

Luna had folded her blanket and placed it on a stool. She reached for her apron and was tying the strings before he'd even poured them water.

"Aren't you tired?" he asked, as he watched her fetch the frying pan from a cupboard.

"Not anymore," she said, moving to the refrigerator and reaching for the egg carton. "I had the best dream. We had a vegetable garden as far as I could see, and I picked carrots as big as a tree. You let me cook them and it was dee-lish-is-ness," she said with flair.

"Dee-lish-is-ness" was her word of the week.

"You don't eat carrots when I make them," he said, watching her assemble the ingredients.

"That's because yours are crunchy." She scooted her step stool closer to the counter and climbed up.

He preferred his vegetables in a form closest to their original essence. "I thought *I* was making the French toast."

"You can do the hot parts. I'll do the rest." Cutting her gaze toward him, she added, "I give more jam than you do."

Chuckling, he slipped off his shoes and unbuttoned his uniform. "Give me five minutes to change. And no turning on the stove. You know the rules."

She saluted.

Walking through the living room, he noted the dolls, stuffed animals, books, and iPad for the streaming network of educational games Hannah had installed. Finally, this place looked like a home. He kept the lights low as he hurried upstairs. Living in an impersonal condo had not been on his list of goals for this age, but he'd never imagined Hannah leaving him either.

Turning on a lamp next to Luna's bed, he walked into his room and shed the uniform onto the pile of others ready for the dry cleaner. Pulling on sweatpants and a denim shirt, he stretched the neck muscles that had formed layers of knots. Even if Luna had not been awake, he doubted he could have gone to sleep quickly tonight. With the foundation award hovering over every thought, the dramas in the kitchen, and the quick death of the bistro, his body rejected most normal behaviors—like falling into bed the minute he walked in the door. He'd still need at least an hour to shuck off the day's details.

Chucking his cell phone onto the dresser, he saw a message glow from the screen. Glancing a second time, he caught Kenny's name and read the text. It featured a link to Alan Gale's review. He almost didn't want to know; he didn't want to care. With the JBF competition in full swing, he wondered if Gale's critique would carry any weight with the judges. He stuck the phone in his pocket and would decide later if it were worth reading.

"Daddy! I'm hungry."

He responded to the siren and hurried downstairs. Inside the kitchen, he saw a pile of bread drowning in egg batter and figured Gale could wait another day.

"What's the secret ingredient?" He regulated the flame on the burner as he glanced at Luna. Her tiny hands could barely stretch around the milk carton. She glanced into her bowl as if she were determining if it was too late to add it to the mixture.

"Cinnamon!"

Judging by the brown tint to the eggs, she'd already dumped in plenty.

He couldn't break her heart by correcting her concoction; he'd have to eat it and begin the narrative that she was a natural cook. He knew the scars from a parent who mocked childhood efforts, and he'd not do that to his daughter.

"Of course, and so what jam are you going to pair with cinnamon?"

Chewing her bottom lip, she guessed, "Strawberry?"

"Sounds great to me. Why don't you find that little jar of your favorite jam in the fridge, and I'll get this bread onto the skillet."

Stepping off the stool, she opened the refrigerator and moved the various containers around until she found the jar she'd bought from a farmers market in the fall. Before she'd closed the door, she'd rearranged the condiments into descending heights. He'd like to think that she was being cute, but she'd done the same things to the items in his medicine cabinet and the objects on his desk at the restaurant.

Before she climbed onto the stool, she yawned again.

He felt like a heel for keeping his baby up this late, but he didn't know how to tell Luna "no." Like a sprite, she flitted in and out of his life, and he didn't want to miss a single smile. God knows he didn't want to bring on her tears.

"Daddy?"

"Yes, baby?"

"Are you going to answer your phone?"

Still remembering the chaos of telling Luna that he wasn't moving to Abilene with her mommy, he could barely connect the dots to a telephone. He felt in his pocket and drew out the device he usually kept on vibrate. Jay's job was to deal with phone calls.

Speak of the devil. "It's a little late for you to be up, isn't it?" he said, as he put the speaker against his ear.

Jay dumped words so fast that Rudy could barely separate one bit of bad news from the other—rather like oil flying off a hot skillet. Apparently, the timing of Alan Gale's article couldn't be worse. Jay predicted news outlets would repost it in the morning cycle.

Rudy went through the motions of cooking the bread and flipping the pieces onto plates, but his mind was not in the kitchen. Even Luna dumping half the jar of jam onto the toast barely registered.

Gale's pettiness about the temperature in the restaurant and the loud guests at the table nearby were nothing compared to his byline credits. The dining experience gave him the platform to announce his new role as marketing director for the James Beard Foundation. Pending the JBF team's response to tonight's dinner, Stella's may be out of the running for the restaurant award.

"Daddy, look!" Luna said, sprinkling table sugar on top of the jam. "I'm a chef too!"

He ended the call and turned the flame off under the burner. "Good job," he said, with a flatness that sabotaged her joy.

"But we're not done." She climbed off the stool and ducked under his arm, lifting his hand to the knob. "We need to cook your toast too."

"We're done, Luna." His appetite vanished. "Eat what you want, and then it's time to go to bed."

"But Daddy?"

He wouldn't look at her. The earnestness in her eyes was too pure to compete with the thoughts in his head. "I said, bed."

She walked over to her plate and stared at it like she wasn't sure what she'd done wrong.

Rudy walked out of the kitchen and wanted to pound his fist into a tree, or a wall, or his neighbor's door where loud music beat a bass note into his side of the sheetrock. But he couldn't do any of that. Placing his hands flat against the door, he leaned his forehead against the surface and tried to breathe, something that would release the tension gripping his lungs.

Tiny arms wrapped around his legs, and he felt Luna press against his thighs like a fairy comforting an ogre. Maybe the whim of being nominated for the award wasn't shot down; maybe there was still hope he'd be invited to cook for the foundation in New York. Maybe . . . maybe this wasn't yet another peg of his life crashing down.

Pushing away from the door, he turned around and scooped Luna up and against his chest. He didn't have words to say to her, just held her tight and hoped that of all things spinning in hurricane colors, she'd be the one constant that wouldn't leave him too.

"You hungry, little one?"

She shook her head. "Not really."

"How about we clean up in the morning?" He started for the stairs. "Maybe we'll even walk down the street and get the donuts you like so much."

She didn't respond with her usual list of toppings like she had every other time he'd bribed her with treats. He'd have thought her quietness was odd, except she asked him to go back for her blanket.

When he found her fluffy bit of fabric, folded in a square on the barstool, she grabbed it and tucked it under her chin. Rudy glanced at the eggshells and milk carton on the counter and wished he knew how to do the father thing better, but at this point, he didn't even know how to manage his own existence, much less Luna's.

This wasn't the life he'd wanted when he left California, and it wasn't the life he'd promised Hannah when Luna was born. But it was the life dumped in his lap, and he'd have to hope he was stronger than the tides pulling him under.

Chapter Five

Lacy buttoned her coat against the wind blowing off Lamar Boulevard and evaluated the restaurant competition, lined with colorful awnings and compelling sandwich boards. The old storefronts, modern bistros, and bungalow housing made West Austin distinctive.

She liked the mix of modern design and 1950s kitsch. Waiting impatiently, she wanted her interior meter to buzz. She needed the affirmation of a good sizzle—like she was about to discover some funky place she could scoop for her followers. Maybe she'd settle for any inkling she was even remotely close to a hot spot. Like others suffering side effects from withdrawals, she'd lost her flair for reading a crowd, and her radar had gone flat. Staring hard at the strange mural painted on the bricks and mortar of a gas station, she waited. Any moment now, she would feel the anticipation.

Or not.

Surrendering to muteness, she glanced around for their restaurant destination but instead saw names she didn't recognize. "Have you been to these places, too?"

"Some." Kali glanced at the signage and then reached into the back of her SUV. "When Jake and I were newlyweds, we'd scoot to the city for our date nights."

Great. Her sister, who gave up a law practice for goat herding, had beat her to this trendy neighborhood. She might as well call an undertaker to bury her career.

AJ English laughed. "You don't have to leave Comfort for good food. Luke and I have become regulars at High Café, and let me tell you, their staff knows we will order the daily specials before we sit down. They introduced me to avocado toast."

Lacy disguised a moan with her scarf. High Café had been the only trendy place to eat in Comfort when she lived there *the first time.*

"The difference is your husband was already spoiled to the surprises of big-city life." Kali opened the SUV's hatch. "Mine lived most of his life on a ranch, so going to Comfort was hardly different from staying home. We needed to expand our horizons."

As Kali and AJ debated the adjustments of their husbands to married life, Lacy tuned down the conversation. *Way down.* Being around happily married people was a torture somewhere between waterboarding and solitary confinement. She loved AJ and Kali, but their joy was sickening.

As one who had spent an unfortunate number of Fridays sitting in Gloria's kitchen, chopping onions or washing the pots, she knew she needed to expand her options. Envying thirty-year-olds was going to send her to a deep, dark place.

Work, that's all she had going for her these days. Rolling her shoulders, she recalled her online investigation of Stella's Restaurant. After the obligatory hours and menu preview, the bulk of the content included generous reviews, photos of interesting dishes, and the words of diners who gushed over the staff. The link to their Twitter feed surprised her because she'd have guessed putting live content on their site was both a blessing—when folks tweeted their praise—and a potential curse.

Returning to the task at hand, she peered into the Tahoe. "Who is going to do the talking when we ambush Chef Delgardo?"

Kali pulled the crate holding bubble-wrapped containers of brie. "You. This idea is your brainchild."

AJ agreed. "I'm here for moral support and to provide logistics on how the Lavender Hill Hall debut is already being discussed in regional promotions."

"And food magazines," Kali added. "My cheese distributor will submit a press release to magazines. He thinks the opening of our event center has visual appeal for a feature spreads in summer issues."

Lacy breathed a sigh of relief that AJ and Kali were not only on board with the off-beat idea to combine a food festival with their grand opening, but also willing to fund the legwork. If this crazy, big plan were to succeed, it would take all of them working double-time to pull it off.

AJ reached for a carton of cheese. "Our architects are excited too. This event will be good exposure for them, and they're willing to underwrite that jazz ensemble Luke met a few months ago."

Lacy moved her fingers through her pocket, searching for a mint. "AJ, you really need to be the one to talk. Your dad is his friend, and he will remember you from catering your wedding."

A wintry breeze spun their hair like whirligigs. They laughed with surprise. Settling their burdens on benches, they finger brushed their hair.

"I thought about calling Dad and asking him to meet us here for a bite. But Dad is in Las Vegas with his girlfriend." AJ hitched the box against her hip and corralled her blonde hair again. "We're the Three Amigos seeing the scary chef."

Kali repaired her ponytail. "He's not scary. He's just . . . demanding. And highly successful. And . . . maybe condescending to suppliers."

With a bag of the mascarpone-cheese containers in her grip, she watched her sister backtrack the selling points. "I thought you said he was pleasant, and you distinctly mentioned handsome." Lacy remembered Kali describing the chef when they loaded the SUV for this delivery. "You said movie-star good-looking."

"Did I?" Kali hit the lock remote. "*Jake* is movie-star good-looking. Chef Delgardo is mildly attractive if you like moody types in need of a shave."

Now she gets down to the truth. Lacy should have remembered her sister knew how to bend facts and spin content to suit her arguments.

"Wait." Lacy stood on the curb and pointed her finger at the two friends. "We need to get our story straight. I'm not even sure why I'm here. You two are the owners of the event center, and Kali has the perfect in to ask the man to be the celebrity chef at the grand opening because she's bringing him custom-made cheese. That, apparently, he loves. And even if she didn't, there's AJ." She shifted her gaze to the friend wearing a chic leather duster. "Who would turn you down? Because of your wedding, you brought Dolly Parton into this man's sphere of influence. If he doesn't fall down and kiss your feet for that introduction, then I will eat my scarf."

AJ glanced at the periwinkle silk wrapped around Lacy's throat. "Did you buy that from Lavender Hill? It looks like something we have in the gift shop."

"Focus." She snapped her fingers. "In May, you'll launch one of the coolest entertainment venues in the Hill Country. Between the lush lavender fields and the dramatic architecture, it will be the birth of everyone's dream-wedding site. And we need this man's star power to bring in the foodies."

"Are you going to tell him the idea today," Kali stepped out of the way of people rushing by, "or wait until he commits to reveal the beginning of what could be the biggest food-and-wine event outside Austin?"

There were a million unsolved details, but Lacy knew she'd landed on the perfect launch idea for the event center when the three of them sat on the back of Jake's pickup the other night, staring at the shell of the building while eating through an order of BBQ. The sunset pricked a memory from a location the band had played for a private party, and, within seconds, she saw white tents, smoking grill stations, and beverage purveyors roll out across the fields surrounding the lavender-topped hills. It was brilliant, but the difference between imagining an awesome party and carrying it out was huge.

"I still don't know why you've voted me the spokesperson."

AJ started walking toward the corner. "Because this plan fell from your brain. As the author, you should be the one to explain the launch of Lavender Hill Hall."

Kali grimaced. "I'm still not sold on that name. I think it's a tongue twister."

Lacy followed Kali and AJ. They at least knew where the restaurant was located. Despite their apparent faith in her ability to concoct a promotional idea, she was lost without GPS. Glancing at the small houses, made cuter by good landscaping and sculptures, she knew she'd never find her way back to this spot.

Her boots thumped the sidewalk as thoughts circled back to the conversation with Gloria last night. Her landlady also saw the broad appeal of the plan and agreed with Lacy that the *Comfort News* should be one of the major underwriters. All Lacy had to do was convince Frank to let her have complete creative control over the media locally and link the serial stories to features in regional papers too. Gloria seemed to think that, with a few well-placed phone calls, reporters would latch on to the feel-good qualities of this story. Frank could be convinced to take part if Lacy proved she had a plan to bring in other news outlets.

She pictured the broadsheet of photos and press releases timed to reveal what could become a regional fixture for tourism and economic development in Comfort. Frank was bound to laugh at featuring this in the paper, and then he'd say "no." For all his expertise in publishing, he was rather stuck on the idea that news had to be black, white, and hard. But she depended on Gloria's insights, so maybe she'd persevere past his first rejection.

AJ and Kali could afford to underwrite the whole event without the *Comfort News* on the banner, but that wasn't the point. Lacy needed this experience to catapult her out of the hills. And she needed Frank to set the launch.

"Here it is," Kali announced, pausing outside a low-roofed building. "I hope the doors are unlocked. I forgot, until just now, that they don't serve lunch."

Lacy took stock of the brick-and-stone exterior, black-framed windows, and the orange awning proclaiming Stella's in a simple block lettering. The first impression was understated. Not what she'd expected from the multi-starred reviews online.

"I read that there was a bakery," she said, glancing around for a second entrance.

"Stella Too." Kali nodded toward the north. "It's a few streets over. We must stop on our way out of town. They sell a bite-sized Bundt cake that is to die for."

Lacy's Keto-friendly breakfast had worn off about forty miles ago. Depending on how long it took to deliver the order and schmooze the chef, she would need to eat something hearty soon. Maybe she should ask one of the staff for their recommendations. When she was in the thick of her influencer world, she'd always tipped extra for information on the undiscovered places. The exposure worked both ways. New restaurants and bars benefited from her endorsement, and she got the edge on her competition.

The exhaustion from chasing the publicity proved a challenge, but the list of contacts was priceless. She had the phone numbers of all the best hostesses and servers on speed dial.

Or at least, she used to have the contacts. Presumably, it was all stored in a cloud until the day she was released from technology prison.

She glanced at the CLOSED sign dangling behind the glass. "Will they let us in without an appointment?"

"I'm texting the general manager now."

The clatter of locks turning on the other side signaled their first win.

AJ winked. "See? It worked. Next time, you can deliver to the suppliers' entrance. We'll ask forgiveness for breaking protocol today."

Lacy had no idea how food deliveries worked. The mechanics of restaurant world were never a priority. She was all about the color and flash, less about substance.

A flurry of nerves skittered around her stomach. Ideas had taken flight so fast over the last few days, she'd not Googled Stella's chef. She regretted trusting Kali's connections to open the conversation. She should have done more research.

A man in a dark suit and elegant tie stood inside the alcove and welcomed them from the cold. His clothing appeared tailored, the wingtips expensive. Lacy didn't think he was the chef, but he made quite a first impression. Taking one of the containers from Kali's arms, he led them into the main dining room.

Shades of peach, amber, and eggplant swirled in watery patterns between the rooms, and the bold, vibrant art popped with colors tinged in acid and metallics. Thick beams overhead were lightened by skylights, bathing the space in warmth. Lacy relaxed. If there'd been a roaring fireplace, she'd have taken up residence.

"Hello, I'm Jay Tumlin, Stella's general manager," the man said, introducing himself to AJ and Lacy. "I didn't realize Kali came with such a beautiful entourage."

AJ grinned. "We're the B team."

"If you're the second string, I don't think I'd survive the first." He held a chair for Kali to sit down. "Where's baby Charlie? I enjoy negotiating contracts with him."

"He's teething and no fun for anyone." Kali slipped her coat off her shoulders. "But I wanted you to meet my business partner in an event-center venture in Comfort, and my sister, who—though she won't admit it—has become our PR officer."

Jay motioned to the bartender to bring them beverages. "Can I offer you any refreshments? I'm going to get these cheeses into Kenny's expert hands, and I can bring you back a sample of what the chef is preparing for tonight's service."

"That sounds wonderful," Kali said. "And is there any chance we could talk to Chef Delgardo? AJ, my business partner, met him in December when he catered her wedding."

Jay handed the boxes off to two staff members. "You're *that* bride?"

AJ held her hands in surrender. "My father met Rudy Delgardo during the days when he was still giving concerts. I wanted to tell the chef how grateful I was for his food magic at the reception and that folks are still raving about his menu."

Lacy leaned forward in the chair and marveled at how easily these minutes rolled toward a natural progression of getting to the man in charge. She should have paired up with these two years ago.

Jay stepped back as the bartender set waters in front of them. "I'm sure Chef can spare a few minutes. Let me visit with him, and I'll be right back."

While they waited, her mind spun with various ways she could create photos in a space infused by this marvelous natural light. Stella's Instagram account must explode with hits. Because she couldn't help herself, she imagined the meal, the candlelight, the gorgeous date, and her posts—#dreamcometrue.

When the whoosh of the kitchen doors reached her ears, she was knee deep in imagined content. *If only she could create.* She'd flirted with an alter ego for a secret online presence, but Woodley's threats felt too real to tease.

Six more months.

She could wait.

Most likely.

When she glanced away from the linen, she caught the gray gaze of a man straight out of the last movie series she'd binged, the one littered with eighteenth-century warrior-monks and dark Italian landscapes. Her tongue froze to the roof of her mouth. Her heart raced. For the finest sliver of a second, she was the damsel stuck at the top of a burning turret, needing rescue by this secret priest of danger.

And then he spoke. No European accent. No hint he carried a saber.

Blinking, she realized the man was still watching her, though he thanked Kali for her gourmet cheeses.

Cheeses?

Catching her breath, she regained her composure. Based on the scruff of beard lining his chin, she'd guess this man was the chef. He was younger than she'd been led to believe, and she was embarrassed to admit she'd entirely based that presumption on the age of AJ's father. Another mistake. Despite stereotyping, this man was fit, intense, and insanely handsome. She'd bet money that he wasn't yet forty.

Listening as AJ recounted the highlights of her Christmas Eve wedding, an event Lacy had attended both as a friend and newspaper contributor, she wondered how she'd missed noticing the chef. That had been just six weeks after her fall from fame, so maybe she'd still been nursing her pride and jealous rage. *Yeah.* She wasn't proud of her behavior that night. Champagne had been gasoline on the flames of her resentment.

But this man. His height, his athletic grace. He would have been hard to overlook.

She must have really been bitter.

As if brisk air swept out her cranium, those memories faded, and what remained was a compelling need to get to the other side of the table to see if this man was as delectable up close as he was from a distance.

Her stomach seized with tension. Her legs felt bouncy. She was fifteen again.

The tinkling sound of AJ's laughter annoyed her, and she fought against a brain fog to focus on the conversation. The chef probably couldn't linger. She'd need to hurry to get her words out. It was her job to ask him to come to Comfort. To work his menu magic one more time.

A flash of heat seared across her nerves. Yanking the scarf from her neck, while struggling free of her coat, she felt both lightheaded and heavy. An ugly sizzle circled her stomach.

Oh no.

In neon colors, she remembered the egg she'd fried for breakfast. It had been sitting in a bowl on the counter. She'd not bothered to ask Gloria for permission to use it—Gloria had a mi casa, su casa hospitality in her kitchen.

Now, she wondered.

Jumping to her feet, she reached for the man—Jay something or other—and begged, "The bathrooms?"

Kali surveyed her sister. "Lacy, are you all right?"

"She looks green," AJ said.

Lacy momentarily fought between flight and remaining the sophisticated professional she'd dressed as today. She could hear her pageant coach yelling in her ear "Never, ever, under no circumstances, run off stage." She ran for the direction the man had pointed. Barely making it to a stall, she leaned over the toilet and let go of the contents in her stomach.

Grasping the seat of the toilet, she waited until the heaving stopped and rocked back on her heels. Spinning paper from the toilet-paper roll, she wiped her face and prayed she'd not made a mess all over the space. Once her eyes cleared, she looked around and relaxed. Until the toilet in the next stall flushed.

Leaning upright, she looked behind her and saw an Asian man dressed in a starched black uniform staring at her with sympathy.

"Oh, no." She glanced around the fixtures. "Is this the men's room?"

He nodded.

She dropped her chin. "Figures."

"You going to be okay?" he asked, looking twice at her face. "That sounded rough."

She stepped toward the sink, washing her hands and rinsing with mouthwash. Weak and shaky, she used their lovely hand towels to dry her face. "I'm sorry I . . . uh . . . didn't mean to . . ."

He frowned in sympathy. "Just be glad no one was using the urinal."

A thin chuckle bubbled in her throat, but she wasn't taking chances on stirring another reaction. "I can't apologize enough. I've never been to Stella's and wasn't sure where the restrooms were."

"You're not the first woman found in the men's room. Sometimes our guests get impatient with the wait and make use of the first available door."

A fragrance of pine wormed through the threads of the towel. If she'd not known before, it reminded her that whoever was behind the creation of this restaurant put care into the details.

"I'd rather not tell anyone that I made this mistake." Lacy glanced at her chest to make sure she'd not ruined her blouse. "People tease me all the time that I couldn't find my way out of a shopping bag. So, can I trust you?"

"I'm Kenny." A small grin warmed his face. "Chef trusts me with his recipes, so you can rely on me to keep this secret too."

She finger combed her hair into order as Kenny stood there, transfixed. Men had stared at her before, but she figured this one was probably waiting on her to leave so he could disinfect the sink.

"You look familiar," he said, glancing at her boots.

In the mirror, she returned his gaze. Sadly, she'd looked into so many faces over the last few years, she was getting less and less reliable at recognizing people. "I guess I just have one of those faces."

"No. I never forget a face." His scrutiny narrowed. "It was somewhere recent."

Considering that she'd not been to Austin in weeks, she doubted his brag. In his defense, in Texas tall blondes with big blue eyes were as common as Cadillacs. She would know. She competed with hundreds of beautiful women, many of whom were quite nice, even without the false eyelashes and teased hair.

The door whooshed open as Kali stood in the entrance wearing a stunned expression. "I couldn't find you anywhere."

It was her childhood all over again. Kali had assumed mother duties somewhere around third grade and never released them, even after their aunt moved in and took over where their momma had left off.

"My mistake," Lacy grimaced, fearing the lecture to follow. "I didn't read the sign when I ran for the bathrooms."

Kenny held his hands open. "And I'm released from the secret."

Kali's eyes narrowed on the man. "Who are you?"

Kenny nodded. "Head sous chef." He walked to the sink and pumped soap into his palm. "Chef's right-hand man, aside from Mr. Tumlin."

"What happened here?" Kali asked Lacy, ramping up her voice.

"Exactly what you have imagined." Lacy stepped around Kenny, careful to avoid eye contact with a man who had paid close attention to her footwear. "I'm sorry I ruined the meeting."

"You didn't ruin anything," Kali said sympathetically. "I'm worried you've picked up a virus somewhere."

She had such a limited circle of acquaintances these days, she'd lay the blame on a bad egg. Before she could fault poultry, the door opened again, and Chef Delgardo stood with a bowl of ice water and a cloth.

"I followed the conversation," he said, entering the small space. "I wasn't sure if you were still feeling woozy, so I came prepared."

Kenny's gaze whipped between the chef and the guest with long, blonde waves. "You know her?"

The chef set the bowl on the counter. "No, but misery trumps introductions."

There was no rock big enough for her to hide. Lacy squirreled into the corner of the sink area and tried to ignore the fact that two strangers and her sister stared at her with varying degrees of sympathy. That they stood in the men's room, and her skin resembled chalk, adding to the dismal impression. Truly, even the weakest contest judge would score her with less than one for deportment and grace, and to be fair, they'd throw her under the bus for not coming up with the right words in a moment of crisis.

"Comfort!" Kenny announced, as if he were a *Jeopardy!* contestant.

Thankful the attention had shifted, she thought at first he was suggesting a strategy for her relief, and then, just as fast, realized that he'd been the one in the designer sunglasses standing behind her at Cup of Joe's a few weeks ago. She glanced at his shoes, seeing sneakers with gold ties. No mistaking the self-confidence of a man with something to prove.

"You were ordering an espresso and got a cranberry-orange scone." Kenny pointed his finger as if she might deny it. "I copied your order because it sounded good, but that was a disappointing scone. Way too heavy-handed with the sugar, and it lacked the depth of flavor one should expect from the tart-sweet juxtaposition."

"You've been to Comfort?" Kali stared at him like this was an impossible coincidence.

Kenny replied with date and time details, but Lacy watched the escape of the chef. His gaze held hers, and despite her recent experience with an upset stomach, she recognized a unique butterfly reaction that had everything to do with the intensity of his smoldering gaze. She wished a million times over that she'd not ruined their interview. The odds of him ever wanting to speak to her again diminished with his every backward step.

"Tell her, Chef," Kenny pleaded with Delgardo. "Tell her, that you sent me back to the hardware store where we cooked for that wedding reception."

"That reception is why we came here," Lacy said, even though her tongue moved stiffly. "We wanted to invite Chef Delgardo to Lavender Hill for the event center's grand opening in May."

At least she could leave with her pride intact. She'd done what she set out to do, tell the Chef he was invited to another command performance. Unfortunately, he was in the hallway, gazing longingly toward the kitchen instead of seeming the least bit interested in the invitation.

Kenny sputtered. "Chef doesn't do catering. That was a one-time special treat."

Kali folded her arms across her chest. "Of course, he caters. We saw on the website he's catered for the governor several times."

"Well, only for special people. He is very particular."

They could battle all they wanted, Lacy thought, as she stepped toward the door. The man in question had bolted. "I need some ginger ale." She tugged Kenny's sleeve. "Any chance your bartender could pour me a glass? I'll pay for it."

Kenny checked his watch. "I'm on the floor, but I'll see what I can do."

Losing patience, she shook her head. "I'll do it myself."

Kenny shrugged and departed the bathroom.

Kali caught the door and stepped into the hall. "That was weird."

"I know, right?" Lacy imagined all the ways this situation could have been done over, beginning with a bowl of cereal. "On the upside, my stomach isn't rumbling anymore."

"No, I mean the way they froze the moment we talked about catering."

Is that what caused the man to lose his composure? She would assume it had more to do with contact with airborne diseases. "I thought we lost the chef the moment the topic turned to Comfort."

Kali pursed her lips. "Yeah, that was odd too. What were they doing in town?"

Lacy remembered eavesdropping on the talk about replacing the electrical panel in an old hardware store. Hardly a location for another restaurant. Unless Kenny planned to go out on his own. Was he leaving Stella's? And why Comfort?

Any chef worth his salt would want to have loyal customers, not a clientele that went to bed with sunset.

As they approached the bar, Lacy ordered a ginger ale, and Kali requested a bottle of Topo Chico.

"Where has AJ gone?" Kali searched the dining room. "She's vanished."

Lacy didn't care. Sipping the fizzy drink helped, but if she never returned to Stella's it would be okay. Mortification topped the list of reasons why she'd avoid this place, although it would be hard to forget the chef. Eyes like that belonged on the big screen.

"Miss?"

She glanced to the bartender. "Your friend is taking a tour of the back of the house with Mr. Tumlin. They should return in a few minutes."

Kali set the bottle onto the polished bar. "I want to see the kitchen too. Which way did they go?"

He pointed toward the swing doors in the far corner of the dining room.

"Be back shortly." Kali hurried across the floor.

Lacy leaned her elbows on the bar and held her throbbing forehead. This disaster was one more on a long list of fails. It might be wise to look for the linking trend and learn to avoid it at all cost, but the only commonality was her own foolishness, and she couldn't ditch that character trait at the secondhand store like she did most of the purses she'd bought in Dallas.

A hand patted her arm, and she looked to the empty seat, expecting AJ or Kali to have returned. Instead, a small girl stood next to the bar.

"I heard you were sick. Here's my blanket. It makes me feel better when I'm feeling bad."

Lacy sat upright, speechless by the generosity of this little human. She accepted the worn fabric and treated it reverently. "So, you heard that, did you?"

The girl climbed onto a barstool. "My daddy's office is on the other side of the wall, and Kenny was telling people about you puking when he came into the kitchen."

This girl seemed too young to be hanging out at work, but what did Lacy know about children? *Zero.* The youngest in her family, she'd never collected the experience around babies that her friends boasted. Which is why she was surprised she'd not dropped Charlie yet. Holding him required all ten fingers and a hip bone.

"So, on a scale of one to ten," Lacy asked, "how bad was the report? Is Kenny telling people I hurled all over the men's room?"

Luna giggled. "I told my daddy to bring you some chicken soup because that's what my mom makes for me when I'm sick."

She wasn't sure which cook was her dad, but she doubted they kept a can of soup in their pantry. All the more reason for her to begin the hike back to the car, whichever direction that was located. "Well, you're sweet to think of that. But I'll be okay. Just ate a bad egg at breakfast."

The girl stared at Lacy's hair as if she wanted to touch it. "You look like Cinderella."

Lacy returned the blanket with due respect. "You're saying that to make me feel better about getting sick in such a fancy restaurant. But I think your blanket had the magic touch. My stomach isn't wiggling anymore."

The girl scooped it close to her chest. "I've had this since I was a baby."

"And how old are you now?"

"I'm seven," Luna said proudly. "I'm in second grade."

And yet it was the middle of the week. "Seven is just the best age. I hope you have lots of fun with it."

The girl's big brown eyes dimmed. "Five was better. My mom and dad lived together then. We had a big house near the park. I was supposed to get a puppy."

"Oh, boy." Lacy didn't know how to handle this confidence. "That's rough. But you know what, a big part of being happy is just knowing how to handle the difficult things that come into your life. Like today. Me getting sick before I ever got to ask my big question feels like a failure, but here I am talking to you, and this makes me feel good."

Luna giggled. "I'm kind of everyone's favorite. As long as I stay out of their way during the service."

"Service? Like a church service?"

"It's what they call the time they're cooking supper and getting it out to the customers."

"I stand corrected."

Luna grinned as if she enjoyed being the teacher. "I have to sit in the break room at night. But it's okay because I have a dollhouse. I finish schoolwork with a tutor and play games on my iPad."

Lacy couldn't imagine why this child stayed at this restaurant so many hours, but she wished someone would reward her grown-up attitude. She doubted many kids would be so long-suffering.

"Luna?"

Lacy and the girl both turned at the sound of the baritone voice.

"Daddy, she's feeling so much better."

Lacy stared at the chef holding a tray with a bowl of soup and a basket of rolls.

"I'm glad." He set the tray on the bar. "I hope I followed your recipe," he said, rubbing the top of his daughter's head.

Inspecting the small plate of grapes and the bowl of steaming liquid, Luna's little brows drew together into a V. "I don't see the animal shapes made of pasta, but it smells good."

"Chicken stock. We didn't have any bits of pasta to use, so this will have to do."

"It's fine, Daddy. The parsley is a nice touch."

A smile flirted around the edges of his lips.

"I see you've met my daughter." He glanced at Lacy quickly, then returned his gaze to the tray, removing the items and setting them on the bar.

Riveted by the aroma of chicken broth, herbs, and vegetables, Lacy couldn't decide what drew her attention the most, the soup or the man who prepared it.

She avoided his eyes in case he'd figure out how he disarmed her with a glance. "So, your name is Luna. That's beautiful."

The girl propped her cheek in her hand. "It's Spanish for "moon." Everyone always asks if Stella is my first name."

Lacy couldn't imagine why.

"Because of the book," Luna continued. "You know . . . *Stellaluna.*"

With limited experiences willfully choosing to read, she knew that if a book wasn't listed in a fashion magazine, she didn't know the title. "I guess I don't know that one."

"Really?" Luna perked up. "You may be the first person ever to not ask me that question."

"But the restaurant is named Stella's."

Rudy wiped his hands on the dishcloth tucked into his apron. "The restaurant is named for my grandmother."

"In California," Luna added helpfully. "She was breel-yi-nant!"

Maybe the stomach condition had been brought on by a virus because she wasn't following the thread. "Who is in California?"

"Stella," Luna announced, like it was a fact everyone should know.

"So, you're not Stella?"

"No, silly." Luna hopped off the barstool. "I'm going to ask Kenny to make me a grilled-cheese sandwich. Can I, Daddy?"

Gulping the ginger ale, Lacy couldn't take her eyes off the chef. He stood woodenly, as if surprised to find himself still at the bar. The awkward pause lingered until the voices of Kali and AJ interrupted.

"Oh, my word." Kali's voice rose as they returned. "That kitchen is a dream."

Rudy turned toward the two women. "Thank you."

AJ's face gleamed. "You must have had an amazing architect. I doubt they overlooked a single detail."

"I couldn't afford an architect when this was being built out, so I planned it myself." He folded his arms across his chest and rocked back on his heels. "After all the kitchens I'd worked in, it was easy to know what I wanted."

"And what was that?" Lacy didn't realize so much thought would go into a restaurant kitchen. But to be fair, she didn't know what sort of planning would go into a home kitchen either.

"Streamlined efficiency and comprehensive workstations for the cooks." He glanced at the stainless-steel kegs lining the wall behind the bar. "Even our wine service is maximized for the least amount of waste and the freshest experience in every glass."

All three women turned toward the bar set up, their gazes settling on the large vats with dispensers tapped into the base. "So, those are *wine* kegs?" AJ asked.

"Yes. It's an air-tight way to deliver wine by the glass." Then he pointed to a smoky, glass-enclosed niche. "We sell by the bottle as well. Not every vintner is inclined to send their wine in barrels. But it is a resourceful alternative."

Lacy sipped her soup before it cooled and decided she'd tackle one task at a time. Eating trumped learning at the moment.

AJ nodded. "Chef, you're the most knowledgeable wine source I've met in a long time. Could we persuade you to come to Comfort in May and be our headlining celebrity chef? We want to host a food-and-wine festival with our venue's grand opening, and you'd be such a draw in your own right, but also your connections would be invaluable to bringing vendors to our kick-off."

Kali speared Lacy with a glare since this pitch was to have been her job.

"No, I'm afraid not," he said, taking a step away from them. "I do wish you the best, though."

Before Lacy could wipe her lips with a napkin, he'd hurried away, and the swish of the kitchen doors echoed his passage.

"Snob," Kali muttered.

"He's not a snob," AJ sighed, "just a busy professional."

"Oh, you didn't hear his assistant say that he only deals with the very top echelon of clients."

Lacy watched the doors swing to a slow stop, wondering about Rudy Delgardo. She wouldn't rule out snobbery, but she doubted smugness rooted his personality defects. The tenderness he showed his daughter contrasted too strongly with his demeanor. No, she'd bet there was a complicated box of puzzle pieces underneath that starched white apron.

An image of her aunt's game closet appeared in her mind, and the stacks of untouched puzzle boxes glowed as if neon. Turned off from such difficult things when she was a teenager, she wondered if—if the stakes were different—could she resist the tangle of shapes today? Swallowing the last of the ginger ale, she decided she probably could. But it was interesting to think about.

Chapter Six

Rudy collapsed in his chair and stared at the calendar tacked to his wall. Three days until he was scheduled to fly, with Kenny and two other cooks, to dazzle the Manhattan-based James Beard Foundation with his Texas-infused menu. He'd mailed ahead the rubs and dry goods. Fresh products would be shipped in dry ice—including the goat cheese Kali Hamilton had delivered today for the burnt-beet salad.

So why did he feel sick?

Not counting the woman who nearly vomited on his feet.

But if he was being honest, she haunted his mind as much as the list of threats waiting for him at the Beard House. Those eyes. He'd seen the inside of a seashell once with the same muted blend of cornflower blue, and he'd longed to own that odd shade, a cross between sapphire and periwinkle. Describing it to a paint salesman, he had desired it for a statement wall inside Stella's and to distinguish his restaurant labels. They'd plied him with a hundred samples, but the color had eluded him—until today.

Until her.

He leaned back, the chair springs screeching against his size. Propping his feet on the edge of the desk, he closed his exhausted eyes and let his imagination run. She was tall and graceful, with movements that evoked a ballet routine. Even running for the bathrooms, she'd maintained an elegance. She was at once artless and entirely composed. Was she an athlete? Maybe a dancer?

He'd never met another person with such a total lack of awareness of their shape moving through the atmosphere. How could she be blind to the wake she left, the stares of every man she passed?

"Daddy?"

His boots crashed to the floor. He turned, seeing Luna in the doorway. An oil stain matted the tuft of her blanket, and he'd have to launder the thing later tonight. "Did you get a sandwich?"

"Yes, but I like yours better. Kenny didn't believe me when I told him you put bacon bits in the cheese."

"Kenny is a purist."

She walked in and curled next to his opened arm. "What does purr-isss mean?'

"*Pure*-ist—means he plays by the rule book. No making things up as he goes."

"But you have recipes, and no one is allowed to fudge a single step."

"Well, that's for consistency, not from a lack of creativity."

Her face wore a question mark, but he wasn't in the mood to indulge her curiosity. So, he tackled the issue that had been burning in his mind all morning. There would be tears, but he couldn't change that. Luna was in that awful space between warring parents.

"Honey, your Aunt Carol will pick you up in the morning. She'll drive you to Abilene and return you to school with your friends."

Clatter in the kitchen reverberated in the office. The fragrance of braising short ribs could not compete with the odor of crushed expectations.

"I thought I could stay with you—*here*—until Mom comes home. I have a tutor!"

"We don't know exactly when your grandmother will be able to walk on her own, so your mom could be a few more weeks. And when the Beard Foundation upped our dates for the competition, it didn't work out for your mom to come back to Texas."

She stared at him like he'd ripped a hole in her dreams.

Rudy tugged her close so he wouldn't watch her eyes fill with tears. "Aunt Carol will bring the baby with her, so you can play with your cousin in the afternoons."

He wasn't sure how much he would have to pay his sister for this over-the-top favor, but he was out of options. Luna absolutely couldn't tag along with him to New York.

"I don't want to go," she moaned.

"And I wish I didn't have to send you back, but you know how important this competition is to Stella's. You've heard us talking about it since you got here, and no one planned for the date change, so we all have to be flexible."

Well, everyone but Hannah. She'd been inflexible since the day she had announced she was leaving their marriage. The offer of marketing director proved too delicious to refuse, and she'd packed their daughter, and all her insecurities, when she moved from Austin.

"Chef?"

Looking over Luna's head, he saw his pastry chef frowning. "Yes?"

"I was asked to tell you the ice machine is making a weird sound, and the ice appears cloudy. Mr. Tumlin is out of the restaurant. What would you like me to do?"

His eyelids drifted down so his frustration wouldn't shoot darts at the woman who'd stayed with him through two restaurants and a divorce. "I've got the number of the appliance tech on my phone. I'll call in just a minute."

She nodded and, sensing that Luna was holding back tears, closed the door.

When the office became quiet, he pulled back and read his daughter's face for the chapter and verse outlining him as hateful. Steely resolve held her eyelids tight. She'd never looked more like her mother. Kissing her forehead, he said, "Sit with me while I try to get the ice guy on the phone. Fingers crossed that he's available."

Luna didn't relax. "I don't want to go home. There's nothing to do. Mom won't be there, and Aunt Carol isn't any fun."

These words echoed from the future, when she'd be a teenager and no longer distracted by pots, pans, and baking cookies. "Some days aren't fun, but how we deal with them reveals who we are."

She paused for a long moment. "That's what the lady said."

He scrolled through his phone contacts. "What lady?"

"Cinderella."

His daughter had a habit of bedazzling words she couldn't pronounce, and now he wondered if she were shifting the habit to people he should know. "Have we met Cinderella? Was she your tutor last night?"

Luna folded her blanket into a tight square. "She's the lady who got sick. The one you made the soup for. That's Cinderella."

Rudy meshed the image of the woman with the unforgettable eyes to the animated character he almost always fell asleep watching. "I can see some parallels, though I doubt she sings with animals. Did she tell you her name?"

"No." Luna shook her head. "But I liked her. She's Cinderella."

"I really don't think a five-minute conversation is the basis for liking someone. She could be a maniac or—worse—a sales rep. Remember the wine vendor who brought you chocolate last week? We don't want a repeat of that disaster."

Luna's lips curved into the smile she reserved for her father. "That candy was gross."

But expensive, Rudy thought. What some people would do to influence him. It was getting ridiculous.

He found the number and placed the call to the technician, insisting the man drop what he was doing and hurry to Stella's. Since he was leaving a voice mail, he didn't guess he'd see the guy within the next thirty minutes.

Luna picked up a pen and started drawing circles on the envelope holding the bank statement. Still in the black, thank God. Fake news from Alan Gale and a fail with the James Beard Foundation could change that bottom line in a heartbeat. Dread soured his stomach, and he knew he had to bring the best food presentation to New York. If they didn't award him restaurant of the year, it wouldn't be for lack of trying.

A curtain of brown hair fell between him and Luna's artwork, reminding him of Hannah's threat to keep Luna booked into camps instead of allowing her to return to Austin for the summer break because, once again, he was giving Stella's a higher priority than his own child. If he didn't carve better time management into his life, he might lose Luna forever.

Scrubbing his hand across his chin, he felt his blood pressure tightening the muscles. Once the award process was completed, and Stella's earned a firm place in the food-service galaxy, he would step back. He had to. Maybe he'd reconsider Kenny taking on more responsibility.

Had Kenny said he saw that lady—Cinderella—in a Comfort coffee shop?

"Daddy?"

"Yes," he responded, shutting down the image of the most beautiful woman he'd seen in years.

"Can we go to the park?"

He noticed she was drawing trees now. There was a winter-storm warning on the horizon, but he was about to deposit his daughter into his sister's hands for almost a week. To Carol's credit, she'd never been to Abilene. He doubted she'd leave the apartment to do anything fun, since that meant loading a baby and gear into the back seat of a rental car.

He stood, checked his watch, and stretched his back. "Let's see what's going on with the ice machine on our way out the door. About half an hour?"

Her frown drew her tiny eyebrows into a pencil. "What if the ice cream truck is there . . . we might have to stay longer?"

It was going to sleet before rush hour, and he doubted anyone would even go to the park with cold winds in the forecast. "No promises."

"You never promise."

"And that way, I don't hurt anyone's feelings."

"You hurt mommy's feelings."

He groaned. "Your mother is good at expressing how she feels. Better than most of the rest of the world."

Her little eyes drew together. "Am I very good at spressing my feelings?"

Scooping her into his arms, he hugged her close. "The best!"

Laughing, Luna snuggled against his chest.

He patted her back, grateful they'd dodged a difficult conversation. Not knowing how long he'd be a champion in his daughter's eyes, he would imprint every one of these hugs into his memory. One day he'd bankrupt the vault. There were no guarantees with the women in his life. For now, he'd invest in her little heart for as long as he could.

Walking into the kitchen, he flagged the pastry chef and announced he'd be going out for a bit. Once Jay was back in the house, he could deal with the repairman.

"Chef."

He saw Kenny walk out from the giant refrigerator. "Are you pleased with the cheese delivery?"

"Yes. The Hamilton woman is reliable. But, if we send this tenderloin order to New York tomorrow, we'll be short for Friday night's service."

Rudy glanced around the kitchen, conducting a mental inventory of who was prepping the seasonal vegetables and which sauces paired best with which items that had arrived this week. His beef provider had already been taxed to provide the menu for the Beard House order, and he didn't have confidence in the quality he'd get if he called a different purveyor. "Let's think about the fish coming in on tomorrow's delivery and ask for extra salmon. Our grilled salmon is popular, and if we make it the special for Friday's menu, perhaps we can move more of it, especially if we bring back the black rice we offered before the holidays."

Kenny nodded. "We've run out of black rice every evening we've served it."

"Make that call to the fish purveyor."

"Me?" Kenny's eyes widened. "I don't order the inventory."

"For today, you do. Unless Jay returns in the next half hour, you can make the call, can't you, Kenny?"

Kenny cut his gaze to the pastry chef, who usually managed the kitchen in authority's absence. She nodded in agreement.

"Kenny?" Rudy reached for his jacket on the hook outside his office. "Can I count on you?"

"Yes, Chef," he squeaked.

"All right then." Helping Luna put on her coat, he added, "The ice machine repairman has been contacted, you're dealing with the fish order, and I will take my princess out for some fresh air. Anyone need anything while I'm gone?"

The usual silence greeted him when he spoke to the staff. They were well trained in following the chains of command, and the only way he knew to keep personnel issues from ruining the culture of a restaurant was to demand everyone stay in their designated lanes.

Ushering Luna to the hall leading past the stock and dish rooms, he focused on the door so that he'd not be distracted by another task. He may be just as awful as Hannah implied, but he was not going to live up to her predictions on fathering. He had enjoyed growing up with a good dad, and he would do right by his child.

At the door, he pushed the security buzzer to unlock the push panel and read this mantra for employees: *Cooking is the art of adjustment – Jacques Pépin.* It was a reminder of the expectations the staff held for the environment in which they served, but also their responsibility to their guests. It applied to his life too. As a stickler for rules, he had to remind himself, almost hourly, to allow flexibility and spontaneity into his thinking. He was most creative when in flawed situations, but he dreaded chaos.

Luna hurried toward the car and banged on the handle as if that would open the lock. He hit the remote and squinted into the low clouds. Sleet might fall earlier than predicted. He'd not taken time to eat lunch, and now, for reasons he couldn't fathom, a hot bowl of chicken soup rooted in his mind. Anything might taste good when sitting next to Cinderella, and he hoped, one day, to see her again.

With an unexpected smile, he climbed into the driver's seat and declared, "This pumpkin is ready to roll. How about, instead of the park, we go to the children's museum?"

"But the Thinkery is so far away."

"Are you really going to try to talk me out of an hour at your favorite place?"

She buckled up and grinned. "Never! Drive on, Prince Charming."

Chapter Seven

Lacy clutched the steering wheel, feeling perspiration dampen her blouse. So much for the efficiency of the organic deodorant a company had sent her to test last year. Stamping on her brakes, she decided everyone on the road was an idiot. Driving in Austin brought out the worst. Or she was nervous. Could go either way with how her gut had been tightening with every mile between Comfort and the capital.

Flashing her gaze to the growing mass of buildings, they reminded her of the tension she felt the first time she drove here for a pageant. Giddy then, she had no clue where she was driving, or that she'd ever need to remember the highway numbers. Now, she cursed that she'd not paid better attention to the route. Kali had told her to arrive before one o'clock to make the delivery. Jay Tumlin made a point that Stella's rarely accepted products after they started cooking.

Buckets of lavender sloshed when she hit the brake pedal again, and she whipped around to make sure they hadn't spilled.

The grid in the trunk of Kali's SUV normally held stacks of cheese products, but today it also carried AJ's offering for Rudy Delgardo. The three of them had cooked up an idea for appealing to the chef and thought sweetening the deal with complimentary lavender stems and wild-berry arrangements for his tables might give them another chance to explain their ideas for the food-and-wine festival. AJ had written a prospectus for the event; Kali had prepared gift boxes of her cheeses paired with fresh fruit, local balsamic oil, and small splits of wine; and Lacy was supposed to present this with more panache than she did the last time she walked into Stella's.

As the only one of the threesome with an available schedule, she'd had a hard time convincing them she was the absolute last person to be a messenger in this scheme, but here she was, praying she'd get to the restaurant in one piece. At least the sun had burned off the rain clouds, and she wasn't battling wet roads too.

It had been a week since their last foray into the city, and in those short days, the weather had returned to the mild temperatures that made Central Texas so sweet. But to be on the safe side, in consideration of her last visit to this restaurant, she'd eaten oatmeal for breakfast.

Now, if she could just find the address before she mowed anyone down.

Honking at a truck blocking access to the turn lane, she felt mildly better. Maybe this panic was merely a matter of nerves. It wasn't like AJ or Kali expected anything significant to happen. *The chef probably wouldn't even remember her,* Lacy thought.

When they'd convinced her to make this trek, she'd gone through her closet and found an outfit that gave her all the feels for a fabulous professional. It had taken some effort to find the bone-leather skirt behind the hangars filled with jeans and T-shirts, but pairing the skirt with a nubby off-white blazer, the white silk blouse she'd bought at Neiman's, and nude boots made her feel like a million bucks. She donned pearls because nothing screamed power like strands of pearls.

Not that she needed to scream. She was just a delivery girl. But the last time she'd been in this restaurant, she'd looked like death warmed over. It was imperative she move up the chain, and this outfit said, Forget the first impression. She might have gone overboard on the pearls, as she was no one's CEO, but sometimes she got started on a project and went haywire. Just like Frank. He was still reeling from the obituary she'd submitted that included the deceased's preference for Frank Sinatra and an enviable streak winning at Spades.

Pulling into a parking space at the back of Stella's, she texted the general manager, as Kali had suggested. Dragging in a deep breath, she flexed her fingers and pictured Rudy Delgardo's chiseled features. Releasing that breath, she hoped he'd say more than three words to her today.

She checked her phone for a reply and worked on her speech. What had AJ told her to say about the fields where they could set up the grill stations for their open-air BBQ? Running her fingers over the pearls, she chased the thoughts strung together. Surely, she'd not be the one to negotiate the terms for the chef to work the event—she was merely to ask for a second opportunity to persuade him. Give the gifts, smile pretty, that was what Kali had drilled.

Ha! Like her smile had any magical powers. It looked good in photos because she'd had a fantastic orthodontist, but it wasn't like she'd saved anyone's life. The basic muscle movements that affected her cheeks and lips were a credit to her father and nothing she'd been able to duplicate, even though others—okay, Amy Marsh—had begged her to teach them the secret. Really, what was so enviable about a smile? It just sort of happened when she felt happy or silly, and those days were less frequent than they used to be.

Climbing out of the SUV and smoothing her skirt, she heard a whoosh, and turned to see Jay Tumlin standing in the doorway.

"Well, this is a surprise," he said, walking over to the vehicle.

Show time. The stage lights clicked on, the sound system hummed with static, and the whiff of anxiety circled her head like a memory from every interview she'd faced, wearing a sash and sitting before a judge.

Lacy popped the remote for the hatch. "I had to find some way to make up for the imposition I caused last time I was here, and Kali and AJ have sent custom gifts for you and the staff."

Shading his eyes from the glare, his gaze raked her outfit, and then he leaned in to see the stems of lavender that were cut to size for the narrow cylinders displayed in the dining room last week. "This smells great."

Matter of opinion, she thought. Lavender in small doses was tolerable. Driving for an hour with the freshly cut stems was like bathing in a trough with them. No offense to AJ and the thousands of people who drove out to Comfort to wander ant-infested fields, oohing and ahhing over the color and fragrance, but she wasn't a fan. It was like the goat farm times two.

Why did perfectly reasonable, intelligent women chuck life in a big city to play in dirt? She just didn't get it. A few more months and her bizarre legal obligation would be satisfied, and she'd be on the fast track back to Dallas. Give her high-rise sunsets any day of the week.

"I hope not too overpowering. We saw, on our last visit, that you liked to pair fresh flowers with your table décor. The natural heartiness of lavender stems seemed like a fit with the California effect." Lacy pulled forward the crates packed with small boxes. "And we made food gifts for all the cooks in the kitchen. We know how hard they work and wanted to thank them for using Kali's cheese products in the recipes."

"Well, that is Chef's genius," Jay said, helping with the crate.

"How did he discover Kali's cheeses in the first place?"

Jay paused. "I'd guess it had to do with his local sourcing of foods for AJ's wedding reception."

"So, he'd agree getting quality local products into the limelight is good for everyone from customers to vendors?"

Smiling, he said, "Save the sales pitch, I'm just the front-of-of-the house guy."

They lumbered into the back of the restaurant with the buckets and crates, and Lacy stole a quick study of the setup. Her pitiful knowledge of restaurants ended with what they served at the table, but now she was curious about the production. Oh, who was she kidding? She'd been obsessed with the chef since the moment he set steaming soup in front of her.

Her internet search had revealed a handful of TV interviews, his starred reviews from regional newspapers, features in food magazines, photos of him and his wife from the Napa Valley jazz and wine festivals, and the re-opening of Stella Too after he'd lost the bakery in a divorce settlement. Gorgeous on film, he seemed downright stubborn about discussing his private life; the exception was the story of how Stella's was named for his paternal grandmother, a native of Barcelona, Spain, and an accomplished cook who only ever knew the farm-to-table format for creating good food.

There'd been a few Instagram photos on his wife's account with him holding Luna as a baby. Apparently, the former Mrs. Delgardo wiped her husband from her life with selective delete buttons. Though it took extreme self-control, she'd stopped there. She didn't want to dive too deep because she knew the temptation to judge. As one who had manipulated images for a certain outcome, she knew how quickly a false narrative could be formed.

One of her resolutions to be a better person, post-Amy Marsh, was to tamp down the tendency to stalk.

As one who would be forever scarred by the opinions expressed, the scandalous events, and the hasty headlines woven into the internet, she wanted to be more open-minded to the old-fashioned approach of meeting someone and beginning with face-value impressions. And her dearest hope was to meet a man who'd fall in love with her before he Googled her name.

These days those options were growing slim. Even Frank used Wikipedia.

"You can set the flowers in the break room." Jay motioned to his right. "I'll ask the waitstaff to arrange them for the tables."

She followed his lead. "If there's space in your cooler, maybe we could store those boxes? Kali took a head count of the entire staff and made one for everyone. There's a split of wine with each box too."

"Wow. I'm impressed." Jay peeked inside a white box. "I wish Chef was here to see this."

Air seeped from her lungs. "Chef Delgardo isn't here today?"

Jay shook his head. "Chef, Ken Lin, and two others are flying home today from New York."

"But this is a busy Saturday. Wouldn't he want to supervise the staff?"

"When Beard House calls, you jump to answer. We've got a foundation award riding on this competition." Jay leaned over to inspect the berry stems AJ had included with the lavender. "We're sick with worry over how the committee will rate Stella's."

"But he's an amazing chef, it says so in all the reviews."

Jay smiled. "I take it you've never tasted his cooking?"

He had her there. Except—

"I have—in Comfort, at AJ's reception. I just remember little about it, as I was working that night."

His gaze returned to the pearls looping over her blouse. "Are you an event planner?"

"No, I'm a . . . reporter." She wished that word fell off her tongue easier. "Taking pictures, mostly."

His eyes narrowed. "Are you reporting on Chef Delgardo?"

"No!" She nearly knocked over a stack of clean linen. "I'm helping Kali and AJ plan their grand opening for their event venue at Lavender Hill. My time with the *Comfort News* is temporary I do something else. They want to begin a food-and-wine festival in Comfort and thought Chef Delgardo would be the natural fit as the featured chef."

"I've gone my entire adult life never hearing of Comfort, Texas, and in the space of five months it's all anyone is talking about." He sat on the corner of a worktable. "What is Lavender Hill, and why would anyone want to go into the middle of nowhere for food and wine?"

This was the opening she'd hoped to have with Rudy, a portal she could leverage to get him onto her turf. She pitched the general manager AJ's unique Lavender Hill story and the marriage of those fragrant acres with her sister's goat-cheese empire. Without getting too lost in the details, she explained that the venue the chef had served from during AJ's wedding reception was almost finished out and how the business partners planned to launch Comfort's emergence as a worthy destination for tourists by creating a mini Austin Food and Wine Festival.

He nodded politely and asked a few more pertinent questions. "Why didn't you tell this to Chef last week?"

"We tried, but he shut it down without many details."

"That's his usual MO." Jay folded his arms across his tie. "He's been under extreme pressure lately—we all are while waiting on this awards process—so, if I had to guess, I'd say he will not want to work that hard for something with risk."

She replayed the tape of the man and his staff that day, but she couldn't get past how he'd brought his daughter to work. How stressful could it be if his kid could play at his feet?

"What's the risk? We're huge fans."

Jay read the label on the wine. "Not from you, but other chefs. The media. It's a new event, there's nothing to guarantee that anyone will drive out to the country for a BBQ."

Lacy bit her lip. Thinking on the fly was her strong suit, but ideas were spinning so fast nothing would settle down. "I guess we just thought he had fun while he was in Comfort in December, and maybe getting away to someplace with less stress would be appealing."

The manger paused, as if replaying memories. "He liked his time in Comfort. More than even I realized."

"So, you think there's a chance? Maybe if we approach him again, after he wins the contest?"

"I like that positive attitude. But I really don't know what to tell you. His life is up in the air these days. I wouldn't count on anything happening."

Lacy added up the expense invested in this visit and hated to think her sister and friend had wasted their money. "Let's not rule anything out." She handed him the prospectus. "Tell me what I have to do to come back and get an appointment with him."

Jay glanced at her with speculation. "You're a beautiful woman, all you have to do is smile, and he'd be willing to talk to you."

She didn't think it would be that easy. "Maybe I'll send in my ugly cousin. That way he would know he wasn't being manipulated."

He didn't seem to sense her bitterness in being relegated to "just a pretty face."

"Luna talked about you all day. You need to be the one to return." Jay stood and walked toward the doorway as if the interview were over. "You might be more influential than you realize."

He didn't know her past. Before she left, she wanted to say hello to the little girl who'd charmed her when she'd felt her worst. "Is Luna around today?"

He shook his head. "Back in school. In Abilene."

"Oh, but I thought—"

"Her visit was a temporary thing, much to Rudy's regret."

All her logical options for returning were dead ends. "Okay, well, maybe I can persuade some guy to bring me here for supper one night, and I can speak to the chef then."

"You're not married?"

"An old maid."

Chuckling, he said, "I just lost ten bucks. Kenny bet me you weren't married."

Any remaining pleasure from this adventure fizzled. "I don't know which is more insulting, being wagered on or going for so little."

"You'd be surprised what the chefs bet on while cooking, but we'll leave that for another conversation." He motioned her toward the hallway. "When you're in town next text me, and I'll make sure you get a good table for whomever you bring along."

Dismissed, she wandered back the way she'd arrived and pushed against the door, reading the poster, *Cooking is the art of the adjustment.—Jacques Pepin.* Maybe that was a truism for her life. Her unconventional childhood, the sidestep into pageants, and her current upended world were twisted in adjustments and disappointments. What she wouldn't give for just one thing going her way.

Climbing into the driver's seat, she checked the mirrors, re-oriented herself to the controls, and then backed out of the parking space, wondering what else she could do in Austin now that an entire afternoon had unraveled. Turning up the radio, she found a station that played music the band had covered last summer.

Dressed for an interview, she needed to make good use of the outfit. Who did she know in Austin she could pop in and ask for a freelance assignment?

Metallic crushing sounds carried over the radio. Her neck jerked forward.

A horn blared.

Throwing the gears into park, Lacy glanced around and saw that she'd crashed into a car. Stunned, she felt her shoulders and chest to make sure she was okay and then gingerly opened the door. First, she saw the front end of the car. Then she saw the back end of the SUV.

She sagged, sure that this was the worst thing that could happen. *The worst is never the worst.*

Lacy rubbed her forehead to scrub away anymore nonsense.

She'd never hit anyone before, but she knew enough to reach for her purse and her cell phone. As she stepped away from the fender, she ran through a checklist. At the top of which was how to explain this to Kali.

The list vanished into the atmosphere as she saw the driver, his expression fuming.

The worst really could get worse.

Rudy Delgardo stared at her like she'd risen from the seventh level of hell to torment him.

With the plans she'd hatched today, she couldn't deny the accusation. But this was not the way she'd wanted to reconnect with the most interesting man she'd ever met.

Chapter Eight

Rudy tumbled out of the driver's seat and slammed his door. After the hell he'd been through in New York, he couldn't believe some numbskull backed into his car. One glance at the torment on the face of the goddess standing next to the SUV and his anger spun loose and flittered away on wings.

Cinderella.

The woman who had occupied a corner in his mind, the off-limits space where he allowed thoughts of life beyond Stella's, had materialized from his fantasy and, for reasons he could not fathom, was standing a few feet away from him.

"Hello," he offered, sounding like a teenager when his voice cracked.

"I'm so sorry," she stammered, hurrying around to see the dented fenders and bent grill. "I didn't see you. I swear, I checked. I can't believe I did so much damage. I'll pay for everything."

White noise. He watched her mouth moving, but he didn't hear a word. Her arms flailed around as she bent down to inspect the front end of his car, but he'd been suspended in a trance. Her hair danced around her shoulders, and the silk blouse gave a glow to her skin that no makeup could duplicate.

She was scribbling something into a notebook and handing him a torn piece of paper when he finally found his voice again.

He reached for the slip and stared at the series of numbers. "Your cell?"

She ran her hand through her hair. "Yes, I know we're supposed to exchange insurance information, but I'll have to call Kali and find out who they use. I couldn't be more embarrassed about this."

Her eyes radiated that unusual shade of blue, calling into his soul like a beacon directing a ship through a storm. "It was an accident."

She rattled off a million more words, but all he could process was that this woman was back in his world. He'd be the idiot if he let her slip through his fingers again.

"How did you get here?"

She stopped speaking and tilted her head to the side. Her hair fell across her shoulder in a wave of gold. "I drove."

"No, I mean—at Stella's. Only the staff park back here."

"Oh," she stammered, and bit her lip. "I brought gifts."

"Gifts?"

"Kali told me to come this way and bring them in through the back. I texted Jay, and he said it would be okay."

"Kali?"

"My sister, the gourmet-cheese maker? The one who makes the goat cheeses in Comfort. We were here last week."

"I remember." He couldn't put a name to a face because Kenny had sourced the local vendors in Comfort, but he'd never forget the three women who blew into Stella's on a cold day. The other two had faded into the background once he met this one, but he'd commit to memory that she was the sister of the cheese maker—that was a thread he might need to pull. "Her cheeses are exquisite."

"She'd be thrilled to hear it. She's proclaiming Stella's patronage on her social-media sites."

"She is?"

"Well, I am, but it's for her benefit."

Questions battled for the queue in his mind, but he knew there were practical matters to deal with first—namely the annoying ding from his dashboard.

"We need to move our vehicles." He gestured to the blocked access. "Let's park along the curb to free space for the staff."

Able to untangle from her bumper with a minimum of ripping, he backed out of Stella's driveway and parked near the little house, home to a pottery studio. The compelling need to cook, to work through his experiences, had subsided, and as he climbed from the driver's seat and studied the damage to his front end, it surprised him how sanguine he felt about the injury. *A body shop could repair this quickly enough,* he thought. Watching her as she backed the SUV into the street and parked nearby, a strange lightness filled him. Electric, almost.

Flexing his fingers, he hoped he could make decent conversation. Rating his past encounter with her, she will have painted him a dunce. Even Luna had teased him about being tongue-tied. *Sweet Luna.* The reports from Abilene spelled disaster, and his sister would never volunteer to babysit again. If only Hannah would return from California.

Studying the poise of the woman walking toward him, he forgot Hannah's complaints. Warmth rolled through him, but he squelched the excitement. This was the absolute worst time to think about starting something with a stranger.

"I have Kali's insurance information." She stopped next to him and offered a small document. "Do you want to snap a photo of this card so you can give it to your agent? They can send an adjuster over, and we'll cover everything as this was my fault."

Kali Hamilton. He read the names listed, but it was just her and a man named Jake. "I'm embarrassed to ask this—" Rudy reached for his cell phone, "but what is your name?"

"You mean in all the chaos of my vomiting in your restaurant you heard no one shout my name, as in, 'Oh, my word, Lacy, are you ruining yet another important meeting?' That sort of thing?"

Her grin teased a response from him, and he rocked back on his heels. "Yeah, that sort of thing."

She offered her hand. "I'm Lacy Cavanaugh, reporter for the *Comfort News* and all-around klutz."

"Lacy?" He ignored her put-down. "I've met no one else with that name."

"Doctors pumped my mother full of anesthesia during my arrival, and she named me after the heirloom blanket my aunt brought to the hospital. I should be grateful my aunt didn't bring something more embarrassing."

She rolled that out so effortlessly that he guessed she'd referenced the story a few times. "I think it's lovely."

"It's not the worst name in the world, but it is hard for people to take me seriously, or maybe that's just my boss." She hoisted her purse strap on her shoulder. "Does anyone call you Rudy, or are you only ever known as 'Chef?'"

He photographed the insurance details and thought about her question. "I'm so used to responding to Chef that I hardly ever hear anyone use my given name. Which is Rudolph. My mother was not strung out on drugs, but she had a fetish for her Belgian roots. Wanted to pass down the names or some such thing."

"Rudolph Delgardo." Lacy tried the name out, twice. "It has a certain ring. Very United Nations."

"Yes, well, my parents met in Brooklyn, which is a melting pot for the world."

"Were you raised in Brooklyn?"

He shook his head. "My parents quickly had more children than they could afford to raise and scurried back to my dad's family in California. They were both teachers and did the best they could, but more times than not, they farmed us out to the relatives in Sonoma when they had to take on extra work in the summer."

"A summer in Sonoma? Try to convince me that was a hardship."

"It was wonderful." Memories of cooking with his grandmother, riding the tractor with his grandfather, and picking fruit till dark collided with soil. He regretted Luna would not know similar memories. "I'm a lucky fool."

Another smile spread across her face. "A sweet childhood is a blessing, right?"

"You've misunderstood if you thought it was sweet, but we were a close-knit group." Not wanting to tread into the dark waters of Delgardo drama, he handed her the card and double-checked that her phone number was still in his pocket. "It will probably take a while to get our insurance companies on the phone, so can I offer you lunch? I happen to know a place close by."

She glanced over her shoulder to a distinctive orange awning over a nondescript back door. "I didn't think you were open for lunch."

"Don't let a little detail like that interfere." He locked his car. "Unless you have other plans?"

Her eyes brightened. "My day was rather uncomplicated until I smashed into your car. So, I'd be grateful for a sandwich, but please don't go to any effort. I've already intruded."

Plane delays and traffic on I-35 seemed like a gift because that twist of fate allowed him to be in the right place at the right time. He patted the hood of his car, grateful he'd traded his BMW after the divorce. This Honda would be cheaper to repair. "I'm sure my car will survive. But I'm starving. I don't eat airline food, and it's been a long time since I grabbed a bagel in Manhattan."

She fell into step beside him. "I confess I get hangry if I miss a meal, so I'm impressed that your hair hasn't caught fire."

He liked the way her eyes were studying his hair. He was the only son to inherit his mother's coloring, and he was teased for being the pretty boy. "*Hangry*?"

"It's that awful combination of being hungry and, like someone flips a switch, every little thing makes you angry until you get food in your stomach. The Cavanaugh women are notorious for hangri-ness."

"My sister keeps snacks in her purse, and this may explain why." He checked the road and led her across to a sidewalk. "Omelet or a sandwich?"

"I adore omelets."

Had he ever met anyone who *adored* omelets? "They're brilliant for using all the odds and ends left after a meal service. Onions, mushrooms, filet minion, gruyere—it's one of my favorite ways to end a long night."

"Rudy—can I call you Rudy? Please know I will eat anything you have available. I'm not fussy."

He rated her expensive clothing and pearls and thought maybe she was fussy, but it drew him to her in a way that seemed to awaken long-dead senses, and he wanted to learn every detail. "Please call me Rudy. My staff uses Chef because I'm a believer that to maintain precision in the kitchen, personality needs to be removed."

Thoughts passed behind her eyes, and he could tell she didn't understand the chemistry of a restaurant staff. It wasn't something easily explained, and he didn't want to waste the afternoon on anything that might bring him back to his current situation.

"You mentioned that you brought gifts." He entered the code to unlock the back door, catching her gaze. "Are you selling me more products?"

She sighed with an exasperation that spoke of good ideas gone wrong. "Our great marketing exercise to persuade you to be our celebrity chef at the Comfort Food and Wine Festival."

Filtering back to the afternoon when she'd fallen from the clouds to land in his restaurant, he remembered a previous request. Holding the door open for her, he breathed in the fragrance of her hair as she passed. *Lavender.* How surprising. He'd have expected something exotic and dangerous. "You're going to ply me with cheese?"

"Plus, wine and cookies." She stepped into the hallway and glanced toward the kitchen. "I brought boxes for your staff. We wanted everyone on board. At the very least they'd sway support, being at the grassroots of something good."

"You assume my staff likes me and wants me to succeed."

She gasped. "Don't they?"

He pulled to mind the faces of those who'd been with him the longest. "I can count on about five people to stand with me whatever may come. The rest of them are biding their time until a better offer comes along."

"Well, five is a lot." She turned toward the break room. "That's more than I have."

He followed her into the cramped space and watched as she set her purse on the table. She was too young and too beautiful to be stained by hardship. What did she know of cruel hands and the fickle nature of consumers? "I would imagine your phone is full of more than five numbers."

"Oh, well, if that's the criteria, then yes. I'm surrounded by a cast of thousands." She lifted one of the white gift boxes and handed it to him. "A token from the founders of the tentatively titled Comfort Food and Wine Festival—even if you choose not to take part."

He opened the box lid and saw the arrangement of cheese, fruit, and a cookie. "Nicely done."

"The wine is a sparkling to pair with the mix."

"From Comfort, also?"

"France." Her shoulders lifted as if she were apologizing. "I don't even know if there is a sparkling made in Texas."

"And yet you're starting a wine festival?" He bit into the cookie, appreciating the balance between salty cashews and brown sugar.

"I'm not the brains behind the operation, and I'm sure that's why they want you involved. You know more about food and wine than the three of us combined."

He also knew the spin his world was about to take. "No more talk of festivals. Let's cook."

Shaking her head, Lacy stepped backward, hitting the wall. "Oh, no. I don't go near an oven. I'll applaud from the safety of the dining room."

He checked his watch, half past one. The kitchen would hum with preparations. The syncopation of sounds always soothed him, but today he was off his groove. Everything felt wrong. He wouldn't trust his instincts.

"There's a chef preparing food to feed the staff for tonight. We'll snitch a few elements from her menu and fix ourselves a plate."

She straightened her shoulders, as if readying herself for any unexpected turn. Which, now that he thought about it, was wise. With everything hovering on his horizon, he should probably suit up in armor.

"I'm fine with anything." She opened her purse and reached around inside. "Do you mind if I call the insurance company while you do whatever magic you do? I can sneak on through to the dining room."

Though ruffled by the incident, she'd not lost focus on following through with the details. He wondered if she knew how efficient she was. "Please take a place at the bar, the staff know they can find me there on the occasions I sit down to eat."

Her look implied she was measuring him against a standard of never veering off course. And she'd be right. He didn't. Precision and repetition were elements of a successful kitchen.

She grinned. "I bet it's something when you let your hair down."'

"I don't understand."

She waved her hand in dismissal. "Don't worry, I've overstepped. Again."

He breathed deeply as she walked past because the fragrance followed like the tail of a kite. Her scent was a flavor profile that seemed impossible to duplicate. But he'd find the source. Bamboo and lavender, with an undertone of what?

Something herbal? Eucalyptus?

Stepping into the kitchen, the staff welcomed him with cheers and clapping. Kenny had beat him to the address. The sous chef, wearing his I LOVE NYC T-shirt, stood near the walk-in cooler, regaling the cooks with big hand gestures and facial expressions worthy of the stage.

"Tell them, Chef," Kenny begged. "Tell them how—against all obstacles—we grilled the tastiest Porterhouse steaks those judges had eaten in ages. They said so themselves."

"Against all obstacles is right," Rudy said, stepping over to a counter where a cook was boiling spaghetti. "Our cold products got misdirected at the Beard House, and we had to improvise in a city where we had no idea where the closest market was located."

Kenny fanned the shock bubbling through the staff. "I was Googling every place I could think of until I remembered my cousin cooked in a hotel near Central Park. He hooked us up with a butcher getting fresh meat at the docks, and we decided to offer a 'meat-lovers-club' menu. Chef pulled off a minor miracle."

Rudy wondered if the miracle would be big enough. Beard House judges rewarded high creativity, not roadhouse cuisine. Lifting a spoon from the drawer, he slipped it into the bubbling tomato sauce and analyzed the texture. It seemed heavy on basil, but that wasn't a problem for his palate. "Salt at the end, and I think you'll find the staff asking for seconds. Please prepare two plates of spaghetti and serve it to me and a guest, in the dining room."

"Now, Chef?" Her eyes rounded in panic. "I haven't made croutons yet."

"Five minutes." He turned halfway and reached for the wheel of aged Parmesan the staff would use when it came time to plate salads for the meal service. "And be generous with this."

The young cook nodded, looking unnerved by the order.

As he checked the progress for the food preparations, he heard Kenny embellishing the horrors of electricity failures and an unexpected delay as the judges lingered in a last-minute business meeting. He and the team might not win this year's award, but he doubted another competitor had faced as many challenges.

And that's why he was sure Alan Gale orchestrated every disaster. The man gloated when he ushered the judges into the Beard House dining room. It had taken reserves of self-control to keep from belting him after serving his plate to the table.

Jay stepped inside the kitchen and nodded toward Rudy. The simple movement conveyed layers of information because it had been Jay who had run interference when Rudy first discovered the cold shipment had taken a detour. Even with Kenny and the other two chefs, he'd have failed if Jay hadn't been navigating plan B from his laptop.

Jay fixated on Kenny's production as Rudy slipped into the dining room. The lure of a beautiful woman outweighed hearing a nightmare relived.

"Chef?"

He turned back at the door. "Jay, thanks for keeping us from a total breakdown in Manhattan. Couldn't have done it without you."

"It's not exactly over."

He glanced to the bar, where Lacy sat holding a glass of wine and then back to his general manager. "What do you mean?"

Jay stepped close and lowered his voice. "Two of the judges were ill last night. They're calling it food poisoning."

Chapter Nine

Lacy opened the umbrella and hurried toward a tree for shelter. The knee-high rain boots—so fashionable in Dallas—now styled various shades of mud. All those glorious photo shoots at Klyde Warren Park, featuring cute looks for the rainy season, seemed a dream from someone else's life.

Knocking on doors and asking neighbors of the decrepit Comfort gas station if any EPA officials had returned to inspect for groundwater contamination brought out those who delighted in mocking someone who matched a scarf with her boots. The men had questioned if polka dots could hold up after mucking through manure.

Dressing for the occasion was the second most foolish thing she'd done today.

The first was telling Gloria that her ex-husband had a cough that wouldn't go away. Frank's hacking habit had produced blood. He refused to see a doctor, saying it was yet another gift from old age. Lacy casually wove the fact into breakfast preparations, and before she could butter her toast, Gloria grabbed a set of car keys and flew out the door.

Shivering because her slicker was suited more for popping in and out of shops than enduring a deluge, she remembered her brave speech about pursuing the story of the gas station. *These old walls will have something to say,* she'd told Frank. He'd chuckled and told her to get her hearing tested. The only saga coming out of this station was a depressed sales price and some hairbrained scheme to install storage units.

Hiding from sheets of pouring rain, she stared at the gas station and wondered why anyone would care if bulldozers knocked it down. The hobbit-sized business had been carved from Texas limestone in a day when no one knew gas tanks would leak and pollute underground water reserves.

As she stood staring at the station, wondering if it could have a second life as a gift shop, a van pulled close to the side of the building where the bathroom door stood ajar. The van navigated the spot with familiarity. A sliding door opened and a young girl, maybe fifteen, jumped to the pavement and scurried inside.

Lacy grimaced. She'd peered into that room last month. That graffiti-riddled closet was its own hazardous-waste site.

Like a revolving door, when that girl returned to the van, another would run to the facilities. She watched this process with fascination, mostly because there were about eight girls crammed into the van, and all of them bore the disillusioned expressions of runaways. White, Black, and Hispanic, the girls appeared malnourished.

They were probably a group going to camp or a school event, but she snapped a photo of the van regardless. The man who crawled out of the driver's seat looked the kind to use the back of his hand when things didn't go his way. She snapped his photo too.

In case one of the girls noted the surroundings, she ducked behind a pickup parked at the lumberyard and regretted that her rain gear bore memorable colors. Her car, parked in the open area, would require her to walk through the driver's sight line. Her gut churned like it did that time she witnessed a band manager harass a caterer—and that incident had later ended in bruises.

"Lacy, is that you?"

Her head jerked around, and she saw Beau Jefferson hurrying across the parking lot. "Hi, yes. Sorry. Is this your truck?"

"Guilty as charged." The brim of his hat offered little protection from the sheets of water. "Why are you standing in the rain?"

"There's a creepy guy over at the gas station, and I'm watching to see what he's doing with that van full of girls."

"Nancy Drew?" His gaze scanned her orange-and-white umbrella and bright green boots. "On acid?"

"Funny." No one in this town appreciated her fashion sense. "But can you peek if they're still there?"

Beau walked to the back of his truck, pretending to inspect a tie-down. "They're pulling out."

"Interesting," she said, moving away from her hiding place. "I guess they made a bathroom stop."

"At the smelliest john in Kendall County?"

"Right?" She thought there had to be more sanitary options than that particular gas station. "Bubba's has several bathrooms, and they're usually clean and warm."

Beau stood at the driver's door. "I can see the wheels turning behind your eyes. You think there's a story."

"Wouldn't you? Those girls didn't look right."

"I didn't see the girls, but, if I don't get back to Lavender Hill, I know one girl who will ring my neck. We're supposed to install drywall today, and I'm trying to find as many tarps as possible so we don't ruin our supplies."

Lacy had stopped by Lavender Hill a few days ago to report on the fallout with Rudy Delgardo. AJ and Kali had been sympathetic, but also determined that if he wouldn't help them, they needed to find another big-name chef soon. Like a woman half-dressed, the event hall had stood tall and proud, but wires dangled from the rafters and gaps pocked the framing. Kali had explained the future installation of doors and cabinetry, but Lacy imagined months of work ahead. She wondered if launching the event center with something as big as a food festival begged for trouble. Actually, she didn't wonder long. She knew they'd started something that couldn't possibly end well.

"Give my best to Colette." Lacy stepped back as he climbed into the cab. "I hope the pregnancy is going smoothly. She looked darling when I saw her a few weeks ago."

Beau grinned. "She's more beautiful than before we found out about Junior."

Lacy waved, pasting a smile on her face. What she wouldn't give for some man to think she was beautiful while growing into a whale-sized human. As he pulled away, she let her lips relax. She couldn't find one man to talk with—what were the odds she'd find one who wanted her to bear his child? She shivered again. Having seen her sister go through a delivery, she doubted she was woman enough to endure pregnancy.

She hurried to her car. Cold to the bone, she missed her Dallas life. With all the traffic, a misty haze would soften the sky during a storm. Here, it was shards of gray slate attacking the soil and anyone who got in its way. Though it had been months since she left, she'd refused even a quick return trip to North Texas. She didn't trust herself not to fall down crying at the threshold of the nearest mall. Besides, if her friends weren't missing her, then she wasn't missing them either.

Folding the umbrella, she wondered if maybe the over-the-top drive to gain followers for her social-media sites had robbed her of genuine relationships. She watched Beau's truck navigate a high-water crossing. Her bond with him went back years. He teased with no real teeth because he'd drop everything to help her in a crisis. Just like he would with Kali and Jake. And AJ and Luke, too.

Pushing the key into the ignition, she realized the people she could count on lived within a ten-mile radius of

Comfort, Texas. Staring out the windshield, she finally comprehended that she'd run hundreds of miles away only to return to the very ones who'd always been here, waiting for her to grow up.

Opening her hands in front of the heating vents, she replayed the scenes where the people in town had welcomed her home without snickering over her flameout, in part because folks in Comfort stared at social media like one might an insect crawling from under a cupboard. Even so, they'd hadn't blinked twice, just welcomed her back and put her to work.

She leaned into the seat, thinking about the skills she'd discovered in herself since going to work at the paper and, most impressive, since she began cooking with Gloria. It's not like she'd learned Latin, but without the opportunity offered here, would she ever have learned she could comparison shop at the market or make an entire meal from scratch?

Not inclined to overthink anything, Lacy appreciated that Gloria had become a mentor when she desperately needed someone in her life. She hoped the guy in Florida wouldn't turn out to be wonderful. She'd hate to lose her new friend.

Backing out of the station's parking lot, she heard a ding signaling a missed call. She paused and dug into her purse for the flip phone. An Austin area code? And they'd called twice.

Her thumb hovered over hitting redial.

She wished it were Rudy calling, even if it were to talk insurance details. Their lunch had ended on the weirdest note. Even though the spaghetti was delicious, his mind had flown a million miles away. What she'd hoped was the beginning of something interesting proved nothing more than a blip.

Her radar must have taken a hit too because she was sure she'd felt attraction. Then, just as fast, the fascination shut off. He'd gulped his food and hurried her out the door without any indication that he'd even remembered she'd damaged his car.

Dropping the phone into her purse, she sighed. Probably a telemarketer anyway.

Later, as she sat at Frank's computer in the office of the *Comfort News*, updating ad information for the next issue, she wondered again about Rudy. There'd been talk about a contest, some restaurant award—James Beard, was it? She opened a search app and researched food awards.

Sipping her latte, she could understand why Rudy and the team at Stella's would want to win this impressive designation. Even though she recognized few on their list of past recipients, it justified the sweat. She hoped he'd get it. Even though she couldn't vouch for his cooking, most of the online reviews were ecstatic. Disregarding the cranky customers and those who loved a platform to complain, the restaurant had a solid vibe.

His rugged face, carved with stress and a few scars, begged her heart to wish him a happy ending. Not knowing the ghosts that dogged his steps, she could appreciate the similarities of their problems. They both had online gremlins fixated on bringing them down. And he had a daughter, which meant the mother was still in the picture, too. She could search online again, but no. He'd pushed her out of Stella's fast on Saturday. Whatever zinged between them had fizzled.

Returning to the InDesign page with layouts for the next edition, she narrowed her gaze on the small details of a promotion for tractor equipment.

The tangy fragrance of tomato sauce, mixed with the aromatics of lavender, swirled free from her memory. As if Rudy sat in the chair across from her desk, she could see torture woven into the grooves around his mouth and knew that his excuse about a kitchen issue had been fiction. Something significant had happened between their banter and his dropping onto a barstool.

She slammed her finger against the save key.

This problem wouldn't get solved today, any more than it would during the other hours she wasted thinking about that man.

Fresh air was the cure. The rain had moved to the east, and she needed to work out the kinks in her back. One perk of living in Comfort was that, with a few steps away from either home or work, she had options for a long, uninterrupted walk.

Dropping her phone into her pocket, she opened the front door and stepped into the grayness filtered from the clouds. The bulbous sky almost distracted her from a distinct odor. Wet animal. There was no disguising a fragrance that lingered long after the perpetrator vanished. An extensive history chasing goats across pastures and corralling them into pens left an impression that no amount of air freshener could erase. She searched the sidewalk, sure that a cow wandered loose.

A small, bedraggled dog rooted in the neighbor's flower bed. "Scat!"

Drue had planted daffodil bulbs there a few weeks ago, and she would scream when she discovered a mutt had messed with her garden. She'd often commented that her outdoor flowers brought as much business to her floral shop as any advertisement she paid for inside the *Comfort News*. Or at least that's what she used as a defense when Frank insisted, as a neighbor, that they should support each other's business.

"Rudy, get out. Scat!"

The dog glanced at her. His eyes brightened. Now, why had she called him that name? Lacy glanced around, grateful no one had heard, and questioned why she'd bothered to name the menace.

The dog barked.

Great. The first name that comes to mind and it sticks to a schnauzer-looking beast. Knots tangled his coat, mud stained his paws, and she was sure there was trash stuck in his beard. The Delgardo family would raise serious questions about her choice to give some Belgian relative's namesake to such a pitiful creature. As he raised his grubby faced and barked again, she could smell his foul breath.

He couldn't know she had immunity to big black eyes and stink. Kali's goats had tried this tactic and failed. Her heart was carved from stone, or so she'd been told.

"Shoo, little Rudy!"

The dog considered her threat factor, then investigated another spot further in the yard. She crossed her arms, irked the dog didn't respect her natural leadership. Maybe she'd lost her touch?

The guys in the band had taunted her with expulsion because she wouldn't let them keep the strays that poked around their equipment van. They laughed at her logic about hygiene issues and fleas, hammering back that every songwriter worth his paycheck had a hound dog. She'd pointed out the obvious—they were a cover band, not songwriters. The issue inevitably dropped.

A childhood spent hopping between addresses taught her that the moment she got attached to some mutt her aunt or uncle would sneak it away, and her heart would break. She needed another disappointment like she needed ten more pounds.

Drue leaned her head, shorn to the graying curls, out of the floral shop. "I have a pellet gun if you think that would help."

Lacy glanced between the dog and the florist. "He doesn't seem to realize he's the intruder in this scenario and that's he's not the lion he sees in the mirror."

"Short-man's syndrome." Drue nodded like she'd seen this trait before. "I've called animal control, but as you can see, that hasn't done a lick of good."

"I've got a broom. We'll force him to move along." She turned back for the newspaper's office.

"I haven't seen Frank in several days. Has the man finally figured out you can handle the paper and taken a vacation?"

Grimacing, she said, "Sick leave. He's working from home in Kerrville. Says he has a touch of the flu."

"Well, he can keep that touch all to himself, thank you very much."

"It's weird, but I miss him around the office." Lacy hadn't lit a candle all week to disguise the smell of cigar smoke. "And he shouldn't trust me with this next edition. Primary races are on the horizon and that looks to be a hot mess. Ad revenue is already up twice as much."

Drue's thick black brows rose high. "Nothing sells papers like contested elections. Buckle in."

She'd been given several writing assignments, and Frank had paid them without grumbling. A few more features and she'd have enough to buy an iPhone without dipping into savings. Text messaging took forever with an alpha-numeric system, and there were no emojis. "If you have any good leads, let me know. I still don't know the names of people who are players around here, and it's hard to judge which letters to the editor are the most important to print."

"It's a hoot you think these ranchers are players, but I'll keep an ear out." She swiped at a honeybee. "People tell florists all the scoop."

Drue talked to a customer who hurried up the sidewalk, describing a funeral arrangement needed as soon as possible. Glancing around, Lacy couldn't see little Rudy anywhere, and she relaxed.

Rolling her shoulders back, she turned toward Fifth Street and the salad lunch that awaited her at High's Cafe. She might live in the back of beyond, but swimsuit season rolled in with the calendar, and she *would* fit into last year's bikini. She would. Even though there wasn't a single person who would notice.

Chapter Ten

Rudy slipped his jacket over his shoulders and stepped out Stella's back door, bound for the bakery. The panicked phone call from his buddy in Manhattan had woken him from a deep sleep and instigated a round of meetings about marketing, considering the backlash from social media rolling out of the Big Apple. The loaner car waited in his reserved space, but he needed to walk the five blocks to Stella's Too. Tension radiated through him, and the only way he could release it between now and meeting with the consultant was to pound the pavement.

Cracking under pressure. A one-hit wonder. Unimaginative and redundant.

The words circled his brain on a loop.

Why the *New York Times* would care about his cuisine was one question, but why they bashed a chef and a restaurant in Austin, Texas, was another—and more disturbing. He had to contain the damage before customers heard the rant.

Some regulars in the Clarksville neighborhood nodded as he passed, but he'd always been too busy to learn their names. He barely remembered what shops were between the restaurant and the bakery. It had been Hannah's idea to branch out with a small market offering ready-made foods and baked goods. He'd gone along because it had opened the door for him to supply breads and pastries to other restaurants, and he enjoyed supporting start-ups. But the struggle to buy out Hannah after the divorce had cost him more than dollars; it had sucked at his soul. Selling the house and the expensive cars helped, but he stayed awake at night, teetering on the bottom line of being a chef-owner, wondering what his life would look like going forward.

All he wanted now was to be free of the pressure. Running two businesses, managing employees, paying taxes, and staying ahead of the inspectors was like a second full-time job. Even with a general manager to run interference, he was never free of the responsibility. Without Luna to remind him that there was a purpose outside of the kitchen, he felt lost—and sinking fast.

Approaching the back entrance of Stella Too's, he breathed in the yeasty fragrance seeping from the ovens and tried to still his angst. On the best of days, he hated marketing meetings. He felt stupid listening to them discuss internet algorithms. He cooked good food and created an environment for people to relax and enjoy themselves. His food nurtured people. It did not need *spin*.

"Chef!"

He wiped his feet on the doormat and glanced at a surprised intern holding a baking sheet of hot almond croissants.

"Sorry, didn't mean to sneak up on you. Carry on, just here for a meeting."

The girl nodded but seemed surprised the boss would peek in on the process this morning. Thankfully, she wasn't chatty. He washed his hands at a sink and glanced through the kitchen at the staff assembling sandwiches for the lunch crowd. Customers complained that Stella's should open for lunch hours, but he found this format to be more efficient than bringing in a full roster of cooks and waitstaff. If today was like most, Stella's Too would sell out of inventory by three o'clock.

He poured a cup of coffee and stood at the counter, searching the bistro tables for the skinny kid who'd met him last fall. The advertising company sent someone new every season. Though he and Hannah had a laundry list of problems, she had known how to put out good ads and stroked the right folks to keep Stella's on the top of the go-to lists for tourists.

If only he knew someone he could trust to manage the public face of the restaurant so he could go back to doing what he did best.

His manager walked over. "Sir, you're ten o'clock appointment is here. She's sitting next to the window. Posting a photo of her cappuccino."

"Why?"

"I wish I knew. There must be millions of photos of coffee foam on the internet." The manager offered him a small platter with their signature bite-sized Bundts, the coconut shavings melting into the warm cake. "But at least she's staging the menu behind the cup, so we'll get some exposure."

Rudy took the platter in one hand. "And that's supposed to save us when customers flock to the next newest-and-greatest food truck?"

"That's what they say."

Rudy never knew who "they" were in these scenarios, but as he was repeatedly told, he wasn't being paid to know. The millennials steered the ship, and it was his job to get on board. Since the girl sitting at the window looked barely twenty, he'd assume she was a genius.

He folded into the chair, feeling as old as his father. Setting the platter on the table and pushing it toward his guest, he introduced himself and waited for her to explain how she would salvage Stella's image after the attack of New York bloggers.

*****

Words. So many words trailed his steps as he walked back to the restaurant. He had watched the girl's lips move, but he still didn't understand when she talked about metrics and key phrases. He asked her to make the bad news go away, and she laughed. She promised even bad publicity was better than no publicity.

Later, as he was inspecting the delivery from the fish supplier, he heard Kenny walk into the refrigerator.

"Who is Alan Gale sleeping with to make this nightmare continue?"

Rudy inspected the last of the salmon and then signed the receipt. Stepping out of the cold room, he nodded for Kenny to follow. The last person he needed gossiping about the James Beard fallout was his fish vendor.

Kenny looked over the scallops before stepping into the kitchen.

Rudy retied his utility apron while he waited for the space to clear of ears. "What now?"

"*CBS This Morning* is featuring the James Beard competition and venturing opinions about who might be the next star chef invited to New York."

"And?"

"Despite the list of highly qualified candidates whom they could discuss, the only thing they can talk about is how we went to the docks to buy our inventory, possibly contaminating the judges with scombroid poisoning."

"Those men did not have that condition. The doctors proved it was an unrelated stomach virus."

"Ah, but the journalists speculate that Chef Delgardo is careless under pressure, and will buy meats from any vendor, risking exposing his customers to unrefrigerated products. They're questioning whether anyone in Austin has ever had a bad reaction after dining here."

Rudy rubbed a vein throbbing beside his forehead. It was culinary school all over again. "That's madness."

"That's the media today."

He sagged against a prep counter. "Every enemy I've ever had will volunteer a story."

Kenny folded his arms. "So, what did you ever do to Alan Gale?"

A hundred images of his onetime friend and classmate flooded his mind. "Why do you assume I had anything to do with turning his mind?"

"Because this is personal." Kenny narrowed his gaze. "Very personal."

The story didn't bear repeating. Kenny cooked well and was pleasant to work beside; that didn't mean he rated as one to know Rudy's dark past. "Don't you have something to do?"

Kenny nodded toward the platter of hand-carved radishes. "Done."

"Well, find something else. The media specialist I talked with today said she will bombard Instagram and Twitter with a whole avalanche of our five-star reviews."

"That's firing snowballs at an inferno."

Rudy turned away. He didn't need his sous chef critiquing his methods. Not today. He needed to discover what Alan wanted from him and solve it soon.

"Chef?"

Glancing over his shoulder for another of Kenny's questions, Rudy controlled his impatience.

"I know someone who might have an idea about moving you onto a brighter radar."

He wouldn't belittle Kenny's contacts. The Lin family had tentacles across Austin and, seemingly, in New York. He had met Kenny's mother, and one glance from her schoolmaster's all-seeing eye had terrified him. Other family members might not be as strict, but he had no doubt they were as nimble at nosing out problems. The last thing he needed was another Lin in his business. "This will blow over."

"No, the internet makes things live forever."

The consultant had said the same words when explaining how good PR can linger on the airwaves as well. Maybe Kenny had a cousin working at Twitter. "Okay, what then?"

"The blonde. Lacy Cavanaugh."

Cinderella? Regret tightened his gut. He'd treated her badly the day she'd stayed for lunch. Since she didn't even call him back after his two attempts to apologize, he figured he had imagined her interest. Though it soothed him to think about her, she wasn't the solution to his current disaster.

"She knows a thing or two about dealing with bad press, and I think you should call her. She might know how to distract everyone from the JBF."

"What did you do, Google the girl?"

"Maybe." Kenny dipped his chin. "I told you I'd seen her before. Now I've remembered why. She's a super influencer. I followed her on Facebook and Instagram. Her clothes are divine, and she's always at the best places. But, what's important to you, is she could write the book on PR spin. How else does she still have fans talking about her when she hasn't posted anything in months?"

Rudy stared, taking new stock of Kenny's strange haircut. Maybe that was considered fashionable? He knew Kenny spent a lot of time on his iPhone, flipping through posts. Any spare minutes in Manhattan were consumed with finding some designer's trunk sale. How any of that translated to him recovering his image as a chef was lost.

"At the very least," Kenny pleaded, "hear her out about the food-festival idea. She's going to a lot of trouble to convince you to join in. She's smart about creating public perception. Give her space to show you how a new audience would care nothing about Alan Gale's comments."

He laughed bitterly. "Talk about jumping from the frying pan into the fire. Besides, you know how I feel about millennials."

"It's because you're out of touch with communicating to the next generations." Kenny grinned. "She could teach you."

Four words that sent Rudy's mind in a direction that had nothing to do with social media or restaurants.

"Festivals are wins. It brings chefs together with people, and it's a media bonanza. You should give it more credibility. I go to the Austin event every year and it's always popular."

Rudy turned away, restacking a pile of dishcloths to keep his focus on the tasks. "Well, they want to do their festival in Comfort which, as you know, is five miles from nowhere."

The silence was noteworthy. Glancing over his shoulder, he saw the crushed expression in Kenny's gaze. "What?"

"You said Comfort was the one place you felt at peace. That it reminded you of the early years in Sonoma before everyone knew it was special."

Rudy had said a lot of things that week he was cooking for the Christmas wedding reception, none of which mattered now. He didn't have the funds to expand. He would have to battle to keep his reputation, and if this bad press turned into a tidal wave, he could lose everything.

"Chef?"

The weight of defeat hovered at his elbow. "What now, Kenny?"

"Isn't this Friday?"

Rudy paused, thinking through the things he'd accomplished since breakfast. "Yes."

"And it's one o'clock."

"What's your point?" Rudy's impatience was close to taking on a life of its own.

"You were supposed to be in Abilene today for Luna's lunch. Isn't it Daddy-Daughter Day at her school?"

Chapter Eleven

Sunshine and wildflowers teased the window overlooking the driveway of Provence Farm. Even a bluebird dipped for a peek through the glass, as if to invite one and all into the beautiful outdoors.

Lacy sat at a desk in Kali's office, laying out a media plan for the weeks leading up to the event center's opening. She stared as if imprinting the image of picnic tables and happy foodies would somehow make the dynamics gel into place. The three friends had brainstormed for days on how to network with Austin and San Antonio newspapers to generate a mention but had yet to land on the perfect idea. The chefs they'd chatted with were enthusiastic about a food-and-wine festival, but seemed to think one of the chic towns, like Fredericksburg or Boerne, would be a better draw. When Lacy reminded them that the new center sat on the perimeter of a sweeping lavender farm in Comfort, they'd smiled their regrets and wished her the best. They had promised they'd reconsider if the festival received good exposure in its first year.

Tapping her pencil against her notepad, she brought her mind out of the sunlight and onto her paper. Reviewing the list of vendors, she starred vineyards that had committed to set up sampling stations. She wondered if it were time to bring in a headlining music act instead of a celebrity chef. If she'd not burned the relationship, she might have asked her friends in the band to make an appearance. But, with Amy Marsh going solo and signing a record deal, all conversations with the band were funneled through an attorney. She wondered if they involved Christopher.

"Hey, can you watch Charlie for a few minutes?"

She glanced over her shoulder, seeing Kali standing in the doorway with the baby. "Sure, do you need to go into town while the nanny is at her dentist's appointment?"

"No, a packaging salesman arrived, and Charlie could not keep his hands off the samples."

Having spent the better part of the week in a quiet office on Main Street, the amount of activity that landed on Kali's doorstep stunned Lacy. It was a wonder she got her work done between visitors and the vet. Lacy reached for the baby. "Come here, cutie."

Kali peered at Lacy's folders. "Still calling your contacts?"

"Yes," she said, tucking Charlie onto her hip. "One good thing from working for Frank is that I've met people in a variety of newsrooms. I regret every complaint I ever voiced about taking over his email."

Kali pushed a lock of hair behind her ear. "How is Frank these days?"

"Not good. The tests came back stage-four cancer." Lacy returned to her chair, afraid she might drop the wiggling boy. "Gloria said he'll begin chemo soon. He's asked me to manage the entire production of the paper for the next few months."

Saying the words out loud made her wonder how she'd ended up in this position. Despite her promise, doubt riddled her thoughts. The past few weeks, he'd offered a crash course in management while he worked from home. Given more and more responsibility, she knew he was in the background, providing accountability. Now, the safety net had folded. Frank had cursed that chemo brain would affect his tongue, and he couldn't guarantee his words would always make sense. The editors of the other papers in Frank's stable offered her their help, and she'd promised to call before she reached a panicked state.

But in the middle of the night, every dream produced one printing chaos or another.

Kali seemed to sense her tension. "Do you want to hang around and produce a weekly paper? I mean, I thought you despised being there."

Lacy had aired those words more times than she cared to admit, but always with the proviso she was biding her time for a better offer. She'd sent out dozens of resumes, but no one had invited her in for an interview. For the present, it seemed her best source of validation would come from a paper that Frank once said he could produce in his sleep.

"I don't hate it, exactly." She found Charlie's pacifier and baited it onto his pouting lip. "Without Frank in the office, I kind of like the editorial control. I'm still plugging in the basic stories he demands, but I can give them my bit of personality, and no one has freaked out."

Kali studied her sister. "That sounds like you like it. Like you like being in Comfort."

"Oh, please, don't read into it. I'm still doing my penance, but it's tolerable."

A breeze blew through the hallway as the salesman propped the door open to roll in another display case.

"I heard Amy Marsh will tour with Taylor Swift." Kali leaned her shoulder against the doorjamb. "She's about to go big-time."

Biting the inside of her cheek, Lacy kept from expressing her opinion. Kali would never blame her, but the sooner Lacy stopped thinking about Amy as the enemy, the sooner she could move past bitterness. Or so Gloria told her. She was still working on the whole forgiveness thing and was finding progress slow. Watching Amy's name pop up on *Entertainment Tonight* proved that her "behind-the-scenes" video peek into Amy's life had done no permanent damage. Tempted to call Christopher and offer this as proof, she didn't because she feared antagonizing someone with power.

"Mrs. Hamilton?"

They both turned to see the salesman poised with his portfolio.

"Gotta go." Kali stepped into the office and kissed Charlie's head. "I'll be half an hour, tops."

"Sure, no problem." Lacy glanced through the window. "We'll take a stroll."

Shuffling through the production area, she found Charlie's stroller at the backdoor. Negotiating it outside, she fought with him to strap him safely into the seat. He'd had a taste of crawling in the grass and, since then, insisted on being in the dirt. Lacy didn't trust him not to put everything he touched into his mouth, so she was keeping him locked down.

Finding her sunglasses, a pair of Ray-Bans she had bought in better days, she pushed Charlie toward the driveway and knew they'd get a nice long walk if she covered the distance from the farmhouse to the road. Years ago, when Kali bought this tired land, Lacy had wondered how the plan to raise goats and make cheese would ever succeed.

Time proved she was not the visionary among the two sisters, but she was a darn good cheerleader. She'd spent all her free time helping Kali, and she had no regrets about leaving two years ago because, by then, Jake was back in the picture. Once that tall drink of Texas cowboy walked through the doors of Provence Farm, she knew he was there to stay.

Pausing, she wound her hair into a ponytail to keep it contained in the breeze. The sun warmed the earth, and the scent of new grass wafted in the air. Glancing around at the foals frolicking in the front pasture and the baby goats being led to a watering hole, she wished she had a camera handy. The lavender-blue tint to the hills, the spikes of green cactus, and the first hints of bluebonnets needed broadcasting to the world. This gift of bucolic earth was reward for enduring the winter.

When she returned to the office, she'd grab Kali's camera and snap a few pictures. She could already imagine the Provence Farm posts—borrowing an idea, she might create something about "happy goats make happy cheese."

Hearing an engine grinding down, she watched a sedan turn into the drive, slowly making its way up the slope. She pulled Charlie's stroller into the grass in case the view of the farmhouse and the ranch distracted the driver. When the car slowed to a stop next to her and a window dropped down, she caught her breath.

"Just the person I was looking for."

Lacy couldn't find her voice.

It had been two weeks and some-odd days since that baritone had curled around her eardrum. She'd thought about him a million times, but never—not in the whole of ever—had she thought Rudy would drive to Comfort. In all her fantasies, they were meeting in Austin at some trendy bar with a jazz combo in the background. He struck her as a jazz guy, not a drive-to-the-country-in-a-rental-car kind of guy.

"You seem shocked." He balanced his elbow on the open window.

She pulled her glasses down her nose to be sure she wasn't daydreaming. "You're the last person I expected to see today, especially here."

His gaze swept the pastures. "It's not the place I expected to find you either."

"I'm sure you know this is my sister's business, Provence Farm. They make your favorite cheese."

"I recognized the sign." He glanced toward the placard tucked into a grove of rosemary bushes. "I've tried calling you, but that didn't work. So, I decided that if I would ever talk to you again, I had to throw myself on the mercy of your sister."

Those words sounded surreal. If she hadn't seen his beautiful lips move, she'd have doubted he had said the words at all.

"You want to talk *to me*?" She glanced at the sky, waiting for something heavy to land on her head. Had anyone ever worked that hard to track her down? No. Never. "But I gave you my number."

"And you've never answered my calls."

"You've called?"

Rudy put the car in park and unfolded from the driver's seat. "I called."

He was even taller when seen outside of a kitchen. This might be the first time she'd seen him in regular clothes, dark jeans and a black sweater with a gray undershirt. He was both unremarkable and stylish in one sweep. Nerve endings bubbled under her skin.

Staring at him now, under the soft haze of sunlight and easy temperatures, she wondered how she'd ever thought he was aloof. He'd driven over a hundred miles to find her. That spoke of a level of interest that exceeded anything she'd ever imagined. And here she was, dumbstruck, while wearing her oldest denim.

Charlie grumbled. Lacy glanced down and saw her nephew staring at her like he was about to demand action. Moving the stroller back and forth, she tried to think when Rudy would have called her. "I don't have caller ID on my recycled flip-phone, and I don't know how to unlock the voice-mail feature either."

Rudy leaned against the door. "I just thought you weren't that interested in returning my calls."

"You left messages?"

"Three or four, but who's counting."

She put her sunglasses on her hair. "Do you want to come to the house? I don't know how much longer my nephew will remain quiet about his walk being interrupted."

Rudy bent down to run his hand over the boy's flyaway tuft of brown. "So, he's not yours?"

"Oh, dear God, no." She knew a fiery color flared across her cheeks; she could feel the heat wrapping around her throat. "I'm not exactly mother material."

He stared at her for a long moment. "And yet that is a healthy baby."

"My sister's son. He eats gourmet baby food."

Quiet for a moment while processing, Rudy stood and shifted on his feet like he was at a loss about what to do next. "I'll meet you at the porch?" he asked, before climbing back into his car.

"Yes. Sure." There was only one other vehicle at the farmhouse. The paper salesman and Kali probably watched this whole bizarre interaction from the conference room.

Lacy's breath exhaled with a quake to her shoes. What would she do with Rudy? What did he want?

Pushing Charlie uphill at a speed that he loved, her mind warped ahead to conversations that may or may not ever happen. Rudy waited for her at the bottom of the steps to the house, and she nearly swallowed her heart. How could a man who spent entire days in a kitchen be that gorgeous? The sunlight picked out the various shades of walnut in his hair, and his shoulders testified to a workout regime.

Charlie screamed. Unbuckling the straps, she was kicked with his moccasins. Grateful for the distraction, she cooed, "Not now, little monster. We're going inside."

He must have understood her words because his arms flailed, and his face squirrelled into a tantrum.

Lacy hugged him close, hoping he'd calm down. "Charlie likes being outdoors." She hoped Rudy's history with Luna would cause him to forgo judgment on her parenting skills.

"It's become a battle. Which is why Kali keeps his playpen in the backyard."

"Here, give him to me." Rudy opened his arms. "Sometimes someone new can surprise them out of their fits."

"Oh, I couldn't possibly."

He scooped Charlie out of her arms and soon had the baby lodged securely against his chest.

Lacy watched Charlie's anger melt as the baby stared in fascination at Rudy's chin, poking a finger against the beard stubble. "You're a magician."

"I assure you, if I were around the kid often this charm would wear off." Rudy turned to look into the baby's face. "Isn't that right, little one?"

Charlie beamed in response.

"I was supposed to be the favored person." Lacy pouted to disguise the howitzer going off in her heart. How could a man who commanded minions be so adorable with an infant? "My babysitting skills will be questioned from this day forward."

Old iron squealed from the front door's hinges. Kali stood inside the threshold, staring in surprise. "Chef Delgardo? I'm stunned. Did you make an appointment? I'm sure my manager would have told me about a product tour."

He shifted Charlie in his arms and turned toward the porch. "I took a chance on finding you at the office today. I pulled out of Austin with little itinerary."

Lacy saw circles under his eyes she had missed the first time she stared at him. His cheeks were gaunt. And she was sure gray hair had pebbled his sideburns since she'd seen him last. Her fingers itched to smooth his hair back into the controlled style he wore at work, not this windblown disarray that scattered her known impressions to the four corners.

"Well, lucky for you," Kali said, opening the door wide, "we specialize in hospitality to the aimless."

Lacy followed him up the steps and through the door, catching Kali's questioning gaze. She had no answers to offer, just a bemused grin for the weird turn of events. In one of her pageants, a popular Texas actor had made a surprise appearance and all the girls had hyperventilated. He'd packed less power than this chef.

Taking Charlie, Kali stepped away, explaining that she needed to get the salesman out the door before she could show Rudy around.

The silence in the front room thickened as Lacy and Rudy stood near the reception desk. Shifting from one foot to the other, she thought through a million stupid things she could say but opted not to expand his already ditzy impression. Having vomited in his restaurant and backed into his vehicle, she didn't need to aim for a trifecta of opening acts.

Rudy didn't seem inclined to chat as he read Kali's biography, framed beneath a photograph snapped while working the Provence, France farm that had inspired her career choice.

Lacy's experience with interpreting men had limits.

Frank implied that she was better suited for networking with the drill-team set. Digs like that one got under her skin because it was discrimination disguised by a joke. Although, if she were candid, she'd admit she got along really well with girls who knew their way around makeup, mirrors, and posturing. But Frank wasn't here, so she didn't have to argue the point.

Mentally, she scanned the morning's headlines and searched for something that might appeal as a conversation starter. Politics? NBA playoffs?

"I was hoping to visit Lavender Hill today," he muttered.

Stunned, she tilted her head to the side, wondering if that request came from the man facing the wall. "You want to go to Lavender Hill?"

He straightened and moved along to scan the featured magazine articles profiling the cheeses Kali manufactured and the unusual entrepreneur behind the success.

She wondered if she'd heard him correctly. Maybe the rumors about chefs were correct. Maybe he was used to barking an order and expecting immediate responses; he didn't know how to deal with a novice who repeated things he'd said.

"I'll see what's keeping Kali."

Before she exited, he asked, "Will you go with me—to see AJ?"

The lavender farm was waking from its winter sleep. Though the weather flirted with those who'd putter in their gardens, it was too soon for serious shoppers. So, it was safe to assume he drove this far into the country in response to the request for the festival and wanted to see the event center—not to see her.

Her pride took the stomach punch, and she had to control a gasp.

Why doesn't someone teach girls to prepare to be the runner-up? Everyone always preaches to reach for the stars, that you can be anything you set your mind on. Don't let anyone tell you otherwise.

Until someone does.

"Yes, I'll go." She found her voice. "Kali will want to come along as well."

It hurt too much to realize she wasn't enough of a draw. *Silly girl.*

Too many pageants had messed with her head, and she would face a lifetime of rejections before she stopped responding hopefully to every anticipation.

Scurrying toward the production area, she ran smack into a cloud of moldy warmth emanating from the stoves. Gagging, she hid her disgust of the aroma and hurried toward Kali's office. The room stood vacant, as did the conference room. Charlie's playroom sat empty too. The only other space on this floor was a break room. Lacy stared through the window to the goat paddocks, wondering if she should wander upstairs to keep from returning to the room inhabited by Rudy Delgardo.

Like every other good thing that had entered her world, she'd read too much, too fast into his interest. What was it going to take for her to learn that no one liked her just for herself? People used her to get to the next big thing. In the yawning emptiness of the last several months, she'd found print media proved the same. It was a who-knew-whom playground among editors.

"Here she is," Kali announced brightly, "looking like a lost soul."

Whipping around, Lacy bristled. Older sisters always thought they knew the truth.

Rudy dwarfed Kali by a foot. His gunslinger gaze unnerved Lacy. It was as if he could stare past the scars and see the orphan still looking for a forever home and someone to trust.

Swallowing, she pretended a flood of flashing cameras waited urgently on her response. The trouble with winning Miss Texas was that the fallout with media and friends set her up for a lifetime of poise and cynicism—both equally dangerous skills for someone who had yet to figure out who she wanted to be when she grew up.

Chapter Twelve

Wind slung dust against the window of Lavender Hill's garden shop. Though the interior felt snug, the chill captured during the last-minute run from the fields still stung.

AJ handed Lacy a mug of Earl Grey tea, sweetened with a lavender-infused syrup, saying, "Who knew a blue norther would sweep in this morning?"

Lacy breathed the fragrant steam and tucked deeper into the chair in the front room. A display of hummingbird feeders and chimes dangled near her head. Rudy perused walls, looking at art and shelves of décor items as if he rarely saw a world outside of a pantry.

Kali sighed as she sat on the arm of the chair Lacy had claimed. "I should have paid closer attention to the forecast before waltzing Chef through the fields."

"The nature of these weather patterns is that they surprise most folks." AJ offered Rudy a mug. "Even the most experienced."

"I was happy to explore. It's much alive now than it was at Christmas." Wrapping his hands around the mug, he added, "But just as cold."

"The locals say that a blue norther brings with it a surprise, but they never seem to think the change is for the better." Kali's focus grew misty. "I'm sure my goatherders are running for the barn and predicting doom." She stood. "I should call them."

"I'll bank on an abundant growth for the gardens. This weather pattern always brings a good rain." AJ drew a chair forward. "The gardens will erupt with color in another few weeks, and I'll begin my busiest sales season of the year."

Lacy listened to the banter with half an ear. She'd once worked in AJ's greenhouse, so she was familiar with the backbreaking work involved when the lavender bloomed. She'd moved countless plants and bags of potting soil into vehicles belonging to folks who drove from Austin and San Antonio. She'd ducked a few weeks ago when AJ emailed asking for seasonal help.

As Rudy asked questions about the business plan, she closed her eyes and imagined his voice reading the headlines of the paper's latest edition. She smiled. That man could make tax returns sound sexy.

It was construction talk that eventually pricked her brain and brought her back to the moment. Before the wind blew through, they'd toured the event center, peeking in at the catering-service areas and built-in bar space installed since the last time she'd been on site. Rudy had asked engineering-based questions she'd never have considered. She'd scribbled "HVAC" and "disappearing stage" onto her notepad to research in the privacy of her office. No point admitting how little she knew.

"I can imagine the large windows in the hall will frame the fields with living art," Rudy said, before sipping the tea. "Will the lavender be in bloom at the time of the grand opening?"

AJ nodded. "We usually harvest the plants in June, so if we time this right, we can show it off with color covering the hills."

"I haven't cooked with lavender, but I imagine there are recipes we could highlight at the festival." He lifted his mug.

"This tea is delicious. Maybe we could offer a cocktail bar with lavender syrups."

Kali returned to the room, her enthusiasm engaged with the conversation. "We could stage a cooking show throw down. Reward the chefs creating the best-tasting lavender recipes with a prize. Maybe even do a baking event for home cooks? Like an old-fashioned pie contest!"

Lacy listened to them bat ideas around but held back from commenting. This still felt surreal. Rudy was standing in Comfort talking about their festival as if the idea had believability. They'd dreamed big and won?

No, they weren't that lucky. The winds howling outside testified to unexpected turns.

Something felt off.

For one, Rudy had implied he'd driven all this way to see her, but as yet, they'd barely had three private moments between them.

Second, he was quite accommodating for a man who was too busy to even give them a second thought the first time they'd asked.

And third . . . well, third, he was ridiculously curious about lavender for a man who oozed male superiority. Even she wasn't that enthused about an herb that grew like wildflowers in this soil. Every time she got a nose full it transported her to Aunt Annalise's dressing table and the talcum powder she had applied every morning. Kali and AJ were around the bend on lavender, but that was their schtick. She expected it. But Rudy? Did a man seem more or less masculine because he knew the flavor palette of an herb?

She'd go with a big check next to manlier. The contrast of edgy, foreign demeanor with knowledge of a tiny plant made him seem like someone who might know other interesting secrets. Her nerves tingled. Now, what might those mysteries be?

"So, Lacy, what do you think?"

Startled, she blinked. Filing away ideas not meant for group discussion, she said, "I think we need to return to the simplest concept and not make this festival more complicated than it has to be."

Three sets of eyes stared at her with varying degrees of surprise.

Kali yanked the mug from her sister's hand and sniffed it for purity. "We wondered if you were ready for lunch. Rudy suggested we drive to Kerrville and visit a friend's restaurant."

Embarrassed, Lacy avoided Rudy's gaze. He had some crazy power over her senses, and she didn't trust herself to behave. "I can't go to lunch. I have to run a final proofing of this week's edition of the newspaper and send it to print."

Coughing to cover her reaction, AJ winked. "Since when do you turn down a hamburger?"

"Oh, you didn't say it would be burgers." Lacy's weakness for sizzling, mustard-slathered beef was legendary. Jake teased that he always grilled two patties for Lacy because one was never enough. "But still, Frank needs me to turn this in promptly, and I don't want to earn a mark for inefficiency."

"You like burgers?" Rudy's gaze seemed to question her taste in food.

This was it—the beginning of the end of her fantasy. In his private life he probably only ate vegan. The blue norther never lied.

"It would be my last meal if I were ever facing a firing squad." She rolled her shoulders back. "With a double helping of fries. And I wouldn't turn down a chocolate pie. If I were being executed."

Kali groaned. "I swear, you've always had the most twisted imagination."

Rudy grinned. For the first time in all the occasions she'd ever been around the stern but stunning chef, he smiled. His eyes lit, and a glow brightened behind those stormy gems, proving he had a powerfully compelling gaze.

Lacy had to pick up one of those breakable art pieces AJ staged around the store to distract herself from staring. "I bet you're too sophisticated to enjoy a good hamburger."

"I've grilled thousands of burgers and consumed as many as I could along the way. I towed a grill trailer to the Sonoma-area farms during harvest to feed the workers picking grapes. I consider a perfectly cooked hamburger a true test of a cook's worth."

Lacy set a porcelain rose on the table. "I always thought the omelet was the true test."

"Depends on if you're talking American cuisine or French."

"Well, around here, they separate the men from the boys based on a preference for ketchup or mustard."

Kali latched onto Lacy's arm and drug her toward the front door. "We're stepping outside, Chef, before you run for your car and never look back on Lavender Hill."

Lacy heard a deep chuckle before the door slammed behind them.

"What are you doing?"

Lacy shook her arm free of her sister's grip. "I'm going to work. Can I borrow AJ's truck? My car is back at your place."

"You know that's not what I'm talking about. Why are you sabotaging the festival? I thought you liked Rudy."

"Have we been given permission to call him by his name yet?"

"Lacy," Kali murmured, before following her sister's footsteps pounding into the gravel compost. "You're not making sense."

Whipping around, Lacy narrowed her gaze on the woman who read the fine print before downloading a new app on her phone. "*He's* not making sense. Three weeks ago, he gave us a solid no when we asked him to headline this event, and now he shows up, out of the blue, like he's all in? Something is fishy."

"People change their minds."

"Without asking us about our marketing, or if we've done a feasibility study, he announces his interest."

The wind wrapped a scarf of lavender around them.

"You've done a feasibility study?"

"Not exactly. But I got event notes from my friends over at Becker Vineyards." She folded her arms over her chest. "The point is why now."

"I thought you'd be dancing for joy. He's the one we wanted from the start."

Lacy turned and walked toward a farm truck, searching the dash for a set of keys. Finding none, she gave up plan A. She'd have to get a ride to Kali's some other way.

Rudy disturbed her on a cellular level. She was both attracted, to a degree she'd never experienced before, and sure he would break her heart. No amount of explaining justified this, but as the wind circled her legs, she knew it was true. The question remained: Could she work with him on the festival and keep him at arm's length? Her track record with disasters proved she was a magnet for mayhem. She probably conjured this blue norther just by fantasizing about the man the moment he stepped out of his car.

"He is here because he wants something out of this." Lacy searched her bag for her phone. "Something we can't see yet. You mark my words."

"He can have whatever he wants. He's doing us a huge favor."

"Is he though? You know he bombed out of the James Beard Awards?"

"How do *you* know this?"

She punched in the number for the one cab driver in Comfort. If she was lucky, he wasn't hauling livestock as well. "I'm a social-media addict, stalking headlines is what I do. The rumors out of New York are bleak."

Kali threw her hands in the air. "I don't care if the Michelin people take back a star—that doesn't impress me. I like Rudy. He's credible. And he'll draw people to our festival. That's what matters."

Lacy didn't agree, but then she was the only one among the team attaching an entire career strategy to May's event. She needed a big win, one with enough fuel to shoot her across Interstate 10 and back into a city, where she could carve out a viable means of income and something resembling the positive role model she'd sworn to be when crowned Miss Texas. Though the pageant committee had not written her a nasty 'gram after the Amy Marsh debacle, she expected one any day.

A sash-wearing ghost nipped her heels every time she checked her email.

What she didn't need, want, or desire was another crash—even one with fallout limited to her personal romantic wasteland. She was sure she'd imagined the smoldering glances today, but to be certain, she was taking a giant step backward. No point tempting Cupid's evil twin.

Glancing to the porch where AJ and Rudy watched this small duel, she doubted they understood how much was at stake. If they did, they wouldn't be smiling.

Chapter Thirteen

Rudy lifted a stalk of Brussel sprouts and studied the buds for imperfections. Clatter from pots and pans arranged for afternoon sauces created a backdrop for the messiness of his thoughts. Setting the stalk on the work surface, he switched his attention to tomatoes. Lifting one of the purple-hued varieties to his nose, he breathed the organic bouquet that sunshine and good soil produced.

"Are you going to make me beg?" Kenny handed him a squash. "I'm not too proud to go down on my knees. I'm the one who showed you her YouTube videos."

"It's been a long time since I've seen you beg. Maybe since the time we knew Sandra Bullock had a reservation, and you were desperate to serve her food."

"I looked very good in the waiter's uniform, admit it."

Rudy shrugged. Kenny was a celebrity hound. He investigated everyone who requested the private dining room. Rudy had never given two figs for who dined at Stella's, unless it was someone who could harm their reputation. Like Alan Gale or his ilk.

"*And* she raved that the wine reduction sauce—*my* sauce—" Kenny added, "was sent straight from the hand of God."

"Now it's permanently on the menu. What's your point?"

"Tell me everything that happened with the Blonde Goddess."

Rudy stacked the vegetables in the box and wiped his hands on his apron. It had been two days since he woke with the bright idea to drive to Comfort. All in all, he'd had better plans.

Something weird had happened with Lacy. He'd seen her eyes light up when he drove to her sister's farm, sure that meant she felt that same sweet torture he did every time she was near, but then her enthusiasm had tanked with each passing hour.

Though he'd tried, they'd had few private conversations. Maybe that was the problem? She needed words.

Hannah complained he was genetically incapable of communication, but he'd always thought that was because he didn't like talking to her. Maybe the problem applied to all women.

Or maybe he felt like a tongue-tied twelve-year-old around Lacy Cavanaugh.

He hadn't done a good job disguising his shock after seeing her with a baby. Thankfully, he soon found out the child was not hers and she wasn't married. Despite her protests, she was good with children. She'd had Luna wrapped around her finger within moments of their meeting. But had he gone wrong then or later?

On the winding drive back to Austin, he'd replayed their moments together. After years navigating Hannah's moods, he was well aware when he was the source of a woman's disdain—whether he knew what he had done to inspire it or not. Something he'd said ticked off Lacy.

And, though he'd not signed a contract, they'd committed him to their food-and-wine festival. Kenny had better be right about creating a distraction to redirect media attention away from the James Beard Foundation.

"If you use her ridiculous nickname one more time, I will not tell you anything."

Kenny pouted. "But that's what her friends call her . . . when she's not around."

"You and I are not her friends," Rudy said with finality. "I'm not even sure she wants to admit she knows me."

Kenny played with the heavy gold chain dangling over the silk jacket he wore. He told people he'd won the piece in a poker game, but Rudy was sure Kenny bought the jewelry off one of his cousins who worked at the mall.

Unlike his sous chef, he didn't rattle when he walked. The only jewelry he owned was a Rolex he inherited from his Belgian grandfather—a banker and a World War II resistance fighter. Rudy's wardrobe centered on two colors he could mix and match interchangeably—dark blue and dark gray. If he owned a shirt in a different shade, it was a gift from someone who didn't know him well.

"Start at the beginning and do not leave out a single detail." Kenny closed his eyes as if was mentally settling into a lounge chair with a tall, cold drink. "What was she wearing?"

Rudy walked to the other side of the kitchen, ignoring Kenny. It wasn't that he didn't know the answer; it was to protect his ego. It had been brought up to him—on many occasions—that he was blind to the nuances of the females in his world. Apparently, he couldn't be counted on to give a compliment, recognize a new hairstyle, or even appreciate when a spouse was under the weather because he was entirely self-absorbed.

And Hannah had been mostly right.

Those early years of their life together, he'd been in self-preservation mode, staking a reputation as a professional chef. Then they'd moved to Austin. He worked sixteen-hour days at a prestigious hotel kitchen. Customers searched him out, requested his special dishes, and in what seemed like a blink, he had investors suggesting he strike out on his own. Between his day job and the private events he catered, it would be weeks sometimes before he had more than ten minutes to find out what was going on in Hannah's life. That was the first time she threatened to divorce.

"What difference does it make what someone was wearing?" Rudy checked the onions being minced by a young chef. Rapping his knuckles on the block, he gave the signal of approval.

"Indulge me," Kenny pleaded.

Jeans that hugged her hips and a shirt that convinced him she'd walked right out of his fantasy. Large hoop earrings that tangled with her hair, and a bloom in her cheeks that makeup couldn't provide. "I refuse to feed your imagination."

"Okay, fine. I'll just go with gorgeous. Now, what happened when you told her our plan?"

"Ah—" He leaned over an induction stove and breathed in the fragrance of garlic and celery simmering in butter. "Didn't get to that point."

"What?" Kenny followed Rudy. "I gave you the talking points. Explanations that you knew about her unfortunate fallout with the media, and you felt in a similar boat? Remember? Then you were to plead with her to work a strategy for our delicious revolution. Simple. A fifteen-minute conversation, tops."

Rudy remembered how his heart flip-flopped when he saw her holding the boy. "Things came up."

"But she's brilliant. We need a genius at the helm of this Twitter war. Her move away from Instagram and Facebook has her fans salivating. Everyone is waiting on her return. I swear, she's more valuable now than she was when she was reporting on the backroom dramas of the band. There's a Facebook group wondering if she's been abducted by aliens."

Rudy thumped the butternut squash, investigating its ripeness. "I forget most people the moment they walk out of a room."

"Well, unlike most Instagram stars, Lacy Cavanaugh was funny. And insightful. And smart. She wrote important things about culture. A talent like that doesn't vanish because Amy Marsh threw a hissy fit about being outed."

Several heads turned their way. Rudy couldn't imagine why the cooks would gasp over this name, unless the woman was someone even worse than Gale. "Who is Amy Marsh and why do we care that she's gay?"

"She's not gay. She's bulimic. And she's a singer." Kenny threw his hands into the air. "I don't even know why I try. You're hopeless."

Rudy grinned, feeling better than he had all day.

"I'll call her." Kenny landed on a new plan. "I can announce she and I will be best friends. Besides, someone needs to inform her that the Facebook group has posted a retrospective of her top-five posts."

"You will do no such thing." Rudy marched Kenny toward the dining room where they'd have a measure of privacy from the curious. As the swing door closed behind him, he rounded up his wayward thoughts. "*I* will call her."

Kenny spun on the heels of his designer boots. "You can't be trusted to handle this. I need to talk to her. I'm almost a 100 percent sure someone who has invented a fake name is stalking the Facebook group on Amy's behalf. They're posing questions about Amy and Lacy that feel way too insider."

"We're not going to interfere in her life."

"Someone has to warn her."

Rudy held his tongue while a waiter approached, laying linen napkins on the tables for tonight's service. After the man moved away, Rudy took a step closer. "If she's as savvy as you say she is, she'll figure out what's going on. In the meantime, we need to stir some attention for this festival. I've promised to talk to Don Hurt and the folks over at Tito's about attending."

Kenny stood still for a long while, an unusual occurrence that should have flagged Rudy's attention. He'd hired Kenny six years ago and knew the young chef better than most. But Rudy was consumed with his own worries. The tweets Alan Gale continued to spew, the silence from the James Beard Foundation, Hannah hammering him about better time management for Luna, and new pressure to create a spring menu for Stella's.

When the bartender brought over the inventory from the distributor, he signed off on the change order regarding the new line of mixers. He glanced around the dining room for some sign that Jay had arrived today and could run interference, while he walked down to Stella Too's and tried to clear his thoughts.

Seeing the head of the waitstaff roll out a cart of glassware, he almost turned away, then remembered Kenny. "You're on the schedule for head chef this week. I'll be in Abilene Thursday and Friday, and I need to know you can take care of any last-minute surprises."

"Yes, Chef."

He did a double take at the odd expression on Kenny's face. "Are you okay?"

Kenny's eyes brightened. "Don't you worry about a thing. I'll cover all the bases while you're gone."

He remembered Jay's confidence that Kenny could handle being head chef, and he hoped Jay was right. Whether Kenny was ready to run his own place was a decision he'd prefer not to make, but surely, he could keep Stella's afloat for two days. "I'm not leaving until Thursday."

Kenny nodded. "Got it."

Rudy stepped away and felt like he'd missed something important. Glancing around the room, all appeared normal for a Tuesday afternoon. It was almost as if he could hear Hannah chuckling that he was about to screw up again.

Rudy tamped down the taunt. She'd been both good angel and bad angel in his conscience for the ten years they'd been together, and no doubt her two sides were something he should have seen when he met her in San Diego. But those heady days, when she called him with an offer too good to be true, were a long-forgotten tale.

"Chef?"

"Yes." He answered the waiter.

"Are we getting more lavender for the tables? Several of the customers commented that they liked the arrangements."

An image of the spiky stems jutting out of the narrow cylinders flitted through his memory. He nodded. *Perfect.* "Yes, I think I can get in touch with the supplier and find out about the next delivery."

Dismissing all other thoughts, he hurried to his office. Closing the door, he reached into his pocket and pulled out his cell phone. His finger hovered over the contact list that featured her number. Would she read his real intention into the call? Would she know how much he regretted the way things ended this weekend? None of that mattered as much as catching her while she was near her phone.

Now that he knew she couldn't access voice mail, he was more determined to know Lacy's schedule and choose the best times to call. He flipped his wrist, reading his watch. Two in the afternoon. Staring at the photo of Luna on his desk for courage, he punched the dial command and waited.

And waited. The endless ringing revealed one of two things. Either she didn't want to talk to him, or she was too busy doing something better. Something interesting.

The one question he'd not bothered to ask, and the first one he should have considered--was there another man in her life? Someone who commanded her attention?

He disconnected the call.

He must be too late. Again.

Chapter Fourteen

Morning light warmed her shoulders but fixed a glare on the screen jumbled with legal notices that didn't seem to fit into last week's line indents. Deciding to close the blinds, Lacy pushed back from Frank's desk and accidentally rolled into his credenza. A stack of newspapers crashed to the linoleum, and the avalanche claimed a mound of personal mail piled on top of his humidor. The pica pole, his archaic tool for laying out newsprint copy, crashed to the floor, ringing her ear. Lacy sighed. One more disaster in a day that had begun with an overzealous rooster crowing from the neighbor's yard.

Bending to retrieve the envelopes, she wondered if there was an order to this mail. Glancing through the bills and solicitations, she hoped she could recreate the organization—if one could call it such—to date delivery. If not, suspicion might set in. Frank would leap to the assumption that she'd picked the lock on his safe also.

There weren't enough scones at Cup of Joe's to counteract the blistering that came from messing with Frank's desk. She barely survived the lecture after organizing the in-box. But, since he'd given her the password to his desktop computer, she'd have to assume he knew that online access to his InDesign account came with certain risks.

Adjusting to his chemotherapy, Frank now spent most workdays weak and immunocompromised. Gloria, his oncology chauffeur, said he couldn't risk catching a virus and that he'd return to the Comfort office at the end of the month, at the earliest. Sorting the past-due stamps, she wondered what she should do about these bills. Frank had been secretive about the business of running the paper, and with other newspapers in his portfolio, she'd assumed he had an accountant tucked away somewhere, writing the checks. Current evidence proved otherwise.

She shoved the envelopes into a plastic sack and would give them to Gloria later. Maybe Frank's ex would deliver the bills, and he could catch up on his bookkeeping while propped in a recliner. It proved harder than she'd thought to picture the curmudgeon wrapped in a blanket with a beanie on his newly bald head.

So much of his spunk came from the flinty shadow he cast.

With a whiff of humid warmth, the front door blew open.

Lacy looked up to see Drue standing on the threshold, flowers disguising her face.

"Lacy, that you?"

"Yes, I'm here. Come on in." She hurried to close the door on the approaching rain. "Oh, my word. Those are gorgeous. Do you need help with a delivery?"

It wouldn't be the first time Lacy had volunteered. Valentine's Day weekend, she and Drue's grandsons had delivered flowers from dawn to dark. She'd delighted in seeing the surprise of folks' faces when they received an arrangement. That time driving the back roads had helped familiarize her with the farm-to-market roads and rural addresses. Living in Gloria's back house had spoiled her from knowing the conditions of those with thin paychecks and large families to feed. After passing several mildew-stained trailers and soulless yards, she had determined to be aware the hillsides housed people across the economic spectrum, not just the ones with million-dollar views and rolling ranch land.

If Drue needed help this morning, she'd be glad to take a few hours away from the computer. Maybe the time away would inspire her for writing headlines this afternoon.

Dark eyes peeked over the top of the white-and-yellow blooms. "I'm delivering! These are for you."

Air whooshed by, and she realized it came from her own lungs. "Me?"

Tottering toward the big table covered with fliers, rulers, and taped photos, Drue sat the vase in the middle of the high school's cafeteria menu. "I rarely get to do something this fun, and I might have gone over the top."

Lacy followed, gaping at the flowers bringing sunshine into the room. "Daisies are my absolute favorite. How did you know?"

Bending over, she stuck her nose into the display. She wasn't sure what she expected for fragrance, but these smelled like toe jam. Rising, she tried to remember the last time she'd held a bouquet of daisies. Maybe the afternoon she'd splurged on flowers at Trader Joe's. Over the years, she'd posted several photos of the posies she'd bought from roadside stands, or wildflowers she'd collected, and because of the likes, made a habit of buying flowers every time she went to the grocery store. The daisies from the Dallas Farmers Market were always a big hit.

Drue propped her hands on her ample hips. "I didn't know your favorite. I guess because I've never asked. But the guy who called in the order said he knew you loved daisies, and that I was to find as many as I could." Drue pulled a handkerchief from her back pocket and wiped her brow. "Lucky for you, I have a friend in San Antonio who owns a wholesale shop and just got a month's worth of orders from Mexico."

Lacy blinked and tried to think who would know her preference for daisies. There was a guy she'd dated a million years ago, but his idea of a nice gesture always involved red roses. A fashion designer once sent her a huge thank-you bouquet for modeling his spring collection, but those flowers were artsy. The guys in the band wouldn't know to send flowers to their own mothers' funerals if she wasn't around to remind them, so this treat wouldn't have come from them.

A card dangled from a spindly plastic stick. She reached for it and read the message.

Drue folded her handkerchief. "So, are you thrilled? Over the moon? Or whatever it is you young people call it these days?"

"I'm . . . uh . . . stunned." She glanced at Drue's ageless complexion, a grandmother of ten, though you'd never guess because her coffee skin boasted zero wrinkles. "Are you sure these are from Rudy Delgardo?"

"He added a nice tip to make sure I spelled the name correctly. He said so few people do."

Bubbles of happiness burst from behind Lacy's heart. A delight she'd not known in years flooded her brain. "Rudy sent me flowers." Her voice sounded odd even to her ears. "I had no idea he cared."

Drue scoffed. "He cares at the high-market rate. Daisies aren't exactly in season."

"How would he even know I like them? We've never discussed it." A dry laugh burst from her lungs. "We have hardly even spoken."

Drue's eyes narrowed. "He's not a creeper, is he? I'd hate to think I got in the middle of some shenanigans. I've barely recovered from that Valentine's fiasco where we delivered the wrong roses to the wrong woman."

Lacy tapped the card against the table, bringing her mind back from picturing Rudy sitting at his desk, planning this order, to the comment hanging in the atmosphere. "I hadn't heard about that story, but it sounds like the funny thing you could turn into a great post. Are you sure you don't want me to come over and help you with your Instagram?"

"Gosh, no. My grands are forever trying to get me onto the web, and I tell them I don't need the hassle. I have enough business doing funerals and weddings to keep me in high cotton."

Questions swirled in her brain, and a red flag waved at her from the distance. Something wasn't right about this delivery, but the daises befuddled her. Starved as she was for male attention, she'd hug the arrangement to her chest if it wouldn't break the stems.

"You enjoy those beauties," Drue said, backing toward the door. "I've got to chase off that dog before he upends my bulbs."

Lacy removed the flowers from the middle of the table and set them on her desk, a second-hand table Frank presented to her on her first full week of work. The antique had never looked better. Staring at the tall peak of blooms and small orange pom-poms breaking up the sea of white, she wondered what she should do next.

Did she write a thank-you note? Call immediately? What was he expecting to happen as a result of sending flowers?

Would they go out?

Her heart did a high kick while rockets flared in the background.

She checked her watch and saw hands pointing to eleven thirty. Surely, he could spare a couple of minutes? Rehearsing a few lines, she found her phone and punched in the number she'd saved as his personal cell. She didn't want to take the chance of calling Stella's and having to chat with the general manager.

This was too personal.

Too special.

Rudy liked her.

Had there ever been any better news?

Butterflies swarmed her middle, but she'd waltzed into more dangerous places than thanking a man for thoughtfulness. She could handle a phone call.

When his voice came on the line, her stomach tightened. "Rudy?"

"Lacy."

"I hope I didn't catch you in the middle of anything urgent."

"Not unless you consider the drive-through line at Chick-fil-A a matter of national importance. Luna swears she will die if she doesn't have nuggets for lunch."

Thrown off that he was with his daughter, she regrouped. "I didn't realize she was with you this week. I wanted to call and say thank you for the daisies. I don't know how you knew they were my favorite flower, but I'm overwhelmed by your generosity. They really are the best thing about my day."

The line hummed for a moment. Thinking something had interrupted the satellite signal, she was about to redial when he spoke.

"I'm not sure to what you're referring."

Little fires erupted everywhere—first her heart, then her lungs. She glanced at her fingers to see if they flared as well. She glared at the flowers and snatched the card from the table. "The daisies? Ordered from Drue's Floral Shop in Comfort?"

"Hi, Lacy!"

She heard Luna's voice in the background, and tears popped to her lids. This situation was sinking. "Please tell Luna I said hello."

He didn't. "Lacy, I don't know where things have gotten miscommunicated, but I didn't order flowers. I was going to call you this week to ask you to bring another delivery of lavender stems to Stella's. But I didn't get around to it. I'm keeping Luna in Abilene for a few days. She had a dentist appointment this morning. I didn't even know there was a florist in Comfort."

So many words and none of them the ones she'd expected.

Swiping the spring of hot tears that spurted with the flood of embarrassment, she tried to salvage this before she mortified either of them any longer. "Well, I'm sure there's an explanation somewhere. Your name was on the card. So, I assumed you'd sent the arrangement. I guess it was the craziest of mix-ups," Lacy stammered. "No harm done. I'll let you go. Now. Goodbye."

"Lacy?"

She disconnected the line before she said something even more ridiculous. Caving into a chair, she buried her face in her hands. Horrified, she rethought the sequence of events, stumped how something so bizarre could have happened.

If he didn't send the daisies, then who did? And why?

Her mind spun odd circles, never landing on logic. Exhausted from the surprise of tears and shamed for having dialed Rudy, she hurried to the bathroom to wash her face. Finding a threadbare cloth buried with the stack of industrial paper towels, she didn't bother to wait on the water to warm. Standard-issue iciness was preferred. Leaning against the sink, in a room she'd once cleaned from top to bottom, she stared at her reflection. The mascara stains, splotchy cheeks, and bare lips didn't register—the hollowness did.

Some mornings she got dressed from rote memory, as if no one in Comfort expected the fashion styling so necessary in Dallas. And they didn't. That level of acceptance had fooled her into thinking she had it all going on, as if instinct trumped makeup and a flat iron.

But seeing the eyes stare back at her from this cracked mirror, she knew the truth. It glared as obvious as that zit on her chin. She'd lost her edge or, at least, the awareness she'd honed in the city. The street smartness about people and timing, the think-before-you-speak intuitiveness fostered from hiding behind a lens and having hours to pen a post.

Was there a name for the disease that turned savvy women into shells? If there was, she had contracted an incurable case. An exposure that must have started sometime last summer, when she'd first set down good sense and flirted with stupidity.

It was bad enough she'd been so consumed by jealousy regarding Amy's rise to fame and—most painful—supplanting her as band favorite that she'd indulged a vendetta to discredit her rival. She never intended their skirmishes to grow into the madness it became, but the battles had consumed her, and before Thanksgiving she'd turned from strategic-marketing guru into a complete maniac. When she discovered Amy's dark secret, she couldn't wait to expose it to fans—and the bandmembers. Boy, had she shown them. *Oh, yeah. Quite the Sherlock.* Setting aside any sense of deportment in her quest to oust this rival, she'd not only thrown Amy's name onto a national platform, she'd personified every stereotype people had about jaded beauty queens.

She still groveled when she realized how far she'd sunk. Even during pageant days, she'd been able to stay above pettiness, in part because the circuit was a means to an end. As someone with no academic achievements to boast, she was committed to winning as much scholarship money as she could.

But the girl in the glass? Hardly the reflection of the former Miss Texas who'd been cautioned to question every phone call, every new friend, for their bootlicking intentions. Nope. All that good training had been wadded and tossed to the wind.

She guessed she should thank whoever sent the flowers for waking her from the weird hole she'd fallen into last summer, but as she wiped her face, she committed to a new path. The price for that foolishness had been paid. She never wanted to feel this gullible again. Pain had a weird finish, as if the first kick weren't bad enough, but the aftertaste brought real bitterness.

Walking back into the office, or "brain center" as Frank called it, she realized she'd been the wrong woman. With the wrong flowers. There was nothing funny about being on this end of a delivery gone wrong.

The door to the *Comfort News* blew open again, and whips of rain dampened the threshold. Jake Hamilton stood with water dripping from his cowboy hat.

"Kali called me from the road and asked me to stop by and grab you. Someone left the gate open at the farm and all the goats have escaped. It's all hands on deck to round them up before they find their way to the highway."

Stuffing the cloth behind her back, she grimaced. "I'm not dressed to chase after goats."

He glanced at her leopard-print mules and skinny chinos, then back to her face. "Are you sick? You look like you've been hit by an ugly stick."

"It's temporary. I recover from these bouts of introspection quicker than most people."

"It's probably those flowers. Kali says daisies make her sneeze."

Refusing to look at the arrangement, she scowled. "I'm sure that's what it is."

"Who sent you flowers?"

"What makes you think they're for me? Could be for Frank."

"No one sends Frank flowers."

"Forget the flowers." Half of Comfort would know about the daisies between now and the time they collected the goats. "I'll finish this page setup and change. I'll get to the farm as soon as I can."

Jake backed out of the door and then paused. "Can you bring a few sacks of sandwiches? Maybe burgers? We'll need to feed folks after a roundup."

"Can't you do that on your way out?"

"I'm towing horses." Jake rearranged his hat for best rain protection. "It's not like you've got anything going on. Come on, help us out."

He was gone before she could protest. No one really understood what she did with her time. They thought the newspaper assembled itself week after week. Ads, legal notices, and copy weren't all that she did with her schedule, but they still regarded her as someone who had nothing to do, biding her time until she got a better offer.

She pursed her lips. That wasn't too far off the mark.

Gloria's voice hammered through her gloom. In her artless way, her landlady had chided Lacy about the depths of self-absorption and the value of investing in something else—anything other than a constant replay of all the unfairness life had tossed her way.

She glanced across the room. The flowers fell into that category.

Or . . . pitying could stop right here. Today.

She stared at the organization she'd brought to the *Comfort News*, the efficiency of production. The buzz of fresh ideas had taken flight. Good had come out of bad.

She'd discovered talents in the ashes of the fire that had tarnished her tiara. As she glanced at the flowers, she realized that Drue had put a lot of effort into the design. It shouldn't be trashed because of someone's cruel joke.

Setting the vase on the desk, she scurried into her raincoat and the rubber boots stored under her desk. The ladies at the library would love something bright in their space. Then, though she was no fan of goats, she would help her sister. Kali had been the mother she'd needed at various junctures in her life, replacement for the nurturing aunt who'd died before she graduated college. If Kali were in crisis, Lacy would help.

And she'd buy sandwiches—not burgers, though.

Just saying the word brought back an image of Rudy standing on AJ's porch, offering to treat them to lunch in

Kerrville. She'd been too proud, too confused, that afternoon. The relish of angst might ruin burgers for a long while.

And she would not think of Rudy if she could avoid it.

Some weird twist of fate had spun her world into a tilt, but in the spirit of new beginnings, she wouldn't whine like usual. Gloria had told her that she'd matured since coming to Comfort. If Gloria saw growth in Lacy, she would run with it.

She opened the door and observed a familiar mutt sitting on the *Comfort News* welcome mat, wearing a muddy grin.

"Shoo!" She snapped. "And I mean it this time. Go away and never come back."

His grin folded into a frown.

"Oh, good grief," she complained, as she locked the door behind her. "I don't like you. And you won't get under my skin."

He yapped a retort.

"You won't," she insisted as she stepped over the dog. "I'm stronger than you and have more important things to do than chase after a lost cause."

Rudy must have thought she was talking to him because he pranced along the sidewalk beside her. As she nudged the library's door open, Rudy sat, rain washing over his bedraggled coat. She glared at him.

"Seriously, leave me alone."

A man in a well-worn leather coat stood on the other side of the doorway. "I can't say we've met, but now that I've seen you, I can't swear to leave you alone."

She glared at the rancher. "I meant the dog."

He glanced around. "What dog?"

She shoved the flowers at him.

Managing to grab the arrangement, he asked, "Are these for me?"

"No, but can you give them to the folks at the library desk for me? I can't risk the dog following me inside. He leaves a mess everywhere he goes."

"All right," he said, with some suspicion. "But I don't see any dog."

She looked behind her and, sure enough, Rudy had vanished.

The second rumor that would spread around town today was that she'd gone mad.

Maybe self-pity was an undervalued attribute.

Chapter Fifteen

"Kenny?" Rudy growled into his phone. "What have you done?"

"I'm sorry. I confess. The grocer sold out of beets, and I'm substituting turnips in the vegetable medley. I know you hate turnips, but it was the only root vegetable he had in quantity." Banging pans and a few swear words carried over the phone connection. "It's chaos here. These people are taking liberties with you out of the kitchen."

He knew Luna listened to every syllable even as she sipped her soft drink. "I'm not talking about vegetables." He barely avoided gritting his teeth. "I just took a call. *About daisies.*"

The clatter of whisks and spoons echoed for a long second. "The rolls are on fire. Must go."

The rolls weren't burning. His pastry chef prepared baked goods in the morning when the kitchen temperatures were coolest. Disconnecting the call, he dropped his cell into a cupholder. *Damn Kenny.*

"Daddy, what happened? Is Kenny in trouble?"

Rudy pictured Kenny taking his campaign to recruit Lacy to a strange new—floral—level. Knowing his sous chef, this gesture should have opened a door, not slammed one shut. "Depends on what happens next."

"Mommy says you can't undo a mistake."

He was familiar with Hannah's standards for behavior. "Well, there's a lot of room to try before feelings get set in stone."

The temptation to gun the gas skimmed along with blood cells pushing against his veins. With Luna in the passenger seat, there was little he could do to release the tension. His eyes cut to the cell. Gripping the wheel, he stared at the wide-open plains and wished he were driving to Comfort.

If he could see Lacy maybe he'd think of something marginally less stupid than the junk that normally stopped up his brain when he was around her.

Why hadn't Kenny warned him about the flowers?

"Feelings." Luna slurped. "Mommy's got feelings for someone. He calls her all the time. It's gross."

Rudy's mind shifted gears. He'd vowed he'd never be the dad that pumped his kid for information, but this was too appealing to resist. "I'm glad she's dating someone. It's about time she was happy."

Luna sighed. "I'm not happy."

As he turned into the hotel's parking lot where he'd rented a room, he glanced at his daughter. "So, is he someone you know? Someone from around here?"

"I don't know. Mommy won't say. She just goes into her room and closes the door."

A long-distance romance. "Well, let's not bother your mom about details right now. She'll tell us when she's ready." The not-knowing teased him. Not because he was jealous but because of the relief. If Hannah could move on to someone else, she'd be too distracted to poke her nose into his business.

Grabbing his phone and his briefcase, he led the way to the hotel room and unlocked the door for Luna. A stale odor assaulted him. God, he hated this lifestyle. Drab hotels, odd dates that suited no one but Hannah, and the constant need to be "the fun parent" because he had to woo his own child into seeing past the stories her mother spun.

He couldn't be fun if someone paid him to take lessons.

He worked, that's what he did. Recognizing beautiful foods in their natural states, knowing how to take a vegetable from the garden to the plate, and bringing deliciousness to every element of the table—that's where he excelled. Learning to braid hair, remembering the names of Disney characters, and finding Luna's shot records required a level of effort he'd never expected. If quizzed this moment he'd fail Fathering 101.

A fighting spirit rose from under the weight of introspection and reminded him that complainers never won. How often had his grandmother drilled those words into his head? He had to work with what he had on hand—like the ingredients that found their way into his minestrone.

"Are you going to do homework?" Luna jumped onto a bed. "I ate my lunch in the car. I'm bored."

"I brought work from Stella's." Jay had sent a list of ideas to consider, but Rudy's brain still imagined Comfort. "But it can wait. Are you sure you ate all the lunch? Even the fruit?"

Luna fell flat to her back. "I don't want the fruit cup."

"It helps your body grow."

"My body doesn't like fruit."

"Your body isn't old enough to know what it likes and doesn't like. You're still discovering food."

She flipped over and propped her chin on her elbow. "I know I don't want to go back to school today. Can't we take a half day, like tomorrow?"

Holding open his briefcase, he glanced at the bed. "What do you mean—tomorrow's a half day?"

Scowling, she said, "Didn't you read the parent's memo? We have a half day because it's teacher in-service day."

Hannah had insisted he take these two days off from Stella's because she had to fly back to California; her mother had developed an infection from surgery and needed another procedure. She'd told him about the dentist's appointment this morning but had failed to mention a change in the school schedule. He'd lined up several online conference calls with vendors tomorrow and registered to take a continuing-ed class in food safety. What was he supposed to do with Luna being out of school for a half day?

Luna sang a silly song while he replayed Hannah's email in his mind. He was not prepared to entertain in Abilene. He'd struggled to find the pony farm for an after-school treat. "I'll call your mom and find out if she's made plans for you, knowing that you'd be off early. Did she say if she'd made plans for the weekend?"

"Daddy, we don't need plans."

For a man who lived by a tight schedule, he needed a plan and a backup before he could relax. "I'll find out what your mom wants."

"I want to stay with you!"

He wanted that too. There was so much he wanted to invest in Luna, but the only way he knew how to communicate was with food. Glancing at the matchbox room, with a minifridge and a microwave, he saw no equipment for real cooking. It was as if someone had stolen his tongue.

Watching Luna roll off the bed and land in a heap on the floor, he wished someone had given him the recipe for making this life work. He held his cell phone in the air, saying, "I need ten minutes."

Luna pouted and then reached for the remote control.

He stepped beyond the door, standing at the railing overlooking the parking lot, while waiting for the call to connect. What he wanted to do was transport Luna to a space where she could play, learn, and live, free of the strain of traffic in Austin and closer than the three-hour commute to Abilene. What he wished for was some place like Comfort.

With the snap of his fingers, he imagined the sunny bistro he'd envisioned at Christmas: a spacious kitchen, wide windows with views of the hills, a dining room that felt fresh and clean and encouraged lingering—a patio bar, too.

His breathing eased. His fingers relaxed their hold on the phone.

There'd also be a house nearby, and he could walk between the house and the bistro, knowing Luna would be safe playing outdoors or curled up with a book on a deep sofa. It didn't have to be a huge place, but it needed to feel like home, with a yard for growing vegetables and herbs and a big, scarred table on a porch outfitted with an outdoor kitchen, including a smoker where he could stoke his award-winning brisket. Luna would like a pool. Was it too much to ask for a vineyard—something sweeping west into the sunset? His grandfather had planted olive trees at the ends of rows of grapes, and he longed to do the same.

An odor of dirt and manure twirled through his brain and easily restored a muscle memory from days cutting grapes from the vines. Luna would complain of the labor, but she'd learn the cycles of life on a small farm.

Comfort reminded him so much of Sonoma. Maybe that was why his mind often switched gears to that limestone-shrouded village and the scrappy people who lived under the live oak trees. Well, if he were honest, there was one woman who anchored that fantasy. But after today, she'd probably sworn off ever speaking to him again.

Even now, as a dial tone rang in his ear, he traveled back to the dusty hilltops spiked with cactus, a thin ribbon of river luring a soul deeper into its valley.

Fifteen arduous minutes later, he returned to the hotel room seeing Luna's lineup of condiments, in descending order of size, outside his sack. Her eyes glazed over as she stared at the screen dancing with animated fish.

He squatted in front of her, interrupting her view. "Hey there. You ready to head back to school?"

"Need to put on my shoes."

"Well, I need to eat my lunch, and you know I can't do that and drive. Remember the time mayonnaise fell from my sandwich onto the steering wheel?"

She smiled. "You said ugly words."

"I walked around all day with an oil stain on my shirt." He squeezed her knee before standing. "Tell me about your teacher while I eat this salad."

Her little voice bounced over her specially crafted words, zinging musical tones through his ears. Luna had depths of creativity, and he didn't want to miss watching them unfold. For him, that presented the assumption they'd be together in the kitchen, but Hannah's father had been a songwriter, and his own father an engineer. Talents grew in a variety of silos. She might require different spaces to explore what was packed under her skin.

Which brought him back to an image of Comfort.

Uncomfortable though he was, he sat at the table pushed against the air-conditioner and opened his salad container. Dousing the lettuce with salt and pepper and a bit of the balsamic dressing, he bit through the meal with more speed than finesse. Luna had unpacked his overnight bag and was putting his clothes in the drawer, as if she needed him to move in.

"Hey, Shortcake."

She glanced up when he used her favorite nickname.

"I just talked to your mom and have some good news."

"Grandma won't die?"'

"Is that what Mom told you?"

"She said I had to pray for Grandma to stay alive until Mom got to the house."

Rudy rubbed his forehead, biting back the truth he wanted to spew. "Grandma is fine."

"She's not going to die?"

"Not today."

Luna sat on the floor. "Well, then my prayers worked. Do you want me to pray for you too? Mom said you are super grumpy and that anything I say can set you off."

A few dozen punishments flitted through his mind, but he hated wasting time thinking of Hannah if he could avoid it. "Pray all you want, but I have a great idea for the weekend. Something unexpected."

"Un-expec-tee-totally?" Her grin spread across her face like butter melting on toast. She reached around him with the remote and shut down the television.

He helped her to stand. "And," he added casually, "we must make a quick stop at your mom's place after school to pack up a few more clothes."

Her head pivoted. "But I brought my favorite outfit."

"Do you have other favorite outfits?"

"Yes. Three. But one is reserved for church, so it stays with Mom because you haven't gone to church in a year—or so Mom says."

He would ignore the jab. "Do you have an outfit you could wear if you were playing with baby goats?"

She paused slipping on sneakers, glancing at him with skepticism. "I thought you said we were feeding ponies."

"Today we feed ponies. But after school releases tomorrow, your mom said you could stay with me the whole weekend. We're going to take a road trip to a town that I think you will really like."

"And that's where baby goats live?"

He nodded. "I have it on the best authority."

By five o'clock Friday afternoon, he had his doubts about his plan. Not only was Stella's in chaos in Austin, an hour away, but Luna was crying. The quaint room at Comfort Commons hotel had a spider on the loose. Kali Hamilton was sick, so she didn't feel she should welcome the Delgardos for a goat tour until Saturday morning. He'd been ready to chuck it all in and pack the car for Austin when Kali mentioned Lacy had a key to the barn.

Lacy. Something about that woman fired his heart in a way no amount of chili peppers could duplicate. She was beautiful and graceful, but those eyes—light, spark flaring, daring him to come closer and risk the singe.

Kali suggested her sister could tour them around Provence Farm with the same panache, minus the teething baby. Rudy didn't need the tour after his previous visit, but if he could get fifteen minutes of Lacy's time, he'd explain about the daisies.

He handed a cold washcloth to his daughter and hoped she'd forget about the spider before the entire hotel complained of her screaming. Luna wiped her eyes and then held her arms up to him like she used to do when she was a toddler. His heart melted. Wrapping her in a hug and lifting her up, he carried her out the door and through the narrow hallway leading downstairs to the lobby. If the janitor didn't produce a spider carcass by the time they returned, he would have to drive back to Austin.

"So, before we go to supper, how about we walk around town a bit? Stretch our legs?"

As they stood on the doorstep, Luna's head popped from his shoulder.

"I like to walk."

"I know you do. These streets are so safe we won't have to dodge city buses."

She squirmed out of his arms, standing as tall as her legs would allow. "Can I lead the way?"

"You don't know where we're going."

Shrugging, she grinned. "I like getting lost."

He let his eyes rest a moment before he answered.

"And you can always find our way back, right, Daddy?"

His ruffled patience settled into its box. He'd walked all over this town during Christmas, getting lost and wandering back to the hotel every evening. "I can get us back to the Commons."

Rudy followed behind Luna, who was too busy skipping to pay any attention to the storefronts and shop windows. This town didn't have the same renovated glam of Fredericksburg, but the roughness appealed to him. The hanging baskets dangling from the streetlamps spoke of optimism.

"Look!" Luna crossed the quiet street and lunged for a row of shrubbery next to an art gallery. "A dog!"

Checking both ways, grateful no one was driving, he saw a bobbed tail wagging from underneath the arms of a half-hearted rosemary bush. The animal could be a coon or a coyote. "Luna, don't—"

She pulled it out by a hind leg and hugged the messy animal to her chest. "He's beautiful."

Rudy hurried to the other sidewalk and saw a small mutt boasting a beard full of dirt and dried condiments. It wore no collar, and the beast had skinny legs and a malnourished body, but his grin stretched a mile wide.

"Careful. He's a stray." Most likely flea infested, too. "Just set him down."

"Daddy, he needs me."

"He doesn't need you. He needs a bath."

"I can give him a bath. With bubbles."

And this is why they'd never replaced the cat. "Please, just set the dog down. He belongs to someone."

The dog lathered her cheek with his tongue. "No, he doesn't. I can tell."

He could sense someone approach along the sidewalk, and he wanted to gather his daughter before the dog reacted badly. "He's not ours. Just let him go."

"Please, Daddy. I love him."

Though it pained him to think through the logistics, he would have to separate his daughter from the stray, and the resulting tears would invite public speculation.

"Rudy? Luna?"

His head snapped around and his heart caved into his lungs. "Lacy?"

Her face drained of color. "What are you doing here?"

"Cinderella!" Luna's grip on the dog loosened, and it struggled out of the embrace.

Staring at her wasn't his best move, but Rudy seemed incapable of inventing a logical reason for meeting in her hometown. Her hair flowed long and loose around her shoulders, her body glowed with the aura of late-afternoon sunshine, and as she walked closer, her steps were those of a queen—Comfort was her town, and she knew how to bend it to her will. Maybe he imagined the last part, but the navy blazer and pale pink jeans screamed modern power suit.

"I love your shoes." Luna crawled across the grass tufts to admire the leopard-print mules. "Did you see my new dog?"

"You mean Rudy?"

"Not my dad, my dog."

Lacy's smile brightened her already mesmerizing eyes. "Actually, I've nicknamed that rascal Rudy, but don't ask why because I'm not telling. He's a stray and a nuisance and digs in everyone's yards. I'm pretty sure he was in a trash can about an hour ago."

"Ewww!" Luna jumped to her feet and gave the dog a scolding glare. "He kissed me."

Lacy's gaze travelled between Luna and the dog, bypassing Rudy altogether. "Well, then that's the best sense he's shown in days."

Rudy's head spun loops of the last few seconds, but Luna and Lacy seemed in sync. Watching Lacy bend to chat at eye level with Luna brought a sense of urgency to say something brilliant. His history of verbal constipation had to be conquered.

"Any chance we could continue this conversation at High's Café?" He rocked back on his heels, disguising the tension pinging through his body. "We didn't have much in the way of lunch and would love your company. I owe you an apology, and French fries might open the door for me to explain what I think happened with the daisies, and why Ken Lin is your biggest fan."

Lacy's eyes rounded. "You had me at French fries, but I'm not sure I understand the connection to Ken."

Luna reached for Lacy's hand. "Kenny works for Daddy, and he's super smart, but sometimes he says dumb things."

"Luna," Rudy warned "this will be one of those adult conversations."

The mutt dropped to his haunches next to Luna's sneakers. "Then can I keep the dog? I could play with him while you talk."

Lacy bit her bottom lip, possibly to keep from smiling. "She's a master manipulator."

"Tell me about it." Stepping aside to let Luna and the dog lead the way to the restaurant, he lowered his voice. "I already dread her teen years."

"Luna, they're not going to let you bring the dog into High's Café, he's got a bad reputation. But if you want to play with him in this open space, your dad and I can sit on their patio and watch you." Lacy stepped over a knee-high railing. "See, you can sit in a chair under the tree."

Luna hurried over to the spot, but the mutt stopped at the sidewalk.

"He probably remembers the cook chasing him with a wooden spoon earlier, but if you feed him some crackers he might stick around." Lacy grinned, as if she had nothing better to do than run interference for his daughter. "I'll find you some crackers while your dad orders us the super-sized fries."

A weight rolled off his shoulders.

The woman, who had countless people following her social-media sites, rounded cracker packages from the tables for his daughter. How had this miracle happened? He had no idea. He wouldn't question the gift. Hurrying inside the restaurant, he placed an order for three grilled-cheese sandwiches, fries, soft drinks, beer, and—just because he felt happy for the first time in days—two slices of apple pie.

No one recognized him. He could blend into the early evening vibe with no pressure to serve a hundred demanding clients. When was the last Friday night he'd not been standing before a hot stove? Filling Luna's cup with a root beer, he couldn't remember. The weekend in NYC still raked coals over most of his recent memories, but he would push that far away from his mind tonight.

There was no guarantee Lacy would linger, so he'd make the most of the moment without retreading a nightmare. Collecting a hand-sanitizer package from the rack of complimentary napkins, he headed toward the patio feeling like a man who'd won the lottery.

Only, when he got to the patio, he saw a vacancy that seared a father's soul—both Lacy and his daughter had vanished.

Chapter Sixteen

Lacy bent over at her waist, gulping air into her lungs. She would wring that dog's neck if she ever saw him again.

"But he was just here," Luna cried, rounding the corner. "How can he be faster than us?"

"Because he's a wizard," Lacy stammered, standing tall and running a hand through her hair to straighten the disarray caused by chasing a dog. "We have to let him go. That dog knows every hiding place in town."

Luna folded down to her knees. "But I wanted to keep him."

"Rudy is nobody's pet. He prefers to live in the wild."

Luna stared at her with watery eyes. "But it gets cold."

"I think our bigger problem isn't finding shelter for the dog but returning you to your dad." She glanced around to see if a large man with long legs, gorgeous hair, and a scowl ran after them. "He's not going to be happy."

Luna stood, resigned to her broken heart. "Daddy's not been happy in a long time."

"Lacy?"

She whipped the other direction to see Anna Weber approaching from the corner. She held hands with her twin seven-year-old daughters, Ariel and Adrian. The girls' soccer uniforms were streaked with mud.

"Well, this looks promising," Lacy said, waving. "I hope all that dirt means you two mutilated the other team."

"Really, Lacy," Anna frowned. "Let's not encourage violence."

Adrian broke free of her mother. "I scored three times and took down their goalie. I was the MVP!"

Lacy high-fived her small friend. "I'm not at all surprised. Ariel, did you have fun too?"

Ariel arrived, but her eyes were less bright. "I slipped in the mud and skinned my knee. I never want to play again."

Lacy identified with the smaller girl. There were no childhood trophies in her memento box. "Well, at least you're trying. I hear that counts."

Anna's gaze took in the confused little dark-haired child hovering behind Lacy. "What are you doing tonight? Playing tour guide?"

Lacy sighed. "My new friend met that scamp of a dog who torments everyone in the business district. She took off chasing the dog, and here we are, both the worse for wear, and the four-legged beast is nowhere to be seen."

"Is it the little Scottie with white-and-gray fur?" Ariel's eyes grew wide. "I saw him running toward the high school."

"That's the one." Lacy reached behind her and drew Rudy's daughter forward. "This is Luna, she's visiting from Austin."

Ariel stepped closer. "I like your sneakers."

Adrian scowled. "That dog snapped at me one time. I'm never going to bring him a treat again."

"We shouldn't feed him," Anna said, with exaggerated patience. "The sheriff needs to catch the puppy. Its owners are probably unhappy he's escaped again."

The girls surrounded Luna and began questioning her about feeding the dog. Luna didn't reply but followed the conversation with fascination.

"Are you babysitting?" Anna lifted her sunglasses and propped them over her auburn hair.

"No, um—" Lacy wasn't sure how to explain this situation. "She's the daughter of, uh—"

"Luna!"

She twisted, watching Rudy race toward them.

Lacy pointed her thumb over her shoulder. "Him."

Rudy slowed when he saw that the group gathered at the corner included his child. His gaze shot questions she knew needed answering.

"It was the dog, Rudy." Lacy explained before he jumped to the wrong conclusion. "Luna saw him bolt and she took off after it. I didn't have time to tell you because I chased her and tried to divert her, and then that rascal vanished, and here we stand. Fortunately, she's forgotten the dog because we ran into my friends, the Webers."

Rudy scanned the mom and daughters with less ferocity than he'd shown her. Lacy guessed that was a parent's prerogative, but she wished he'd not jumped to the worst-case scenario. She was still within sight of the café.

"Hi, I'm Anna."

He shook her offered hand. "Rudy Delgardo and my daughter, Luna."

"We've just met," Anna replied with an easy smile. "It looks like our girls are about the same ages."

"Your daughters play soccer?" he asked.

"It's a little-league team. We're walking to the café for post-game treats since they won their game."

"I'd love for Luna to play too, but she's been reluctant." Rudy patted her shoulder, as if to remind her he had arrived. "Team sports don't appeal to her."

Anna whispered conspiratorially. "One of mine didn't want to play either, but I knew she needed rattling from her comfort zone. The other one is a natural. She'll have to be reminded there's not a product-endorsement contract offered in elementary school."

Rudy's face crinkled with delightful layers as he smiled.

Lacy contained her wonder at the difference. A cue played between her ears, reminding her she was not the one who'd made him grin.

Rudy's shoulders lost a notch of mistrust. "Well, join us. We've just ordered, and I'm sure the staff wonders where we've disappeared."

Watching Rudy and Anna evaluating each other, Lacy thought, *single parents must have a radar pinging signals from other frazzled DIYers.* Loss, betrayal, and something final flitted through Lacy's mind. She wanted to shake off the sting but couldn't. It was as if she'd seen a photograph drift from the future: Rudy and Anna, with their instant family.

Admittedly, Rudy and Anna would be perfect together. Their coloring matched, they were both intelligent, and their girls could become lifelong friends. They both needed to get unfocused from their jobs so they could see the bigger world picture. Yeah. They were a match made in co-parenting heaven, and she felt like the biggest heel for wishing they'd never met.

"Okay." Anna's smile confirmed that she'd just made the best decision of her day. "The girls already seem to be friends."

Rudy sighed. "Well, let's hurry. The food won't be as tasty if we let it get cold."

"And he would know." Lacy laughed, sounding brittle. "He's a chef."

Rudy cut his gaze to her like she'd revealed the password to his financial records.

"A chef?" Anna's eyes widened. "I'm not much of a foodie, but I appreciate how much work and creativity must be involved. So much pressure, too."

Rudy nodded as they started walking toward High's Cafe. "This is the first Friday night I've taken off in months."

Anna gasped. "I can't imagine."

"It's brutal. But it's the only life I know. Every season is a new challenge in creating a relevant menu."

Anna asked questions about his training and the restaurant, and he answered with candor. Lacy chewed the inside of her mouth. She'd never had opportunity to have a genuine conversation with the man, and the depth of his thoughts astounded her.

Envy consumed her heart.

There was really no other conclusion: Anna had become her frenemy.

While a cloud skirted the sun, they both angled for the same man. Twenty-four hours ago, she'd have sworn she never wanted to speak to Rudy again. But one smoldering glance from him and she was putty.

And also, a third wheel.

Anna and Rudy talked as if they'd become instant friends, whereas Lacy couldn't seem to get a simple sentence from him. Groaning, she aimed for logic. Rudy didn't belong to her—quite the contrary based on the flower fiasco. She needed to throw cold water on her face. Something to wake her from this reaction.

Hello? She was not thirteen, she reminded her inner child. And this was not summer camp where the skinny girls always got the guys. They were all reasonably intelligent adults. Or at least Anna and Rudy seemed certifiable. If the jury could read her thoughts, they'd send her for counseling.

Anna giggled.

Really? Thirty-year-old mothers should not giggle when asking about a man's work schedule

"He's not alone in the kitchen. You should meet his sous chef. What a hoot!" Lacy stepped between them to be the middle of the sandwich. "That Kenny, he's something else, right?"

Rudy sent her a glare. "Kenny is on probation right now."

"Then who is running the kitchen tonight?"

"Well, he is, but he's not at the top of my list of favorite people."

"If he bombs out with you, he could always go into flower-arranging." Lacy ignored the laser beams directed her way. "He's got a real talent for over-the-top designs."

Anna's head swung between them as if someone replayed Wimbledon.

"I can explain," Rudy said, gritting his molars.

"Well, all is well that ends well." Lacy stepped up to the curb of the restaurant. "The staff at the library loved the daisies."

Anna gasped. "Are you talking about *those* daisies? I saw them yesterday and couldn't believe how gorgeous they were. Drue outdid herself. That arrangement must have cost a fortune."

Adrian and Ariel held hands with Luna. "Can we order hot dogs?"

Rudy stopped at the gate, spying his food order sitting on one of the patio tables. "Start with what's already here, and then we can move on to the next course."

"French fries!" The girls dived for the table.

Anna grimaced. "We can't eat your food."

"Nonsense," Rudy insisted. "Let them tackle this. I know I need that beer now more than ever."

Lacy saw that he'd ordered two. To prove she was not a small-hearted person, she threw her arm wide and gestured to the patio. "I'll bet Anna wants the other beer. Nothing like sitting on the sidelines throughout little league, listening to all the armchair coaches to bring on a need for Shiner Bock, am I right?"

"I'd love one," Anna nodded, eyeing the glass hungrily, "but you drink that one, and I'll go inside to place our order."

No way. It was too soon to be alone with Rudy. "Let me treat the girls. I haven't seen them in ages."

"You bought ice creams last week." Anna pointed to the table. "Go, eat your sandwiches before the girls scarf them down."

Within a second, she and Rudy stood on the porch, the giggling girls huddled around the table. She should apologize for having caused him a minor heart attack when Luna had vanished, but she couldn't express the sentiment.

His scowl was mostly unreadable—except for the part where he wasn't sure he liked Lacy very much.

"Anna is great," she said, for lack of anything better. "Such a good friend, and wow, one heck of a mom. She runs a small publishing company—classical music and really old hymns and things—and keeps up with the girls, too."

Rudy stared like he was waiting on something to congeal.

She squirmed. "I'll see if Anna needs any help with the glasses," she said, avoiding another moment dodging land mines.

"Lacy, about the flowers."

Cold fusion hardened her feet. *Oh, yeah. Those.*

Rudy's gaze landed on the ceiling fan spinning overhead. "Kenny thought he was helping inspire you to get involved with Stella's social-media issues. He said we should hire you. He didn't mean to imply . . . um, I'm . . . he wasn't suggesting that I was interested in you or that— "

He. Wasn't. Interested. With those words, her ears closed off the debris ricocheting from her heart to her ears. His honesty provided the reality snap she'd needed. The disillusionment of the Amy Marsh debacle had so clouded every pocket of her brain that she'd indulged the fantasy that because this man had been nice to her—just nice, not flirty or suggestive—he must be in love with her. How stupid could she be?

Swallowing every crooked emotion choking her, she took a few steps backward. "Hey, look. That dog is back. Luna might take off again. I'll let you chase her this time."

Rudy's head turned to the yard space, and he made a beeline for his daughter.

Releasing her breath, she felt blood return to her extremities. That beast had saved her. She'd have to treat him the next time they crossed paths.

Ducking indoors, she eavesdropped on Anna bantering with the salesclerk and snuck behind the book racks, toward the bathrooms. She could ghost through the back door without having to explain why she could never again show her face to Rudy Delgardo.

Chapter Seventeen

Lacy rolled over in her bed, toward the bleating ringtone. Reaching her arm from under the comforter, she patted the nightstand, searching for the annoyance. No one should be allowed to call before seven in the morning.

As she leaned onto her elbow and flipped it open, she saw the time inched toward eight. This had better be good.

"Lacy?"

Ugh. "What."

"So, that answers my question if you're up already."

Falling against the pillow, she tucked the phone against an ear and draped the other arm over her eyes. "Why would I be up? I'm a childless adult in a house with an air conditioner I can drop to frigid temperatures. This *is* my only pleasure."

Kali chuckled. "Well, with air conditioning like that I can see why you'd sleep late."

She wasn't interested in banter. She'd popped awake last night, replaying her disastrous hour with Rudy, and no amount of middle-of-the-night insight could make up for the junior-high exit. "Get on with it."

Charlie screamed in the background. "I need your help."

Her nephew had vomited on her the last time she heard him cry like that. "I'm not available."

"I wouldn't want you to babysit. He's got a temperature. Jake has already left for the ranch, and it's going to be an hour or more before he can return. I've got appointments at the farm, and I'm really hoping you can go place nice for me at the office while I wait for Jake to take over with Charlie."

Groaning, Lacy sat up. "Cancel them."

"I can't. Two different customers have driven in from great distances. One should be there at nine, the other is scheduled for ten." Kali held her breath. "Please say you'll entertain them until I can get there."

Rubbing her eyes, Lacy put her feet on the cold floor, then snatched them back under the covers. "I can't believe you booked clients for Saturday."

"Things we do for difficult customers."

Lacy pushed hair out of her eyes. These were not her customers. "You used up your allotment of favors when I chased goats last week."

The pause lasted more than a beat. "Allotment? You mean like the amount Jake paid that crazy-expensive attorney, Christopher Woodley?"

And there was a nail in her coffin. "I'll be there by nine. But I make no promises to be charming."

"Open the front door, show them around the cheese-making room and the storage units. I have one client who wanted to see the goats. He has a child tagging along."

Her ever-so-slight resolve tanked. Children and goats should never mix. "How soon until you can get there?"

"Just hold things together—that's all I ask.

Later, with her to-go cup of coffee from Gloria's kitchen and a handful of freshly made beignets, Lacy drove along the driveway, careful to avoid potholes. She'd been so preoccupied with Gloria's comments this morning that she had almost forgotten to be angry at her sister for drawing her out of bed. But Kali's evil ways were slippery, and Lacy was easy pickings.

Gloria. Could she be more stunned about *her* morning news? Despite years of bickering, Gloria announced she'd already packed a bag and planned to stay at Frank's house for the next week. Once Lacy confirmed they weren't talking about some new "Frank" Gloria might have met on her Silver Singles app, she'd stopped asking questions. Apparently, there was room for only one Frank in Gloria's orbit. He'd grown so weak from his last chemo treatment that he couldn't help himself to the bathroom. Lacy had questioned if the drastic step of moving was necessary since there were visiting nurses for this problem. Shock of shocks, Frank refused to let some stranger in his home to see him at his worst. Gloria had gotten Frank through so many ugly years, there were no mysteries left to surprise. She'd been voluntold.

Lacy had to add a double shot of espresso to her cup to process the disbelief.

Not only was she on her own for supper for the foreseeable future, but Frank's cancer would interfere with whatever was happening with Gloria and Mr. Miami. Although, the man Lacy had stalked via his Facebook page didn't have near the tug on Gloria's heart that a sickly killjoy with newsprint-stained fingertips did.

Dang. She'd pinned a lot of hope on Mr. Miami. He had a super-hot—and single—son. Lacy had longed for a double date.

Stepping out of the Ford's seat, she studied the unfamiliar sedan in the Provence Farm lot. Blowing air from her lungs, she assumed Kali's first customer arrived early because they couldn't help themselves. Checking her watch, she was five, maybe fifteen, minutes late. Sometimes tourists stopped by begging for a peek into the manufacturing center or thinking there would be a gift shop filled with goat figurines. Though there wasn't an official shop, Kali was always quick to give away a small block of cheese as a means of thanking them for their time.

The stand-in would sadly disappoint the visitors.

Dusting her hands on the back of vintage jeans, Lacy scooped her hair into a high, messy bun and propped her sunglasses on top of the pile of hair. She'd left her house with the minimum of makeup because, well, it was her day off. She'd run through her stash of expensive samples she'd collected from modeling in Dallas and had purchased makeup from the drugstore last week. Mascara wasn't nearly as exciting when it came in a two-for-one deal. Since she was already out the door, she'd drive to Kerrville for groceries later. Maybe wander around the James Avery store. There was an ice-cream shop downtown. She'd need a reward by then.

Fragrance from the herb garden blew by on the breeze. It would be another gorgeous Saturday in the Hill Country. *Yay for me,* she thought grumpily.

Stepping over the gravel in the drive, she wondered why she felt sour. Besides the obvious missed adventure with Chef Gorgeous, she had heard good news last night. Christopher had called. He could hardly contain his surprise to tell her she'd been liberated.

Amy Marsh's family had called back the hounds.

The "insignificant" video had made America fall in love with the Texas songbird, and her fame crested with the contest win. She had a record deal in the works, TV appearances lined up for months, and a boyfriend. Amy had pleaded with her father to release Lacy from the confines of their legal agreement.

Daddy did.

That announcement called for champagne. But all she had in the minifridge was mineral water and ginger beer, neither of which felt celebratory. Instead, she'd plowed through a bag of potato chips and countless chocolate candies left over from Valentine's.

Christopher gleefully surmised, now he wasn't her legal counsel, that they should go out sometime. He had to be in Austin in a few weeks. How about the symphony?

She invented the first excuse that made sense.

She wasn't sure that he bought her apology of not being a fan of classical music, but he didn't linger on her questionable music tastes. He leapt onto a travelling art exhibit as an alternative. Giving in seemed the quickest way to exit the awkwardness, and realistically, her social calendar had holes all over it, so why not?

Climbing the steps of the porch, she gazed across the front pasture and watched the foals eating hay and young goats chasing dandelions. Hallmark didn't have moments this good.

"Lacy?"

Whipping around to face the drive leading back to the barns, she saw Luna Delgardo dragging a goat by a leash.

"Um, hello." She blinked twice. So, this was the client with a child Kali had mentioned, conveniently without naming names. "What are you doing with Mrs. Bilbo?"

Luna drug the reluctant goat toward the porch. "I'm playing."

"I see that. Did you mean to keep one?"

Luna's bright expression dimmed. "Mom won't even let me have a dog."

Lacy stepped off the porch to meet Luna halfway. "So, what were you going to do with the mutt we chased last night?"

"I was going to keep him at my dad's house."

"It sounds like you have a plan." Lacy glanced around the yard, searching for the man who'd claimed her dreams last night. "Is your dad here?"

"He's chasing a rooster that got loose."

Suddenly, the sky gleamed with high-intensity lights and a grin popped free before she remembered that Luna's father made her angry. Maybe watching him capture a known escapee would be worth the incoming dent to her pride. "Let's go watch."

Luna shook her head, and braids swished around her shoulders. "Daddy said bad words."

"Even better."

As they turned toward the corrals, she scrutinized a tall man in dark jeans running for the tree line. This wouldn't end well. Lacy knew Jake had clipped the rooster's wings because the scoundrel had a history of heading for the high branches, and once the rooster realized he was about to be caught, he carried on like a woman accused of shoplifting—not that she had a video of that high-pitched denial on any of her photo threads. None that she could ever—legally—post, anyway.

Lacy tugged Luna back toward a corral. "Let's not crowd him. That rooster has a pecking problem, and I, for one, don't want to get attacked."

"Is Daddy going to get bit?"

"Only if he thinks he can reason with the bird."

Luna glanced at Lacy with confusion.

"Let's sit. This could take a while." Luna followed Lacy toward the bench and settled on the seat to watch things unfold. The goat nibbled on Luna's sneakers.

"We missed you last night," Luna said, dragging the momma goat closer.

Not sure how to answer, Lacy paused. Taking a moment to think through her options, she glanced away and saw Rudy, holding the rooster clutched to his chest and walking toward the barns. "Oh, my word. Your dad caught him."

Luna jumped. "Yay! Daddy won."

She could see Rudy's hair standing on end and dirt streaking his cheek. The rooster had calmed, and no one seemed to be bleeding. "I think he might have."

Lacy caught Rudy's gaze.

"Don't say a word," he growled. "I don't want to have to explain if this monster ends up in a soup pot."

Lacy covered her smile with her hand.

"But where are you going to take him, Daddy?"

"Good question." He manhandled the squawking bird. "Lacy? A suggestion that doesn't involve a chopping block?"

"Last stall in the green barn. It's his roost."

Head held high, Rudy marched toward the barn like this was his normal Saturday routine. Who knows? Maybe he had farm skills she'd never imagined.

Lacy glanced at the girl. "How about we return this one to her baby, and then we can make a snack? I have a feeling we'll need to give your dad some space."

"But I don't want to give her up. I caught her and everything."

And Lacy was quite sure that explained how the rooster escaped. "Mrs. Bilbo needs to feed her baby, and she has a lot to tell her friends. Let's return her to the barn, and you can come another time."

Luna's expression caved, but she didn't argue. "Babies needs their mommas."

They walked into the green barn, and Lacy unlatched the lock on a corral filled with fresh alfalfa. Opening the gate a fraction, she urged Luna inside. "If you'll take the leash off her neck, we'll move her into the pen, and you can give her and the others their vitamins."

While Luna petted a baby goat, Lacy scooped a handful of foul-smelling treats and handed them over the gate. "They will come running when they see you have these, so just give one to each, okay?"

Luna giggled as goats swarmed her.

Feeling a warm presence behind her, Lacy fought the urge to turn. Yesterday still stood between them.

"Did your sister send you?"

For a man covered in rooster feathers, he sounded imperious. "She's running late. I'm here to cover the office until she arrives." Lacy replied.

She watched Luna while waiting on his words. Impossible though it seemed, she was intensely tuned to his breathing. He might be the most aggravating man she'd ever met, but it would take a while to forget him.

His silence stretched longer than her patience. Relieved that he wasn't demanding an explanation for her disappearance last night, she was alternately worried that Anna's charm had more than made up for any worries that Lacy had either been abducted or was the rudest woman in town.

Luna fell to her knees in the messy corral, giving in to the nudges and nibbles of baby goats.

"I'll be inside if you need anything," she said, stepping to the side. "Be sure you lock up behind Luna. Kali won't be happy if her goats get loose."

At the door, she heard his voice.

"Lacy, wait."

She turned back, seeing Luna chased around the pen by baby goats. Hard to tell if the squealing came from the seven-year-old or the soft-fur kids.

"We need to talk."

Did they? Weren't they back to the stiltedness of their first meeting? Seeing the stormy hues of his eyes after his rooster rundown, the fantasy of him as a knight returned with Technicolor. "Talking doesn't go well between us."

"We've had our share of miscommunications, I know, and I made a mess of things last night. But I need your help, and that's what the daisies were about."

Daisies. How could she forget the pyramid of flowers that sent her imagination straight to the corner of happy and baffled? "You ordered them, or Kenny?"

"Kenny did, and he knew they were your favorite because he's one of your followers on Instagram."

Hearing that a sous chef in Austin followed her account provided its own weird blip, but to know he stalked her posts enough to recognize her flower preferences made her rethink the level to which she might have overshared her personal life. "Okay, that mystery is solved. But I have no idea how I can help you. You're the one with the uber-successful career."

His lips pinched. "That's a tough subject right now, as I'm being trashed by a food critic with a national platform, which is why Kenny thought you would make a good sounding board."

The hackles on her nerves stood and took note of how her disaster was now a resource for others with reputations tangled by media. "I don't know what I can tell you since I went dark after my fallout."

"Kenny thinks absence was a stroke of brilliance. He says your Facebook group has grown with folks wondering about how fabulous you're going to be when you return."

She laughed. "People think that was a master-planned strategy?"

He ran his hand through his hair, straightening the unruliness. "I don't have a Facebook account, but my wife did, and she was a fanatic. Kenny is too, and he's often telling me what's going on in the world based on what he's seen online."

She'd avoided reading hashtags or checking her groups for fear that she'd not be able to resist restrictions. But, if Christopher said she was free of future legal action, surely that meant she could resume her old life—minus any Marsh-related posts.

Gloria had told her the fast from social media was doing good, that her brain was reconnecting with the natural world instead of technology. Today, those virtues collided.

Rudy needed her help.

Intriguing. And dangerous.

In the dark hours before dawn, she'd admitted she had some bizarre crush. He'd not done anything to encourage it, but the infatuation grew organically from the fertile seeds in Lacy's imagination. She'd promised herself to take up some challenging new hobby to distance herself from the obsession. Pickleball seemed an option.

A few hours later, here he was, circling back to those daisies.

She glanced down at the leather thong sandals, frayed jeans, and a T-shirt that had been washed so many times the blue had faded to white. She was 180 degrees different from the girl who knew how to stoke a photo and a tagline for maximum impact.

"Daddy! Look!" Luna shrieked. "They're trying to catch me!"

Both adults turned to see delight fan from every tiny footprint racing through the sawdust.

"That's what is real," Lacy said, in a moment of insight. "That's what is important. The folks who follow you on social media would prefer to see genuine content than something manufactured."

"Luna is in heaven. I wish she could live like this every day." Rudy reached for his cell phone and started a video. "But that doesn't change the fact that I have an enemy, and he's using Twitter to vent."

An algorithm for a scheduled sabotage would not be hard to create on Twitter. "Don't you have a media consultant or an advertising firm that could handle this for you?"

"They don't seem to appreciate how personal the vendetta is, and I'm clueless to know how to combat this guy outside of a kitchen."

"What makes you think it's a man?"

"He dined in Stella's recently, and he's on the board of the James Beard Foundation. I know it's Alan Gale."

Luna crawled over the pen railing, exhausted from her race from death by nibbling.

There were a million knots to unravel before she felt strong enough to tangle with hordes of foodies that followed Stella's on Twitter. "I don't know if I should get involved—"

"Lacy?"

They both turned to see Kali standing under the arc of the barn door, outlined by sunshine.

"Hello, I'm sorry we got here a little earlier than I'd predicted." Rudy shoved his phone into his pocket. "I apologize if we've created havoc with your goats."

Kali stepped closer, her gaze reading Lacy's face for clues. "The babies love the attention, but I hope your daughter has a change of clothes. She's going to have goat poop all over her pants."

Luna giggled. "Goat poopies."

"You must be Luna," Kali said, as she leaned against the pen. "Your daddy told me you love animals and wanted to see the farm. I hope you're okay with doing a little work, too. It's time to feed the big goats."

Lacy knew there were goatherders on the payroll to manage the maintenance of animals, but her sister would play up her Farmer Kali role today. The break gave Lacy time to figure out what she was going to do about Rudy. Based on the shared eye contact, he might be a little affected by their morning too.

She didn't trust her gut anymore. What if he was really sending telepathic messages that she was a nutcase? Anna might have told him of their escapades crashing wedding receptions, which would confirm his impression. A wise woman would back away. The man had a full plate and a daughter that needed his undivided attention. As a child who'd fallen between the cracks, she recognized the scars on Luna.

Lacy held her palm toward Kali. "Do you want me to use your phone to take pictures of you and your helper with the goats? That would make darling content for your followers." And before Rudy could object, she added. "And I'd keep her face off camera to protect her privacy."

Luna must have grown up with a camera in her face because she assumed a pose and a smile.

"See, my little sister is the guru of all things Instagram," Kali said, while reaching into her back pocket to retrieve her phone. "And if I have any credibility on my page, it's because she's given me a presence in the last few months. Imagine what she could do for us with the food-and-wine festival."

Rudy's expression bordered on unreadable, but he followed them outside to the big pen. Lacy stepped to the other side of the dirt path, aiming the camera lens for the best angle. Rudy held back, leaning against a mud-stained golf cart, and folded his arms over his chest while he watched his daughter climb the railing. Stress evaporated from around his eyes.

Lacy snapped his image before he noticed.

She'd email it to her computer, then delete it from Kali's photos before her sister figured out. Not that Kali didn't suspect. There was a ridiculous setup for this meeting—was Charlie even sick?

But keeping things from her sister was a guilty pleasure. Kind of like the chocolate she hid in a ginger jar, but with fewer calories. She'd hold her cards closer to her chest now that Kali was trying to manipulate things. Snapping photos of Kali and Luna, she set up several shots that caught the morning light dappling across their dark hair. Because she felt a pull, she turned her gaze toward Rudy and saw him studying her with unrepentant interest.

Swallowing, she glanced at the phone to see which photos were the best and reminded herself that he was a single dad. Nowhere on her list of potential men to date did she have a category for men with children. Maybe because she was so insecure around little ones? Or maybe because she was so high maintenance, she knew she could never be happy with a fraction of a man's attention.

Cutting her gaze, she saw his attention fixed on Luna. She patted herself on the back for dodging potential dings to her heart. Rudy was a committed dad; after his restaurant and his ex-wife, he'd not have energy left for a girl with a complicated history, particularly since drama followed her like bad perfume.

Now that Kali was around, she could ease away from the situation and head to the grocery store. She forced her mind to picture the list of veggies and fruits instead of how the sunlight bathed Rudy's hair in raisin tones.

Handing the phone to her sister, she said, "I uploaded a cute picture and a tagline. If you like it, you can hit the send button."

"Oh, it's darling. Thanks." Showing the picture to Luna, Kali added, "Can you stay for a few extra minutes? I think my ten o'clock arrived early, and I don't like to give two tours at once."

Lacy read the gleam in her sister's eye and didn't know if she should shut the matchmaking down now or grab the extra minutes as an opportunity to apologize for last night. Either way, she felt stuck. She had a flimsy alibi for leaving, and her heart was greedy for one more chance.

Luna looked at her with wary eyes.

The kid didn't have confidence in Lacy's sticking powers. Thankfully, she was too young to read all the online articles detailing everyone's opinions about why Lacy ran instead of seeing something through. But then, how many of those folks had to walk across a bright stage wearing nothing more than a bikini and high heels?

That form of torture had a way of changing the way a girl saw the world.

And this particular girl didn't need any more headaches.

Chapter Eighteen

"Is your grilled-cheese sandwich supposed to be on fire?"

Rudy handed Lacy a spatula, saying, "Butter burns fast. It's hardly a fire."

"There's smoke." Lacy flipped the egg-coated bread sitting in foamy butter. "And when I'm cooking, that's considered a bad thing."

He leaned over her shoulder, deliberately close enough to notice her eyelashes, the flawless skin over her cheekbones, and the bow shape of her upper lip. His gut tightened. "That's usually when things get interesting," he said, unable to control the tremor in his voice.

"That's because you're a chef, and your mistakes get labeled as brilliant new developments." She plated the Monte Cristo sandwich. "Whereas, when I cook, things rarely turn out the way I had thought they would. Like how a snack for your daughter has turned into second breakfast."

"Hey, it was your sister who upped the game by providing fresh eggs and the cheese." He tore a bit of the parsley found growing outside Kali's back door and tossed it over the crispy, battered bread. "But I'd like to hear more about your cooking and your thoughts about food."

Stepping to the side of the stove in Kali's test kitchen at Provence Farm, Lacy wiped her hands on the dish towel and opened a bag of chips. "I can't imagine why you'd want to hear my thoughts. I'm not sophisticated. I eat a lot of junk food, and I'm sure my preferences are elementary."

It was this idea he wanted to combat with guests at Stella's. Everyone thought they had to develop a high-priced palate, but his goals were more basic. He wanted to make sure ordinary people were happy spending their hard-earned cash on a dish of his food.

When Lacy had volunteered to come indoors and make them a bite to eat, it had thrilled him. Most people refused to cook around him, assuming he'd grade their skills. If that thought had crossed her mind, she'd kicked it to the curb.

Torn between sitting in the sunshine and seeing what she would create, he gave in to a need to hover over her shoulder while she whipped out something that didn't come with a pedigree. Her recipe involved white bread, ham slices of adequate quality, and thick mayonnaise that listed sugar as a primary ingredient. He'd never tell Kenny that his blonde goddess ate like a 1950s housewife.

Kali and Luna entered with a basket of eggs they'd collected from the coop. Kali offered mozzarella she'd been perfecting, and within moments, they'd flipped a basic sandwich into a dressier dish. Lacy insisted she wanted to learn every step.

Watching the way her hands generously filled the plates with the chips, he liked that she ate the chips spilled to the counter. She also seemed unconcerned that her hair had slipped off-center. *Perfectly imperfect.*

"Will you serve this with a beverage?" he asked, looking around for a kettle to boil water for tea.

Lacy leaned into the refrigerator and hooked three bottles of Dr Pepper in her grip. "We have our poison. If you want something else, make it."

Kali took a plate and set it at the small table. "I'll drink water. I'm still dehydrated from that head cold."

"Daddy, can I have Dr Pepper?"

He should say no since she was about to consume hundreds of calories of fat, salt, and sugar, but watching Lacy pop the top off, producing the resulting hiss that fired up his taste buds, he couldn't resist. "We both will. Who was it that told us Dr Pepper makes everything better?"

"That old man at the zoo!" Luna grinned. "Daddy and I love the zoo."

Kali settled Luna in a chair. "Are you staying the whole weekend?"

"I have to drive her back to Abilene tomorrow, so we're cramming as much country life into our day as possible."

He knew Lacy was paying attention to the conversation, though she seemed to struggle with the last bottle cap. When she'd disappeared last night, he'd been both alarmed and oddly turned on by her petulance. He'd never known a woman who'd made a silent exit the most mesmerizing feature of a night. Anna Weber was intelligent and a devoted mother, but he'd felt about as motivated to keep the conversation going as he felt when the city food inspectors popped in on his kitchen. The minute he realized Lacy wasn't coming back, the sun had dropped from the sky.

He'd not expected to see her this morning, but when she walked through the yard, everything in his world made sense again—even that one-eyed rooster.

Kali set a stack of plaid napkins on the table. "Luna is a natural with animals."

Thrilled she'd enjoyed herself, he also beat himself up that it had taken this long before he recognized she was better suited to a barnyard than a ballet studio.

Lacy sat next to Kali, and that meant he could sit across and watch the sisters. There were similarities in their bone structure, but whereas Kali was dark haired and brown eyed, Lacy was golden light—and those unforgettable eyes. Lacy bit into her sandwich and groaned in delight, snatching a string of dripping cheese and wrapping it around her finger. She was a greedy eater. Blood rushed over his nerves. "I take it you approve of my hijacking your recipe?"

Her tongue darted out to lick melted cheese from her lip. "This egg batter is a dream."

No prize meant more to him. "And you said I used too much butter."

"I'll never question your butter usage again."

He enjoyed thinking they'd cook together again. Maybe tonight. He glanced at his plate, realizing he was starving. The awkward evening and Luna's before-sunrise awakening were forgotten.

The conversation easily bounced around goat care and cheese making before he realized that Lacy hadn't said a word. She seemed to enjoy the banter, but preferred being a spectator instead of commenting on the shelf life of Brie.

He needed her to speak. Her voice, warm and silky as if it had been braised in a slow oven, was one of her sexiest qualities. "I'd like to know how this idea for a food-and-wine festival is sketched from your point of view." He stole a chip from Luna's plate. "You seem to be the one with the marketing background."

Lacy's hands flew into a surrender. "Not me. AJ and Kali have a much better grasp on what guests would want to see and do at Lavender Hill. My skill set is in copying whatever people have posted to Pinterest or their Instagram stories about festivals."

He doubted she copied anyone. "But you have a master plan, right?"

"Define master plan."

He glanced at Kali. "You've written out your agenda, who you'd like to feature at various stations, and what you will offer that differs from what they do in Austin?"

Kali sent her gaze to her sister. "Have we done that?"

Lacy shrugged. "I wasn't sure we even had Chef Delgardo secured until you mentioned it earlier."

Luna grew still. "You're going to work for my daddy?"

Lacy laughed. "He will work for us."

Rudy leaned back and draped his arm around Luna's shoulders. "Would you like to draw pictures of the goats? I brought your paper and pencils in my backpack."

She nodded, picked up her plate and moved it to the sink. Before Rudy could finish the last of her sandwich, she was through the back door, the screen slamming in her wake.

"She's a darling girl, Chef."

"Thank you, and please call me Rudy. I only stand on ceremony when I'm in the kitchen with the staff."

Kali nodded in deference. "It must be hard to raise a child around a restaurant. I can barely balance my baby, and I have a nanny who works on-site."

Rudy grimaced, remembering all the babysitters since the divorce. "It's a challenge. I don't have Luna with me as often as I'd like, and when she's in town I try to spend as much time with her as I can. But Stella's is a demanding place, and I have to supervise the kitchen, even if that means a late night."

Kali refilled her water glass. "Do you have a nanny?"

He wished he had a wife to share this life, but that dream was way down the list of options that might make his days more pleasant. "Potentially. Kenny Lin's mother is driving him crazy since she retired. She's going to meet with me next week and see if she thinks I'm worthy of her time."

Lacy chuckled. "That sounds like a backward interview."

"You've not met Mrs. Lin." Rudy wasn't sure Luna was ready for a grandmother who would starch the bed linens. "I'm desperate for someone who will put my ex-wife's mind at rest. Hannah won't let Luna come to Austin unless I have a qualified sitter, and Mrs. Lin is my best shot at getting Luna for the summer."

Kali nodded as if she understood. "I'd have been lost without Lacy these last few months. My nanny has children of her own, so when her kids are sick or need to go to after-school events, I have to call in the backup."

Lacy waved. "That would be me. I'm the understudy. The runner-up."

"You have a day job." Kali swiped at her sister's shoulder. "Otherwise, you'd be my first choice."

"As if I have any qualifications. I was the runt of the family. The one least likely to be remembered for after-school pickup or rehearsals."

"That only happened once," Kali insisted.

"Four times, but who's counting?"

Rudy enjoyed this glimpse into their family. Growing up in a noisy household, he understood inheriting his brother's clothing or missing a meal if he was late to the table. He had the unfortunate quality of being fascinated by the kitchen at an early age and delighted in cooking with his grandmother, which made him an easy target to be dubbed "the sissy."

Kali raised a finger in the air. "Pardon me for prying, but why does your ex-wife get to call the shots on what you do when you have custody of Luna?"

Rudy hadn't thought about the custody arrangement since he had sat in his attorney's office. "I really don't have a good answer for that."

"Kali is a former lawyer, and even though she breathes cheese fumes, she can't seem to get away from sticking her nose into everyone else's problems." Lacy smiled indulgently. "I'm exhibit A, if you need to feel less violated by her curiosity."

"He doesn't have to answer," Kali justified, "but as a mother who would fiercely protect her child, I understand the dilemma of wanting to micro-manage childcare. I also know the law, even under amicable divorces."

His divorce wasn't friendly. Hannah had wanted out, said she'd felt second place to Stella's. She filed the papers, she moved to Abilene, and he had to pay the attorney's fees. Once the collateral damage settled, it had left him nearly bankrupt.

"But because we really don't know Rudy as a friend, let's not ask him to reveal his deep, dark secrets, okay? I think we should talk about the festival and get some details ironed out." Lacy glanced to him, then let her gaze hover somewhere near the messy stove. "It would help to know what your experience and expectations are before we go crazy with our plans."

Relieved he'd dodged having to discuss his private life with an attorney, he recognized he owed the pass to Lacy. He imagined most people would have thought she'd be too self-absorbed to run interference. Intimidated when Kenny told him she was a former Miss Texas, he soon found out she was as down to earth as anyone he'd met. Nice to his kid, kind to his staff, and able to laugh at herself, he immediately shifted her to his mental column of surprising females—a distinction she held exclusively.

While rearranging the salt and pepper shakers, he said, "I have zero experience with food festivals, and my only expectation is to get out of this event with some heightened media attention and influence for Stella's."

Lacy leaned her elbows on the table. "You don't have any experience?"

Kali sighed. "Lacy, don't get fired up."

"But we need someone with credibility. That's why we went after him. We thought he was a more-affordable version of Don Hurt."

And now he knew where he ranked. "Thanks. I think."

"I'm sorry, she sometimes speaks before she thinks," Kali explained. "We wanted you because we like the way you cook. And we felt like you might indulge us because you'd been so kind to work AJ's wedding reception."

Rosy hues circled Lacy's throat, rising to color her cheeks. He'd need to remember she bloomed when she was angry. "You're starting out, creating something new," he said, hoping to regain his integrity. "I think it's safe to say you could take a risk on me, someone willing to come alongside.

Neither of us really know what we're doing, but it's food and wine and people coming together in a beautiful setting to see a brand-new venue. Can we really screw this up?"

Kali pushed back from the table. "I need to walk. Having been in bed for the last two days, my brain is mush. I'll look for Luna. You two figure out what we need to do first and then email me and AJ with the details."

Lacy jumped as if electrocuted. "You can't dump this on me and Rudy. We're not the ones who wanted to pull this off."

"I'm not *dumping* anything other than some initial logistical planning. AJ and I will still write the checks, make the phone calls, and advertise. But she's with Luke at a jazz concert. I'm still on the mend. So please, y'all just tell us what you think needs to happen next. We'll go from there."

Rudy heard the screen door announce Kali's exit. Oddly, he wasn't as sore about this development as Lacy. The idea they'd have a quiet conversation around a table leapt straight from his dreams.

"The Hill Country is beautiful," he said, stacking plates. "It looks like Napa Valley used to look before the wine industry flipped that place on its head."

Lacy stood, moved to the counter, and opened and shut drawers, looking for something.

He needed to say words, anything, that would keep her in the kitchen. "I think the festival might be a peek back in time. The unjaded, natural approach folks in Austin would drive out here to find."

Lacy found a notepad. "What did you just say?"

"Peek back in time?"

"No, the unjaded part," she said, with a thoughtful pause. "That's a great angle, kind of like the old ranch concerts AJ's dad used to host for his music roundups."

"I remember those." Rudy realized she wouldn't sit again. He stood and lifted plates toward the sink. "That's how I got my start catering in Texas."

Her gaze bore into him, and his blood zinged.

"Another great story," she said as she scribbled. "One that we could use in preparing our vendor packets—particularly, if I could video you cooking in a free-range format that might inspire foodies to rediscover a chuck-wagon menu."

"I'm not cooking biscuits."

She grinned, and his knees went weak. Lacy's megawatt smile could light a stadium.

"Austin does a BBQ throw down. What if we hosted a living-off-the-land food festival—fish, venison, vegetables, and even buffalo?" Pacing the kitchen, one hand whipped the air as if trying to catch the thoughts. "And we could offer wine pairings along the way. We don't have to bring in a huge number of winemakers, just those willing to offer vintages paired with the various food stations. Folks buy a ticket to enter and eat a progressive dinner along the way."

He wasn't proud of this, but if she kept staring at him with that gleam in her eye, he'd agree to anything. Being in the same space when she was dreaming out loud was like putting Wolfgang Puck and Thomas Keller in a cook-off—there were no losers.

"This format keeps our overhead down, our expectations more directed, and we plan our stations based on what the chefs want to prepare. We don't have to guess a menu because it's all locally sourced."

She thought like a general manager. Jay should hire her for Stella's. Then he could look at her all day long and find a million ways to be near her. "I don't see any major flaws," he said, when it was apparent she was waiting on him to answer. "But let's brainstorm a little more."

"Kali had some venison in this fridge that a game hunter provided. She planned to cook with it, to test a cheese pairing, but didn't know how to cook it."

He followed her to the refrigerator, leaning close enough to smell sunshine in her hair. "If that's fresh meat, open it. If it's been there a while, you'll really need to incinerate it."

She pulled out a packet of butcher paper and checked the date. "He brought it by the other night when he dropped Jake off."

Rudy took the package and opened the tape. "Deer filet medallions. Interesting."

"Interesting how?"

"In the sense that I haven't eaten something like this in a long time." Rudy's imagination fired. "Where does Kali keep her seasonings?"

"Whatever she has would be in the cupboard by the stove. She uses this small space to test products and serve samples to salesmen."

Rudy glanced around the space remodeled with leftover appliances and cupboards. It reminded him of the space where his grandmother cooked. "Are you in a rush?"

"What do you have in mind?"

He found a sauté pan, oil, salt, and pepper. "Back by Kali's screen door was an herb garden. Will you pinch some basil, parsley, and chives?"

She seemed hesitant. "Okay, but what are you doing?"

"We're going to cook."

"We are?"

"I think best when I'm cooking, and your idea of a hunter-and-angler menu is intriguing. Let's see if it can be done."

"Now?"

"Why not?"

Her eyes swept the room. "I can't think of anything else I have to do, so sure."

How she had a free Saturday was not a gift he was going to question. "And shallots, if your sister grows them."

"She does!" Lacy snapped her fingers. "They go into one of her cheese spreads."

While Lacy disappeared, Rudy washed his hands and tried to suppress the euphoria. Creating while cooking and having a beautiful woman to impress were two challenges he welcomed. Gathering ingredients, he tossed the medallions into Worcestershire sauce to marinate while he thought through his approach.

He opened the window, allowing an air current to remove the smoke if his methods turned messy, but also because he enjoyed hearing the farm noises and conversation connecting him to those outside.

After several minutes, he'd gathered what he needed, and the meat had come to room temperature. Lacy reappeared with a basket of herbs, a jar of buttermilk and cream, and two loaves of French bread. "I wasn't sure what you might need, so I grabbed things I thought were handy."

"Bread?"

"In case we need something to go with the cooked meat. She has a wonderful dipping oil, and I snagged a bottle of wine from her office. Salesmen bring her a plentiful supply of products."

"Will you dice the shallots and herbs for me?"

"My hacking wouldn't win any prizes. How about you cook? I'll video."

She made more notes on her paper, but he didn't want her on the other side of the room. "Bring that wood square over. We're not looking for perfection, just something roughly chopped."

He pulled the block closer so she'd brush against him while she worked. Glancing at the vented hood and the cupboards, he thanked God for small kitchens. "How old are these bouillon cubes? Late 1990s?"

Chuckling, she cut her gaze to the jar. "Can't be that old. Kali bought the place about five years ago."

"You never know." Unwrapping the foil, he dropped the cube into a sizzling pan of melting butter. The space exploded with beefy aroma. "Do you eat much venison?"

Lacy shrugged as she peeled the skin off a shallot. "Not really. There have never been many hunters or fishermen in my world."

He poured cream into the pan. "Pass the mustard."

She did and added, "My parents died when Kali and I were young, I was in kindergarten. Our aunt raised us after that. The only man who ventured into our world was a widower who married my aunt when I was about twelve. He brought his two daughters into the mix, and there was too much estrogen in our house for him to compete."

"But surely you've dated some rugged Texas cowboys?" He held his palm open toward her. "Pass the shallots. Isn't this smelling rich?"

She nodded. "No cowboys. No fishermen. No one for the longest time because I was on the pageant circuit until I finished college, and then I rode off into the sunset with some friends who had started a band, and that got a little nuts, but I assure you, none of them were into eating deer meat. We lived off Whataburger and whatever two-for-one deals we could find in the towns we played."

Adding the medallions to a separate pan of melted butter, he angled the handle to avoid splatter. Recollections of cooking on the fly when he was in culinary school and the days he spent inventing recipes when investors first talked to him about opening a restaurant came flying back to him. A few years rolled off his shoulders as the muscle memory responded.

"What about you?" She handed him minced garlic and chopped basil. "Do you hunt?"

"I barely make it out of the kitchen to find the dry cleaners. I don't have time to walk in the woods, even less to sit in a stand and wait on a deer to stroll by."

"Can I use your phone to snap photos?"

He reached into his back pocket. "Sure, but don't you have a cell phone?"

"Remember, I've gone old school. My phone has no functions besides calling and texting." She opened the camera feature and set his iPhone filters. "Mind if I snap you making whatever it is you're creating?"

"It's a version of steak Diane, but I make no promises it will turn out like the old standby." He glanced at the salt and pepper shakers. "I wish I had cumin, but we'll get by."

"Stand closer to the pan, I want to focus on your hands adding the garlic."

Obeying, he sprinkled garlic into the sauté pan with the onions and aromatics, then used the same fork to check the meat. "And what are you going to do with these photos?"

"I'm not sure yet, but I think people who might be inclined to come to a food festival would love to see a starred chef cooking wonderful foods in a kitchen that looks like what they have at home. Or—" she glanced at the corners stuffed with thin cupboards and a salvaged sink, stove, and refrigerator, "even less than what most Texas households have at home."

"You overestimate people's interest in cooking."

"Clearly, you haven't binged on the Food Network."

Hannah had watched those shows. She used to say he needed to be more approachable to restaurant guests, like the chefs on TV. He'd refused. Chatting with guests meant less time overseeing preparations.

Observing her zip around, aiming the camera, he'd never realized how satisfying it was to watch someone do something for which they had a skill. Wouldn't Kenny like realizing his favorite influencer produced segments behind the camera, too?

Tasting the sauce, he added a pinch more salt. The medallions needed a few more minutes of cooking time, but the aroma confirmed that they'd absorbed enough of the Worcestershire to mask any gamey fragrance.

"I couldn't wait a minute longer," Kali said, entering the kitchen with Luna in tow. "I could smell meat sizzling, and I had to know what you were creating."

Lacy set his phone on the counter, far away from the splatter. "We're experimenting to see if a hunter-and-angler menu might be the distinction for our event at Lavender Hill."

"Like surf-and-turf for the Hill Country set?" Kali came closer to peer around Rudy's shoulder. "Oh, wow."

"Kind of just like that," Lacy said. "Do you have any cheese we could pair with the venison and French bread?"

"Do I have cheese, she asks." Kali spun around and headed out of the test kitchen. "I'll grab the pickles we preserved a few weeks ago and some simple goat cheese. I don't want to compete with that sauce."

Luna sat on a chair and dropped her sketches on the tabletop. She organized the condiments by size. "I found another momma goat, and Miss Kali said I could name the baby."

Lacy glanced to where Luna squared the napkins. "What are you going to name it?"

"MacDonald."

"MacDonald?"

"You know," Luna sang, "Old MacDonald had a farm, Ee-Ii-Ee-Ii-Ooh."

Lacy cut her gaze to Rudy.

He smiled at the shared misgivings. "Don't ask her to explain. I'm surprised she doesn't name the thing after a Disney prince."

"It's a goat, not a thing, Daddy."

He removed the medallions and let them rest on a plate before turning the heat off underneath the sauce.

Kali returned with a jar of homemade pickles and a plastic carton. "Let's see how these things pair together."

Rudy glanced at the jar of dills. "I'm sure it will be perfect."

"Is that the venison Jake's horse breeder gave us?" Kali asked Lacy, as Rudy poured the sauce over the meat and sprinkled it with a scissor of parsley.

"I'm sure what we're about to eat is nothing like what the breeder had in mind, but yes, it is the same. Jake will wish he'd been here for this moment."

"Jake is up to his eyeballs in clinging baby boy. His last text said that Charlie only wants to sleep on his chest."

"Aww," Lacy smiled. "And that's a problem, how?"

"Well, Jake was going to gather the tax paperwork for the accountant, and that's not going to happen from a recliner."

Lacy wrapped an arm around her sister. "I know how you must hate missing out."

"Are you kidding? Wait until I tell the production staff that Rudy Delgardo made culinary magic with their products. Do you think I want to miss a bite of this creation?"

Lacy winked. "Charlie has been trumped for the first time in his brief, beautiful life."

As they prepared a sample plate and served the food in a style reminiscent of family dinners, Rudy felt an electric current he'd grieved as forever lost. The helter-skelter world of Stella's during service hours had stolen this experience, and with no one at home to indulge his experiments, he'd forgotten how satisfying it was to watch someone consume his dishes, even if it was a cobbled recipe.

"I've died and gone to heaven," Kali whimpered.

Lacy scooped an extra spoonful of sauce into her mouth, as if she might starve without the rich, creamy mix. She hurried to the notepad and scribbled a list of ideas onto the page.

He bit into the meat, thinking it wasn't half bad.

Luna's curiosity brought her to the stove. She found a spoon and gave it to him with an unspoken command to give her a sample too. Luna's palate might be underage, but she'd tasted some fine cooking in her life. He hoped she'd cook alongside him one day and bring him full circle with the memories of cooking with his grandmother.

Ripping the page from the pad, Lacy held up her trophy. "The Hunter Gatherer Food Festival at Lavender Hill!"

Kali wrapped her arms around her sister and squeezed her tight. "Brilliant! It's perfect."

Lacy looked over her sister's head, finding his gaze, and grinned. "What do you think, Chef? Can we do it?"

There were a million things they'd not considered, liabilities to vet, products curated, but he wouldn't put a dent in their enthusiasm. Not when the vibrant world of Lacy Cavanaugh colored his with hues of light and life. He'd do anything to make sure she smiled at him, like that, again.

Chapter Nineteen

Lacy sat at Frank's desk, staring into the computer layout for the next edition of the *Comfort News*. It was impossible to figure out word counts and font sizes while her mind replayed the most flawless Saturday of her recent life. Though she needed to edit for punctuation, her imagination returned to the Provence Farm test kitchen.

Had she not known how the day would end, she'd have said seeing the ultra-confident chef covered in rooster feathers ranked as the number-one memory. A messy Rudy, with hair blown out of order, was an image she'd savor. The aroma of onions, garlic, and butter tugged her memory back to the kitchen. But cooking together? That experience outdid every slow dance and moonlit walk she'd taken with any other guy. Standing close to him gave her a flush, and, well, she'd never think about food preparation the same way.

Their long walk around Comfort later in the afternoon involved a lot of brushing shoulders and hushed conversations. She'd forced her hand not to reach for his as they wandered the back streets. But Luna's skipping ahead kept the tension simmering and safe. Parental responsibility must have been at the forefront of his mind.

She twirled a long piece of hair around her finger. Had she ever met a man so hard to read? So unpredictable? So utterly fascinating?

The rub, though, was they'd pulled out of town last night with no promises to return. Double-checking her phone, she didn't see a missed call either.

Clicking over to the flat plan of the newspaper, she inspected the layout of each page instead of the gritty work of proofing. Focusing today was more difficult than usual. When the phone rang, she reached over the plate of sandwich crumbs and answered Frank's 1980s-era desktop unit—the one with more buttons for associate lines than a two-desk shop required.

"*Comfort News,* where all the news you need is right at your fingertips."

"That sounds even cornier now than the day you pitched it." Frank's voice resembled tumbling rocks. "Give it up, Cavanaugh."

She'd missed this geezer. "I can get away with whatever I want because you're not here to answer the phone in person."

"Don't tempt me. Gloria has hidden the keys to my truck, but I'm not above hitching. That's how I got to Marfa back in the seventies."

"And do you think *I* want to answer to Gloria for you going AWOL? She's terrifying when she's angry."

"Don't get me started." Frank coughed, and it sounded like he hacked up a lung. "Now, tell me the headlines for the next edition."

"I sent you a screenshot."

"I've pushed some button on the computer and resized everything to midget status. So I called instead."

Lacy leaned back in his executive chair and studied the keyboard. Frank was nimble with computers. He must be struggling with what Gloria referred to as his "chemo brain" if he couldn't fix a sizing issue. "Okay, let's talk through the layout."

While scanning the pages for Frank's approval, she cleaned spacing issues and several misspellings. As editor for the last several editions, she'd learned to format, felt comfortable inputting the columns from area writers, and knew her reports of local events were concise—or at least nothing he would disapprove. As long as a pandemic or national crisis stayed away from Texas, she could keep this up for a while.

"You know, Frank, you owe me a raise." She'd sent him two emails detailing how her additional work warranted a competitive salary. He'd cut her checks, but she knew it did not represent her worth. "I've more than proved myself to you in the last six months. Did you ever think you'd turn the entire production over to me when we first met?"

"Gad, no. I wasn't sure you'd last a week."

There was a compliment in those words, she was sure of it.

He coughed again and sighed from the effort. "I guess," he said, "if I'm being honest, you're as capable as anyone to keep the paper going."

She glanced around the room and wondered if continuing as the editor was something she could visualize. Could she sit at this desk, week after week, proofreading obituaries and writing reviews of the high-school-choir competition? Even after a total overhaul of décor, there was still the matter of living here. Charming though it had been for her penance, she needed the stimulation of a city.

"Christopher Woodley called a few days ago," she said. Frank knew the family well and had hinted that if Woodley got his act together, he should marry Lacy. She'd endured that advice, hiding her scorn. Christopher was an acquired taste. Besides, Frank had no business matchmaking when his personal life echoed for miles. "He said I had met my obligations to the Marsh family, and I was no longer *frozen in limbo*—his words, not mine." She waited on a reaction. When none came, she continued. "I assume I have served my internship in Comfort."

Frank's silence stretched so long, Lacy wondered if he'd fallen asleep. It had happened before, twice since he'd begun chemotherapy. While he may or may not be unconscious, she swallowed her trepidation, and spoke the idea brewing in her heart for weeks. "I know it may be a while before you can return to the desk, so I can stay until you return. But you must pay me a legitimate salary."

Just as she thought she'd have to put the receiver down and hope that Gloria would find him with his cell phone opened, he sniffed—loudly, like his emotions had gotten the better of him. Lacy stared at the receiver, unsure what to do with a man who leaked tears.

"Okay."

She washed that word through her mind, wondering if there were codicils attached to the letters. "Okay, what?"

"I've been giving this some thought. Well, more thought than I'd wanted, but you know how ruthless Gloria is when she gets an idea. I'd like you to stay on as editor, with a complete benefits package, while I put the paper up for sale."

"What?" Panic lit her nerves on fire. "You plan to sell?"

"Lacy, I'm not getting better. Doctors tell me that even if the tumors shrink with the chemo, my lungs will never recover, and it's just a matter of time."

She collapsed against the desk, resting her forehead in her palm. "I had no idea it was this bad."

"I've kept it quiet. Gloria warned me against setting off a firestorm. Doctors tell me I can't ignore it anymore. I'll bundle all the community newspapers and sell them as a set or individually. Whatever offers come forward."

She reached for a tissue. "I'll help however I can, you know that."

"Gloria will stop by with paperwork to get you enrolled on the insurance, like the other editors, and you can stay as long as you want. I'm hoping you might buy the paper. You've done a good job with it, and everyone in town likes you."

She stood and would have paced the room, but the land line acted like a leash and jerked her to the desk. *Buy the paper? Had he lost his mind?*

"Lacy, I'm whipped. Had to get my blood drawn this morning, and it winded me. Think on things, and when Gloria stops in, she can tell you what I've mapped out, okay?"

"I'll be here." Looking at the blue screen as it wavered in her gaze, she swiped her cheek. "She can text when she's heading this way. I can meet here or at the house."

"I knew I could count on you. Even if you are a spring chicken."

Disconnecting the call, Lacy walked to the wide window and gazed on the tourists strolling Fifth and Main Streets, shopping bags and Cup of Joe's distinctive coffee cups clutched in their grips. Her heart, swollen with surprise, ached for Frank. What must it be like to wake to a dawn with few tomorrows?

With her mind spinning through the possibilities of staying on, it was a wonder she recognized the van that pulled to a stop in front of the empty store across the street. She might have dismissed it had half a dozen hungry-looking teenaged girls not fallen from the sliding door. The driver barked at them, and they cowered on the sidewalk.

That hooked nose and greasy hair seemed eerily familiar.

As the man threw open the driver's door and marched around to corral the girls, she remembered seeing him at the gas station on a rainy day. Different teenagers, same van, similar method of operation.

Hurrying to the desk, she snatched the camera and returned to snap pictures of the man pointing into their faces before he unlocked the shop. Opening the newspaper door, she propped it with a brick to stay in place and broke off dead blooms from Drue's potted geraniums. Covertly, she snapped images of the van.

Had she ever noticed if anyone worked across the street?

Stepping into Drue's Florist Shop, she saw her friend assembling an arrangement at the long, wide worktable in the middle of a room, surrounded by buckets of blooms.

"Hey, can I spare you for a second?" she asked.

Drue set down her clippers and pushed up glasses that had slid down her nose. "Only if this involves coffee. I'm about to die of thirst."

"Come to the window and tell me if you've ever noticed this van before. And if you've seen folks using that shop across the street."

Drue stretched her back and limped forward.

"What's wrong?" Lacy could see pain gripping the soft skin around those deep, chocolate eyes. "Is it your feet?"

"Knees." Drue stopped beside the rack of greeting cards. "I'll have to go see a doc. My Arthur is acting up."

Lacy didn't know who Arthur was, and she wouldn't ask. Too much bad news had already made her question the risks of growing old.

Leaning close to the blinds, Drue narrowed her gaze. "I've seen that van a few times. Figured he was a workman doing stuff in Mrs. Upchurch's shop. That used to be the sweetest little antiques place, but she passed on a few years back, and no one has readied the place for a new lease."

"That man is not a repairman."

Drue cut her gaze to Lacy. "What are you talking about?"

"Call it female intuition, but the driver of that van is running an operation, and it involves teenaged girls."

Drue sucked in her breath. "He's a pervert?"

"Or a pimp." Several years ago, she'd been educated to an underbelly that preyed on runaways. "I think we need to call the police chief."

Drue blanched. "Based on what?"

"Because you and I are about to walk over there and knock on the door."

Throwing her hands in the air, Drue scowled. "I'm not walking over there. I've got work to do."

"He could be using this street to traffic girls."

"I don't know what you're talking about." Drue scurried to her worktable. "And I don't want to know. We have no business sticking our noses into that shop."

Lacy couldn't ignore the apparent red flag about girls being moved through Comfort. At the Miss America competition, one of the contestants had a platform of educating people to the signs of human trafficking, specifically the young runaways who fell for the lies spun about the sex industry. Stunned by the eye-opening material, Lacy had asked more questions and discovered the staggering statistics.

She'd have to research later, but her heart went out to these girls who may have fallen under the spell of an "older boyfriend" or "uncle" who manipulated them into believing he offered a way out of their circumstances. If this was what she suspected, the "way out" was a one-way street of corruption, pain, and defenselessness.

Without a strategy, Lacy would play dumb, hoping the truth revealed itself. Reaching for the knob, she paused when Drue called her name. She could already imagine the headlines. Copy wrote itself in her imagination. Would Frank allow her to produce an article about sex trafficking?

"Don't do it, girl," Drue cautioned. "Call the police and let them handle this."

"By the time they get here those girls could be halfway to San Antonio. I'll be careful. I'll be neighborly and see what's what."

Drue's warnings trailed Lacy's shadow like unravelling ribbon.

Crossing the street, she bent over, picking up a coin from the pavement, and snapped a better image of the van's plate. Then, with bravado she borrowed from her pageant years, rolled her shoulders back, pasted on a smile, and pretended like she had valid reasons to waltz into a shuttered business.

After a quick prayer and visual check of which pocket was disguising her camera, she pushed open the door and stepped into a room emptied of most furniture except a free-standing counter. Mildew pockmarked the walls and dead air made the room feel thick. A thin yellow light radiated underneath an office door at the back.

Muted voices carried, and she could hear a woman barking orders.

What would Frank do?

Wiser after her days writing text for legal decisions, she memorized physical details of the space, the building blocks for a report about an event no one would want to believe was happening in their hometown.

A young girl's yelp resolved all her concerns.

She might be wrong about what she suspected was going on behind that door, but she'd not be able to look at herself in the mirror if she didn't investigate.

Heavy footsteps stomped along the sidewalk outside the shop. Putting a hand against her racing heart, she stepped behind the door, hoping the next person would breeze past.

The door pushed open wide and banged into her face.

Gasping, she grabbed her nose. She'd have yelled had she not remembered the people in the backroom.

A Kendall County deputy stepped inside, his gaze sweeping the storefront.

"Lacy." He removed his sunglasses, propping a hand on his holster. "I saw you sneak in here, and I thought you were chasing that dog again."

Letting her blood pressure unlock her voice, she made an obvious glance around the abandoned room. Covering her face in case her nose started to bleed, she whispered, "Not this time."

"You thinking of moving the offices over here?"

Men, so pragmatic. "I'm curious about some strange people I saw unlock the door and rush in. A man and young girls. I think he's trafficking runaways."

"One glimpse and that's the assumption you imagine? It's quite a leap."

"I witnessed a similar situation a few weeks ago, with the same guy. Same van. Something's off, for sure. And if it were your sister being moved into a backroom by a greasy-haired pimp, wouldn't you want to know what was happening?"

Laughter drifted from the back room. Lacy stiffened. Fingering her bruised nose, she looked him in the eye. "I have no idea what's really happening. But my gut tells me, there's something off, and Comfort is too ideally suited on the interstate for this not to be a legitimate question."

"You sure?" His eyes narrowed. "I saw stuff like that happen in Afghanistan, and the sheriff sent us all to sex-trafficking training so we'd recognize the signs. Not everyone takes this seriously."

She nodded to the back. "We're burning minutes here."

Deputy John Mayne followed the motion of her head. He handed her a handkerchief. She took that as a sign he'd indulge her sleuthing. She felt like Jessica from those old *Murder, She Wrote* episodes that played on late-night cable.

"Can you arrest them all? Right now?"

He cut his gaze. "That would be the Comfort police's call, they'd want to make that move. But I can intercede and at least get the girls with an advocate, if they want one." Deputy Mayne surveyed the room, then silently walked to the door. He raised his fist and knocked before he shoved against it with his shoulder.

Lacy stood behind him, stretching up on her toes, watching people scramble like roaches stunned by daylight.

An alleyway door flew open. Men ran outside. A woman, wearing a make-up belt, a camera setup, and light stands all glowed as if primed for video making.

Mayne evaluated the room.

Why wasn't he leaping to take somebody down?

Costumes littered the floor and the woman was shooing girls out the back door. They didn't seem happy to have this moment interrupted. Even the young girls threw Lacy an evil gaze, before hurrying toward a vehicle.

Car doors slammed, and wheels spun against the alley drive.

Maybe this wasn't the nefarious setup she'd suspected? But those girls definitely looked under consenting age. A cloud of sweat lingered, and the deputy stepped further into the room, kicking aside feather boas and lingerie.

He headed to a corner where two girls huddled behind a Victorian chair. Snapping a photo of the room, Lacy took as many pictures as she could, in case the deputy needed evidence later. Tiptoeing, she stepped over the candy-colored pajamas on the floor and snapped closeups of the staging area. She could see the deputy had bent to talk to the girls, so she leaned around the back door, looking to see if the creeps lingered in the distance. She pursed her lips, wishing the deputy had whipped out a gun and chased those guys.

"Lacy?" Mayne called her back into the shop. "Can you sit here for a moment? I'm going to make some phone calls."

Glancing at the girls, she could see them clinging to each other for dear life. Tempted to beg off, she swallowed her reservations and nodded. He stepped into the front of the shop, and she eased over to the corner, wondering what she could say to make the girls feel safe.

"Hi," she murmured, pulling the chair away from the corner and sitting on it like she wasn't horrified by the people who'd used this prop. As if a genie had pulled back a curtain from her past, she remembered a kind pageant coach who would sit behind stage and calm contestants between events. She channeled some of that woman's poise. "Everything will be okay now. Please don't worry."

Staring at her through teary mascara, the girls seemed about thirteen. They didn't appear inclined to believe her.

"I mean, I guess I can see why you're worried, but Deputy Mayne is a good guy, and he'll make sure this ends well for you."

One girl buried her face in her knees and wailed. "He's going to throw us in jail."

The other one whimpered. "They warned us that if we didn't do what they said the police would lock us up forever."

Lacy glanced at the deputy and wondered how someone would not trust this man. But God only knows what lies these girls were told. Or how they were even lured into doing what they were about to do. Her stomach pitched, and she tried to remember what it was like to be fifteen. "Seriously, I know this seems like the worst turn of events, but it's not the worst," Lacy hurried to say. "Things will get better for you."

"My sister," one of the girls said through clenched teeth. "They took my sister."

She knew more girls had entered the shop than the two that had been left behind. Glancing around the room, she wondered what had happened to the driver of the van. "Is anyone else here?"

The girls shrugged as if they didn't know or weren't going to say.

Wondering what was keeping the deputy, she sat straighter and took a second glance at the space. She didn't feel like she should peek into the bathroom or closet because these two might take off, but she didn't know if the deputy had a full grasp of the situation either.

Come Monday, her first line of business was to trash this flip phone and get one with a camera and apps; the need to be the first to post this scoop was as tangible as the perspiration dripping down her spine. She didn't understand the urge to write about this story, but she felt a burning need to broadcast a warning to the community. Her blood pulsed with the beat of significance. As soon as she could, she'd find a keyboard and pound out the words to sum up this experience. Maybe, just maybe, she could shine a light on a topic that every parent and teacher needed to take seriously.

Mayne hurried into the backroom, his cell phone clutched tightly in his fist. "Police have been notified, and I can handle the girls until they get here. You can take off."

Dismissed? From her own investigative story? *Oh, no, no, no.* She was the eyewitness. She had a story to tell. "I'll stay, John. You might need help."

"I appreciate the offer, but you don't have the creds to be drafted. The sheriff is calling the appropriate services to get involved." Mayne opened the doors of the bathroom—littered with more clothing and makeup—and the storage closet, emptied except for trash. "I can't believe you thought you could walk into this situation."

"I was going to save these girls from a pimp!"

Mayne glanced back at her, his brow rising toward his hairline. "You know that for a fact?"

"Well, not exactly, but I'd seen the van before and knew the driver was moving teenaged girls in a fashion that didn't seem on the up-and-up."

He inspected the camera tripod and backdrop without touching anything. "You were right to be suspicious, but you should have mentioned it last week when I saw you at the county-commissioners meeting."

Being scolded in front of two victims seemed unnecessary, but maybe even those in uniform could be unhinged by scraping the surface of something with the potential for criminal layers. "Maybe so, but timing seemed essential."

"You're pretty, except for your purple nose," one girl said. She glanced at the deputy, then back to Lacy. "Does he like you, or what?"

Lacy felt to determine if her nose was broken. "He's a friend and a good guy. He'll make sure you two get good help."

"We just want to get to my sister. She's in the other car."

Mayne paused. "What other car?"

"The one they keep out back. They promised to take our pictures, then move us to the next stop where we get to pick out some new clothes."

He whipped out a notebook. "What can you tell me about the other car? How many girls were here?"

Lacy stood so he could have the seat. Despite his warning, she was going to stay close. Maybe the girls needed a female to make them feel safer, or he'd need a witness. Either way, she couldn't walk away. Never before had she felt so useful or so justified by the curiosity that bedeviled her into poking her nose into things that always bit back.

Stepping into the bathroom, she reached for a paper towel and dampened it under the tap. Seeing her reflection, she knew an element of satisfaction that she hadn't felt in a long time. Finally, Lacy Cavanaugh had a purpose.

Wailing sirens broke Comfort's quiet, and she stepped back into the room, waiting for the next development. She couldn't help wondering if there were multiple men involved, driving different cars. Might someone hover around to come back and collect these girls? She leaned out the alleyway door, scanning the lot.

Local police and someone that she'd swear was a Texas Ranger entered the space. An explosion of conversations changed the temperature of the room. Mayne stood and provided a physical barrier for the girls so they weren't overwhelmed. He briefed the ranger, the sheriff, and the police, then motioned around the room and toward the door, updating them on the details.

Lacy stepped back as Sheriff Weston surveyed the dirt-packed parking area and alley to Main Street. "What are you doing here, Lacy?"

She'd met the sheriff several times, most recently at a re-election campaign event for County Judge Brenda Jefferson. "I saw the van out front and recognized it from a previous encounter. There'd been a bunch of girls that time too, using a bathroom at an old gas station. I thought it was odd that he'd have access to this shop, so I came over, all neighborly, to see what was going on."

"And he busted your nose?"

"Deputy Mayne opened the front door and it hit my face. On accident."

The sheriff glanced at her quickly. "You say there was a van out front?"

"A brown minivan."

"It's not there now." Sheriff Weston motioned to two deputies. "We'll need to have the state troopers put an APB out for a minivan."

Lacy raised her hand. "I have a photograph of the license plate."

Three speculative gazes focused on her bruised face. She raised her camera from her pocket. "I took photos before I snuck in."

Chapter Twenty

The ceiling fan in Cup of Joe's stirred the air over the heads of guests, teasing some of the early spring temperatures from the open doorway of the shop. Lacy leaned back in her chair, inhaling the aromas drifting over from the coffee bar. What she wouldn't give for a scone, but she'd had difficulty snapping her jeans this morning and would cut back where she could.

Breathing blueberry pastry from a nearby plate would have to suffice.

AJ sat a mug in front of Lacy and then collapsed in the chair across the wooden table. "Spill. The. Beans."

Lacy glanced around the crowded room before her gaze settled on AJ and Luke English sitting across from her. "Don't you want to wait for Anna and Kali? They're collecting their coffees. That way I don't have to repeat everything."

"Please," AJ groaned. "Like you haven't told this story a hundred times already. Is it true the *San Antonio Express-News* picked up your exclusive story and published it as front-page news?"

Luke folded his hands together. "We drove from the airport last night when AJ's phone started blowing up with the text messages."

"I bet you'll win some journalism award for your scoop. Who knew? You've become an investigative reporter. I can see the made-for-TV movie now, 'Beauty Queen Detective.'" AJ held her mug close to her lips and blew on the steamy surface. "Teasing aside, I'm glad they caught the creeps."

Lacy tapped her icy fingers on the table. She wished she could feel so sanguine.

Within hours of the story going live on the *Comfort News* website, folks had threatened her for exposing the community to speculation and insult. She'd been called a traitor and accused of spreading lies. Even Beau texted her to ask if she really thought a place as safe and boring as Comfort could allow something so awful to happen on home turf.

That was before she started feeling the cold stares of people who may—or may not—be associated with the trafficking ring and may—or may not—be planning revenge for the one who busted the story.

Still, she wouldn't dial any of it back.

Lacy discovered facts about trafficking were worse than those first headlines. The more she read about the topic, and the longer she sat on the other side of the yellow crime-scene tape listening to police reports, the more she understood her personal responsibility to educate and expose a network that preyed on teenagers.

Three articles later and a handful of interviews with leading experts, she'd created a series of powerful articles that got the attention of editors, publishers, and broadcasters across the state. The penalty for her crusade stung almost immediately.

Labeled a fraud and a purveyor of "fake news," she'd quickly found out that most subscribers want their headlines presented with sunshine and positive outcomes. Telling the truth came with a heavy dose of scrutiny. Chatter from those that questioned her right to spread such "lies" also came laced with warnings.

Sheriff Weston posted a security detail to the bungalow until he felt sure there wouldn't be blowback from those threatening her. She hadn't slept more than three hours since this barrage started.

Sighing, she said, "See, you already know the details. I don't need to add anything more."

Luke stood as Anna and Kali joined them at the table, saying, "We know what we read in the papers and on Twitter, but that's hardly the same as hearing it from *the eyewitness*."

"Yeah, it's that eyewitness part that I wish I'd played down. Someone might track me to Gloria's house and make me pay for exposing this group."

Kali put a hand to her forehead. "You didn't tell me that you were being *threatened*. Is this *normal*? Why would you be a target? You're telling the story, not making it happen!"

Anna leaned forward putting her hand on Lacy's wrist, insisting, "Start at the beginning. We haven't seen you in almost a week, and I feel the world has spun off-center in the blink of an eye."

Lacy glanced over her shoulder, checking to see who might be watching. "It was as innocent as I reported in Friday's edition. Something didn't seem right, and I stepped into the shop. Thank God, Mayne saw me and wondered what I was doing. Once Frank gave me the go-ahead to run with the story and use photos that didn't implicate the victims or the police, I replayed the incident in print. The photo of the license plate was the key element that allowed the state troopers to capture the van driver. As soon as he was captured—and reminded of his rap sheet—he made a plea deal in exchange for names and locations involved. Then the various agencies descended within hours to shut down the human pipeline." Lacy sipped her coffee, hoping caffeine would kick-start her flat feelings. "After my reports went live on the wire service, other reporters jumped onto the topic, and they're keeping the next phases of the investigation on the front burner."

Luke sighed. "You did what we all wish we had the courage to do—step in we see something our gut says is off and intervene for the victims. On behalf of those girls' parents, let me say thank you."

The what-ifs were never far from Lacy's mind. She'd had an unstable childhood. If it hadn't been for a compassionate aunt, she might have been a runaway too.

"Wow. No one will question your media credibility now," Kali said with awe.

Anna grinned. "To think we know the next Barbara Walters."

"Who," Lacy asked, "is Barbara Walters?"

Anna shook her head. "I forget sometimes that you're still a baby."

"Almost twenty-eight," Kali corrected. "Maybe we can time her birthday with the food festival. You all need to hear the big idea Lacy invented. It's brilliant, and our celebrity chef is all-in, too."

Anna paused before setting the cup in its saucer. "Is the celebrity chef Rudy Delgardo?"

Kali winked. "Ta-da! We've snagged him and the title of 'Comfort's Hunter Gatherer Food Festival' for our grand opening at Lavender Hill. It will be off the charts. I can't wait to spread the word with my vendors."

The shift in the conversation surprised Lacy. All she could think about for the last thirty-six hours had been worry for those girls. She'd prayed, and begged John Mayne for details. The best she could hope for was that they'd really been placed in a safe house or turned over to an advocacy group. Running her fingers through her hair, she wondered if playing a small part in their rescue was ever going to be something she'd recover from.

Kali's enthusiasm for the festival sounded like clanging bells in her ears.

Or maybe it was a means to distract from the terrifying reality that, as parents of young children, they'd have to anticipate evil reaching a gnarled finger out towards their babies. An image of Luna's trusting face flashed before her eyes.

Rudy would tear apart someone who threatened his child.

"Rudy Delgardo is a lovely man. And so kind, too," Anna said with astonishment in her voice. "I hope he's not dating anyone because I might chase him."

AJ chuckled. "Well, that would be a surprise. I haven't seen you interested in a long while."

Lacy barely followed their conversation, save thinking that no one really saw Rudy as she did. He may not be able to communicate well, but she knew enough about him to know he was a warrior beneath that apron. Those eyes of his revealed depths in his soul.

"Well, since the girls finished kindergarten, I haven't had a moment slow enough to consider it," Anna said, "but I'm telling you, the man I met the other night is a keeper. The real test, for me, is how a man treats his children. This guy was great. I can't imagine why his wife would have let him go."

"I know, right?" AJ leaned her elbows on the table. "He's dreamy."

Luke cleared his throat. "I'm sitting right here, ladies."

AJ cut her gaze to meet her husband's. "Feel totally unthreatened. But I'm not blind."

Lacy stirred the foam into her coffee, filing away her movements from the last three days. The adrenaline had faded, the compelling need to write had subsided, but the ghost of a reporter hovered over her shoulder. It whispered into her ear the moment she sat in Frank's chair. Since that first day, she'd poured a whole new level of commitment into everything she produced for the paper.

This was no longer a fill-in while she waited for something better to come along. She almost suspected she'd found her calling.

Oh, who was she kidding?

Tomorrow, someone would send her a link to Nordstrom's shoe sale, and she'd be back in the throes of figuring out summer-fashion tips.

"Lacy?"

She glanced and caught AJ's questioning gaze. "Yes?"

"We were wondering what you would do for an encore. You laid out the plans for our food festival, were offered the newspaper to buy, and scooped a story about sex traffickers in the Hill Country. I'm sure you've got something else up your sleeve."

Lacy sighed with the weight of the anticlimactic. "My attorney told me I'm off Marsh Family probation. I can leave Frank and resume my Dallas life if I want it."

For three long seconds, the only sound was the fan blade slicing air overhead.

"What? That's huge!" AJ reached across to grab her arm. "What a blessing!"

Smiling, she knew she should leap, but with the elements of the last few days, returning to the way things were seemed meaningless. She missed the glamour of Dallas, but she couldn't say Comfort had been dreary. Not anymore.

Their chatter about Amy Marsh, the outcomes of national talent shows, the state of the media these days, and how they would channel all their energy into the festival ran over her head like waves hitting the shore. She'd been swimming in the Gulf of Mexico a few times. The solitude of being under water was a feeling she'd found nowhere else in nature.

She longed for that bliss.

The silence.

The weightlessness.

The feeling nothing sharp could touch.

She should leave town.

Drive to Florida, maybe the beach. The time away could organize her thoughts about what she would do next, and the break would put her mind at rest so she could sleep. Could her car endure the trip? When was the last time she had the oil changed?

Luke pushed a plate of scones her way.

She nodded her thanks, but her appetite had vanished. A cold energy buzzed through her bloodstream. It was as if she ran on a battery she hadn't known she possessed.

Anna finished her coffee and then announced she had to hurry to her office. Kali followed soon after because she had to shop the grocery store since Jake was home sick and begging for homemade chicken-noodle soup.

Lacy pushed back from the table, too. There wasn't a pressing appointment on her calendar, but she felt like a sitting duck in front of the plate-glass window at Cup of Joe's. Better to hide at the newspaper office, emailing columnists about next week's edition.

Saying goodbyes, Lacy scanned the caffeinated crowd, surprised she knew most of the faces. In six months, she'd become a local. Many had congratulated her on the scoop as she walked in. Others expressed worry over what the world was coming to. She had no answers, only the hope that this was an isolated incident. It was small solace that the perpetrators were outsiders.

Collecting her purse, she noticed AJ and Luke studying her. "Are y'all staying for a bit?"

Luke rose. "We'll hang around. AJ's dad wants to talk about hospice care for his mother. Inez has gone down fast."

"Well, I'm sorry to leave you with those prospects. If you want to stop by and talk about the festival later, I'll be at the newspaper. Rudy's parting advice was to plan small this first year and revisit afterwards to see if there's a market for continuing this type of event."

"Good advice," AJ said. "Take care."

Luke stepped forward. "I'll walk you out."

"Oh, there's no need. My office is just blocks away."

"Humor me."

She wove a path through the chairs, and when they came to the door, he tugged her elbow. "I didn't want to say this in front of the others, but you may have a bit of delayed shock. Nervous? Sleeplessness? Loss of appetite?"

She glanced into his eyes and saw a wealth of experience she didn't know he possessed. "Yes."

"Walking into a scene like you did will create baggage." Luke paused while a couple entered the shop and moved to get in line for the counter. "You should leave town for a few days."

She hurried to speak, but he lifted a hand as if directing traffic.

"You're going to list reasons you can't, and I will advise you to go anyway. Take your laptop if you can't unplug from the newspaper. I think you need to look at buildings and faces that won't remind you of what you witnessed."

Processing his words gave her a measure of peace. Maybe she wasn't a freak for freezing up after seeing those girls loaded into a squad car.

"And to convince you this won't hurt your pocketbook, I'll offer you the downtown apartment AJ and I lease in Austin. We don't have plans for the next month, and we can drop the keys off later this afternoon. It overlooks the lake, and I think long walks will do you good. Don't argue, just say yes."

Austin?

Like a breeze blew through to scuttle the cobwebs forming in her imagination, she pictured all the things she'd enjoy in the capital. Stella's topped the list. If she stayed in Austin, she could walk or Uber without worrying about getting on the wrong highway and ending up in Dripping Springs. Her old nightlife-seeking genes wiggled an affirmative, but her conscience pictured Frank holed up at the cancer center.

"I don't know, Luke. That sounds wonderful, but—"

"No buts. I've seen this reaction more times than I'd like to admit, and you need a break. Maybe some anonymity, too. If you don't say yes, I'll tell AJ, and she'll make you come work the lavender beds because she thinks pulling weeds is the answer to all of life's problems."

Lacy knew AJ's philosophy about gardening. "Okay, maybe. I'll need to talk to my publisher and make sure I can do the work off-site."

Luke's eyes widened. "Even though you've been given the green light to return to Dallas, you're still hanging around to help with the newspaper?"

It surprised her too, but she'd grown accustomed to Frank, his grousing, and his long-standing battle with what people should read—and what they were willing to buy—in print. She wouldn't let him down when he needed her most. "I guess it's still a novelty. I'm sure I'll drop it the moment I invent the hashtag to announce my return."

"I always knew you'd blossom again, with followers hanging on your every tweet."

"And yet we didn't meet until I spiraled from the height of my fame."

"Hey, you were up there—that says something."

"It says I needed to grow up and do real things."

Luke grinned. "First, get out of town. Then you can do all the real things you want. With a byline that's gone viral in the media, I'm sure you can get any job you wish."

Whether his enthusiasm was born out of their friendship or a real trend, she wasn't going to guess. It was nice having someone on her side who thought she had earned her chops. Kali was always her supporter, but it meant something weightier to hear a word of praise from someone who hadn't been raised to nurture a baby sister.

Stepping out onto the sidewalk, she breathed begonia-scented air spinning with the hanging baskets and wondered if Luke could be right. Could she investigate a job in the news industry?

Morning sunshine warmed her shoulders, and her burdens shifted.

Luke was probably right. The worst was behind her.

Chapter Twenty-One

Someone grilled hamburgers nearby, and the aroma hovered like the laughter floating through Zilker Park. Rudy swallowed the desire for charcoaled beef along with the memory that Lacy ranked them in her top food group. Thinking of her was counterproductive to the work ahead this week but preventing her image from entering his mind proved impossible. It didn't help when Luna continued to ask when they would next see Cinderella.

"Daddy, watch me!"

He set the wicker basket on the table and observed Luna executing a near-perfect cartwheel. She'd bragged that she'd learned this skill on the school playground, and Rudy was grateful she seemed to have made friends. He'd worried that her shyness had turned crippling.

When Hannah dropped Luna off yesterday for spring break, it was with a list of strict instructions he'd dutifully taped to the refrigerator in his kitchen. Mrs. Lin took one look at the list and crumpled it into the trash. She insisted that no one need teach her how to care for a child.

Rudy was glad Hannah was halfway to the airport when Mrs. Lin found it. Their introduction had gone smoothly, but Mrs. Lin's eyes had narrowed to slits when Hannah rattled off Luna's hang-ups.

"Fresh air is good for little girls," Mrs. Lin said, unpacking the basket.

He wasn't sure his daughter would eat the cold lo mein noodles and dumplings packed for their maiden outing, but he wouldn't complain. He'd hired a grandmother for a two-week trial, and so far, she'd met with everyone's approval. That fact should be enough to celebrate, but he squirmed as he felt like the one under the microscope.

In the days since she'd moved to the upstairs bedroom, Mrs. Lin had given him a note with required household products, repairs outstanding at the condominium, and a roster of activities she'd escort Luna to, along with the estimate for their expenses.

The saving grace was that Luna had instantly fallen in love with Mrs. Lin. The two bonded, and in some weird parallel universe, they were of a like mind.

Today, Mrs. Lin decreed he could drive them both to the park. And he'd obeyed.

"Daddy, I want to go to the playground!"

"After we eat lunch," he said, noting that Mrs. Lin had packed glassware, flatware, and placemats too. "And then, for dessert, we'll find the ice-cream vendor who mixes the M&M's the way you like it."

"No ice cream today," Mrs. Lin amended. "Too much dairy affects her bowels."

Luna's bowels had never been a topic of conversation before. "Well, this is my day off too, so we'll figure out what is the best treat for all of us."

Mrs. Lin pursed her lips. "No dairy."

Rudy rocked back on his heels, worried he'd missed something in his daughter's diet. Or was this one of the famous Lin doctrines Kenny had warned him could not be questioned? Kenny made Rudy swear hiring his mother would not impact his sous chef status with Stella's. At first, Rudy had laughed, wondering what could be difficult about a grandmother. Since that unfortunate miscalculation, he'd considered whether he was even the one in charge anymore. She'd instructed him to avoid stocking soft drinks and prepackaged snacks, and that Luna would have a firm study time every evening after supper. Informed that he must purchase a world map, they had tacked it to a door so Luna could learn how to pronounce the names of countries and continents.

Swatting a fly, Rudy thought noodles were the least of his problems. Luna crawled across the table to help set out plates, and he watched Mrs. Lin fawn over his daughter.

He'd give up whatever power was negotiable to maintain stability. Hannah could no longer question Luna's safety. Mrs. Lin was the key to his summer plans, maybe to the rest of Luna's childhood.

Breathing the grass-scented air, he released the stress of the official notification announcing Stella's was out of the running for the James Beard Award. The codicil promised they might nominate him in future years, which was a minor comfort as Alan Gale had signed the letter. There was no way he could lobby his complaint of backroom shenanigans without being blacklisted.

The feisty tweets about Stella's uneven quality had quieted.

Reservations were back to sellout status.

Financially, he was running in the black again.

He shouldn't grumble.

But his pride stung from knowing the upheaval of the last few months was caused entirely by a man with a grudge. A hint of honeysuckle reminded him of California and an insult from ten years ago.

Rudy had not known when he started dating Hannah that she'd previously dated Alan Gale. It had been early in the relationship when Gale tracked them to the Malibu bistro, insisting Hannah give him a second chance. When she pointed to Rudy as her excuse for turning him down, advertising that she'd found someone more reliable than a freelance journalist, he'd turned volatile.

It was the second time the two men, who'd met at the Culinary Institute of America, had been interested in the same woman. The first time, Alan chased the girl and won her—only to divorce shortly thereafter. Rudy didn't care and never asked why. In Malibu, Hannah chose Rudy over Alan. He'd wondered what sort of revenge Alan would require. The attention flattered Hannah, and she told him not to worry about it. Alan would have to move on.

What she'd not counted on was that a chef never forgets: not the ingredients that fail, the cooks who can't be trusted, the managers who cut into the profits, or the passions that drive people to take incredible risks.

But then, Hannah wasn't a chef.

"Mr. Delgardo, sir. A plate, please."

Mrs. Lin handed him a serving of dumplings, noodles, and some sort of slaw. Not his favorite, but he didn't dare insult his cook. "Thank you."

Luna had scurried around to sit on the bench next to a bottle of chilled Topo Chico—the beverage preselected for their meal. He wondered if he had to wait to sit until Mrs. Lin sat; the protocol for a nanny was new material.

A large black Labrador ran past their picnic, trailing a leash, and the voices in the distance indicated that the dog was being commanded to return.

"Daddy! He's lost." Luna jumped from the table. "He doesn't know they're looking for him."

"Oh." Rudy swallowed a forkful of noodles. "He knows."

In the blink of an eye, Luna ran in the direction of the dog, calling after it as if he'd respond to her fairy voice better than he would the people shouting from the bend.

Dropping his plate to the table, he yelled, "Luna, come back!"

"She will return," Mrs. Lin announced, unconcerned. "She will not go far."

Says the woman who chose not to read the paper delivered to his doorstep. He read every word about the sex traffickers that had been in Comfort within days of their visit. He vacillated between being proud of Lacy for writing an article picked up by the Austin paper and stunned she'd had the gall to walk into a dangerous situation. Could her pluckiness have rubbed off on Luna?

No. His daughter was a leap first, think second kind of girl. A dangerous combination in a large public park.

He chased Luna's steps, eating up the distance faster than her little legs could run.

She called the dog, and he knew she was headed toward the bike path along Barton Creek. Overtaking her near the path, they watched the dog sail into the crowd of people meandering at the water's edge.

"Daddy, I almost got him," she panted as she stopped short of the path.

"He is not ours to get."

Teenaged boys following ran toward the water's edge, yelling for Bevo to return.

"The dog belongs to them." He scooped Luna into his arms, hugging her close. "You've got to stop chasing after dogs. This is not your problem to solve."

"But I love them. And they're lost."

"They're not lost. They're having the time of their lives before they get leashed again."

Luna pouted. "I was so close to catching him."

They both watched the dog leap into the water and splash through the shallows.

"Rudy?"

Stunned, he froze. Had he imagined her golden voice? Did fear for Luna make him drag a fantasy to life? She was in his head not ten seconds ago. It could be a reaction to stress. Turning toward the folks jogging along the path, he saw a tall blonde in spandex jogging attire. "Lacy?"

She met them on the grass, bending a bit to catch her breath. "I can't believe that in the thousands of people I've seen today, I recognized you." She tweaked Luna's ponytail. "And the little princess."

"Cinderella!" Luna scrambled to the ground and wrapped her arms around Lacy's legs.

He glanced down at his navy T-shirt and dark jeans, knowing he'd be easy to overlook. He wasn't supposed to be in this spot at this minute. If not for that stupid dog, he'd be swallowing noodles and figuring out how to make conversation with a woman who recited a grocery list like a drill sergeant.

"What brought you to Austin?" he asked, downplaying the heartbeats racing in his throat. "Are you training for something?"

"Trying to get back in shape after months of eating three square meals in Comfort."

"But here? Surely there are running paths nearer your house."

She paused like she was thinking through potential routes. "I could do laps around the high-school field, but I lost the enthusiasm for red dirt." Checking her wristband for the measured distance, she glanced back to him. "I've been staying in Austin for a few days and trying to figure out what to do with the rest of my life. Jogging seemed a good idea."

She was here. In his neighborhood. His heart hummed with an energy he hadn't felt in a long while. Maybe since the last time he stood next to her. "And you haven't been to Stella's?"

With a smile, she deflected the scolding. "I ate there the first night I arrived, but when I asked Jay if I could see you, he said you were at the bakery preparing kolaches for a fun-run the next day."

Why wouldn't Jay have told him? "The staff at Stella Too's caught a bug, and we had to disinfect the kitchen and bring in help to fulfill a huge order. A nightmare, but somehow we pulled it off."

"All's well that ends well, right?" Lacy's eyes brightened. "Somewhere in all of that you have Luna with you again."

"Spring break." He motioned for them to step out of the way of the crowds. The shade trees welcomed them in. "Luna's mom took a trip to New York, and we get a practice run for our summer."

"We have Mrs. Lin," Luna announced, "and she is going to be my nanny. Now I can come stay whenever I want because she will keep me while Daddy works."

"Well, that sounds perfect," Lacy agreed. "I'm sure she's delightful."

"Come meet her," Luna insisted, tugging Lacy's hand. "She's made lunch, and we have a picnic."

Lacy wiped perspiration from her brow. "Oh, I couldn't. I'm a mess."

"Mrs. Lin packed hand wipes because she said we must not catch germs."

Rudy could hear the echo of the lecture about viruses and thorough handwashing. "We really would love your company," he said, "if you can take a break."

A fresh flush of color turned Lacy's cheeks rosy. "I don't have any plans. I was just killing time."

Luna tugged her deeper toward the trees. "Then come this way. We were eating lunch. Then this dog ran by, and I had to catch him."

"You were chasing another dog?" Lacy glanced toward the water. "I saw that beast fly like a bullet out of the woods."

"You know how Luna is about strays."

"Oh, I remember," Lacy chuckled. "And just so you know, little Rudy has been rounded up by the police and taken to the vet for a cleaning and checkup. Hopefully, they'll find him a permanent home."

Luna clapped her hands. "That's the best news. Maybe we can adopt him." She turned to her father. "Can we, Dad? Please?"

"Absolutely not." Rudy motioned for them to join him on the dirt path. "Mrs. Lin would not welcome a dog."

"Do you know that or are you just guessing?" Luna asked with suspicion.

Lacy laughed.

Her amusement was the most wonderful sound. But then, he was susceptible to thinking anything Lacy did was stunning.

They returned to the picnic area, Luna skipping ahead because she said she wanted to be the first to tell Mrs. Lin about finding Lacy. Rudy wanted to reach across the slight distance, hold her hand, make sure she wasn't a figment of a stress-induced moment. He'd regretted leaving Comfort without a plan to see her, but towing an active child, he doubted he could pull off much of a Romeo effect. Lacy probably dusted her hands together that night and said good riddance to Hurricane Delgardo.

He glanced at her, caught her gaze, and smiled. She smiled back.

"Daddy, there's plenty to eat!"

Whispering, he gestured to their table. "My advice, take nothing she says personally."

"Luna?"

"Mrs. Lin." Rudy approached and made introductions. In a move he could never have expected, Mrs. Lin recognized Lacy.

"You are the one my son admires. He asked my advice about sending you flowers. You like daisies."

Lacy's features momentarily froze, maybe processing a response.

"Lacy is a friend of our family, Mrs. Lin. Kenny was hoping to send flowers to invite her to help us promote the restaurant. Kenny wasn't pursuing Lacy."

Mrs. Lin's raisin eyes narrowed. "He calls her a goddess. That does not sound like a friend of the family. It sounds like courtship."

"Kenny is—" Rudy stumbled for his next word.

"Kenny is a gentleman," Lacy interrupted. "You raised him to observe the nicest courtesies. The flowers were so lovely. And yes, because of the gesture, I will help Rudy, Kenny, and *all* the staff at Stella's with whatever they need in the ways of social media."

A tight breath eased from Rudy's lungs. It was the first he'd heard of the battle Mrs. Lin waged to force Kenny into dragging a bride to the altar. She must not know how much Kenny would rather own a restaurant than a dowry. But he'd not be the one to burst that bubble. No way.

"And I'll be in town for the next week or so," Lacy added, glancing at him. "Maybe we could meet to discuss the details for the campaign as well as the food festival in May."

"Yes. Any time. How about tonight?" Scheduled to work, he would rearrange every calendar if she said yes. "We could try one of the new restaurants downtown or go to a favorite place you enjoy."

"Sure." She grinned. "I'd rather you cook. That Saturday still ranks as one of my favorite afternoons in a long while."

"I'd like that too, but since Mrs. Lin has moved in, she's made me aware that my kitchen is not big enough for her automatic rice cooker. I've already hired a contractor to add another workspace.

"Here. You eat this. It will put meat on your bones."

Lacy glanced at the plate Mrs. Lin thrust at her.

"I'm trying to get the meat off my bones," she said, accepting the plate. "But this smells delicious, so I'm willing to break a few rules."

Mrs. Lin smiled.

Actually smiled. *Had he seen her teeth before today?* He sat down on the bench, weary from figuring out women. He'd thank God that Lacy was running by at the same moment Luna was chasing a dog and leave it at that.

Dragging a long pull from the Topo Chico, he ran through the staffing options for tonight and decided who he'd call in. Watching Lacy settle next to Mrs. Lin and keep a conversation going was nothing short of a miracle. He'd felt like everything he did around the nanny was wrong, but with the Blonde Goddess she was smiling and petting Lacy's ponytail.

Luna bit into a grape, watching the twosome as well. "Lacy is nice."

He looked down at his side. "Yes, she is."

"I want to be like Lacy."

"Okay."

"Can she stay with us?"

"We're out of bedrooms, and you're now sharing my bathroom."

"She could sleep with me."

Luna's twin bed had sacrificed essential real estate to a stuffed-animal collection that threatened to overtake her mattress. "That's not going to work, besides, I heard her say she has a place to stay."

Luna popped another grape into her mouth.

His phone rang and as he checked the caller ID—Don Hurt. His friend and fellow chef had created a wild-game restaurant at the top of everyone's list. He'd have to ask for a reservation during the conversation. They could call it research. He wasn't sure he could call it a date.

That would get back to Hannah.

Rising from the table, he walked to the tree line to finish the call.

Returning a few minutes later, he saw Luna sitting next to Lacy, and they were looking at her phone. The laughter was contagious.

"What's so funny?"

"Goat videos," Luna said. "Lacy is posting these to Instagram, and lots of people are watching the babies chase bubbles."

Lacy glanced at him. "I got a little desperate in thinking of ways to help Kali promote her cheese business. This has worked wonders."

He leaned over Lacy's shoulder and watched. "How long can they keep this up?"

"As long as Kali keeps blowing the bubbles. They'll tire out in a minute, and it's like when one goat goes down, they all collapse. Four-legged dominoes."

Distracted by the slim lines of her neck, he paid little attention to the goats. Since no one was paying attention to him, he indulged the moment to note the threads of gold in her hair and the delicate curve of her ear.

"You're staring," Mrs. Lin snarled.

Walking around the table, he collected the plates and dumped the trash. There would be a lengthy walk to the car, but they'd pass an ice-cream truck, and he'd indulge his daughter—her bowels be damned.

Maybe they could offer Lacy a ride. Maybe she'd spend the rest of the day with them, and then dinner could become an extension of a day that would bleed into the weekend.

"Can you join us for dessert? There's a great food truck near the parking lot."

Lacy turned her iPhone around and apologized for the dings signaling texts and reminders. "Sorry, but I've got to run. I'm meeting someone at the Bullock Museum for a traveling art exhibit, and I have to shower first."

"Oh," he said, unable to mask disappointment.

"On the upside, he works for a law firm, and they're considering being a sponsor for the food festival."

"So, you're not on vacation?"

She groaned. "I'm more or less working remotely."

"Comfort is so comfortable, why would you want to leave?"

Her face clouded over. "Things have become complicated lately, and I needed a change of scenery to figure out my next steps."

That sounded odd, but he figured that he wasn't an expert on her life, so there were volumes that could tangle as quickly as angel-hair pasta. Watching her rise with the grace of someone who could make exercise look effortless, he wondered what she meant by figuring out her steps.

"I made a reservation for us tonight. It's Don Hurt's place. We can ask him to help with the food festival, so we can call this a business meeting." He stuffed his hands in pockets, nervous she might remember she'd already planned an evening that included something far more glamorous than dining at Falcon Ridge. "I can pick you up about seven."

She bit her lower lip. "That may cut it close, but if I'm running late, you can text me an address, and I can Uber there."

He wondered who he was competing with to secure her attention. He pictured some grad student, filled with the dreams and hopes of a life just beginning. Glancing at the knife and burn scars on his hand, he knew he was too old to think he could offer anything to a girl who could pull the world by a kite string. He was a dad. A chef in the precarious balance of owning a restaurant and maintaining salary for employees. He barely had room for a few hopes, much less dreams. Most of his hours centered on making Stella's grow so he could put a daughter through college one day.

"Sure. I'll text you later."

Luna kissed her cheek. "Love you, Lacy. You're the best."

Lacy hugged his daughter and smiled. "You say the sweetest things, kid. I hope to see you again before spring break ends and you go back to your mom's."

Without consulting her dad, Luna grinned. "Let's see each other every day."

"You'd tire of me after five minutes." Lacy backed away, thanking Mrs. Lin for lunch. "Bye, Rudy."

He watched her walk away, wishing he'd said something poetic instead of let's have a business meeting. How stupid could he be? Feeling Mrs. Lin stare through his skin, he'd guess he was about to find out how Kenny could have swooped in with ten times more style.

The urge to punch something lingered in his limbs all afternoon.

After his shower, while combing his hair, he saw the reflection of a man whose face told a hard story. Scrubbing his hands over his chin, he should shave, but a waitress once told him he looked mysterious with a bit of stubble. If he were going to win a second date with Lacy, he needed every ounce of help he could gain.

It seemed unfair to have met someone like Lacy this late in his life. She lit a fever within him. If he'd ever felt this stinging awareness with Hannah, his memory had traded the experience for reality—two months after he and Hannah had stopped dating, she had called to tell him she was pregnant.

Running a hand along his cheek, he felt the stiff bristles of gray popping through the brown, and he wondered how long it would be until his hair reflected the steel of his thoughts. He leaned closer to the mirror and checked his sideburns for any evidence that he stared down the pike at forty.

"You look like Prince Charming, Daddy."

He double-checked the knot holding a towel around his waist. "I thought Prince Charming had blond hair."

She blinked. "He does? I've always thought he looked just like you."

"You're an angel, little one. Did you know that?"

"I've heard that before, but you can say it as many times as you like."

He kissed her forehead, smelling the fragrance of her freshly washed hair. "I'm guessing Mrs. Lin is going to let you watch your movies tonight since you're already in your pajamas?"

"Her burs-sur-ee-itis is acting up after walking through the park today, so we'll have breakfast for supper and watch TV." Luna glowed. "Doesn't that sound like fun?"

He'd rank it slightly above torture, but this is where he and Hannah had always differed about parenting. Having not grown up with a television, he didn't understand the vacancy that occurred when someone sat down in front of a box and gave over their thinking to a bunch of actors. His perfect evening was music, puzzles, books, and hitting the sheets since he was usually awake before dawn. But, as he learned seven years ago, babies reset the schedule.

Sending her downstairs, he stood at his closet door and wished for something a little less dark in his attire. Life rarely happened outside of Stella's, and he had few outfits without cooking stains. Reaching for a tweed sports coat, he paired that with a navy button-down and jeans with a bit of fade. Stretching to a top shelf, he pulled down a dusty box. Don would give him grief if he walked through the doors of Falcon Ridge without cowboy boots.

He'd texted Lacy the address, and twenty minutes later waited on the curb at the restaurant so he could greet her taxi. Half a dozen cars pulled to the curb, and couples piled out, talking and checking their phones for reservation confirmations. He'd never stood outside Stella's when guests arrived, but one night he should. It might be enlightening to hear what people expected of their encounter.

Checking his watch, he knew Lacy still had ten minutes before she'd be fashionably late. He didn't know if that was still a thing, but with the thickness of Austin traffic, it might be a legitimate issue. A Mercedes pulled to the curb, and he glanced away, distracted by tourists snapping selfies.

"Rudy!"

He watched Lacy rising from the car, assisted by someone in a suit. The man, about thirty, leaned close to her ear as if begging her to reconsider. The filmy cocktail dress and spiky sandals hinted they'd been to a party.

"Sorry I'm late." She found her balance on the sidewalk. "Christopher could not tear himself away from the featured artist at the museum, and I thought we would never make it on time."

Jealousy wove around his heart, squeezing his voice in the process. "Christopher?"

The man stared at Rudy before he offered his grip. "Christopher Woodley, Lacy's attorney and guide to the finer works of Texas artists. We were at a private reception, and when you can get that close to a genius, it's hard to watch the clock."

Particularly when one had to surrender a beautiful date, Rudy guessed. He took stock of the competition and felt on an even playing field. Woodley might be younger and have less baggage, but his eyes said he knew Lacy was too good for him.

Rudy stepped out of the way of people passing by and realized that Woodley wasn't hopping in the driver's seat. He would have to shake the guy. "I hear you're considering sponsoring our food festival? Let me say a big thanks in advance—it takes a brave man to support a cause just getting started."

Woodley's eyes widened. "Well, nothing is official."

"I'll not ask you for a check tonight," Rudy said, remembering the awkward months when he recruited investors for the opening of Stella's. "But it's a comfort to know you're in the background, ready and willing to see this event succeed. I know I speak for Lacy and her sister when I say, well done."

Lacy was biting her lip to keep from smiling. "Yes, thank you, Christopher. I'll be in touch about an underwriter's form and a logo for your firm so we can advertise your support."

He blanched. "Well, I need to run it by the senior partners first."

Lacy stepped across the concrete and stood next to Rudy. "And thanks for the art show. It was quite the afternoon."

"Okay, yes, well, maybe we can get together again soon. I'm here at my parents' place, overlooking Lake Travis, for the next several days. Legal conference, you know."

"Yes, you mentioned that a few times." Lacy waved her fingers. "Thanks again for the ride. I hope you've not gone out of your way."

Christopher read the Falcon Ridge signage. "I wonder if I could grab a bite to eat at their bar?"

"Reservations are already on a waiting list," Rudy said with apology. "I had to pull some strings to get a table for me and Lacy."

"We should hurry, Rudy, don't you think?"

He saw the twinkle in her eye. "Yes, I think we should. Goodbye, Woodley."

And before the man could respond, he wrapped his arm around Lacy's waist and directed her toward the black door. Tipping the doorman, they were led to the front of the line where the maître d' greeted him warmly. *As well she should,* Rudy thought, *since she used to be a hostess at Stella's.*

"Your table is waiting," she said.

They were seated in a comfortable booth against the enormous windows of the wine room, a bottle of champagne chilling in an ice bucket on the table.

"Oh, my," Lacy sighed as she leaned against the bolstered cushion. "I'd never considered the perks of dining out with a chef. That champagne looks top drawer, as my aunt used to say."

Happy that it impressed her, he smiled. "My grandmother used to say 'top drawer' too. I asked her what that meant, and I've never forgotten how she explained that people in the old country kept all their belongings in one trunk or bureau, and that the top drawer was reserved for their best possessions."

"My aunt was from France, and though she'd lived in the United States since she was a teenager, she was always whipping out phrases and expressions that Kali and I had never heard. Our mother, her sister, was French too, but I was too young when my mom died to know if she used the same sayings." Lacy picked up the menu, disguising her face. "I've never been here, what do you recommend?"

He guessed that meant the conversation was over. Maybe later he could circle back to hear more of her childhood. The scars from past years ran deepest, at least that had been his experience. Thankfully, he had a trusted babysitter for Luna and a friend at the bar, so he could take his time unravelling the mystery of Lacy Cavanaugh.

He rolled his shoulders back, confident the night would be memorable. Sipping the honeyed bubbles, he just wasn't sure to what extent.

Chapter Twenty-Two

Lacy rolled over in bed, opened her heavy lids, and squinted at the sunlight warming the ceiling. AJ and Luke's condo sat fourteen floors above downtown Austin and close enough to the lake to let fresh air stir the curtains. She'd slept with the windows open because the temperatures had turned cool, and the air felt good on her skin.

A smile eased across her face as she remembered the night before. Turning over, she looked at the other pillow.

Her phone started ringing Kali's specific tone, and she reached to the nightstand to catch it before it went to voicemail. "Morning, Sunshine."

"You sound groggy. Are you still in bed? I've been up for hours."

"You have an infant. What crisis has gripped you now?"

"Besides the fact that Jake had to leave at midnight because one of his mares was in breech, and the foal had the cord around its neck, I've been agonizing for that momma all night. The vet saved them both, but still. It was a touch and go."

Lacy sat up and propped the pillow between her head and the wall. "You people have too many animals in your world, I don't know how you manage."

"I don't either, but that's not why I'm calling. I saw the text you sent last night about meeting Don Hurt and how he would help promote the festival. Did he really offer his posse of grill buddies and their tricked-out tailgating trucks?"

"For real. It was like some magic moment watching Rudy and Don break down the food and beverage requirements. I could barely get the notes typed into my phone fast enough. Don attends the Austin Food Festival, so he gave me a list of things to do and not to do. It was like a crash course in event management while eating the best supper I could have imagined. The chef sent out samples of food for Rudy and me to try, and I gained pounds sitting there. Don't get me started on the wine."

"Please. I ate egg salad last night. Do not tell me about the luxuries of fine dining. I might scream." Kali yawned. "But I must know how you ended up at a swanky restaurant with our favorite chef."

Snuggling into the covers, Lacy replayed the sequences and may have revealed too much. Kali pronounced that they'd be an item by summer.

"We can't date, Kals." Lacy would like nothing more than to disagree with herself, but she knew the obstacles. "I'm sure he sees me as a flighty airhead. He and Don were using terms last night that I'd never heard before. I've never felt more out of my league."

"Well, there's the age thing too."

Lacy tossed the covers back. "What age thing?"

"Well, isn't he, like, forty?"

"Thirty-eight."

Silence stretched between Austin and Comfort.

Finally, Lacy stood and walked into the bathroom, staring into her sleepy reflection. Without mascara and eyeliner, she looked twelve. "Please don't say he's too old for me."

"I've always thought you needed someone mature, someone who could reign in your enthusiasms and keep you on solid footing. But he's got a lot in his world. Maybe too much for someone who just wants to have fun."

"What do you mean," Lacy paused, looking deeper into the mirror, "just wants to have fun?"

"Well, your influencer thing. Now that you've bought the new phone and watch, and all the toys you used when you were a fashion-and lifestyle guru, it will be back to the party scene, right? I'm surprised you haven't leased an apartment in LA already. Wasn't that your big dream?"

Those aspirations had been pinned to a corkboard in her home office at the W. "I can't afford to go to California. I've been living off my savings while in Comfort. Without advertisers sponsoring my sites, I'm posting for my own vanity."

The echo of those words circled her brain—*posting for my own vanity*. Had she said that out loud? One evening, with wine and the reliable rhythm of the porch swing, she and Gloria had dissected the motivations leading her to switch from posting images about the band to offering photos of herself, posed around Dallas, wearing this or that style so smartly. Finally, she admitted the effort smacked of personal validation. Gloria had asked her a haunting question—what had she put on Snapchat that would improve anyone's life?

She'd not tagged any health tips. She'd not introduced followers to any physicians with the latest and greatest breakthroughs. She'd not even posted anything about voter awareness or safety tips—but her followers had known where the best clubs were, what one should wear for brunch, and how to trick out a Stars jersey with high-heeled boots.

Not a single warning about a 1-800 number for guys and girls afraid they were being groomed for trafficking.

Hanging her head over the sink, she didn't want these introspective feelings today. She should be dancing on clouds after her evening.

"Listen, I gotta go, Kals. I'll call you tomorrow."

"Wait, send me and AJ an email with the outlines of what Don Hurt said. We're meeting with the ad company that designed our business logos and then a banner company to get estimates on signage for the event hall."

"Sure. I'll be in touch."

Dropping her phone on the counter, she brushed her teeth and washed her face. Thoughts collided behind her eyes, and she hated the self-doubt tugging at her conscience. Questioning her character before coffee could only lead to misery.

But she couldn't stop the flood any more than she could hold back the sunshine.

Worries for those teenage girls followed her to the gym. Later, as she stepped out of one of her favorite stores, without a single purchase, she felt anxious wondering how *safe* was the safehouse.

"Lacy, wait up!"

She groaned. Had she tagged herself on Facebook? *No.* She'd turned off all location alerts when setting up this new phone. Turning around, she watched Christopher hurry across the street. His ripped jeans hugged his legs, and his Sketchers revealed thin, white ankles.

Propping a straw bag higher on her shoulder, she itched to be on the move. "What brings you here?"

"Brunch. I saw you walk out of the Urban Outfitters and knew I had to catch you." He took off his sunglasses. "I had a good time yesterday and hoped we could go out again. Are you free tonight?"

A million reasons screamed inside her head, all of them bringing a dark-haired knight riding to the rescue. They'd parted with a kiss and a promise to see each other today. The invitation was unspecific, but he'd asked her to stop by the restaurant at noon. She hoped that meant she'd be busy the rest of the weekend.

"Sorry, but I'm heading to a job. I'm helping a restaurant fix social-media issues and set them up with a food stylist."

"Great use of your talents. Maybe I could meet you there? I'm always looking for somewhere to wine and dine Austin clients."

And she walked right into that one. "You should definitely add Stella's to your list, but aren't you tied up with your legal conference right now?"

"I'd skip a session to spend time with you."

She could hear Frank urging her to date Christopher: stable, smart, and loaded with earning potential. Wasn't that what she'd always said she wanted?

She blinked and pictured their future together—desirable address, all the right schools for children, expensive travel destinations, and someone to foot her credit-card bill. With the job offers she'd received recently, she could work as much or as little as she wanted.

Frank's silent whisper advised, *Don't screw this up, kid.*

Frank. She had the prospectus for the Comfort newspaper on her desktop. She'd read it twice, surprised by the reasonable price he'd attached to the product. He'd built a small publishing empire with little more than grit and hard work. Surely, she should give his advice credibility?

Though the art exhibit wasn't her thing, Christopher hadn't been boring. He knew a lot about painting, kept up a running commentary about the folks who gathered at the museum, and introduced her around—never once mentioning Amy Marsh when people asked how they had met. Her nerve endings didn't dance, like they did with Rudy, but he was pleasant.

She'd give him a second chance. "We could do drinks Sunday afternoon, if you're available."

His smile stretched across his face. "I'll *be* available. I'll text you with details once I decide on a location."

She glanced at her watch. "I have to go. Enjoy your brunch."

"I will, and you look great."

Glancing at her yoga pants and white sneakers, she had to wonder about his taste. She was the carbon copy of every other woman bouncing around downtown this morning, nothing Instagram worthy.

Taking off, she hurried toward the condo and then turned left in case he followed her. She didn't like Christopher knowing where she stayed. No reason for the caution, but she'd yet to shake the sense she was being followed. Those small-minded pests who'd trolled her sites had gotten inside her head. Sheriff Weston said no one would know she was in Austin unless she advertised it.

Running through the shower and changing into white jeans and a boho-chic blouse, she coiled her hair around a leather scrunchie and chose dangling earrings. Paired with her expensive sunglasses, she was sure she could hang with whomever she might meet at Stella's. Even Kenny.

Climbing out of the Uber and standing at the front door of the restaurant, she was surprised at how dark and unwelcoming it seemed. Tempted to text Rudy, she re-read the hours sign and guessed she should have gone to the back door. By the time she walked the half block around, her thongs were covered in mud, and a splatter of something oily had ruined her jeans. A kale smoothie had long since worn off, and she would kill for Dr Pepper.

Also, Rudy hadn't arrived.

Kenny led her to his office where she could wait. "I don't know where Chef is. He's usually one of the first people here on Saturday because he likes to enjoy the kitchen before it becomes a storm center."

"Could I go to the bar and fix a soft drink while I wait? It's so hot today."

Kenny glanced into the small office, checking to see if the chef had snuck indoors. "Sure, make whatever you like. Just don't mess with the bartender's order. He can tell if someone has put something out of place."

Setting her bag on the floor next to Rudy's desk, she stopped at the handwashing sink to rinse away the perspiration. Though stained from the walk, she didn't mind spending more time in the Clarksville area. It had been easy to imagine Austin before progress uprooted the bungalows and old trees to build high rises.

Pulling a familiar label from the mini refrigerator, she popped the top and drank right from the can. No need to bother with a glass when she would consume this beverage in less than five minutes. As she glanced at sunlight pouring in behind the shelves of bottled liquors, she thought the colors created an artsy element often overlooked. She reached into her back pocket, retrieved her phone, and set the camera for portrait, focusing on the shafts of light.

"An artist at work?"

The phone almost slipped as she whipped around to see Rudy standing in the shadowed dining room. His black T-shirt, jeans, and boots were his casual uniform. The leathery volumes of his face screamed stress.

"I got a little distracted by the light." She picked up the can and stepped away from the bar, hoping he wouldn't see her nervousness. "I'd never noticed there was a window before."

"A happy coincidence, not a well-planned design element."

Gone was the loose-limbed man of yesterday. Rudy's shoulders were taut, and his eyes lacked humor.

"Don't lie, Rudy," said the short woman who stepped from behind him, entering the dining room wearing a sundress and chunky high heels. "I moved the bar there to capture the light, instead of positioning it closer to the front door. Which is what *he* wanted. Never let a man design a space. They always default to efficiency and cost."

Reading their faces, it was clear these two shared history, but she struggled to figure out how the woman played into staffing. She'd thought she'd met everyone when she delivered the gifts all those weeks ago.

"It turned out to be a good decision, I guess." Lacy didn't move any closer. Rudy's body language screamed cantankerous. Her plans for a Saturday videoing him cooking with the staff and scheduling his Facebook posts flitted away like a Parmesan curl on spaghetti. "Did I arrive too early?"

The woman positioned herself so the amber light from the bar shrouded her with a color. "I'm Hannah Delgardo, and you are?"

Her knees buckled. *Luna's mother.* No mistaking the resemblance. "I'm Lacy Cavanaugh. I'm—" She scrambled to come up with a title that filled in the gaps of her nonexistent business card. "a social-media consultant and a coordinator for the Comfort Hunter Gatherer Food Festival. Rudy's helping with the event, and in exchange, I'm helping him with social media for the restaurant."

She glanced at her ex-husband. "Well, lucky you."

Rudy stood silently, as if waiting on a verdict.

Lacy didn't understand the dynamic between Rudy and Hannah; he'd been vague on the details of his personal life, but she wasn't blind. These two had recently exchanged heated words, and Rudy came out with a loss. Her heart went out to him, and Luna too. It couldn't be easy strung between two headstrong people.

"Actually, I'm the lucky one," Lacy inserted. "I've never planned an event of this scope, and my friends who own the event center are super excited about Chef Delgardo's talent being a draw. Surely, you must know what a coup that is for us?"

"He's just failed the James Beard Awards, so I'm not sure what sort of *coup* you're looking for, but he's not as grand as you might think." Hannah's smile froze her cheeks. "He's on the fast track to has-been status."

"That's enough, Hannah." Rudy stepped closer to the bar. "Lacy need not discover how bitter you are within moments of meeting. She's a bystander."

"There are no spectators in the restaurant business," Hannah replied. "Everyone reacts to a hiccup. We all saw the drop here after a few biting tweets."

"You know nothing about Stella's anymore." Rudy's eyes stormed. "And it's time for you to leave."

"You'd like to think," Hannah snarled. "But I have friends who work here. They tell me things."

Rudy pointed his arm toward the front door. "I'll call Mrs. Lin to get Luna packed. I can't promise she won't cry. She was looking forward to the list of activities Mrs. Lin had planned. And she'd settled into the new routine."

"The sooner Luna learns life is not fair, the better." Hannah smoothed the skirt of her dress. "As a single mom, I deal with her tears all the time."

Rudy didn't rise to the bait, and Lacy privately clapped. In the brief time she'd known him, he had proven a devoted father. Luna seemed well adjusted, so if anyone had issues, she'd assume it was the mother—a woman apparently reluctant to leave her ex alone.

"So, *Lacy*, I hope you don't get too upset, but Rudy spends all his time here. I'm not sure when your food event is, but he's not going to spare you much effort. Stella's is his life."

The only way to get this woman to move on was to prove there was nothing for her to see. Lacy pulled out a chair and dug her phone from her bag. "Oh, I'm not worried. It's enough to have his name associated with our event to get other chefs interested. When you get one famous person on board, others can't wait to jump in also." She set her phone on the table. "Now, if you'll excuse me, I have to set up a conference call. *Bon Appétit* magazine is salivating over this partnership."

Hannah's smile faded. "Well, I have to get back—so much to do as well. I can't stay."

And yet she didn't move.

Lacy picked up her phone and displayed the keypad. "Chef, should we set this call in your office?"

"Yes, whatever you think is best." Rudy's eyes softened. "You're the expert."

She was glad he played along. "Glad to help. Such a worthy cause." Walking toward the kitchen door, she added, "Nice to meet you, Ms. Delgardo. Good luck with Luna. She's a doll."

The air froze.

Lacy had made a fatal mistake, but it took her a moment to figure out what she'd said wrong.

"You know my daughter?"

Reeling from the setback, she dialed back to a memory from her pageant days, that delicate chaos when the answer that fell out of her mouth had nothing to do with the question asked. Lacy kept her expression neutral. "Chef was babysitting the day our event committee arrived for a meeting. That he could manage a curious child and three women bent on a mission was a masterful display of patience and fatherhood. We knew then he was the chef for our event because we'll be a family-friendly festival."

Tension relaxed.

Lacy sighed. "I have a nephew so I can appreciate the balance."

Hannah backed away, but her gaze held Lacy and Rudy hostage. "What date is your event?"

"Last weekend in May."

Hannah paused. "Oh, that's too bad. He'll have Luna then. I guess you'll find out just how good he is at managing a full plate."

Lacy grimaced. "We must hope he can find a way through."

Rudy stepped closer to where she stood. "That phone conference?"

"Must hurry," she said, with an added frown.

"Goodbye, Rudy. Don't forget what I said about the background check on your nanny. I want to see it ASAP."

Lacy watched the mother leave. It was only as the front door swooshed closed that she released her breath. "That was crazy."

"Welcome to my world." Rudy headed toward the swing doors. "The office?"

She followed, hoping he wouldn't be too disappointed when she revealed there wasn't an interview.

Kenny stood next to a counter, wiping away crumbs. Maybe it was the sight of tiny, toasted bits of bread, but her nose found the trays of cooling rolls and the basket of yesterday's baguettes, and her stomach lurched. Bread had always been her weakness. And butter. Thick, creamy, salty butter smeared over a piece of warm toast. Nirvana.

"You bake here?" She heard the longing in her voice and hoped Rudy would steer her toward an office instead.

Kenny chuckled. "Our first-time guests almost always worship the pastry chef. She makes magic with dough."

"I thought you had an actual bakery where bread would be baked."

Rudy reached into his apron and withdrew a notepad. "We do, but our chef likes to prepare here because it's quiet and cool in the mornings. She has the place to herself and is much happier that way."

Watching him scribble a note, she saw the addition was one more on a lengthy list of reminders. She wondered about his methods for maintaining staff. Toss in his family, and now the food festival, and she wondered that he didn't show her the door. He was the last man in the city who'd have time for a casual date.

When she glanced up from watching him write, she saw his eyes fixed on her.

She forgot her hunger for bread.

"The office," he suggested.

"Yes." Following him to the glass-enclosed space, she knew there'd be no real privacy, but at least their voices would be muffled from the noise of cooks beginning the day's meal preparations. "Every time I'm here I realize there are so many more layers to running a restaurant that I'd never considered."

"Most are things they don't teach in culinary school, either."

Rudy closed the door as she settled onto the chair across from the desk. "Just to be clear, there's no phone call with the magazine. I invented the distraction."

"I figured."

"And I'm sorry I complicated an already hard situation."

Rudy sat on the corner of his desk, a leg dangling close to hers. "I'd never intended for you to meet Hannah. She flew back early and was mad because I've met her ridiculous requirements for keeping Luna over the summer. She was looking for me to fail. Something new to hold over my head."

Lacy leaned back in her chair, relieved she wasn't in a custody battle. The spikes in these taunts caused wounds. "It sounds like Luna is the one who gets hurt."

Rudy ran a hand over his beard. "I wish I knew the real reason Hannah cut the week short."

"This happens often?"

"More times than I can remember. It's a power play, which is why I refuse to push back. I hope she'll tire of the game and let Luna have some continuity."

Sitting forward, she put a hand on his knee. "Luna adores you. It shows every time I've seen you together."

He paused. "I'd be lost without her."

"Well, let's make sure there's nothing that stands in the way of her spending the summer with you." Lacy may not have walked in his shoes, but she knew what it was like to not have a father. "How can I help?"

Standing, he walked to the window overlooking the kitchen. "Thanks, but I think keeping Luna's life as uncomplicated as possible is the best I can offer her right now."

His words rolled through her brain, landing on a tender memory from the park yesterday. "By uncomplicated do you mean that you don't want me spending time with her?"

He whipped around. "No, that's not what I meant at all. I like you, Lacy. And Luna thinks you're a princess. You're now part of our complicated world if you're willing to stick with us."

A knock against the glass shattered Lacy's surprise.

"Chef?"

They both glanced at Kenny. "My mom has texted that Luna is throwing a tantrum about having to pack. What should she do?"

Rudy sighed. "Let her kick. Hannah started this when she came back from New York earlier than she'd arranged. She can deal with the outcomes."

Kenny blanched. "My mother doesn't allow tantrums. *Ever*."

"Then I'll trust her to deal with it. Luna needs to respect her authority, or this will never work in the long term."

Shaking his head, Kenny stepped back into the kitchen.

Rudy held his hand toward Lacy, inviting her to stand. "I love my daughter, but she won't control my reactions. That's why I've hired Mrs. Lin. I finally met someone who can be a reliable nanny and allow me to run my business."

Regretting the loss of his touch, she reminded herself that his life was too complicated for a romance. Even if she was aching to see where they might go. Better to switch to the thing she knew she could control. "In that case, let's set up some short films for Instagram."

He held open the door. "Come help me choose ingredients. We'll determine recipes after we see what the delivery truck brought us in the way of vegetables. Then we can talk about what to cook."

Busying herself with the phone, she peeked at him asking, "Do you always wait to determine your menu based on what's available?"

"Always." He stepped into the kitchen, seeming to bask in the normality of noise. "I have basics that can be produced because the food products are available year-round, but we invent menu specials based on what the grocer has in his inventory."

"So, you're at their mercy?"

"I prefer to think of it as a challenge. I keep my expectations sensible and let myself be surprised by the offerings." Pointing out a delivery box sitting on a counter, he glanced in. "He's going to provide what is growing seasonally, and that allows me to offer my guests fresh recipes. Along with the favorites everyone loves."

She wondered if he had a recipe for balancing his personal life too. Or did he make that up based on what was going on around him? "I read many of your online reviews, and guests frequently mention your French Fries. What makes them so special?"

He shrugged. "I have no idea. We get potatoes, peel them, cut them, soak them in some ice water. They look rather imperfect, but I prefer that."

"You mean the fries don't come frozen?"

He selected a big Idaho potato from the box. "We cook from the original form."

"I adore French fries, they're my comfort food when I'm stressed."

"We'll make some today." He winked. "Not that you're stressed around here, right?"

Kenny sorted the vegetables into stacks, pulling leaves and stems as he inspected. While he and Rudy discussed the delivery, she studied the kitchen. The rolling racks with the bread drew her eye, but then she saw the footprint for cooking stations within the bigger space. A bricked pizza oven anchored one corner, and industrial ovens and ranges divided the three remaining areas. Underneath the stainless-steel shelf that circled the room, filled with plates, pans, and transparent storage bins, she saw that one range had a wide griddle and space to cook multiple products under a monstrous vented hood.

Every area had a supply of seasonings and oils, bowls, and utensils.

He nudged her shoulder. "Ready to get to work? You'll need an apron. Wouldn't want to ruin those jeans."

Kenny whispered loudly. "Love the wedges, too."

Six months ago, she would have happily promoted her shopping links to anyone who wanted to copy her style. Today? She felt chagrined. Her wardrobe was designed with whatever was easiest to reach and appropriate for the weather.

"Point me in the right direction, Chef, and I'll suit up."

Kenny set down an artichoke. "I'll show you the lockers. You can store your purse in my cubby."

In the hallway, Kenny closed in on Lacy's shoulder. "Can I post a photo that you're in our kitchen today, working with Chef? I don't have a ton of followers, but there are some folks who'd think this was a kick."

"I don't mind, but between you and me, I haven't announced a return to my sites. I haven't figured out what I'm going to do yet."

Stepping aside so another cook could pass, Kenny asked, "You will go back to Insta, right? You made it all so fun."

Fun. Not meaningful. Not life-changing, just lighthearted banter that distracted folks from important stuff in the world. "After six months away, it feels a little frivolous."

"What would you do," Kenny showed her into the break room, lined on one wall with locker space and pegs for coats, "if you didn't show everyone the latest looks from Texas designers?"

She pulled out a small ring light and a portable microphone and set her bag in Kenny's locker. "I'm swamped with the food festival, so maybe I'll showcase area growers and restaurants."

"You mean like a critic?"

She laughed. "I'm only just now understanding that there is more than one kind of salt. I'm the last person who should critique someone's cooking. But—" The idea bloomed in her mind. "I could be—in my goofy way—a portal for introducing followers to the food scene around them."

Kenny stared at her like she'd become a blemished tomato.

Shrinking from his gaze, she wondered if there were already a hundred Austin bloggers doing the same thing. TV jobs had flooded her email, and even an investigative-reporters pool in Dallas, but she wondered if she could dive into those careers. "I don't have to decide anything today. I still have a rural newspaper to run, so this thing I'm doing for Stella's today is on the side."

"Did you know Chef had once considered opening a bistro in Comfort?"

She slammed the locker with too much force. "Rudy in Comfort?"

"Yeah, he was serious, too. I worked with him on the wedding feast, and he was inspired." Kenny reached for a spare apron and showed her how to wrap it around her waist. "I expected him to announce he was chucking this to become a farmer or a vintner. He brought back soil samples to have them analyzed."

Tying the apron ends into a bow, she pictured Rudy working in a restaurant set in a town favoring bacon-centered menu items. Wearing his white chef's uniform, he'd stand on the sidewalk, begging tourists to discover his menu. The ranchers wouldn't race over for truffle potatoes or salmon. They'd probably rally to High's Café to protect them from the invader.

She hated that pitiful image for Rudy. "Not all dreams come true, do they?"

Kenny stepped aside so she could move from the room. "Mine haven't. I always thought I'd be a head chef by now."

"Really?"

"I guess I could if I invested in my own place. But I'd rather work for Chef and not have all the pressure he deals with every day." Kenny sighed. "But, man, you should have seen us at the James Beard. We fired on all cylinders."

Hannah's words taunted. "But I thought Stella's was out of the running."

"Yeah. Some judges got sick."

"So, was it your cooking or because judges picked up a stomach bug?"

"At first, they blamed us, our products. But it was a virus going around. The news came too late to change our place in the judging. But who knows, maybe Chef will do it again. I don't know."

Filing away those details, she'd pen her posts to counter feedback from those who may have heard about the James Beard competition.

Kenny checked his phone. "Aw, man. Mom is ticked. She and Mrs. D must have butted heads." Panic played behind his eyes, as if he were the one who would pay if his momma were unhappy. "I can't deal with tears, you know?"

There had been some knock-down, wailing encounters with her sister and two crazy cousins, but she had a hard time picturing Mrs. Lin pulling anyone's hair. "Who's crying now?"

"No one, yet. But if Mrs. D keeps stirring stuff up, Mom will quit. She'll move back in with me. Then I'll be the one crying. I'm twenty-nine. I'm too old to live with my mom, you know?"

Patting his shoulder, she bit back a smile. "I'm sure you're going to be fine."

"Fat chance," Kenny said dragging his feet. "Mom is loaded and owns a big house. She's renting it to my cousin right now because she's moved into Chef's condo, but if she quits, she will kick me out of my room. I need Mrs. D to back off."

"Try sending her daisies."

"What?"

Lacy grinned as she entered the kitchen and saw Rudy had set a dozen Idaho potatoes on a chopping block, along with a razor-sharp knife. He admired her apron while tossing a peeler in his palm.

"The worst is never the worst," she said. "So maybe this will blow over."

"Said no one ever." Kenny sighed. "She's all yours, Chef. I'm stepping into the cooler to chill my nerves."

Rudy's smile was for her alone. "Best news of my day."

Chapter Twenty-Three

Standing in Gloria's kitchen, surrounded by all the latest gadgets, should feel inspiring. But Lacy stared at the brutalized potato in her hand, thinking this process did not feel as efficient as it did when she was with Rudy. Everything seemed better with him, but he'd insisted that making French fries was entry-level cooking. So why did she feel so inept?

"I don't think we're doing this right," AJ complained as she shook out the tension in her hand. "My potatoes are limp."

"We're going to quick-fry them, then keep them warm in the oven, and fry them again." Lacy fished a handful of spud lengths from a bowl of starchy water. "Trust me, I know what I'm doing."

"Trust you?" Kali laid a knife down on Gloria's heirloom chopping block. "I don't even know how you lured us here to cook tonight. Wine must have been mentioned. AJ, was wine mentioned?"

"Wine was mentioned." AJ chuckled and lifted her empty glass. "But I'm all for pretending I didn't hear it the first time."

Lacy tossed a dishcloth at her sister. "Cooking is a process, not a means to an end."

"Oh, one weekend with Chef Delgardo and now she's the expert." Kali tipped a bottle of Fume Blanc to her glass and poured generously. "Or was it two weekends?"

Lacy studied the thermometer in the deep pot rather than answering her sister. The less those two knew about the time she spent with Rudy, the better.

As it was, she was a little fuzzy on the specifics.

After that first supper at Falcon Ridge, the days rolled into one bliss-colored montage of cooking, eating, and talking. Somewhere along the way, she'd started thinking of Rudy as a friend. Probably too soon, but he was as fascinated with her story as she was with his. And, icing on the cake, he had no clue about Amy Marsh. Even cared less after hearing the messy legal issue. He'd walked into his home kitchen, tuned the radio to some classic-rock station, floured a board, and begun making pasta. The more they'd kneaded dough, the more she vented about how hard it was to create a voice in a world jam-packed with people yelling for attention on various media platforms. As they were hanging strands of linguine to dry, he'd said, "Quit yelling."

Stop competing. Just like that.

She'd stared like he was the second most brilliant human being—after Gloria, of course.

The thing she appreciated about an older man was that he'd figured out listening was as beautiful as sharing. He talked, too. Their hours together weren't one sided. She knew volumes about the history of food and cooking methods, but very little about his past, and that was okay, for now. It would come out one day.

The afternoon she'd spent with Christopher paled in comparison.

Eventually, Luke needed the apartment for his Austin meetings, and she'd run out of reasons to stay away from Comfort. Rudy needed to deal with the onset of the South by Southwest tourists who'd booked reservations months in advance. She'd packed her luggage, loaded into the Ford, and returned to the cottage behind Gloria's house, only to discover that Gloria had moved to Frank's. Permanently.

She wanted to be with Frank through the hard weeks and months ahead, as he had no one else, and there was plenty of room in the enormous house in Kerrville. Since that had been their home when they were married, she'd said it felt like sliding on a favorite pair of slippers.

Insisting Lacy live in the bungalow, Gloria enjoyed thinking the house was occupied and being useful instead of collecting dust. That meant learning to use the lawn mower and pulling weeds in the garden, but Lacy considered labor a minor exchange for the privilege of luxurious bedding, big-screen TV, and a kitchen that should be featured in a design magazine.

"What else are you dropping into the boiling fat?"

Lacy glanced over at Kali, who should have shaved Parmesan for the French fries. "I have green tomatoes I bought at the farmer's market. They're prepped and on a cookie sheet."

"You shopped a farmers market?" Kali set down the grater. "Seriously, I don't know who you are anymore."

AJ held her wineglass close to her lips. "We're witnessing the second coming of Lacy Cavanaugh."

"Funny," Lacy said, careful to dab the potatoes with a paper towel before she dropped them into the oil. "I assure you, nothing so transformational. But though I came to Comfort kicking and screaming, I have to think the last few months have been good for me. Maybe I've grown up. Who knows?"

"Ease me into this." Kali read the label on the Parmesan cheese. "You're about to tell us you're moving to Austin? Please, at least, say you'll wait until after the food festival? We can't pull this off without you."

"I'm not moving." She watched the potatoes fry. She'd thought about relocating. She'd checked rental rates, followed up on the job offers from local TV stations, and considered sharing an apartment with a college friend. Nothing felt right. She'd lived on her own too long to settle in with a roommate again, and the idea of primping every day for a news camera felt daunting. Driving back to Comfort, she'd wondered if she'd lost her mind. Everything she'd wanted was being offered to her on a platter, but she held back. "I'm not opposed to borrowing your condo next time you guys have a free weekend. It's expensive to stay in the big city."

AJ toasted Lacy with her glass. "Anytime. Luke's there more than I am because he has clients in Austin. I go during the slow season, and we all know I won't see slow again until mid-July. I kind of wish we'd waited to offer the food festival in the fall when I'm less busy and the weather is kinder."

"But we'd miss out on potential summer revenue," Kali insisted. "I have talked with three brides who are driving in next week to check the space for their weddings."

"I'm not sure who's going to rent it right off the bat. It will still smell like sawdust. And it will cost a fortune to cool, too. Have we figured utilities into the rental fees?"

Kali shrugged. "I've given it a good guess, but we won't know a definite cost until we've hosted a few events."

The three women grew quiet. Popping oil made the only sound.

Lacy lifted the slotted spoon and pulled a few samples out, checking the crispness and accidentally spilling the fries to the counter. "For the cook," she claimed.

Kali sighed. "I wish I'd filmed this. Jake will not believe Lacy is cooking."

AJ picked up the salt grinder, ready to sprinkle the fries being transferred to a paper-towel-lined tray. "Sure he will. Look at all she's accomplished since she's been home. Shaping up our little newspaper and making it feel fresh. Getting you and me onto social media, to the point that we need to hire someone to post content every day, and now we're weeks away from launching a food festival." The golden potatoes piled on the tray, and AJ snitched one even as the salt melted. "Oh. My. Word."

Lacy grinned, knowing Rudy would pat her on the shoulder and remind her she knew more than she gave herself credit for. He'd teased her that all she needed was practice and a willing audience. "Kali, grab that bowl and we'll mix the fries with the cheese, a little truffle oil, and some fresh garlic. Then you'll think you've died and gone to heaven."

Five minutes later, Kali was groaning in delight. "Please tell me there are more fries?"

"Nope." Lacy wiped her salty fingers on a dishcloth. "I had to buy the potatoes in Austin because I knew they wouldn't have this type at Safeway. But the next time someone heads near a high-end grocery store, we'll ask them to bring us back an inventory."

"What if we had a French fry station at our festival?" AJ ran her finger through the remaining cheese and oil. "We could sell them in those cute paper cones, and kids would beg for them."

Soon the conversation dovetailed into details and the timeline. Construction boomed ahead of schedule, so they could move the furniture they'd ordered and set up booths for the vendors who wanted to be indoors. Lacy couldn't wait to tell them about the chefs she'd called and the connection she'd made to a local hunting club. Fingers crossed, they hoped to have ten cooks with travel trailers and a variety of menu items. AJ agreed to send each cook a generous bag of lavender herbs in case they were willing to mix their recipes to highlight the lavender farm.

"But we still haven't settled on a name for the event hall." Kali finished the last of the fried green tomatoes and leaned back in her chair. "What do you think if we offered a naming contest?"

Popping the top on a bottle of sparkling water, Lacy poured bubbles into their glasses. "That might be fun, but you could get weird suggestions too."

"I'd want us to have final say on any name." AJ sipped her water. "If we're investing in this building, we should get to name it. I still like Lavender Hill Hall."

"A mouthful." Kali picked up a pencil. "Let's table the idea for now."

Lacy glanced at the notes laid around the table. "But we have our plan? Our duties?"

AJ and Kali nodded. "We'll handle the logistics, you handle the PR."

They made it sound so easy. As if a carefully worded email could round up the region's reporters, bloggers, and vendors. Most of those professionals were immune to the deluge of cute prompts and gifts designed to influence them. She'd have to invent something unique to be worthy of viral attention.

"I'll work with the designer to get the website perfected and set up the remaining social-media accounts." Lacy wondered if she could lure any of her Dallas friends to come south. "I want y'all to have a Pinterest page too. Brides will want to see the possibilities here, and we may have to stage a few bridal portraits at the start, just to show the potential. We can create a page on the website for links for those who sign a release form to share their photographer's work."

Kali scribbled a note. "I can call a photographer in San Antonio and tell her we'd like her help to lure her upcoming portraits to come west. Brides in the lavender field would be an unforgettable collection. AJ, are the plants blooming yet?"

"It's early. Another few weeks and there will be more color."

Imagining the shots staged with soft lighting, happy brides, and pops of color in the bouquets, Lacy imagined a list of hashtags as she collected the plates. "I'm willing to model for you, if you need something to post on the site a little faster."

AJ and Kali glanced at each other. "The Blonde Goddess as our featured bride would be a triumph."

The sooner that moniker vanished, the happier Lacy would be. The months away from the fashion epicenter of Texas had softened the color of her hair and reminded her why she'd never loved high heels. Those closest to her may have not noticed the changes, but she'd let go of some of the sass and vinegar, too.

"At the very least I'd be agreeable to being staged for various settings. No groom, of course. But with the strings of lights installed next week between the event hall and Lavender Hill's shop, we could set shots with the plants in the garden center and even around the fire pit."

Kali clapped. "I wish I wasn't so much shorter so you could borrow my wedding dress."

AJ brightened. "My dress was for a winter wedding, but I bet we could ask Colette if she knows someone who would loan us a dress. As our architect and decorator, she's bound to have connections."

"We'll need a florist on the cutting edge of design." Kali turned to Lacy. "Do you have friends in the floral business? Besides Drue. I don't think she's done anything original in ages."

A memory of a white tower of daisies came to mind. "Let's not write Drue off. I'll visit with her and see if she's willing. She could pull something together quickly."

They made a few notes about advertising the bride's-room setup and also decorating a groom's room at the event hall. They giggled about whom they might recruit to be the fake groom in the photos, and Lacy begged them to stop. Deputy Mayne was the leading contender, but she'd not talked to him since the arrests. He'd been interviewed by every news outlet in the region, and she'd facilitated some follow-up stories in the last two editions of the paper, but that was as close as she wanted to be to the realities of the extreme sadness of human trafficking. She hoped when the perpetrators went to trial, she'd be far away from the media circus.

AJ stood and reached for the wine bottle. "This is fantastic. It's like everything has finally gelled. We have the chef, a roster of cooks with grill trailers, wine vintners willing to participate, the construction is on target, and our website is almost ready to go live. What could go wrong now?"

Chapter Twenty-Four

Rudy helped the busboy carry the trash bags to the dumpsters, enjoying the heavy lifting. He'd like to toss several more bags, possibly a few bricks, to ease the tension in his shoulders.

Meal service tonight had been predictable. Numbers were down after the South by Southwest festival, and several of his staff asked for time off. But a slow night was not the root of his dysfunction. Something crueler brewed.

Something rotten.

Stella's had reached a plateau, and regular customers ordered their favorite menu options without interest in the specials. He'd asked Kenny to scout the competition and see if they'd overlooked a food trend, or if the moderate profits resulted from levelling after a busy year.

His normal, rational thought processes didn't tame the taunts from Hannah.

After ten years, he had thought he'd seen all the mysteries in his ex-wife, but he'd misjudged her. These phone calls and emails about the tanking of his reputation following the James Beard fiasco were part of a scripted plan. That nervous tick in her voice gave it away. But why?

He'd compensated her for Stella Too's, a requirement of the divorce agreement. He'd never missed child-support payments. What more could she want?

"Chef?"

He glanced at the busboy, reflected in the glow of a security lamp.

"Do you want me to deliver the leftovers to the shelter since Kenny isn't here tonight?"

He nodded. "Keep what you'd like for your family. I hear your mother is still sick."

"Thank you, Chef."

He stepped indoors, grabbed his keys and wallet, then helped the busboy load pans into the backseat of a compact. He set the alarm on the building and watched the taillights disappear. For the first time in days, he was alone.

Cooler air circled him, and the silence of the night softened the edges of his thoughts.

Pocketing his keys, he started walking. Pacing his steps, he applied logic to ideas that defied any order of fairness. What was Hannah's point in hurting him?

Had he been so horrible to her that her revenge wouldn't be complete without cutting off Luna and taking away the restaurant? He'd failed their relationship more times than he could count, but he'd not been unfaithful to Hannah. He wondered if the same applied to her. The rumors had been hard to ignore, but he never pursued them. He hadn't wanted to ruin his wife; he'd just wanted to be free of her unhappiness.

Running his hand through his hair, he remembered her calling to announce the pregnancy. He'd already moved to Texas by then, accepting a position at the Barton Creek Resort. A fresh start, that's what he'd told his grandmother.

Hannah followed him to Austin, moved in, and they were married within weeks. Their marriage surprised his parents, but they understood and welcomed another grandbaby to their growing brood.

The days working the hotel kitchen were long, hot, and repeated weekend after weekend. About a year into it, some regular guests approached him about opening his own place. They'd courted him with a kitchen where freedom and money were not limited, and he'd jumped at their offer with both hands. Hannah had gloried in the dramas of opening a restaurant in an up-and-coming neighborhood, but eventually she grumbled. He was at work more than he was ever at their apartment.

Luna was a colicky baby; she didn't sleep well, and never wanted to be out of her mother's arms. He'd not been sensitive, but Hannah's flights away from home began before Luna's first birthday, and it took him a while to appreciate how motherhood drained her of energy.

A dog skittered by, surprising him. Snapping away from questions with no answers, he reached into his pocket to pull out his phone. Almost two. No wonder he was spinning circles in his head.

Disgusted with how he'd wasted a walk on unproductive thoughts, he unlocked his car and threw himself into getting home. Mrs. Lin would snore, and he could sit and nurse a whisky while he dug through last month's financials.

But even in his living room, every thought returned to Hannah.

Diminishing reservations—she'd been the administrator of all their advertising.

Waitstaff slipping away—her best friend had been head hostess.

What clue was he missing?

He set aside Jay's notes and wondered if there had been significant press from the James Beard fallout. Calling up Twitter on his laptop, he read through the Stella's posts, seeing nothing unusual. There were a few tweets tagging Stella's and smearing them with lies about inspection reports. He followed back to see who sent these, but it was some random person with a temporary history. He couldn't determine anything significant about the account. Maybe Lacy could dig better, but he'd write this off as nonsense.

There were several tweets from Alan Gale with the usual posturing, and he'd dismiss them by considering the source. Other than those, there wasn't anything as dangerous as what Hannah had alluded.

His eyes blurred reading the screen, and he shut down his laptop with a thud. Unhooking the buttons on his uniform, he slipped the shirt off and tossed it into a pile for the dry cleaner. Rubbing his eyes, he longed for something he didn't know.

It hovered beyond his periphery, and he could almost smell warm, summer grass—like the pastures surrounding his grandmother's property in Sonoma. A simpler time. A curl of fragrance wove around his mind. Was it lavender?

Swallowing the last of the whisky, he dropped the glass in the sink and shut off the lights in the living room. As he climbed the stairs, he remembered the last time he'd smelled something like that, and he'd been with Lacy.

He wondered what she was doing now that she'd returned to the newspaper office. Picturing her in that environment didn't add up, but she sounded energized about the community and the ideas for progress she wanted to inspire. Or maybe he was painting everything she said in lilac colors because being with her was like sitting across from the embodiment of his best dreams.

Scrubbing a hand over his beard, the bristles startled his nerves.

She'd been through tough times and could smile, finding the humor in being banished to a small town, doing things she'd never imagined were in her skill set. It was like she'd found solace in Comfort. Her trials had weaned her off things that brought her trouble, and she'd found hope for better days.

He needed comfort in his life too. Or maybe he just needed Lacy.

Walking into his room, he didn't bother with the lights. He could feel his way around the routine. Falling onto his bed, his imagination settled into the comfortable niche he'd carved for her. The fantasy of a vineyard, a house, and restaurant where dining rooms opened to the air, customers were always happy, and he could live every day basking in the glow of a woman who had unlocked his heart and gave him back the gift of laughter and love.

Chapter Twenty-Five

Lacy sat across from Frank in his spacious living room. Perched on the edge of the sofa, she looked at the shell of a man sitting in a club chair with a blanket over his legs. She'd once thought he would never choose to smile. Now she wondered if he even could. Shorn of his hair, gaunt beyond belief, his eyes glassy orbs in a face held together by leathered wrinkles, he gripped the hand of a woman who'd shown him immense kindness and forgiveness.

Lacy glanced at Gloria, brightened by the colors in her dress, and saw a strength in her eyes that was big enough for both of them. This is who Lacy wanted to be when she grew up. Not only was Gloria intelligent, savvy to the world, and fit, but her gray hair was stylishly cut in a swingy bob and her makeup always made her skin glow like she was lit from within. Months ago, she'd assumed that there was nothing Gloria couldn't accomplish once she put her mind to it— the woman had conquered making croissants, and that was epic. But this? Returning to a man who had few friends and offering him care at his weakest time? That, she didn't understand.

Frank had called this meeting an hour ago, and she had dropped her work at the office to drive Interstate 10 and be at his door five minutes before he expected her. She knew how pleased he was when someone came early to an appointment. Timing was everything with him, and he had no patience for lollygaggers. She'd had to Google that word the first time she'd heard him use it.

Frank handed her a letter, addressed to his attorney, and she knew from experience this meant she was to read the contents and not bother commenting because it was a done deal. The man was a master with words, and she'd never dream of editing him. But as she read the sentences, she wondered if this was real. She flipped the letter over, looking for the punch line.

"Frank, this is insane." Lacy wanted to run, cry, scream at the unfairness of life. Instead, she reached across the space and wrapped her fingers over his twiggy bones. "You cannot gift me the newspaper."

"I can do whatever I damn well please," he said, with a fraction of his usual vinegar. "And I want you to have it. It won't make you a fortune and will probably cause you no end of indigestion, but you've got the spirit of a communicator, and if anyone can make that thing work, it will be you."

"I have no words."

"You don't need any, other than 'thank you.'" Frank's best offer of a grin widened his mouth. "What you did with that story about the girls, caught in a trafficking sting was top-notch reporting. Though it kills me to say, I couldn't have done a better job."

Praise from the one who'd taught her—could any words mean more?

"Though I don't understand it, that experience has changed me."

"It's honed you. Focused you. You're a natural-born observer, and that's the key ingredient. Technique can be taught, instincts can't."

She looked down at her soft, pliable fingers wrapped over his bony ones. The contrast resonated in her heart and gave her a sense of belonging.

"I have no intention of staying in the Hill Country." Lacy mostly believed her words. She'd had a callback from a TV station in Waco, and the Dallas paper wanted her to drive in for an interview. Every time she pictured herself in a courtroom or chasing a police car to a crime scene, she saw a vast blankness. Squeezing her lids shut, she forced herself to walk in the shoes of reporters and, inevitably, she'd trip over something simple. "I'm going to make my way in a place that knows how to think in twenty-first-century lingo. This paper would tie me to Comfort."

"Then hire someone to run it for you and keep the proceeds." Frank glanced over at the contract Gloria had set on the table. "I know you need a source of income, and this paper can keep a roof over your head."

Letting go of his hand, Lacy leaned back in the chair. She was breathing his oxygen, and it made his words sound sensible.

Gloria smiled with serenity. "I'm going to need someone to rent my house. I'll stay here, even after . . . and I want you to live in the bungalow. You love the place like I do, and those walls need someone who is sympathetic to their creaks and groans."

Lacy put a hand on her feverish forehead. "This conversation feels weird."

"Well, I feel weird, but there's nothing to be done about that," Frank said. "I trust you, and I think you're up to the task. I'll parcel off the rest of the papers, as I think I've got a buyer for the one here in Kerrville. But I'm giving you the *Comfort News* because it needs you as much as you need it. Locals respect you, and that's a big part of making a community paper work. Besides, if anyone can figure out how to make newsprint successful in this age, it's going to be someone young and courageous."

A film of tears blurred Frank's image. "How can you say that? I came to you at the lowest point in my life and fumbled every task you gave me."

"And yet, you were brave enough to expose something everyone else had turned a blind eye toward. We don't have enough folks like that in our world, and I know I speak for Comfort when I say, that's the kind of person we want reporting the news."

Wiping her cheeks, she processed his words and tried to make sense of the emotions.

Gloria sat down on the sofa, sinking next to her. She wrapped her arm around Lacy's shoulders, leaning close to her ear. "You may not think this is what you want for the rest of your life, but maybe it's what you need for the now."

For the now.

Later, as she walked out of the limestone-and-wood ranch house, she kicked at the gravel and breathed deeply of the scorching air blowing across the hilltop. Staring over the split-rail fence that separated what passed for a yard from the pasture, she wondered what had just happened. She'd driven here to comfort Frank. Her gifts had been another can of his coffee and cigar-shaped chocolates. He'd laughed until he started hacking, and then Gloria had to give him a hit of oxygen.

Somewhere between delivering Frank the mail stacked on his desk and sipping the chamomile tea offered, she'd been gifted a newspaper. Christopher had drawn up the paperwork, and all she had to do was sign to receive a pocket industry with one employee.

Lacy walked to the fence and propped a heel on the bottom rail for support. Leveraging herself off the ground, she gazed beyond the cactus and weathered lavender shrubs to see the long view. The clock tower at city hall, cattle ponds, roads winding in, out, and around the town, and rooftops galore. What she didn't see were skyscrapers, a pollution cloud, or traffic. There were pros and cons to be considered in accepting Frank's gift.

"Lacy?"

She turned around, seeing Gloria step off the front porch and cross the gravel. "Please don't tell me there's more. I'm barely holding myself together as it is."

"He hated for you to see him like that, but it couldn't be helped. He's a proud man. I know you understand."

She brushed her eyelashes free of the damp. "If he's gifting me the paper, does that mean he's not going to recover? Even just a little bit?"

Gloria placed her hand over Lacy's on the rail. "Life is a vapor, and no one is promised old age."

She shook her head, picking up a scent of the dreaded lavender. "I can't bear that right now. Frank is rock solid. He's like Mount Rushmore, all the heads rolled into one craggy mess."

Gloria chuckled. "He'd like that analogy, but it would go to his ego to find out you respected him that much."

Lacy stared into the distance. "It's funny, isn't it? When I first came to Comfort, I couldn't stand Frank. I thought he was a dinosaur and a grump. I watched the clock to flee the first moment the hand marked my daily hours."

"I'm sure he was aware. Nothing gets past him."

She turned to stare at her friend. "Even you?"

A smile played on Gloria's lips. "That's a story for another day."

Stepping away from the rail, Lacy pushed hair behind her ear. "I can't do it. I can't take the paper."

"Don't make any decisions right now. Let the news settle on you. Think, ponder, and play with the ideas." Gloria folded her arms over her chest. "You're a bright girl and probably have a million offers sitting on your desk after that story was picked up. But life is more than a shiny ball. It has edges, holes, and deep caves. Make a choice based on where you feel most grounded. Okay?"

That was impossible. The only place she felt grounded was here among the friends who'd seen her through her worst.

As she crawled into her car and raised the air conditioner to its highest blower option, she watched Gloria enter the house. With the high pitch to the roof, the dark wood, and enormous windows, it really looked more like a lodge.

Lodge. The word zipped through her mind, looking for a partner. She backed around the driveway and wondered why the letters flashed with neon colors. Then it hit her. Lavender. Frank grew lavender? How strange. What was he thinking? Lavender and lodge were about as manly as—Lavender Lodge!

She smacked her hand against the steering wheel. Why had they been so hung up on calling the Lavender Hill event center a hall? They could name it's sweeping roofline and gigantic windows a lodge, a barn, or a shed for that matter. But the double Ls would make an intriguing logo, and alliterations were easy to remember. *Lavender Lodge*. It rang with possibilities.

She'd have to call AJ and Kali with the idea on the way back to Comfort. But would she tell them about Frank's offer? Was she ready to hear their lectures about how she wasn't old enough to run a paper? Or that she was too flighty to settle down and follow city-council meetings? Or that she'd always sworn she'd never live in Comfort?

Yeah, that was the sticking point.

Driving down the hill, she knew she wanted to call someone. She needed to vent these things, and her current sounding board was sitting next to Frank's chair, checking his levels.

Second choice for understanding listener who didn't judge? Rudy.

He was so far outside her circle that he could see things clearly. He'd been intuitive about showcasing his sous chef on Instagram because Kenny would love the attention, and followers would like to see someone having that much fun with his work. When she fired up the laptop, she'd check Stella's newsfeed and stories to see if the magic formula for scheduling images had brought in as many new followers as she had predicted.

Driving into town, she pulled into a parking space near Red Bird's Soda Fountain. An ice-cream treat felt necessary after the shock she'd endured. But before she could pull the door open, her phone rang. Fishing it out of her purse, she checked the caller ID and saw a name that made her freeze.

She glanced around, wondering if she was being pranked.

As the tune continued to ring, she debated whether to answer. She would have thought she'd deleted this number, but when she activated a new iPhone all the old data stored from her previous phone downloaded.

Moving over to the awning's shade, she pushed answer and decided that if this day were going to get any weirder then this call made sense. "Hello?"

"Lacy."

"Amy."

She practically conjured Christopher's face and could see him staring at her agog. This wasn't breaking any of the family's mandates for her behavior. Besides, hadn't he told her all was forgiven now Amy had won the talent contest? Yes, he'd said those words.

She had nothing to fear.

And yet, her stomach knotted into a ball.

"How are you?" Amy Marsh asked with the same breathy airiness that led everyone to assume she was fifteen instead of twenty-nine.

Wow. After all the name calling, media shaming, and potential lawsuit, Amy was asking how she was? Like they were friends?

"I'm a little sweaty, Amy. It's ninety degrees here in the Hill Country. How are you?"

Amy tittered, like she'd always enjoyed Lacy's humor. Which she had, at first. Then the competition to win the hearts of the boys in the band started and then the Instagram spat. This wasn't one of those cases where when old friends reunite, it's like no time has passed. Not only had time passed, but so had a sentencing phase. Something was behind this random call, and she'd bet a double-dipped mint chocolate-chip cone that it was bad.

"I'm in a treatment facility in Santa Fe."

Surprised, Lacy held her breath, knowing there'd be more.

"And part of my wellness exercise is I have to make peace with the past." Amy sighed. "And that means forgiving you."

Releasing her breath, she tried to imagine Amy—raven-haired and fragile—submitting to the authority of a licensed counselor. Amy always fooled people into thinking she couldn't make her mind up about anything, but Lacy figured out that was a ruse to disguise how she controlled her choices and the people surrounding her. Remembering the lesson, she steeled herself for the real reason behind this phone call.

"And have you?"

"Have I what?"

"Forgiven me for revealing that your figure was carefully crafted, not a legitimate disease that cripples girls?"

The silence wrapped the miles in a gossamer banner of truth and cruelty. Lacy had exposed a lie and paid the price for it. She'd never fallen for the cries that Amy was caught in a cycle of purging because she'd lived with Amy for eight months in a travel trailer. She knew the truth.

"I have dealt with the issues I have with my parents, and part of that is finding out what was at the root of my weight roller coaster."

Lacy would site an unlimited supply of Doritos and six-packs of Miller, but she'd stopped caring about Amy's lack of self-control when she watched the girl rope the bandmates into carrying her load of work because she was "sick." On the pageant circuit she'd met too many girls caught in the grips of actual bulimia and anorexia to not recognize when someone faked a disorder. She was insulted on behalf of every girl who sat with a ghost every time they went to a table.

"I hope you've found what you needed, Amy. I mean that. Food is a necessary element of living, and there is real beauty in the process of preparing it and serving people who appreciate the effort. I hope you can enjoy that someday."

"I will. In a way, I have you to thank for that."

Observing a family pile out of their minivan and rush for the door at Red Bird, laughing about their reward for a morning of swimming lessons, she found words to reply. "I can't imagine how you'd thank me after I exposed your private life to the band's followers, but I'm grateful you can see positive come out of the year we knew each other."

"I ended up on top, so that worked out well for me. I'm also a size four now and have never looked better. My agent thinks I should apply for the next season of the *Bachelor* and see what a ratings boom that could become for me and the network."

Willing away the image of Amy sitting at a Santa Fe spa, sipping cucumber water, and gloating about her successes, Lacy squinted into the sunshine and imagined a happy place. Stella's came to mind. She could almost smell the focaccia bread and garlic butter.

"Lacy, are you there?"

"Yes, I'm glad you didn't suffer from the exposure on my site."

"Your Instagram accounts? Oh, please, like I didn't know you were following me around with a camera? It was so cute, how you thought you were in on some big secret. It was my thrill to get the better of the Blonde Goddess. God, how I hated that name. The guys drooled over you every time you walked by, blindly updating your posts and staging little scenes like you were some up-and-coming fashion designer."

Lacy stared hard at the Ford she'd bought a few months ago. "You manipulated me so I'd film you?"

"I have a disease." Amy sighed. "I don't do anything on purpose."

Every nerve cell stood tall and waved a flag to expose Amy for the fraud she still was, but a calming breath settled everything back in place. She wouldn't poke this bear. She'd put her life back together after Mr. Marsh had bullied her into a corner. She was about to inherit a newspaper. There was a sliver of a chance she and Rudy Delgardo would see each other again.

She. Would. Not. Rise. To. The. Bait.

Another deep breath.

"Of course, you do," Lacy said, forcing sincerity into her voice. She wanted to own these words, even if she had to leverage some of Gloria's strength. "And it's important you find the tools you need to succeed."

"Oh, dear." Amy chuckled. "Lacy Cavanaugh has become one of the good girls? Is that why you wrote that little report on—what was it—prostitution? Trying to out another girl just trying to make it in this world. I mean, I know you're scraping to get by and desperate to make a name for yourself, but that seemed a little far-fetched in a backwater town. I don't know why you always need to be the center of attention, but really, throwing insinuation and speculation around has got to stop."

Gasping, Lacy filed through her known connections to guess at who had sent Amy the articles. She'd not have found them sitting in a coffee bar in Los Angeles, scrolling through Snapchat.

Amy sighed "I'm at peace with how I was a trigger for your need to sensationalize things—my therapist says, talent always instigates jealousy in others—but, seriously, throwing that sweet, little town under the bus, and then suggesting that some young girls—probably trying to get into a legitimate modeling agency—were somehow being brainwashed? That's a stretch, even for me, and *I* live in Tinsel Town."

"I'm not going to argue with you about something for which you seem to be blissfully ignorant, but I will ask you to leave me alone." Drawing in a breath, she added, "I hope whoever is recording this call will note that *you* called me. Goodbye, Amy."

"Wait!"

Though it pained her to pause her finger over the disconnect button, she did. Instincts hummed that there was more to this call than checking off a box for a therapy session. "Yes?"

"I just want to say," Amy's voice dropped to a whisper. "I will come out on top, Lacy. Nothing you do, no amount of effort you put out, will *ever* overshadow me. You may think you're prettier, but I have the better gift—I'm smarter."

Silence buzzed in Lacy's ear, and she dropped the phone in her purse. Stung, but also rattled, she tried to guess why Amy still wanted revenge. Was winning the top prize, sitting on a pile of cash, and being American's darling not enough? No, it would seem that some people had a bottomless need.

God help her, she didn't want to ever become *that* person.

The legalese might cause her to stumble, but the reliability of providing the news, instead of being the news, was where she wanted to be. She'd sign Frank's contract tonight.

The mint-chocolate-chip buzz had evaporated. Tempted to return to the office and dig her frustrations into the template for next week's paper, she decided to walk along Baker Street instead, pounding pavement and staring into the storefronts as she let her thoughts fly. Hammering little images of Amy's face into the ground helped, but it didn't give her the satisfaction she craved.

She saw a reflection in the window of a shop and almost didn't recognize the disturbed woman staring back. That scowl was going to leave permanent grooves in her forehead. Rubbing at the wrinkles, as if she could make real life go away, she pursed her lips to bring back a rosy color and realized a truth her aunt had frequently stated: winning too much too soon could turn a person. Better to be the one everyone wished had been selected than the one they regretted choosing.

Turning away from her image, Lacy no longer wondered how she was going to compete against the Amys of this world. She'd redirect all that misspent energy into discovering who she was and how she could carve her own way forward. It might not be easier, but it was bound to be better than the hollowness she felt chasing fame.

Chapter Twenty-Six

Gathering with AJ, Luke, Jake, and Kali, Lacy stood on the drive of Lavender Hill's garden center and admired the pewter metal roof and copper downspouts of Lavender Lodge. From this angle, the lavender fields spilled away in even lanes, and their fragrance settled on them in a blanket of sunbaked goodness.

Jake held a chilled bottle of Veuve Clicquot they'd open to christen the building as soon as Beau and Collette drove in from San Antonio. Lacy held the basket of glassware.

A painter stood on the scaffolding, finishing the last strokes of an enormous mural, scrolling "Love grows here" along the side of the building. Lacy couldn't wait to post the first Instagram photo.

Tomorrow, when they staged the bridal photos, they'd shoot images in front of this wall. Latching onto the public-relations efforts proved she had skills communicating the brand of Lavender Lodge, but time would tell if the "love grows here" logo had sticking power.

"I'm excited," Kali beamed. "It's like the reveal party when we were expecting Charlie."

Jake side-hugged his wife. "And equally expensive."

Luke laughed. "Hey, the surprise supper for Beau and Collette had to happen tonight because she's about to pop with their baby. I'm not holding my breath she will feel like walking around to show off the details."

"It's been killing me to stay off the property this week while she decorates and completes tasks on the punch list." AJ nudged Lacy. "Some of us were tempted to sneak in, but we controlled ourselves."

"Barely," Lacy added. She'd lost steam for sneaky maneuvers because she was enduring a course in newspaper management from an instructor who wheezed. "Your saving grace is that spring overwhelmed you with customers and you're too exhausted to move in the evenings."

Luke nodded. "It took a caterer to make tonight's dinner party worth her while."

Ice bolted through Lacy. The freeze was a reaction to the word catering, not an uninvited image of Rudy, looking sexy in a black uniform with a long white apron.

Suddenly, she longed for the chef in a way she hadn't indulged for days. Between learning how to work with vendors who supported newspaper production, mowing Gloria's lawn, and collecting trash cans for her neighbors who were too old to roll them along their driveways, she was never able to call him at a time convenient for idle chatting.

He hid his phone in his desk during the hours he supervised the kitchen. Texting at odd hours seemed his first line of communication. With a few finely crafted cooking terms, he could make her think of things not edible. Putting a hand over the butterflies in her belly, Lacy watched the Jefferson's SUV drive toward Lavender Hill, spewing dust and gravel in their haste.

"Do they know we've named the place Lavender Lodge?" Jake asked. "We're going to have to explain the double L brand on the cookies if they haven't already heard."

"They know." Kali waved. "They agreed Lacy's wording was perfect."

Lacy tucked that sideways compliment into a pocket for later enjoyment. She'd not done many things perfectly during her time in Comfort, but suggesting the winning name gave her deep satisfaction.

While everyone hugged and teased Beau about being days away from surrendering his role as apple of Colette's eye, Lacy stepped back and shot a few images of the three couples bathed in a sunset glow. Their years of friendship, and now the joint effort at creating a building together, gave them an intangible bond that would lead them through life's moments.

She'd ask their permission before posting this to the new Lavender Lodge Instagram account, but she wasn't sure she'd tell them about the hashtag #lifegoals. They didn't need to know how jealous she was of their happiness or their settled status.

Committing to this nook on the Guadalupe River would be a death sentence for dating. All the good guys were taken, except the ever-present Deputy Mayne. He was easy on the eyes, if a little slow on making conversation. Besides, he was panting after Anna these days. Lacy had seen them chatting at last week's soccer game.

"Come over," Colette called to Lacy. "Let me take your picture. You look gorgeous. And I can't believe I'll ever be able to fit into a dress like that again."

The glistening halter dress, dug out from the days she'd haunted Neiman Marcus sales, was a go-to guaranteed to make a girl feel like a million bucks. The silky fabric twirled around her knees, and she always paired strappy heels to add even more length to her legs. Tonight, in honor of the location, she'd dug out her favorite cowboy boots instead. The juxtaposition between glam and ranch summed up the conflict in her soul these days. She wasn't sure what style bloggers would say about the pairing, but after all this time, she didn't care. They protected her toes from pebbles.

Digging into the basket, she pulled the champagne flutes and gave Jake a dishcloth to contain the cork when he twisted off the top. Passing around glasses of bubbly, they toasted a crazy, big idea that almost never happened.

"To AJ being so mad at Luke she decided to fund this thing," Kali toasted.

"That's how you remember it?" AJ asked, laughing.

"Of course." Kali sipped the golden liquid. "I think we were standing on this very spot when you turned to Colette and said, 'Let's do this.' That may not be an exact quote, but Colette and I were both stunned."

Colette Jefferson sipped her bottle of water and smiled. "I couldn't believe she said yes. I was sure she'd need months to think through the pros and cons of building an event center next to the lavender fields."

AJ shrugged then looped her arm through her husband's. "What can I say? My best decisions are the spontaneous ones."

The conversation nosedived toward how each couple almost didn't make it to the altar. Some stories don't bear the repeating, especially when Lacy's love life inspired no one.

Wandering to the end of the driveway, she stepped through the carport where Lavender Hill's composted soils were stored in wine casks, and she stopped at the edge of a sweeping hillside carpeted in young lavender blooms. A breeze stirred hair hanging loose behind her shoulders, and she wished for someone to share this moment.

They were here celebrating the birth of Lavender Lodge, but another fresh beginning hovered on the horizon. Though she'd not announced it, she'd signed the contract and mailed it to Christopher to file. The next edition would list her name at the top of the banner. Terrified of the responsibility, and despite all the middle-of-the-night misgivings, she was no longer a girl without a plan.

It had killed something within her to turn down the Dallas reporter job, but at the end of the phone interviews she never felt the same thrill of the scoop as the folks who led the conversations. Even with the lure of a salary, she'd already dreaded the idea of nosing into tragedies and fallouts. At least in sitting in the publisher's chair, she could choose which stories would get priority treatment, not be on the end that had to satisfy the news desk and the advertisers competing to outwit their adversaries.

Her caveat was that if she despised this job after a year, then she could hire an editor or sell the paper. But the unbeatable bonus was she'd live with her network of friends and family, she could watch Charlie learn to walk, and she could shepherd the event center along with nudges from local headlines.

It would be too easy to fall into despair that she had no one special to share recent ventures with, but for whatever reason, this just wasn't her time. Being single wasn't the end of the world. And when she wasn't hanging around the cheerful couples, she liked that state of mind. Just self-centered enough, she liked everything the way she liked it, and in this scenario, no one complained about dishes left in the sink.

She blinked away the image of Rudy's enigmatic eyes.

He wasn't in a place to begin something frivolous. If he took the plunge into a relationship, he would tow a child, a business, and an ex who still pulled strings. He'd made no promises he would pursue her, and she'd made none in return.

But still.

"Lacy?" Kali glowed. "I can't wait a moment longer."

Hurrying to join them, Lacy stepped over the flagstone path connecting the Lavender Hill shop to the outdoor patio decked with couches and bistro tables, lit by rows of string lights.

An arching, covered drop off-area connected the white-painted ranch house to the property and highlighted the front of the event center. That's where the bride's room and overflow bedrooms could be rented for accommodations. Colette said the muralist was busy removing her gear, so they'd enter through the rear patio because the three-story windows overlooking the lavender fields were most impressive at this time of day.

Lacy admired the fire pit at the far end of the patio. There was also a grill station built into the space that was ideal for outdoor catering. It took no effort to imagine Rudy and Kenny inhabiting that space with their tubs of marinated meat and a giant pepper mill, flames licking the grates. Her stomach growled, and she realized it had been hours since she ate anything more substantial than the granola she sampled at the Eighth Street Market.

Beau walked ahead and pushed back the disappearing glass sliders that united the indoor and outdoor spaces into one expansive room, as he did, he waited for Lacy. "Hey, I'm sorry for the texts I sent, accusing you of making stuff up about Comfort."

He was always going to be her friend, even from opposite sides of the table. "You are entitled to your opinions. Last I checked, it's a freethinker's paradise around here."

"Yeah, but it was more of a case of just because I didn't like the news, didn't mean I had the right to criticize it. I did some fact checking, and you were correct. That trafficking is nasty business."

She wished more readers were as openminded as Beau. "Thanks, that means a lot to me. I'm just getting started, and sometimes I overstep in my enthusiasm."

"Never stop overstepping on the truth, okay?"

She grinned. "Promise."

They entered the spacious indoor space on flooring recycled from wood harvested from area barns. The chandeliers were custom made with bits from recycled rakes and shovels and dripped with diamond-shaped crystals.

Colette had installed custom-crafted carpet along the walls, and the tufts and art of varying shades mimicked earth and sunlight. The wall carpeting absorbed sound and created an undulating form of art. The space was simple and efficient, yet a stage for any type of event.

"This is fantastic!" Lacy said, surveying an upstairs room with a ping-pong table. "You've thought of everything."

Kali wiped tears from her cheeks. "It's more than I could have ever hoped."

Colette collapsed into a leather recliner. "And I'm done. Between the last details and this baby, I could sleep for a week."

"Sleep now," Jake said, "because you won't once Jefferson Junior arrives."

Luke lifted his flute in salute. "And to celebrate this fine accomplishment, AJ and I are inviting you all back to our house for supper. We wanted to thank Beau and Colette for taking on this project and exceeding our expectations."

Beau grinned. "It was our pleasure. It gave me a reason to drive back to Comfort every week, and I can't tell you how much I miss this place. We're buying a cabin to have a getaway place for summers."

Lacy asked everyone to pose for photos. "In the spirit of celebration, do you mind if I share some of the pictures in the newspaper, as a forerunner to the ads about the food festival?"

"Sure," AJ said, "but won't Frank call this fluffy stuff?"

Returning her phone to her small bag, Lacy debated what to say. She didn't want to piggyback on their big night. "He won't mind."

"Since when?" Jake asked. "Frank has pushed back on anything that you've suggested."

"Frank isn't calling the shots anymore." There, she thought. Enough to stop the conversation without giving too much away. "Do you want me to turn out the light, Colette?"

"Hang on, everyone." Kali's eyes narrowed on her sister. "Why isn't Frank interested? Has he sold the newspaper?"

Lacy bit her lip. "Um, yes."

"Why didn't you say anything?" Kali emptied her glass. "Have you met the new owners? Are they going to let you run with the ideas you had for making the paper more reader friendly?"

Lacy glanced around the room decorated with antlers and vintage beer signs. "I've got a green light."

She closed the door behind them, wondering again why she so was so hesitant to tell them. Easiest to say she didn't want to distract from tonight's celebration, but underneath all that nobility she knew she didn't want to invite their second-guessing. The threat of failure smelled closer than she wished.

After ambling downstairs, they took another glance around the catering kitchen. Would Rudy approve their ideas? She didn't know how architects researched their plans, but she'd been to several party venues where it was apparent someone should have consulted professionals.

Snapping an image down the hall to the dramatic windows, it took less than a second to picture guests at the hunter-gatherer festival wandering around with plates of food. Luke had hired a jazz performer, and she'd bet they would position the musician on the corner stage.

Climbing into their cars later, everyone followed AJ and Luke to the dirt-topped road leading to their farmhouse. Parking near the oak tree, Lacy glanced across the valley and wished to one day have a home of her own. Moving into the bungalow was incredibly comfortable, but Gloria's perfume still hovered in the rooms. She wasn't sure what she could afford when the charity ran out, but she knew she'd want a modern space.

Two cars parked near the kitchen access, and she assumed those were the caterers. Someone had moved a dining table to the English's front porch, outfitted with linens, candlesticks, and crystal.

Kali and Jake climbed out of his truck, while Luke whistled for Beans, the family dog. Lacy didn't understand the fascination with dogs. Gloria had insisted on a no-pets contract when Lacy signed the lease for the guest house, and she'd not given it a second thought. Caring for animals, save what she'd learned rounding Kali's goats and chickens, had not been part of her education. Four-legged Rudy was a strange exception and she didn't like him anyway.

Climbing the steps to AJ's porch, she watched Colette and Beau park. They were opposites who seemed to make things work. Maybe it wasn't such a stretch to think that Rudy could get past their age difference, then they could have a chance too.

But Rudy came attached to a seven-year-old. Shuddering, she only recently figured out how to keep Charlie from slipping in the bathtub. She was the last person who should apply to become a stepmom.

"Come inside," AJ called from the open door. "We'll have cocktails in the living room and a special mocktail for the mom-to-be."

Lacy smiled at Colette's effort to waddle across the yard. "You want me to insist they make that a double?"

Colette rolled her eyes. "Between my heartburn and stretch marks, I'm not sure I can endure anything more than ice cubes."

Beau grinned, as if he couldn't be prouder of her suffering. "She'll forget all of this the moment Junior arrives."

Colette slugged his arm.

They moved into the foyer. Lacy stepped backward so Colette could clear the table boasting flowers and bridal photos, and when she did, she bounced into another person.

Turning to apologize, she saw eyes she dreamed about every night. "Rudy?"

He wore a gray T-shirt and a dishtowel tossed over his shoulder, but his smile radiated a look that had nothing to do with food. "At your service."

Chapter Twenty-Seven

Nerves skittered under Rudy's skin. He didn't doubt his abilities to cook for this party but hearing Lacy's voice shot his senses to high alert. The years rolled away, and he was thirteen, cooking an entire menu for the first time. Lacy wouldn't critique his risotto like his grandmother, but still, he wanted to please her to a level that defied logic. He needed her affirmation in a way that seemed to hold the world in balance.

Lacy had asked so little of him, but he didn't trust the goodness. His grandmother had had exacting expectations, and he'd overcompensated. The seeds that grew from that stone-and-spit soil in his soul taunted that he couldn't quite measure up. He'd have to work harder, faster, and with more skill—every single time. Over the years the taunts had somehow morphed into Hannah's voice, and somewhere along the way, he had begun to expect all women to grade him with a measuring stick too high for him to ever achieve anything of lasting value.

He didn't know what he expected from the surprise of meeting Lacy two months ago, but she was different, totally refreshing—the kind of woman he didn't know existed. It wasn't even her beauty that distinguished her because Texas seemed to be overrun by gorgeous women. No, it was an intangible resilience running hot under her fragile confidence. Her arms were always reaching for something new; she wasn't beholden to repeating the same tried-and true techniques every single day. Light followed her; she was the stars and the moonlight to the dark places in his heart, and he hoped they'd find some way to see each other after the festival.

Even Luna liked her. She'd drawn images of Cinderella with a wiry-haired dog, and he'd have to site blindness not to recognize a chef and a little girl in the royal family.

But he had to survive tonight. Then tomorrow morning, over frittatas, he could lure her back to Austin and into his life. From the moment Luke English had called to organize the surprise for their business partners, he'd planned this menu for Lacy. His only demand in agreeing to the request was that his role remain a secret. The element of surprise would reveal what their words had stumbled over these last few weeks.

Today in AJ's kitchen, when he and his youngest chef unpacked their equipment, AJ had chuckled and said Lacy would smell this ruse a mile away. She promised to keep the surprise but gave Rudy some details regarding festival promotions and development of the Lavender Lodge website, including the warning that Lacy would model a wedding dress tomorrow. She said she didn't want him to freak out if he happened to take a turn around the property and see her with the photographer. Though Lacy seemed immune to the effects of her exquisiteness, others had been known to gasp when she walked into a room.

He had plenty of experience being left speechless by her presence and having watched her approach the English's farmhouse minutes ago, he better understood AJ's warning. But he wondered if he was the only one who recognized how delicate she was underneath the glamour.

He wouldn't claim expertise because even now, in the English's foyer, he stood dumbstruck. A gold dress hugged her body, and his thoughts faded. The worn brown boots emphasized the shape of her legs and her seemingly innate ability to mix odd elements of wardrobe and make them sing. *Sing?* What glop did his mind produce now?

Her perfume floated under his nose, and he forgave himself.

The only thing grounding him was that he knew she was far more than a pretty shell; she was a lonely soul in search of mooring. If he were free to propose, he'd stop at nothing to put a ring on her finger. But his baggage weighed more than any dreams of happily ever after.

When she turned, her eyes wide with surprise, weights rolled off his shoulders. Her skin looked kissed by sunshine. He steadied her with his hands, his fingers memorizing the silky texture of her arms.

"I'm astonished," she said, her smile melting across her face. "Who's at Stella's tonight?"

"Kenny is running the kitchen. He needs the practice."

Leaning toward him, she said, "Then I hope he masters it. You could have a life if you didn't have to be in the restaurant every evening."

Seeing the years spill ahead in her eyes, he wanted more than anything to meet that goal, but even without Stella's, they'd have hurdles. "Jay tells me every week I have to learn to trust Kenny. We're getting there."

The urge to pull her closer, tuck her under his chin, and wrap his arms around her was too fascinating. He'd embarrass himself if he didn't bring some space to his thoughts. Stepping back, he reminded himself he had all night. This would be a supper with several courses.

Best of all, he didn't have to return to Austin until tomorrow afternoon.

"Will you introduce me around?" he said, removing the dishcloth and wiping his palms. "I've met AJ's husband, Luke, but everyone else looks like family."

"No. All friends. You'll like them. Luke and Beau are closer to your age than mine."

He brushed his lips against her ear. "You calling me an old man?"

"Does anyone question the Eiffel Tower? Some things are ageless."

"And I'm not one of them," he said with a chuckle.

Her grin lit a new fire in his soul, and he wrapped an arm around her waist. They followed the others into the living room, and he dropped his hand. He wasn't ready for her friends to analyze their relationship.

AJ raised a glass to Lacy. "See, we pulled off a surprise. And not just for Beau and Colette."

Lacy giggled. "I don't know what you're talking about, but I know we'll probably eat the best food we can imagine, so thanks for importing the talent."

"Plus," Kali rushed over, "we can iron out the last of the details before the festival opens in ten days."

The men introduced themselves, inviting Rudy to sit. He poured generous glasses of lavender-infused tonic and gin and settled on the sofa next to Lacy. Within moments the chatter about the event center bounced around the room, and no one seemed uncomfortable with him in the mix. Lacy included him in the talk about how the guests and cooks would move around the Lavender Hill grounds, and Jake had corrected some parking issues, asking his ranch hands to look at the pasture where they would let guests self-park.

It seemed to Rudy they'd anticipated every angle. Lacy had taken Don Hurt's suggestions to heart. Short of a downpour, he couldn't imagine what would interfere with the debut of Lavender Lodge.

"And what is it you want me to do?" he asked, as Lacy reminded everyone of their tasks.

"You're the celebrity judge. I'll escort you around with a grading sheet for categories of best tasting, best use of lavender, best presentation, and most original. We'll have prizes, a case of wine for each winner, and then everyone is free to mingle and buy products from the vendors."

Kali added, "And we're offering a drawing for those that want to enter to win a free event rental at the lodge."

"You are?" Lacy asked. "Since when?"

"Since right now. AJ and I were so amazed by what we saw tonight that we think a giveaway will be a brilliant way to induce someone to plan their wedding this far out in the country. Maybe we could expand it to online participation, too?"

He watched Lacy take the idea and spin it through the troubleshooting tracks in her mind as she asked more questions of AJ and Kali.

"Chef?"

He glanced up and saw his cook standing in the doorway. He'd brought the girl along because she took directions well and was willing to wash dishes, plus she had relatives in Fredericksburg so she could bunk with family for the night.

"May I serve the appetizers?"

He nodded, and she entered the room bearing a tray of bacon-wrapped shrimp.

Lacy bit into the shrimp, groaned, and looked at him with that gaze that said he could do this every night of the week. She had no idea how her thoughts reflected in her eyes. That's what made her so different from other women he knew; she didn't hide or posture. She was what she was, and if someone didn't like it, they could leave.

Within moments everyone asked questions about his cooking, his recipes, and his preferred methods. This reaction played out in the restaurant too. He answered, feeling the questions were friendly and less like someone wanted to copy his technique.

Luke reached for another shrimp and asked Jake when he'd last had something this delicious.

"I guess the last time we ate at Stella's," he replied. "We drive to Austin, or used to before Charlie was born, for special occasions. Beware Beau, your days of living it up are over."

Beau nodded. "I've been warned. But we're so stinking excited about this baby, I'm willing to endure any disruption to our patterns so I can have Colette's mini-me running around."

Colette smiled. "He's so sure the baby will look like me."

"I can only hope," he corrected. "God knows we don't need another one with my mug."

"Babies are wonderful," Rudy offered. "It's humbling to become responsible for another human. But don't be fooled, they will drain the life out of you. My daughter was colicky, and we could almost never make her comfortable."

The energy in the room stuttered to a halt.

He'd said something wrong; he just didn't know what.

He glanced at Lacy for help. "Luna can come to the festival, right? She's excited."

"She's welcome." Lacy wiped her lips with a napkin.

Beau leaned forward, resting his elbows on his knees and spearing Rudy with his gaze. "I didn't realize you were married with a family. I was thinking there was something brewing between you and Lacy."

Rudy sat forward. "Divorced. Almost two years. My daughter is seven and lives in Abilene with her mother most of the time."

Colette tugged Beau's shoulder, as if drawing him back into the couch. "Her name is Luna?" she asked. "That's lovely. We've collected an entire roster of names, but we're going to wait to name the baby after we meet him."

"We did the same thing while waiting on Charlie," Kali added. "There was a running joke about what we would call the baby, but when he was born, we named him for Jake's dad."

Rudy scanned the room, assessing their expressions. The women seemed friendly, but the men bore gazes that threatened to drag him out back for a beating.

Lacy scooted to the edge of the sofa and stood. "I need to find a plate because I'm going to make a mess. I shouldn't be allowed to eat away from a table."

Rudy jumped. "I'll help you."

He followed her through the dining room. "Tell me, what did I say that killed the room?"

"I don't know what you mean. Weren't they just talking baby names? I hate those conversations because they go on forever, and I'm the last person in the world who should ever be charged with naming a human. Look what my mother named me. I'm a walking joke."

"How so?"

"The rumor is my mother named me for the blanket my aunt brought to my birth. And what's as bad is she named my sister a name she got from merging my father's name, Liam, with her name, Karin. I can't tell you how many times I've heard Kali explain to folks who questioned the spelling of her name."

"You couldn't ask your mom for a better explanation for your name?"

"My folks died when I was young, so my aunt raised me. She vowed we'd have no more of the names nonsense going forward."

Thankful to not be the reason for Lacy's abrupt departure, Rudy relished the glimpse into her past. She didn't offer them often. "A blanket, huh? That's tough."

"What was tough was getting through junior high with an odd name, twenty extra pounds, and stringy hair. Add weird step-cousins, courtesy of the man my aunt married when she was forty, and I was officially a freak."

"You mean stepsisters?"

"Oh, no. Kali and I weren't getting any closer to those girls than was necessary. We referred to their dad as our uncle, and that made them cousins. It kept the balance of power in place."

He chuckled, remembering the chaos of his family. "A coping mechanism?"

"I was living a nightmare until I graduated high school."

He handed her a stack of small plates. "What happened then?"

"Well, I grew boobs and hips for one thing. Dropped forty pounds and turned into what Aunt Annalise called her 'swan.' Which means I was the proverbial ugly duckling."

Rudy would have thought someone had spoiled her since childhood for those blue eyes. "Well, you got your revenge on all the kids who teased you. You won Miss Texas."

"Fat lot of good that did me when I flamed out last fall."

"But you landed on your feet, right? You've become a reporter, and that's difficult to accomplish."

"Can I tell you a secret?" She paused. "Don't tell the others, but I've inherited the newspaper. I'm the new editor and publisher of the *Comfort News*."

Time stopped.

The gut punch yanked his breath.

A publisher? That sounded permanent. The thing he'd thought was an internship while she figured out her next move had become a career? She'd never move to Austin now.

Though fragile as phyllo, his ideas for the two of them had played in his mind all day. He'd . . . well, it didn't matter now what he'd hoped because she would live here.

"Congratulations," he said with more confidence than he felt.

"It was unexpected, but I think I can make it work. I've been looking at new columnists, and if I take transition easy, I hope to swing the subscription rate in a year."

He glanced around the dining room at the antiques and art, trying to find an object that would distract him from saying something stupid. His gaze shot back to her blonde hair flowing in waves behind her shoulders. "You'll be great at it. Look at how you've already raised support for the festival, and that was something you invented a few months ago."

"You're a big part of that too, Rudy. If I couldn't have dropped your name, none of these cooks would have given me the time of day."

"They would have if they'd seen you."

She shook her head. "The more important thing is that we had credible support and an excellent plan. If this works, maybe we'll do it for a few more years."

Stepping into the foyer, he watched her walk into the living room, a queen among her subjects. She might have no clue the power she held, but he knew those people would protect her with their dying breath.

A green ribbon of envy wove around his heart. Lacy didn't know it yet, but she was as much a part of the fabric of this community as her sister and their friends.

The hills had claimed her.

This was the sign he'd needed. Lacy was a blip, a sunray on a cloudy day, a lovely distraction on his bumpy road to supporting himself and Luna. He should be grateful she had told him her decision. It would alter his plans for tonight's forecast of a full moon.

"Chef? The vegetables are ready."

Recipes arranged themselves in his head. He had a job to do. "I've heard supper is ready to serve." He took the dishcloth, wadding it between his fingers. "If you'll make your way to the front porch, Clarissa and I will serve you a menu that Lacy once told me was her favorite meal. Since she's done so much to get this food festival going, I thought it fitting to customize the evening to fit with your wonderful lavender products."

Kali applauded. "Oh, how fun."

AJ leapt from her chair. "I knew I could smell lavender. Cinnamon, too?"

"Yes," Rudy nodded, stepping back to give them room to ease toward the front porch. "Part of the marinade for the lamb shanks. We used cumin, paprika, and a superb wine, but the cinnamon cuts the spiciness and blends well with the lamb."

"I can't wait," AJ said as she passed by. "I will be one of those nerds who takes pictures of their plate."

Lacy patted his arm. "I can't believe you remembered me telling you about that meal."

"When a lovely woman tells you what she likes to eat, it becomes a mission to make her happy." He smiled to disguise the chip in his heart. "I hope you're pleased."

"I am," she said. "It's crazy sweet you put so much thought into this."

Beau stopped beside him, raking his gaze along Rudy's fitted T-shirt. "I'm watching you, bro. You may think we're a bunch of bumpkins who can be fooled with fancy food, but we take care of our own. I think you know I'm talking about Lacy."

Rubbing his nose to keep from saying the first thing that came to mind, he stifled his reaction. "No one thinks you're a bumpkin. Yet."

Beau's eyes lit with firecrackers. "You see it stays that way."

Watching the rest of the men file out, Rudy wondered if they all thought he was out to take advantage of her. He could compete in a restaurant, but if he had to battle in the Hill Country, he'd lose. No six-shooters sat packed in his arsenal. The only tool he'd find hanging from his belt were tongs.

And he was a little bitter that no one would stand up for him.

Chagrined, he remembered how Jay and Kenny had his back when Hannah's attorney served him divorce papers. He wasn't alone. He had friends. Scrubbing his hand along his jaw, he cursed his attitude. It was this setting, these vibrant people. They seemed to live a rare existence, and he'd be lying if he denied it didn't appeal to him. The limestone fragrance from his fantasy vineyard drifted through his mind.

Hurrying to the stove to check the baking sheets filled with the crusty remains of golden potatoes and bright green beans, he grabbed the mint he'd brought with him. "You've got the serving portions separated for the men and the women?"

"Yes, Chef," Clarissa said, cutting her gaze to him.

Tearing bits of the herb onto the lamb shanks she'd positioned on each plate, he nodded. "Then deliver baskets of bread and salted butter to the table. I'll finish this."

Wiping a cleaning cloth around the perimeters of the plates, he wondered what the dinner conversation would be tonight.

Not that Jefferson intimidated him, not entirely. But he knew it wasn't right to prolong things with Lacy if they didn't have an actual future. Now she had a newspaper to manage, she'd have no time to meander around his kitchen and snap images for their website and social media, which meant they had zero reasons to drive the hundred miles each way to see each other.

"Chef, are you ready to serve?"

He nodded. "Take these two plates, this one to the pregnant woman and the other to her husband, they are the guests of honor tonight."

"Yes."

"And the wine is on the table?"

"Breathing, but I think they've already poured their glasses."

"This will be a busy service. I'm leaving you to cover second helpings, the cheese and salad courses, as well as clearing the plates." He toned down his demands when he saw the dread in her gaze. "I'll help with the dessert, as we'll need to torch the sugar."

"Yes, sir."

He glanced across the kitchen, making sure flames were off at the stove. He saw the vanilla-bean-and-chocolate custards cooling on the counter. The tubs with the supplies he'd brought from Stella's were on the table, ready to be repacked after service. The room was small but efficient, updated with high-end appliances but not stuffy. The screened door brought a breeze into the room and kept him on a distanced but friendly basis with the family dog.

Chalky shades of orange disappeared beyond the screen.

He shook his head and picked up the heavy plates. This was not the time too long for something that could never be.

Stepping onto the front porch, crowded with a table of contented people and the first shadows cast by the string lights and candles, he smiled because he knew they would remember this night. "Cheers, friends. And save room for dessert. I'm offering black-and-white crème brûlée."

"That will make our customized cookies look pitiful," Jake moaned. "But I'll take a crème brûlée every single time."

"I'll eat Lacy's portion since I know she's not going to want the calories," Beau said, staring at his bountiful plate. "We hauled a wedding dress from San Antonio, and rumor is she's supposed to fit into it tomorrow."

"Hey, I can eat anything I want." Lacy reached for her wineglass. "I sent them my measurements and was told the dress had an elastic waistline."

Beau eyed the breadbasket close to Lacy's elbow. "I'm not sure I'd be so confident. That designer is nothing more than a twig."

She laughed. "You take care of yourself, Jefferson. And I'll do me."

Rudy served Luke and AJ while Clarissa finished the place settings.

Settling into a chair next to Lacy, he reached under the tablecloth and squeezed her knee. "Don't tell me if you hate this food, I'll be crushed."

She laughed. "I doubt anything could crush you. You're a warrior chef."

How little she knew, but he wouldn't argue. It soothed his spirit to have her think he was brave, daring, and able to defeat enemies. Lifting his wineglass, he saluted her. "To ever after."

Chapter Twenty-Eight

"To ever after?" Kali sat her mug on the table in the bride's dressing room at Lavender Lodge. "What does that mean?"

"I hope it means what it usually means," Lacy murmured.

"Me too," Kali sighed.

AJ stood behind Lacy, hooking the wedding dress together. "Stop speaking," she urged. "Breathe in."

"I'm holding my breath," Lacy whispered.

"Almost there," AJ said, squeezing the fabric together.

The hairdresser pleaded, "Don't mess up the curls."

AJ's elbows knocked Lacy's hair over her shoulder. "Did you pay a deposit for this dress, Colette? Because Lacy may own it after I rip this seam to shreds."

Colette snapped a photo with Lacy's iPhone. "It's supposed to have some give, you know, for dancing and comfort."

Lacy shook her head as if to say there was no room to move.

AJ relaxed. "Finally."

"Don't move," Colette commanded from the recliner. "I want to see the full effect."

"There's no effect," Lacy grumbled as she turned to face her friend. "I'm still wearing sneakers."

"I can't see your feet." Colette adjusted the phone for another angle. "But then, I can't see mine either, so we're even."

Kali stood, her hands clasped over her heart. "Oh, Lacy. You look gorgeous. Like an actual bride."

Stepping to the full-length mirror, Lacy felt a strange warmth fill her heart and fire up her imagination. *A bride.* Blinking fast to hide her reaction, she buried the longing that someone would want to spend the rest of their life with her. "Colette, leave me the designer's card so I can tag her in the photos. Is the photographer here yet?"

AJ nodded. "Drue delivered your bouquet. I love what she did with that wild mix of bright flowers. Color will pop in all the pictures."

They'd scanned several Pinterest pages looking for the right contrast with the deep-purple hues of the lavender fields. "Drue said if we chose soft colors and leafy bits, what's popular right now, the bouquet would fade with the backdrop. I told her, whatever she chose, to go big."

"You're so smart about these things," AJ said. "I can't believe we get to play dress up today. I *love* owning an event center."

They had no reservations, and few people knew about the location. But seeing the smile on her sister's face held back the words. No one needed a reminder of how fast this thing could flop. "The vendors want exposure to your future customers. It's a win for them when they get top billing on the lodge's list of services."

The friends followed Lacy out of the white house, and to the front entrance, where several cars had parked willy-nilly in the pasture. They greeted the photographer who'd already scouted locations and lighting, and also the rental company, which had brought a green-velvet couch and a wedding arch for props.

"I have the shoes," AJ called, lifting a silk bag holding Lacy's favorite strappy heels. "Kali has snacks."

"I can't eat a thing today," Colette groaned. "I almost popped last night. Beau says we'll never eat again, and that's saying something because we're staying with his mother and everyone knows Brenda is a fantastic cook."

After the shock of seeing Rudy last night, she'd warned herself to put the brakes on her imagination. If they were to have a future, it couldn't be rushed—too many complications, like careers and his child, stood between them. But when she woke this morning, none of that mattered. He was waking up in Comfort too.

Bringing her mind back to the task at hand, she needed to get through this morning before she could figure out what last night's smoldering glances meant. Lacy glanced across the Lavender Hill grounds. If they didn't start shooting photos soon the sun would bake every smile. She talked poses with the photographer, and he agreed they should begin in the lavender fields.

In a matter of minutes, he positioned his videographer in one location and climbed onto a small stepladder, directing Lacy to walk and spin, letting the dress flow against the lavender mounds, while she carried the weighty bouquet. A breeze lifted her curls and blew them around her throat, adding movement to the shots.

Everyone called out commands to Lacy to turn this way or that, but she listened only to the expert. He had an enviable list of photo credits. The others were armchair quarterbacks.

In the distance, the hum of a golf cart crested the hill, and they all twisted to watch Luke and Rudy ride into the scene.

Her heart flip flopped. Her stomach took flight. Was her palm sweating?

After the Jeffersons left last night, and Kali and Jake had followed, she and Rudy had loaded Clarissa's car and then strolled with AJ and Luke around the property. They agreed that wandering after that feast would help digestion. Talking in the dark seemed to loosen normal constraints. Luke shared some issues from their early days of a long-distance romance, and AJ added how surprised she'd been that the man she'd never have guessed could be hers, had waited for her to come around. Lacy presumed that they could see she and Rudy were holding hands, but they didn't mention it or the silence when Luke asked Rudy if he'd ever marry again.

When Rudy walked her to the car, they'd kissed as if he were leaving for war instead of an address on the other side of town. Rattled to her soul by the power of that kiss, she couldn't imagine why he'd looked so sad. All she could think of was how soon could they find a way to merge their calendars for their next date.

Braking near the back of the Lavender Hill shop, Luke scooped Beans off the floorboard. "Look, y'all. I brought a groom!"

Everyone turned to see AJ's big, fluffy Goldendoodle dressed in the same bow tie he'd worn at their winter wedding.

Kali clapped. "Oh, that's darling. Let's get Beans into the photo."

Lacy's gaze glued to Rudy. She didn't know he owned a shirt in a color other than black or gray, but what denim did for his eyes was lethal.

He rose from the golf cart as if shaken by her appearance also.

The photographer paused. "I have a better idea," he said, following Lacy's gaze. "You, there, at the golf cart. You're the right height. Will you stand here with Lacy and let me pose her around you? I'd like her peeking over your shoulder."

Oh, no. No. No. Lacy wouldn't survive having Rudy within arm's reach while wearing a wedding dress.

Rudy didn't seem to think twice. He stepped forward, his cowboy boots eating up the distance. "You look like the happy ending straight out of a Disney movie," he said, stopping short of scooping her into an embrace. "And I should know because I've seen them all multiple times."

Tangled emotions lifted on a balloon's ribbon and floated away overhead. "Don't make me laugh. Seriously. I might burst a seam. This dress is so tight."

Those words drove his gaze right to her bust, the silk gathers barely containing her flesh. "You're amazing," he said quietly.

Heat flooded her cheeks.

"Here, you be the groom," the photographer pulled Rudy's arm and moved him to face the hillside. "Oh, my. You are so chiseled. The bride will come in close, like this," he said, dragging Lacy against Rudy's chest. "Put your arms around his neck, one hand into his gorgeous hair and let the other arm dangle the bouquet down his back."

"I'm so sorry you've gotten roped into this," she said, feeling a million layers of awkward. "You and your gorgeous hair."

"My hair never gets the attention it deserves." He winked. "Luna would say this is as perfect as perfect could get."

"She would not."

"Would too." His lips brushed her cheek. "She calls you 'Cinderella.'" Wrapping his arms around her waist and tugging her close, he added, "And, so you know, I'm always Prince Charming."

Lacy should have glanced toward the lodge to see the stunned expressions on her friends' faces, but her eyes searched Rudy's, forgetting every reason she'd ever considered for why they should not be together every day for the rest of their lives.

The photographer snapped them from several angles and rearranged her in unique ways but never seemed to hear the words Rudy uttered for Lacy's ears only. She wasn't sure she'd remember everything he poured into her soul that morning, but she was left in no doubt of his desire.

"Fine. I think we have plenty here," the photographer said, sending the videographer away. "Let's shoot in front of those windows. I want to catch the light before the sun washes out the background."

Gathering her wits, Lacy wiped her brow. How did they go back to normal after these last few moments?

Rudy kissed her cheek, careful not to smear her makeup. "I came to say goodbye and bring you coffee."

"Goodbye?"

"Jay called saying Hannah and her new boyfriend made a lunch appointment to explain how they would go to my investors and ruin me if I don't hand Stella's over to them."

Ice-cold water. That's how she would recover from Rudy's whispers. "Can they do that?"

Rudy's hands fisted before he stuffed them into his pockets. "No. But they don't know that yet."

"I don't understand. Where is this coming from?"

He sighed. "She's bitter because after the divorce I bought her out from owning the bakery, Stella Too. She wanted to turn it into a bar or something, I don't know."

"Can you give her the bakery to make her go away?"

"I'm not doing that. That shop supplies area restaurants with breads and pastry goods, like a commissary, and we sell from a walk-in counter too, so it's good for the neighborhood."

Lacy's mind spun with the implications. "How are you going to stop her from taking over your restaurant?"

Rudy glanced over his shoulder and motioned to Luke that he was ready to leave. Leading her out of the lavender mounds, he said, "Two years ago, after the divorce was final, I met with the investors who'd help me fund the restaurant as a start-up. To protect Stella's from ever being in this exact position, I sold my share of the partnership to them. They formed an LLC and made Jay not only the general manager of the restaurant but also the representative for the owners. I'm executive chef."

She didn't comprehend the business arrangement, but she felt sorry for him—he no longer owned his dream. "And Hannah doesn't know this?"

"No idea. We've been watching her threats and feeding her along so we can better understand who her financial backer is and if they pose a serious threat."

"The pushback from the James Beard Award?"

"Yeah, that was unexpected."

"I'm so sorry."

"Why? You came along as a blessed disruption from all this madness, but you're not involved."

"I guess I thought all you had to do was cook and take care of your daughter. I didn't realize there was so much drama in the background."

"I didn't want you to know, hoped I never needed to tell you. But after last night, I knew I had to be honest about my life. So, you could see that I'm not the guy you deserve."

His words made her stumble. Grabbing his arm, she asked, "Where is *that* coming from?"

He let his gaze roam the clouds before he brought his focus to her. "We're both locked into worlds that can't mesh. I have Stella's, and now, you have the *Comfort News*. With the responsibilities of running a newspaper and the distance between us, we're not going to have time to see each other often."

Feeling as if her body coiled into a fight-or-flight paradox, she replayed the sentences to make sure she'd heard him correctly. "We can figure things out. We don't have to decide today. Do we?"

"It's best not to start something we know won't finish well."

"But what about all the things you just whispered to me? We have the potential for something fantastic. Let's give this time."

"Time is the one thing we don't have. You're going to have to dig in to do your paper justice, and I'll have to pull overtime to keep Stella's afloat after Hannah's backstabbing."

"But—"

"No buts, Lacy. I gave in to my needs when you walked into my arms just now, but that was begging for torment. It will haunt me knowing I can't have a future with you."

He'll be *haunted*? He was the only man she'd met who helped her face her past and figure out who she really was. "Is this because I'm too young? You think I'm still a child?"

"God, no. You're one of the most brilliant women I've ever met. We have an age gap, and it plagues me to think that, had we gotten together, you would have missed so much of life because I'm already inching toward forty."

"I'm okay with meeting halfway. I like that you're older. You make me feel safe, like you've seen the world and have figured things out." Her heart cracked. For the first time since she'd left the strange reality of the pageant world, she'd met someone she could love, and he didn't think she was worth the effort. "Why, Rudy? Why now?

He reached for her hand. "Because if we wait any longer it will hurt too much."

They paused at the golf cart, where her heart shattered to the ground. "So, you're breaking up with me before we ever start dating?"

Color darkened his cheeks as he released her fingers. "I'm incredibly attracted to you and, in another universe, would chase you to the ends of the earth. But my responsibilities are to Luna. I'm using Hannah's dealings to gain primary custody of my daughter, and I can't do that and fall in love with you too."

Fragrance from the lavender oils distilled in AJ's barn drifted to them, wrapped them in a lavender-infused cloud. The heat warming the soil seemed to release all the mosquitos and gnats, her white dress a magnet for every annoying element that could possibly torment her while she read the expression of a man she'd hoped to love.

Luke approached them, smiling. "You are gorgeous, girl. I bet big bucks that photographer asks you to model another time."

Rudy and Lacy didn't say a word; they stared at each other, dueling in a silent battle.

Luke waited for a moment before speaking again. "Rudy? You ready to get on the road? I gave AJ the coffee carafe. I know you're on a tight schedule."

Rudy backed away, his eyes never leaving Lacy's. "I'll return for the food festival. Luke said Luna and I can stay with them, so I'll see you then. Okay?"

Nodding, she'd need armor to endure. Watching him fold his body onto the seat, she knew she'd never be the same. The golf cart backed away with a beeping alarm and then vanished along the route it had arrived, a stream of dust marking the trail.

"Lacy?"

Kali's concern cracked the tide of heartbreak, and Lacy batted a tear from her cheek.

"Are you alright? You seem shaken."

She'd filled second place several times during pageants, but the pain of not being chosen still stung. "Overheated. I'll be all right in a few minutes."

Kali stepped closer, weaving her arm around her sister's waist. "For what it's worth, you and Rudy make a striking couple."

"We're not a couple," she hissed.

Kali's eyes widened. "But I thought—"

"Just leave it alone, all right?" Lacy marched forward, heading toward the flagstone path.

"How can I leave it alone?" Kali matched her steps to Lacy's strides. "All you two needed just now was a preacher, and we could have called this simmering love story done."

Lacy cursed.

"Okay, that was rough. But I'm your sister, and I know when you're hurting."

Lacy spun around. "I don't need your smothering right now."

Kali stopped following. Stepping into the air-conditioned coolness of the lodge, Lacy saw people gathered near the windows, waiting for her to pose. They must have witnessed the last several minutes because they braced their gazes for impact. Even the dog stood still.

AJ opened a thermos. "You want to tell us what's gone wrong?"

Bristling, she shook her head. "Let's get this over with."

"I can't work with that attitude," the photographer complained. "What happened to my bride of ten minutes ago?"

The dream-come-true experience of standing in Rudy's arms, hearing him describe her body, was a memory that would both thrill her for months to come and kill any hope she'd meet another man who could make her feel treasured. Lacy kicked off the shoes and tossed the bouquet on a table. "She's left the building. Work with what you have or call this shoot cooked. I don't care."

Chapter Twenty-Nine

Lacy stood beside Frank's hospital bed, stunned that the man who had stomped around Comfort with a cigar in one hand and an editor's pen in the other had deteriorated into a toothless bird. Twiggy, the man propped on pillows, strung with IV lines, bore no resemblance to the curmudgeon who had owned the *Comfort News*. Tempted to put a hand on the blanket covering his foot, testing if he were real, she resisted. Men who powered through covering terrorist attacks, economic crashes, presidential races, hostage situations, and epidemics would not want to be pitied.

She'd come to ask his permission to publish public-service announcements about human trafficking in Texas and the 1-888-373-7888 national hotline number, but now all she wanted to do was flee. She'd never been this close to someone who was this close to death. Hiccups of tears filled her throat. Embarrassed by her fear, she chose to look away from the pale skin stretched across his cheeks.

"He'd be glad to know you were here," Gloria said, adjusting his blanket.

"Is he asleep? I made enough noise banging into the bedside table to wake half the floor."

"He's sedated." Gloria adjusted the knitted cap over his head. "The pain levels are excruciating."

Lacy sagged, oddly relieved he wasn't gone. Afraid to ask how much time remained, she glanced around the room reading the space for clues. What if Frank never left this hospital? She'd missed being involved in her aunt's treatment because Annalise wanted to die in France.

That helpless feeling returned in spades.

Seeing the staunch resolve in Gloria's expression made her wonder if people were born able to endure sadness or if it developed as a result of endless heartache. "How do you do it?"

"Do what, dear?"

"Take care of him." Lacy glanced at her landlady, a woman who had won many awards for leadership in the banking industry. "You divorced ten years ago."

Gloria shrugged, her shoulders disappearing into the cashmere wrap. "He needed me."

He needed me. Such simple words to carry such heavy implications. Had she ever met someone for whom she'd set aside her plans to clean away the sick and war with a fever? The sacrifice did not compute. Frank spoke in surly sentences. His opinions, once formed, took on barnacles. In the months she'd known him, if he'd done anything kind for Gloria, it had been under the radar. She'd have bet money they avoided each other. So, how does a broken relationship boomerang?

"But what happened? If you love him enough to nurse him through cancer, why did you split up at all?"

Gloria motioned to a chair. "Pull up a seat. I get tired of standing, and I can't sit unless everyone else is seated, too. Southern manners go to the bone."

Scooting a chair closer to Frank's bedside, she asked, "Are you staying healthy," concerned Gloria had overdone the caregiving. Skin sagged around her chin, and her hair was flattened on one side.

"I'll feel better once I replace the mattress in the guest room. I never realized the thing was a brick."

Lacy smiled, knowing if Gloria waved a magic wand over Frank's house, the rooms would be magazine-worthy within weeks. "So, what gives? Despite appearances to the contrary, you two obviously still care for each other."

The older woman smiled with a grace born of forgiveness and mercy. "It was all a misunderstanding."

A misunderstanding?

Lacy waited. The details hovered in the room between the beeps of the heart monitor.

She'd not seen a photograph of Frank and Gloria from when they were younger, but Gloria's beauty still radiated from an engaging smile and eyes that didn't miss a trick. Every day, she walked a two-mile circuit even though her feet hurt from years of wearing pointed-toe shoes. "Contracts get broken over misunderstandings," Lacy said. "I feel like it would take more to force someone like you to leave a marriage."

Drips from the morphine IV underscored the pause.

"He was a real catch, back in the day. Handsome, intelligent, and a smart aleck who couldn't resist picking a fight. Frank used to come into the bank and cash the smallest of checks so he could flirt. The other tellers thought we were a comedy until he dropped on one knee at the bank vault." Gloria's face dissolved into a memory. "We married within weeks, against my parents' wishes. Frank came from the other side of the political table, and my father was the mayor. He wasn't keen on me crossing party lines."

Lacy wasn't sure why that mattered, but then her only father figure spent most of his free time hiding in his workshop, carving projects he'd give away to people who wouldn't critique his methods. "Your parents broke you up?"

"They came around eventually. Probably would have happened sooner, but we weren't able to have kids, so the usual softness that happens with grandchildren was delayed until my sister got married." Gloria reached across the space and took Lacy's hands within her own. "I think that's why I'm so invested in you. You remind me of myself when I was your age, and maybe the child I wished I'd always had."

Speechless, Lacy looked at their hands knit together. Old and young. Soft and firm. With no urge to pull back, Gloria's words washed over her heart. All the years she'd longed for a mother washed over her in a swell of feelings.

"Sorry, didn't mean to get overemotional," Gloria said, leaning back and letting go. "As you've warmed up to Comfort and developed the confidence you got from working at the paper, it was easy to think you were a lot like Frank and me. Strong-willed, spicy, but sweet as sugar, a perfect recipe."

"Those qualities may have come factory installed, but I can see where you have helped soften the rough edges." Many times, the best part of her day had been sitting at the table talking to the woman who comforted, listened, and gave advice when asked. "You'd have made a wonderful mom."

A long moment drifted into another.

"I'm from the generation that watched every known structure our parents enjoyed crumble. I missed Woodstock, but I've lived through the fallout—spiking divorce rates, abortion frenzies, school shootings, and twenty-four-hour television. Good lord, I was born before Google!"

"You predate the internet?"

"Honey, cellphones were the stuff of science fiction when I was a kid. I wonder what sort of things you read when you were growing up. Was Nancy Drew still popular?" Gloria fiddled with her wristband. "Frank and I, well, we turned all the attention we would have given to kids and funneled it into our careers. I became one of the first female bank presidents in the region, and Frank published the *Austin American-Statesman*. We were envied for our success."

Lacy didn't realize Frank had published that prestigious paper, but then she'd never researched him. Maybe she would have given him more respect had she not thought he was inches away from becoming a vagrant.

"About ten years ago, we realized we had so completely drifted apart that we didn't notice each other anymore." Gloria picked at her fingernail. "He missed my birthday, I ignored his. He started buying small papers and travelling around the area, gone for a week at a time. I told him he could find an apartment in the city to save wear and tear on his truck." She took in a deep breath. "And he did."

Lacy couldn't imagine how a marriage fizzled. Gloria was such a loving homebody. Wouldn't Frank have fought to eat one of her home-cooked meals?

"Our attorney said we had one of the most amiable divorces he'd ever litigated."

There were many words Lacy would assign to Frank Bachman; "amiable" wasn't one of them. "He'd surrendered. Why?"

"He'd heard, through the grapevine, that a man—a friend of mine in Rotary Club—wanted to date me. This friend had told his friends he thought I was the wife he needed after his first wife had passed away. I guess Frank chose not to investigate that lead and decided I needed to be free to marry a wealthy rancher since I liked living in Kerrville more than he did."

Lacy blinked, picturing the hilltop home with the million-dollar views. "But he got the house."

"I know. My trick backfired. I'd hoped if he won the house in the settlement, he'd want to win me back too. He built that house for me." Gloria sighed. "Water under the bridge now."

Lacy listened to the steady rhythm of the heart monitor. "You never stopped loving him."

"I never did." Gloria wiped a finger underneath her lashes. "And he still loved me too."

"How did you find out he still cared?"

"Oddly enough, it was you." Gloria rolled her neck. "He'd called to tell me you were coming to Comfort, being dumped on him, he groused. Would I give you a place to stay because he didn't think you'd last more than a few days, a week tops?"

"Sounds about right."

"As soon as I heard that resolve in his voice, that dismissive attitude about a girl he'd never even met, well, I'm afraid it brought out the worst in me. I determined to prove him wrong."

A shimmer scooted along Lacy's spine. She wasn't sure why she should be nervous about being a bone in a fight, but it did make her second-guess those cooking lessons.

"But, you being you, Lacy, surprised us both." Gloria smiled. "Your remarkable spirit, your work ethic, and your grinding need to prove yourself overwhelmed us both. Frank would call to ask if I'd seen the same traits in you that he had, and well, one thing led to another. When we both agreed you were the daughter we both would have wanted, it cracked open the vault I'd sealed shut."

Lacy sagged forward, draping her elbows on her knees, stunned.

"And then he was diagnosed with lung cancer."

"And so here we are," Lacy said, glancing at the beige blanket tucked into the corners of the hospital bed. Her eyes filled with tears, crushed to discover the family she'd always longed for, weeks before it would be forever altered. "All together."

Gloria nodded. "Please don't cry for us. We're an old pair of so-and-so's, and we made plenty of our own mistakes. But God brought us you, and it's allowed us to make peace with the past. We're both so grateful you came into our lives."

Tears broke through her thinly patched heart, and she fell into Gloria's lap bawling. She cried for her empty childhood, her aimless wandering, looking for somewhere to belong, the surprise of pageants and the resulting emptiness that followed, and even for her most recent heartache, the loss of a man she'd begun to love.

"I can't do this," Lacy gulped. "I can't let him go. I can't run the paper."

"You're going to do just fine, Lacy Cavanaugh." Gloria petted the long, blonde strands as if she'd only begun to feel silk. "You're stronger than you realize."

Later, with eyes swollen to watermelon puffiness, Lacy entered the cool darkness of Gloria's home and looked at the creamy-white walls with new appreciation. This three-bedroom bungalow had been a haven from a broken heart. Gloria had gambled and lost and created a space here where she rebuilt her sense of self. The pink cabinets, thick Turkish carpets, and posh fixtures were all such a contrast to the early-nineties ranch house on top of a hill overlooking Kerrville. It was as if Gloria had distanced herself from who'd she been while living with Frank, pushing the boundaries, hoping the essence of a sassy bank teller still existed.

Lacy fluffed a silk pillow on the sofa, hugging it close to breathe in Gloria's scent. Her mind replayed the conversations, the complex thoughts, the hope they'd remain lifelong friends. A chunk of her heart fell into place, and a feeling of wholeness drifted within reach.

Her phone dinged a familiar chime. Kali was texting—*Open the front door*!

Lacy looked around, unaware she'd been standing in the living room while evening settled around her. She bent to flip on a lamp and then another, while hurrying to the door. Yanking the knob, it stunned her to see Anna, AJ, and Kali staring at her with mixed expressions, ranging from hostility to awe.

The most recent edition of the *Comfort News* landed against her chest, the one featuring the event hall and the photo of the three couples admiring their dream come true.

Grabbing it, she glanced at the color photo, happy the image printed correctly.

"You. Are. The. Publisher?" Kali growled. "Seriously?"

"Why didn't you tell us?" AJ added. "This is big news."

"I'm so proud of you, I could just cry." Anna reached forward to hug Lacy. "I'm miffed I wasn't the first to know you'd bought the paper, but I'm still happy."

Lacy sighed. She stepped back, holding the door wide. "Come in. I'll tell you the whole story."

"You'd better open a bottle of wine." Anna winked. "It's the only thing that might dampen Kali's fire."

She knew. You didn't live your whole life in someone's shadow without learning their blind spots. "I bought wine, cheese, and a wonderful bread when I was in San Antonio returning the wedding dress. Give me five minutes to wash up, and I'll meet you at the table."

Anna stopped her. "You've been crying."

"Part of the story."

She heard them move into the kitchen, opening cupboards, hunting for the essentials, and hurried down the hall to the room she'd taken when Gloria handed her the keys. Sliding out of the sandals and the dress she'd been wearing all day, she changed into shorts and a workout top, piling her hair into a messy topknot. Washing her face, she rubbed in moisturizer and leaned closer to the mirror, seeing freckles dusting her nose.

She'd pay an exorbitant price for taking on the paper and Hill Country living. Freckles would be the least of it. With the blink of her lashes, Rudy's face materialized from the mirror.

Turning away, she checked her cell for messages, and when her screen glared back blankly, she tossed it onto the bed. She didn't understand how he could switch a gear and decide she was extraneous, but she wouldn't waste another minute waiting for an explanation either.

Her plate groaned with responsibilities. The lonely life of six months ago couldn't find elbow room today. And, to top it all off, Christopher was driving to Comfort tomorrow to see how she had settled in with the new role at the paper. He'd boasted he felt proud, since he felt like this new chapter was his bragging right.

Whatever. He was good-looking and charming; she'd make do with the inconvenience.

Entering the kitchen, she saw her sister had assembled a board of cheeses, pickles, grapes, and crackers. AJ sliced wedges of the sourdough and slathered butter on them before popping them into the toaster. Anna poured generous glasses of sauvignon blanc into Gloria's finest crystal.

"Make yourselves at home," Lacy said, with some derision. "Should I call in an order of Chinese? It feels like you're not leaving soon."

Kali pointed to a cane-backed chair. "Sit."

"You don't get to boss me in my house," Lacy grumbled. "I should get to play hostess."

"You do busy work instead of answering direct questions, so we're streamlining." Kali set the board on the table. "Besides, I saw a pan of lasagna in the fridge. We won't starve."

Gloria had made and frozen several containers one winter weekend, and much to Lacy's delight, she was able to shop the deep freeze instead of figuring out how to cook for one person. That didn't help her tonight, but then it was time to come clean. She'd not meant to keep this news from her best friends, but if it turned out to be another screw-up, she didn't want to hear them say "I told you so." Again.

She reached for a glass of wine. "Where do you want me to start?"

"Elephant in the room?" Anna asked. "I never really knew what happened at the bridal shoot a few days ago, save hearing that you and Rudy looked like star-crossed lovers in a lavender field."

"Not going there . . . at least not now." Lacy sighed. "Let's start with me meeting Frank Bachman and almost quitting three different times on the first day. I couldn't deal with his arrogance, but I also knew he was the gatekeeper for the only open door after the Amy Marsh fiasco. So, I pressed on, and that's what lead to me becoming publisher."

Chapter Thirty

Rudy glared at his laptop. He willed the emails to explode and the menus to write themselves. Glancing at his watch, he pushed back from his chair and entered the kitchen. Kenny tasted the sauces while a roster of cooks filled the gaps prepping vegetables, stocks, and salads for later tonight. Normally the clatter of pots, pans, and knives was the soundtrack to his happiness. Today, it echoed his aimlessness.

Jay pushed through the swing door, catching Rudy's gaze. "She's just pulled up. You ready?"

He drew in a breath steamed by the aromas simmering in the pots. "As I can be, I guess. Everyone is in place?"

Jay nodded. He'd notified the partners, warning them of the takeover threat, and called in the attorney who'd drawn up the paperwork buying out Rudy and making him executive chef of Stella's, Stella Too, and any other enterprise Delgardo fancied. The partners had faith in the chef's work ethic, character, and culinary genius as well as ready cash to explore any endeavor with merit. They'd written Hannah Delgardo off as a mercenary ex-wife who'd been fed a lie about how easy it was to yank control of a money-making enterprise.

Today would be her education.

But first, Rudy had insisted, he wanted to hear her out. There was more to this bid, he was sure of it.

Wiping his hands on an apron, he tossed it to the laundry basket and entered the dining room behind Jay. There'd be no homey welcome, no sampling of beverages and appetizers. Even the lights were off to signal she was an intrusion, not a guest.

They gathered near the front door. Rudy nodded to the wait staff setting the tables, and they returned to the back of the house.

The door opened, bringing a gasp of street heat into the restaurant. Hannah seemed immune to the temperature. Along with an assessing gaze and unbridled confidence, she wore a black sleeveless blouse, showing off her pretty shoulders, tailored slacks, and stiletto heels. Her eyes, though. They were marbles. He'd seen her hire and fire staff with such a look, and he knew she'd come to the meeting today expecting to get what she wanted.

What he didn't anticipate was the man who followed her through the door.

Hannah smiled as if she were already the owner of Stella's. "Hello, Rudy. You remember Alan, don't you?"

Rudy offered his hand, a willing combatant in a duel. "How's New York treating you?"

"Better than I could have ever imagined," Alan Gale replied evenly. "Better than Austin is treating you."

Rudy brushed his fingers along the hem of his uniform, removing any lingering stain from the grip. "That's saying something because life here is good. Very good."

The two newcomers shared a gaze that suggested they were working from a script that would change his attitude. Swallowing his dismay, he realized he'd, once again, underestimated her. She'd returned to Gale. Or the worm had tracked her down, but either way, he'd missed an important clue in understanding what drove Hannah's desire to strip him of the restaurant. How long had they been planning this?

Rudy gestured behind him. "I've invited Stella's general manager, Jay Tumlin, to this meeting because anytime someone wants to talk business, I want him at the table."

Hannah nodded. "Jay."

Jay tipped his head, leading them away from the front of the house. "Won't you come through to the bar? We're setting up for full reservations tonight, so I don't have a table to spare."

Rudy's mind whirled with the implications this farce was nothing more than a do-over from the fights picked in culinary school. If he'd had any doubts about the James Beard Award, the truth was clear now. Gale had abused his power on their committee for revenge. Driving down a candidate with bad press had to be an ethical violation, one he'd remind the board of at his first opportunity.

The man standing in front of him wore the chip on his shoulder from their twenties. It had gouged a permanent place and would likely remain until Gale made peace with the reckless choice of buying meat from a backstreet wet market all those years ago, a decision the CIA had called into question regarding his ethics as a chef. As Rudy had driven him to San Francisco that weekend, he was deemed complicit. They were both expelled.

Today, they were older, graying, and scarred, but Rudy had one thing going for him that the other man did not, a reason to live on the high road—Luna.

With a critical eye, Hannah's gaze took in the table arrangements, including the lavender buds in vases. "Budget must be tight if you can't afford roses."

Rudy had seen her negotiate before; he'd not rise to her bait. Instead, he focused on an accessory he'd not noticed the last time they were together. "Are congratulations in order?"

She blinked. "What do you mean?"

His gaze swept to her left hand.

Straightening her shoulders, she smiled, but her eyes didn't light up. "Yes, Alan and I are engaged."

Rudy swallowed his revilement that she'd exposed his daughter to this man on a regular basis. "Color me surprised. I wouldn't have thought you two had opportunity to reconnect, what with him living in Manhattan."

"Hannah is a powerful woman and hard to forget. The moment I'd heard you dumped her, I hurried to her side to remind her how much I'd always cared."

Searing his gaze on Hannah, Rudy would ignore the lie. "That seems like a lot of long-distance travel would be involved. Were you really in New York when you told me you were in California with your mother?"

"My *travel itinerary*," she hissed, "is none of your business."

"It is when it involves the stories you tell Luna."

Jay walked behind the bar and removed glassware and poured tap water into the basin. "Perhaps everyone is overheated?"

Accepting the glass, Rudy stood tall. He hoped this would be the last time he had to endure either of them in this restaurant. "We have a busy evening ahead, please get to the point of this meeting."

Hannah gulped the water.

"For some time now, I've been looking to leverage my experience into owning a restaurant. I've decided I want yours." Gale withdrew a letter from his suit coat. "I've been watching your profile in the media, and complaints are stacking. It would seem that you've lost your knack in the kitchen and are using inferior staff to make your returns work. No disrespect intended, Mr. Tumlin."

Jay's crooked smile brightened the dark room. "None taken. I hire the waitstaff, and Rudy and I conduct extensive background checks with the house staff. We have a pristine organization."

Gale pursed his lips. "Except your sous chef is freelancing with a food truck and using his mother to make products. At Delgardo's condo. How is that pristine?"

Rudy could tell this was news to Jay, but neither of them reacted. He'd seen evidence of enormous amounts of rice being prepared in his home kitchen, but if he gave it a second glance, he'd assumed Mrs. Lin was cooking for relatives. One of Kenny's cousins owned a food truck. Rudy felt safe assuming Kenny helped cook there on his days off.

"If tattle-telling on a sous chef is all you have, let me show you the door." Rudy checked his watch. "If you're quick, you can still get out of town before traffic backs up on MoPac."

Gale laid the envelope on the bar. "In my years as a critic, I've seen restaurants come and go like waves on a sea. I can always read the signs." He paused for effect. "I'm here to make an offer to buy you out of Stella's. Hannah and I are financially prepared to make an investment, we have big ideas on what this market will respond to after a renovation," he gestured to the cozy colors, "and as a sign of good faith, we'd consider you as executive chef, at salary."

"How kind," Rudy said, between gritted molars.

"Hannah has such an aptitude for management," Gale said, touching his fiancée's waist. "She'd run the day-to-day responsibilities."

Reaching for the envelope, Rudy glanced at his ex-wife. "So, you factored everything into the accounting, including replacing my grandmother's trust fund, what you insisted we use as seed money?"

Hannah's eyes narrowed. "Not every risk can be regained, Rudy. You made that decision free and clear."

"Did I?" Rudy remembered a sequence of events where Hannah fanned the notion that this investment was what Stella would have wanted for her favorite grandson. Not that he'd ever thought he was the favorite, but he was the only one who shared her passion for cooking. "It was to have been Luna's college fund."

"Luna is young. She has ages before we have to worry about college. If she even wants to go beyond high school. You know, she's developed learning issues."

Luna's reading grades were a concern, but like her OCD tendencies, ones he expected would settle once balance was restored to her home life. Rudy handed Jay the unopened envelope. "I'll give your suggestion fair consideration, but don't hold your breath. Stella's has a healthy prospectus."

"Not if you keep getting trashed on Twitter," Gale said, raising his palms upward, as if some unkind fate controlled tweets.

"I have hired a forensic expert, and we have data suggesting the Twitter comments are from manufactured accounts originating from one lone computer." Rudy watched his opponent's gaze twitch. "In Manhattan."

"You can't discover that detail."

"Very little on Twitter is organic material anymore." Rudy replayed Lacy's explanation verbatim. "Much of it drives marketing. You would understand, as you manage the James Beard account."

Gale didn't blanch. "I have an intern who handles social media."

"I'd like their name, please, because I have issues with the truthfulness of their content."

"I'll refer your complaint to the appropriate channels."

Jay coughed, as if refereeing.

Tension rose with fiery licks, but he had the upper hand. He didn't need to drop kick Alan Gale; the man should live with his cowardice for using a woman to front his vendettas. "Be honest, this exercise today is nothing more than you trying to bring me down to your gutter. You've been jealous of my hard work, and instead of doing right by industry standards, you've snaked around looking for any other means to swipe at me."

"You flatter yourself, as usual."

Rudy took a step closer and lowered his voice. "And yet your infectious, greedy fingers follow my footsteps. They say friends make the worst enemies, and you are living proof. I'm only sorry Hannah couldn't see through you the first time."

With a sardonic laugh, Gale said, "And yet she keeps choosing me over you. What does that say, Delgardo?"

There was a grocery list of items he could site as reasons for Hannah's unquenchable thirst to be at the top, but he was no longer interested in them. She'd made her choices, and being a trustworthy partner was not one of them.

"It says that you're not getting your hands on Stella's." Rudy's fists clenched. "I will put up every means possible to you keep you, and your future wife, away from this doorstep."

Hannah gasped. "You can't do that. We have a legitimate offer."

"And yet, you forget, it's not for sale," Rudy said tightly, "I have a question, Hannah."

"Yes?"

"Who is watching our daughter?"

She waved away his concern. "My babysitter, not that it's any of your business."

"Your babysitter is my business. You made it such when you'd bring Luna to me instead of hiring someone in Abilene. I'd like to see the background check on every person you hire from here on out. Isn't that what you said to me about Mrs. Lin? Fair play. I'll expect criteria for babysitters, after-school pick up, and whomever you decide to use while you're on your honeymoon." He'd reread their divorce decree the other night, grateful that he'd had a conscientious attorney when his world upended. "I have legal rights, and I demand accountability."

"Or what?"

"Or I withhold child support."

"You wouldn't dare." Hannah's eyes flashed. "I'd throw you in court so fast your head would spin."

A man stepped forward from the shadows. "That's actually within his rights as father."

Hannah's hair followed the quick spin of her head. "Who are you?"

"Martin Goldsmith," the man offered his card, "an attorney representing Stella Restaurants, Incorporated."

"Stella what?" Hannah sputtered.

"The conglomerate that owns this restaurant, the bakery, Stella Too, and anything else that develops from this brand. Mr. Delgardo is *our* executive chef, and we're extremely pleased with his performance and the returns on our investments."

Gale and Hannah exchanged a furtive glance.

Jay handed the envelope to Goldsmith. "This offer is insulting." Jay turned his gaze on Gale. "When I share this information with the investors, they will question your credibility to even be reliable as a food critic. They're already investigating malicious intent during the James Beard Award process."

Martin folded the paper closed and shook his head. "Mr. Gale, you may think this offer was made in good faith, but I researched Mrs. Delgardo's financials prior to this meeting, and your name is listed as co-owner of her home in Abilene. The mortgage predates her divorce from my client. That calls into question her truthfulness about listed assets and what she cited as grounds for child support."

Hannah took a step backward. "What are you saying?"

Rudy reached for a water glass, suddenly parched. "He's saying you've lied to me, Hannah. From the reasons for the divorce to the truth about your assets. Those details give me all the information I need to appeal to a judge to have Luna's primary custody awarded to me." When her eyes squinted to slits, she was beyond reasoning; she'd resort to raising her voice when her arguments no longer got a reaction. He sighed, knowing he'd won. "Call your attorney, we'll set up a meeting."

Chapter Thirty-One

Drue pushed through the door of the *Comfort News,* her arms burdened with buckets of roses. "Don't leave yet," she said, peeking over the top of white and pink blooms. "I saw you loading your car. I've got to send these with you. AJ ordered them to go into the mix with her wildflower arrangements."

Lacy glanced from the box of Lavender Lodge event folders she'd designed and printed. "Good timing." She checked the wall clock. "The rental company arrived an hour ago with all the folding tables and chairs."

"I sent my grandsons to help with setup. Kali said if they'd tear everything down Sunday, too, she'll pay them and that they could eat as much BBQ as they wanted in between. Let me just say, those boys can put it away."

"She appreciates the help. We're all frazzled figuring out how to do something we've never done before."

Drue set the buckets near the door. "I'm praying the weather holds. As long as we don't get one of those blue northers you should have a good day tomorrow."

The last thing they needed was some unexpected cold front to send all the guests running for cover. She unplugged her phone charger and set the camera in her tote. She was shooting pictures around the property to upload and boost on Instagram and Facebook, hoping to convince folks looking for last-minute fun to choose their festival.

It was worth a try.

Driving out of town, she thought about the last-minute appeals she could make to television reporters and bloggers. Whether she could find ten minutes to sit down and shoot emails was debatable.

Backed up on the driveway, Lavender Hill shoppers swarmed AJ's garden store. Many walked the lavender fields beyond. Parking in the pasture, Lacy hauled as much as she could to the front of the lodge and would double back later for the flowers. Nodding to the wine vendors arranging their tasting stations, she glanced over the event hall, staged with tall tables. Beyond, they positioned even more tables and chairs on the patio.

She almost wished they'd planned a demonstration area so that Rudy could show off food preparation techniques, but they'd saved the idea for next year—if there was a second event.

"Lacy?"

She turned, seeing Luke holding an industrial-sized box of napkins.

"Where do you want these?"

They'd not discussed things like cups and napkins, other than that they needed them. "I guess in the kitchen for now. Have you seen Kali?"

He grimaced. "She left here, in tears, about twenty minutes ago. The rental company's invoice was twice what she expected, and she said it was the last straw on a day that has spiraled from bad to worse."

Lacy guessed that would be her fault, too. "Who is running today's setup?"

"You are?"

"Me?" Breath strangled in her throat. "Kali and AJ mapped the logistics."

"AJ is up to her eyeballs in customers today." He nodded toward the fields. "The posts you've put up have brought folks from as far as Houston. The problem couldn't be better or the timing worse."

She leaned back against a wall. "I can't do this. I can't see this through."

"Well, you're the third leg of this stool. You'll figure something out." Luke checked his phone. "I can stay for an hour. How can I help?"

She brought out the latest to-do list, scanned it for the most pressing needs, and latched on to Luke's arm to drag him with her to make sure the delivery of the portable toilets and picnic tables were in place. She would track down their day-hire police officer to direct traffic and clear the driveways.

Anxiety, pressure, and fear of failure swirled in a vat sitting right above her stomach. She'd never felt so ill prepared. Even the first Miss Bexar County competition hadn't been this torturous. As she scanned the pasture being marked for grill stations, she wondered if AJ and Kali regretted listening to her.

Dragging buckets of roses over to the Lavender Hill shop, she handed them to the head salesperson and told her to let AJ know Drue had provided them.

Betty nodded. "You want to take these Lavender Lodge plastic cups over with you?"

Her arms ached from carrying the roses, but she picked up the boxes she could manage. "Maybe one of the garden crew can bring the others over later."

Betty returned to checking out a customer, while Lacy took a call that confirmed details with the security crew, met the electrician who'd run extra lines from a generator out to the grilling area, and hurried to connect with the air-conditioning mechanic, who assured her there was enough tonnage to keep everyone inside the building comfortable.

As she wiped sweat from the back of her neck, she watched a Mercedes cruise into the Lavender Hill parking area and stop near her Ford. She'd invited him to come early but didn't believe he would. Lifting her hand, she flagged him down.

Christopher Woodley dropped his window. "I'm not going to say I got lost, but I would have been here sooner had I used GPS instead of trusting my navigational instincts."

"You're not late. The beer guy is mounting kegs. At the very least, I can offer you a beverage for your troubles."

"Then my timing is impeccable."

As he climbed out of his car, she could tell he'd dressed for labor with boots, Wranglers, and a polo shirt. "I have to make some phone calls," Lacy said, leading him away from the parking area. "Can I ask you to go into the event center and familiarize yourself with the kitchen? I've called a caterer to deliver lunch for the crew. We'll need to set the plates and napkins on the counter. They'll be here any minute."

He whipped off his sunglasses, tucking them into his collar. "I was in charge of fraternity tailgates in college, I've got this."

"Best words I've heard all day."

She walked toward the ranch house and entered the cool shade with a sigh Reaching for her cell, she sent reminder texts to the reporters she'd emailed earlier and confirmed directions with two of the cooks who'd called to ask if they could park their grills this afternoon.

Hanging up from a call to the ice company, a familiar number popped up on her screen. Her worries bundled into tight rolls constricting her heart. If she waited much longer, the call would go to voicemail. "Hello, Rudy."

"Lacy."

Lord, help her. His voice sent shivers down her spine.

"I hate to bother you when I know you're deep into last-minute details, but I talked to Don Hurt five minutes ago. He'll call you, but I wanted to give you fair warning. He's won't be able to make it tomorrow. Seems he was double-booked and can't get out of the other obligation."

No hi, hello, how are you doing. Nothing to indicate their last conversation hadn't been tear-soaked and filled with longing. Shutting down the images of a white dress and a man in blue denim, she brought her mind back to the pressure cooker. "The way this day is going, I'd be surprised if anyone shows up."

Rudy paused. "I told Kali I'd be late tomorrow. I have to drive halfway to Abilene in the morning to get Luna."

"What?" She stomped her foot into the carpet, curses floating on her tongue. Kali hadn't told her anything about a change with their keynote celebrity. "We had you scheduled for opening remarks at ten in the morning."

"I can't get there before one o'clock at the earliest."

She glared a hole into the wall of the living room. "Rudy, this has been on your calendar for months, why the change?"

"In a word, Hannah." His pause zinged with tension. "She says she's too sick to drive Luna to Austin this week. I'm meeting her babysitter halfway in the morning."

"Are you kidding? Luna doesn't have to be here, but you do."

"I'm doing this event as a favor for you, so I don't have a set schedule, right? Besides, I have to collect Luna now because her school is dismissing early since there are reports of a highly contagious virus." The sound of kitchen clatter rattled in the background. "I'll likely have her for several weeks, so I don't want to mess this up."

Viruses, inconveniences, ex-wives, and childcare formed a snowball nowhere near cooling off her temper. "So, Luna is your top priority." She bit her lip, knowing her voice sounded shrill. "Just to be clear."

"She is, yes."

If Lacy needed a neon sign to show her she'd never rate with Rudy, this was it. There was a limit to chemical reactions and hope. Reality bit her butt and cackled, *Better luck next time.*

But for her, she couldn't imagine a next time. Rudy had unlocked rooms in her soul she'd thought permanently shuttered. "Okay. Fine. Whatever. You do what you need to do, and we'll make the best of things until you arrive."

"Lacy?"

"That's what you wanted me to say, right? You don't want to hear me complain or beg you to reconsider." She picked a decorator's pillow from the sofa and squeezed the stuffing, hard. "Look, we've got a lot going on here right now. I need to get on it. You and Luna get here when you can." *The worst is never the worst.* "I'm sure it will all work out."

She disconnected the call and hugged the pillow. It was the height of selfishness to wish Rudy would call back and say how much he missed her and would drop everything to be with her. But he didn't. He wouldn't. He was a good father, the kind of partner she'd want if she were a mother.

Tossing the pillow, she shook her shoulders, loosening the knots that had doubled down into her neck. She wished she knew how to do this better—to be the mature one, the giver. But making peace with Frank's terminal condition, Gloria's story, and her growing ulcer confirmed she was shallow. A lightweight. Hardly the type to stay afloat in the deep waters of a committed relationship.

Knocking rapped against the front door.

She tugged on the knob and saw Christopher, holding out a Styrofoam container and saying, "The caterers arrived. I thought you'd like to eat too."

"I'll grab a bite later."

"I was afraid you'd say that, but you need fuel for the rest of the day. So, I brought my lunch too. I didn't think you'd sit there and watch me eat without wanting something too."

Compromising, she knew he was right even if he would be the punching bag for her mixed feelings. "Come in, I'll give you the five-cent tour of Lavender Hill's B and B." She lifted the lid and saw salty chips, a crunchy pickle, and a sandwich taller than it was wide. Her mouth watered, and she accepted that he'd rescued her from an acute case of hangriness. "This is the ranch house Kali and AJ saw that started them dreaming of an event center."

Christopher whistled as he took in the kitchen outfitted with white subway tiles, stainless-steel appliances, and marble counters. "They know how to renovate a place. These wood floors are beautiful."

"Those are original, but they were buried under linoleum. The architect who designed the event center renovated this place too." Lacy swallowed a gulp of tea. "Oh, to have her brain power."

"I'd hire her in a heartbeat."

Lacy unwrapped the parchment from around the sandwich and paused before biting into the wheat toast. "Get in line—they have a waiting list. She designs, and her husband builds the plans."

While she chewed through the deli meat, she thought about Colette and hoped she'd be okay. Beau had texted that she was having contractions. They'd stay in San Antonio instead of driving to Comfort for the festival.

How ridiculous would she feel, how mortified, if they'd spent all this money, invested all this effort, on her grand opening idea, and no one actually attended? It would be worse than the Bexar County pageant talent competition where she'd warbled a cover of a July Sands hit song—barely rating a two from the judges' panel. This spectacle would carry far more expense and dents to lifelong friendships.

Christopher returned from inspecting the bedrooms and baths to pat her on the shoulder. "Hey, why the long face?"

She nibbled a chip. "Processing. This day isn't rolling out as I had thought it would."

"Well, since no one has done this before, I didn't think there was a precedent." He smiled. "On the upside, no one can compare it to anything, either. You get to establish the standard."

"That sounds terrifying."

"Amy Marsh going on the *Bachelor* is worse. Do you know how those other girls will tear her apart? She's too innocent for that crowd."

A chip caught in her throat, and she disguised her surprise at his comment with coughing. "I didn't realize you were a fan."

Christopher glanced around the room. "I'm definitely on Team Lacy. But I hate seeing folks fed to the sharks."

"Amy can hold her own." She should have guessed that Christopher was attracted to celebrity. Hadn't so many of his questions been about the folks she'd met and the places Miss Texas was invited to attend? "At least by this time tomorrow the food-judging portion of the festival will be over. The rest of the day will be a free-for-all."

He pulled out a barstool and sat. "Any chance I can talk you into supper tonight? I brought a cooler with takeout because I wasn't sure what the offerings would be in town."

Her phone dinged, and she saw a message from the photographer. He included a link to some of the best photos from the bridal shoot. Closing her eyes, she debated whether she should peek. There wasn't time to give them their due, and Christopher would peek over her shoulder.

Her nerves hummed with indecision. Rudy had been eye candy that morning.

Flipping the phone over, she ate the last of the chips and tried to remember his question. *Supper*? "I'm grateful you're here, and if we're not exhausted by tonight, I'll take you up on the offer. I can throw in a salad and a cold beer. Are you staying overnight?"

"I could." His eyes gleamed. "I wouldn't mind staying with you."

And that was a *no*. "Sorry, I don't do sleepovers."

Backing up a bit, he repositioned his expression. "We can negotiate that another time."

She'd let him think rejection was a matter of persuasive skill, but the truth was Christopher would be forever stained by her first impression. She hadn't warmed up to a patronizing man, and she didn't think she ever would.

"Thanks for lunch, I didn't realize how hungry I was. Do you want to walk over to Lavender Hill? I have to track down AJ."

"I'd follow you anywhere."

She glanced at him and would have laughed at the sappiness, but his eyes were sincere. *Dang*. "You won't say that after you see my sister's goat farm. But for today, we'll stick to AJ's lavender fields."

Christopher asked a hundred questions between the house and the garden shop, and she'd gladly turn him over to Luke or Jake if either were around. A chatty man could be so annoying.

In a sweat-soaked T-shirt and shorts marred by dirt, AJ limped around the greenhouse, finding a shady spot for them to sit.

"What happened?" Lacy asked, watching AJ wince as she sat on the wicker rocker.

"I pulled my back lifting planters, and I have pain shooting down my leg." She wiped her brow. "I now know what my grandmother meant when she used to say she had a hitch in her get-along."

Christopher wandered over to the colorful display featuring native plants.

AJ leaned into the arm of the rocker and whispered, "Remind me why your attorney is hanging around?"

Lacy wished she had a better explanation, but she was too wired to invent one. "He's got a crush, and I'm trying to decide if it's worth pursuing."

"And Rudy?"

Lacy blew a strangled breath through her lips. "We have too many obstacles, not the least being he's a dad."

"I didn't know that stopped people from falling in love."

It didn't, but for reasons she couldn't explain, Rudy couldn't manage both. "He's got to battle his ex for custody, and there's no room left for me."

Pursing her lips, AJ thought for a moment. "I've never seen you give up easily."

"I'm trying to be mature. Responsible. Or whatever it is when you let someone go because you know they have too many other things fighting for priority in their life."

"Honorable. I believe that's the word."

Honorable. Rolling the word through her mind, she pictured the warrior monk she'd first envisioned when Rudy walked into Stella's dining room that long-ago morning. He'd brought with him the fragrance of grassy hills and campfires. One look into his stormy eyes and she'd hop on his horse, hang onto his waist, and ride with him wherever he went.

Images from a hundred romantic movie endings blew through her mind, but a nagging doubt trailed behind. What if he'd never had anyone fight for him?

"Lacy?"

She glanced at Christopher, who stood holding a pot planted with a mixture of blooming red and pink flowers. "Sorry. Catching a moment of aimless thought before we get back to work."

AJ climbed out of the rocker, groaning a bit. "We're in our busy season around here, otherwise I'd give you a tour. Wander around, everyone else does."

Christopher glanced at the crowds but didn't move.

AJ unfolded a list from the papers stuffed into her pocket. "Notes for the most critical things in our setup today, but I feel like you've done most of this already."

Scanning the bullet points, she felt a huge measure of relief. "All that remains is to assemble the arrangements for the vintner tables. Are we going to borrow some of your planters to stage at the entrance and ticket area?"

Christopher leaned in. "Are you charging folks to enter?"

"A small fee, to cover security and expenses we didn't expect."

Christopher nodded. His affirmation grated on Lacy's nerves, as if he'd never expected her to give serious thought to running this event as a business.

AJ picked a dead bloom off a geranium, saying, "Anna is organizing a supper for Luke's jazz musicians who are here to play for the event tomorrow. Do you and Christopher want to stop by? It's about six, something simple to welcome them to the area."

"Sure," she said, grateful for a change of subject. "I'll ask if she needs help."

Later, after they'd arranged the welcome tent, she cleaned the bathrooms while Christopher swept grass clippings from the patio. Grungy, they separated to freshen up before meeting at Anna's address.

She yanked her car door open, feeling a roll of heat greet her. Before she sat down, she took one last glance around the fields, already dotted with tents. No turning back now. Whatever happened, she'd done the best she could. It was going to be a crazy twenty-four hours, but not anything of the scale of the Titanic or Hindenburg. If everything crashed tomorrow, no lives would be altered. It was just about eating comfort foods in a great location with friends. Then, come Monday, once everything was put away, she could figure out how to manage the rest of this life.

For reasons that still stunned her, she'd chosen this neck of the Hill Country to make her home. It better not let her down.

Chapter Thirty-Two

Cars, trucks, and SUVs lined the road leading to Lavender Hill. Some locals rode over on horseback to see what the fuss was about. Lacy stood at the welcome tent, fixing wristbands on guests as fast as she could.

"This turnout is nuts," Drue laughed, handing maps to those passing through the tent. "Never in a million years would I guess that folks would drive to Comfort for some fancy-schmancy BBQ."

Kali gave coupons to a family towing dogs on leashes. "It's only eleven, and we've already made enough to reimburse the cooks for their expenses."

Nervous tension still coursed under her skin, but Lacy didn't worry about the turnout any longer. Between the lodge and the garden center, there were almost a thousand people gathered on these five acres. Sunshine bathed the lavender fields in vibrant colors, and the jazz tunes drifting over the tops of the grill tents added the perfect touch.

The walkie-talkie clipped to her shorts buzzed, and she stepped away to hear an update from security. Flagging a volunteer driving a golf cart, she asked him to deliver cases of water to the patio where they were already running low.

Christopher offered her a can of lemonade. "I found this at the bottom of an ice chest and grabbed it for you."

Leaning into the side of a pickup truck, she popped the top and let the sweetness cool her throat. "Thanks for being here. You were such a help to get the musicians on stage."

"Call me a roadie. It's more fun than sitting at a desk."

Chagrined for thinking so little of him yesterday, she said, "Most people wouldn't give up a weekend to work this hard, but I'm grateful. Did you see the Austin news team? They said this should make tonight's broadcast."

He toasted her with his beer. "Did you finish your projects last night? I hated that you left the supper so early."

Did he know the hours she'd wasted mooning over the photos of Rudy posed in the lavender fields? No, he couldn't. She'd stopped short of posting those to the website because it felt too personal to open the images for world critique.

"And where's your celebrity chef?" Christopher asked coolly. "I expected him at the kickoff."

Adjusting the brim of her ball cap, Lacy gazed toward the tents. "Oh, some complications. He's supposed to be here for the judging."

"And you're sure there's nothing between the two of you? I saw him at Falcon Ridge, and I'm good at reading juries. That man was into you."

For something to do, she checked her cell. "Friends, that's all."

Christopher nudged her shoulder and pointed to the road. "So, who's that?"

She turned, watching a bus navigate the backlogged cars. "I don't know." Listening in on the walkie-talkie chatter, she got the impression it was a tour bus. "I'll investigate and be back in a few minutes."

Before she could move far, guests were asking for a first-aid station, then someone else told her a bathroom was clogged. She ran interference and forgot the unexpected bus.

Later, as she stood in the building letting her T-shirt cool in front of a fan, she glanced over and saw a mob hurrying toward the patio. Stepping away, she wove through the crowd, praying someone wasn't on the ground with a medical emergency.

Coming to the center, she saw the TV-camera crews fixated on someone and as she broke through the line, she gasped. A brunette in a short leopard skirt and black camisole signed autographs for fans.

"Amy?"

Handing a CD cover back to a guest, Amy Marsh glanced toward Lacy and grinned. "Surprise! I couldn't wait to get here and celebrate this big day with you."

Blood drained, pooling inside Lacy's feet.

"Imagine my joy when I saw on Insta one of my best friends was hosting a big Texas tailgate." Amy smiled for the cameras. "I cancelled everything in L.A. and made my daddy send a plane. I wasn't going to miss your shindig. After all you've done for me, I was going to be here for you."

This nightmare sucked air from her lungs.

Amy slithered through the teenaged girls to stand beside Lacy, wrapping an arm through hers. Pouting, she asked, "Aren't you happy to see me?"

Cameras lenses whirred, whispers buzzed, and a foam-covered microphone was jammed in front of her face, but Lacy had no words. Legal documents flashed through her memory.

Amy propped her hand on her hip. "And to top it all off, today is Lacy's birthday. I guess you could say I'm her gift." Turning away from the camera and lowering her voice, she whispered, "And I'm going to hijack your moment. *And* you won't be able to post anything about it. The Blonde Goddess has been silenced on her big day. Gotcha."

Processing what Amy's presence really meant, a sinkhole formed in her chest. She'd done all this work to stage an event bright and unique—worthy of going viral—and a Marsh family attorney would monitor her image.

Like flashlights at a concert, she noticed a hundred people holding their phones to record and photograph these moments. Her ulcer seeped with the worry that somehow, she'd walked into a trap. But no, everything was above board. She'd had no idea Amy would arrive. Really, who could have seen this coming? As long as she didn't post a picture or an innuendo about Amy—oh, who was she kidding? Everyone here would light up the internet with Amy Marsh's name.

A reporter asked Amy questions about her upcoming tour and rumors of a romance on the *Bachelor* set, while Lacy scanned the crowd for Christopher. Maybe he would know how to respond within the boundaries of their mediated agreement with the Marsh family. She'd have to feel her way through these next minutes and pray she didn't step in something she couldn't wash off her feet.

When the microphone swung her way, Lacy said the first thing that came to mind. "We're so thrilled that an exceptional Texas artist has come to Lavender Lodge, and it's my birthday wish that she'll be one of our celebrity judges. Wouldn't everyone like it if Amy Marsh did the honors?"

Clapping and cheers washed over her, and she used the distraction to disengage from a woman here to set a disaster. A glimpse of Kali's stunned expression met hers from across the patio. "Find Christopher," she mouthed to her sister.

Kali nodded and slipped behind a hunter in camo attire.

Heartbeat racing, Lacy backed away, hoping to dodge the reporter. Wild thoughts bombarded her brain, and none of them made sense. She wouldn't waste time figuring out Amy's intentions. The best use of this chaos was to avoid repeating past mistakes. First, she'd text the girls assigned to post pictures from today and insist they resist every temptation to mix an image of Amy with the Lavender Lodge brand. Second—oh. She had no idea what to do next.

"Lacy?"

That tiny voice cut through the conversations and darted into her heart. "Luna?"

Turning, she saw a tall knight being dragged forward by a miniature princess. Luna's violet shorts set boasted Cinderella in her magic kingdom. The frilly purple bows holding her pigtails against her head completed the ensemble. Rudy wore his basic uniform of gray shirt and jeans, but the lines around his eyes were new and spoke of sleepless nights.

Feeling his pain, she pasted on a smile. "You're earlier than I had expected."

"Daddy raced to get here," Luna announced. "He said we couldn't let you down."

A chunk of ice melted from her around her heart. "Thanks, the day just took a turn for the weird, so I'm glad you made it."

"We didn't let you down, did we?" Luna's eyes rounded. "We saw the TV cameras and Daddy said we might be too late."

Lacy grabbed Luna's other hand and pulled them into the event center. "Listen, whatever happens, just play along. Someone terrible has arrived, and I can't promise this thing is going on as planned."

"Like an evil stepmother?"

Lacy glanced at Luna. "Just like that."

Rudy chuckled. She would ignore the deep, rolling timbre. Inviting him into the mix of this awful dream would be like tossing kerosene on Don Hurt's grill.

Christopher appeared before her, staring at the threesome holding hands. "Lacy?"

Without having time to explain, she announced, "Amy Marsh is here."

"*The* Amy Marsh?" Christopher's head swung around the perimeter, searching for the face featured on magazine covers. "How did she get in?"

"That doesn't matter. I need to know what I can or cannot say and still be above any backlash from her father."

"How am I supposed to know?" Christopher demanded. "I thought she'd moved to California."

"She's here, and the darling of the TV cameras. Twitter will blow up with the news."

Rudy interrupted. "I can see why you're upset but let me help. She can be a judge with me, and that will distract her for an hour."

"Already done. I threw that notion out as soon as I realized I had to say something, anything."

Rudy's expression narrowed. "Then I must make sure she oversees the taste test of the BBQ sauces. These guys usually go heavy with their jalapeños."

"I love that you have a dark side," Lacy said, before she realized how much she confessed. "In the meantime, Christopher, you glue yourself to her and distract her from upstaging events. Rudy, find Kali and get your official judge's pin. I'll keep Luna with me."

Christopher and Rudy sized each other up, but no one offered an alternative suggestion. They divided, and Luna hurried to match steps with Lacy.

"Do you have a poisoned apple?"

Lacy glanced down at her tiny companion. "Tempting, but no. We'll have to use our brains, instead of fruit, to solve this one."

Luna sighed. "If only we had a fairy godmother."

"We do!" Lacy dodged a family balancing plates of brisket and slaw and nearly crashed into a couple pushing a dog in a stroller. "Follow me."

Sweat dripped along her spine. If she were to prevent Amy from undermining months of hard work, it would require the insight of someone who'd worked far more hostile takeovers.

"Gloria!" They scooted to a halt at the Becker Vineyard serving station, waving down the volunteer pouring wine into sample cups. She'd worn a purple blouse to blend in with the team. "I was afraid you'd already left."

Smiling, she gazed from Lacy to Luna. "It's nice to be away from the hospital. Frank has a wonderful nurse. I think I'll stay all afternoon."

"Perfect, I need your help."

"And who is this angel?"

Lacy picked Luna up and set her on a stool. "This is Rudy Delgardo's daughter, Luna. And she believes in the power of princesses."

"Always good to rely on a higher power." Gloria winked. "I guess this means your chef has arrived."

Gloria knew the gory details of their story, but there was too much madness stalking the event to correct any details about to whom he belonged. "Amy Marsh has surprised us all by rolling in, and the only reason I can think of for her to fly halfway across the country is to damage something important to me."

"A logical guess, in light of your history."

"So, what do I do about it?" Lacy twisted her hands together. "What plot can I counter with to prevent her stealing the attention?"

Gloria lifted the vineyard apron from over her chest and gave it to the next shift volunteer. "Why do anything?"

Dumbfounded, she said, "Because Amy has malicious intent."

"Mali-eee-ishness." Luna grinned.

"Yeah, that too."

Gloria patted Lacy's arm. "Darling, sometimes letting someone take the upper hand and watching what they do with it is the better use of your conscience."

Music from the jazz group's guitarist filtered through the air, and Lacy wondered if she misunderstood.

"Anything you counter, she will stab back against. Why give her that much influence? Let her hog the limelight. As a matter of fact, direct even more attention on her. She'll post all the moments to her accounts, and by nightfall, the thing she intended to use to hurt you will become a blessing for Lavender Lodge."

"You mean . . . do nothing?"

"Life is too short to chase every insult. If you don't respond to her taunts, she'll stand alone with nothing but ugly words for company. You have a lot more to take care of today than wasting it on revenge."

Luna's eyes glued on Gloria.

Maybe Gloria was right. Amy was up to something. Since she had no idea of the specifics, maybe it would be best to give Amy the stage. Besides, Mr. Marsh couldn't sue if she didn't respond with anything slanderous.

"Luna, would you be willing to sample sno-cones with me?" Gloria asked, bending to knee level. "I have coupons I haven't used yet and overheard kids talking about a tiger flavor that sounds delicious."

"Can I, Lacy? Please?"

"Let's go together. I need to remind the chefs that judging is about to begin."

They headed outdoors, toward the pasture filled with trucks, trailers, and tents. Mesquite-scented smoke lay heavily over the heads of those ambling past, samples of barbecued venison and buffalo already the crowd favorites.

"I see Daddy!"

And with him was a none-too-happy Amy Marsh. Her strappy shoes were no match for the dry grass and pebbles. Kali led the pair to each station, giving them the overview of the contestants. A TV crew followed in their wake.

Lacy held back. If she didn't get too close, Amy wouldn't taunt her with whatever grenades she'd packed. Glancing at Gloria's contented countenance, she would borrow a slice of grace from someone who'd walked difficult miles.

Luke ambled over with Beans on a leash. "I'm surprised E! hasn't followed Amy to Comfort. Most likely, she sent a press release of her intentions."

"She would?"

Luke shrugged one shoulder. "If I were her PR manager, I'd do it. Your video gave her national attention, of course they'd want to see what you might do for an encore."

All the more reason to take Gloria's advice. "I could dig out my tiara and really make it a show."

Chuckling, Luke handed her his bag of French fries. "I'm sure there's a Blonde Goddess meme out there already. Try these. The guy said they're truffle fries. I'm in love."

"My daddy makes truffel-iscious fries."

Luke grinned. "If your daddy is Chef Delgardo, I'd say you were the luckiest girl on the planet."

"He is!"

Luke winked. "How smart am I?"

Lacy snitched a few of the potato treats. "I have to get to work now. It's showtime. Luna, do you want to come with me?"

"I'd rather get a sno-cone."

"You go with Gloria, and I'll catch up with Kali. We'll meet up again in a few minutes."

Weaving through the cooking tents and passing the hot grills, she still felt amazed an idea born on the back of a pickup truck had grown into a thousand people eating and laughing. It was too good to be true.

Kali caught her gaze and motioned to the rear of the group. "Christopher had a word with Amy and told her if she stirred up trouble today, he'd call her management company."

"How did she take that news?"

"Oddly enough, I think it excited her. She's hanging on his arm and smiles at him like he's dreamy. Does she know he likes you? Is she using him?"

There was no telling what Amy had cooked to serve today. Lacy took the clipboard from her sister. "What are the odds we can get through the tastings without an incident?"

"You have Rudy on your side, that trumps everything."

She hoped Rudy was on her side. After the way they'd left things on the phone, she wasn't sure where she stood with him. "I'll have a word with the TV crew, review the procedures with them, then we can get started."

Approaching the jumble of media, tourists, and fans, Lacy stepped up to the platform that also functioned as a backdrop for those who wanted to take selfies with the *Love Grows Here* logo.

"Welcome, everyone," she said, after tapping the microphone to make sure it was live. "We have a beautiful Hill Country day to celebrate the beginnings of good things growing at Lavender Lodge. We hope everyone has time to tour the event center, eat tons of good food, and enjoy the lavender fields next door. It's taken a team of volunteers to pull today together, but we couldn't be prouder to have two special guests as our celebrity judges at this first-ever festival.

"You all knew we had invited award-winning chef Rudy Delgardo from Austin to be with us today. He's a rising star in the food industry and a Texas favorite for farm-to-table cuisine. You'll want to follow him on Instagram and watch the behind-the-scenes videos inside his restaurant, Stella's. No promises on the recipes for those famous dishes, though.

"*But*, as a surprise feature—and every great event always has a secret up its sleeve—we share with you the beautiful and talented Amy Marsh as co-judge for the BBQ tasting! She flew in from California today, an example of her generous spirit, and y'all give her a big Comfort welcome to let her know how much we appreciate her!"

Amy cut her gaze to Lacy, her eyes wide. Lacy winked and blew a kiss, sealing an end to the duel she'd begun a year ago.

As the jazz band's tunes sailed across the fields, adding a soulfulness to those gathering around the food tents, she led Rudy and Amy to the first station where a chef from Helotes had prepared grilled trout. With a megaphone, she called out the contestant's number and handed the criteria to the two judges. Rudy stepped under the pop-up tent that sheltered the table, eager to see what the chef had created.

"I don't eat fish." Amy folded her arms. "I didn't sign up to be a judge, either."

"I'm sorry to put you in a spot. I was so excited when you arrived, I wanted to give you the biggest opportunity to shine. If you'd rather judge on presentation you could avoid having to taste anything you didn't want to eat."

A reporter hurriedly wrote Lacy's comment.

Amy leaned in close, saying, "Don't think this is over."

"You seem to have landed on top, Amy. I can't imagine what more you could want."

The seconds beat slowly. "I want this," she gestured to the crowd, "your ability to land on your feet."

As musical notes circled her thoughts, she wondered what Amy was talking about. "Then you'll have to truly forgive me for that video last year. It was through the fallout of that experience that I learned what was important. If I've 'landed on my feet', as you say, it's because I have really great people in my life, and they've shown me the way forward."

Amy sneered. "So, you believe that sappy 'Love grows here' slogan?"

"I do."

"You're worse off than I realized." Amy flashed a smile for the TV camera pointed her way. "You beauty queens really do have syrup in your veins."

Christopher inched past the onlookers, touching Lacy's elbow. "Everything all right here?"

"Peachy," Lacy said, with an added dose of sweetness. "Amy doesn't want to eat the fish, so will you escort her along the route, and we'll let her judge the food items with the most visual appeal. She can give the blue ribbon at the end."

Lacy stepped away from the tent, needing a dose of fresh air to soothe the ache pounding behind her forehead. Rudy analyzed the trout and seemed capable of handling the tastings. She'd move near the next grill master's team and ride out the minutes without the glare of spectators.

A bolt of fur flew past her feet and forced her gaze to follow its trajectory across the grass and between the legs of guests.

"*Rudy,*" she hissed, watching the dog aim for the tent with the grilled trout.

Within seconds, Amy screamed, tossing napkins into the air. The papers landed on the grill, shooting orange flames into the air. The dog circled the tent, yapping and stirring everyone into a frenzy. Folks backed away, tripping into the strings and stakes holding the tent steady. It collapsed suddenly, capturing people in a tangle of fabric. Guests ran hither and yon as news cameras captured the flight.

Once the fire was suffocated, the cook batted away the poles and flags, and righted the table. Christopher and Amy reacted to the food spilled onto their clothes with a vocabulary that surprised most. A four-legged beast whizzed free of the tenting, a prized trout caught between his teeth.

"My dish!" The cook chased the whirling mutt. "Catch that dog!"

Luna bolted after the cook, shrieking, "Rudy-toodie! I love you!"

Echoes of Rudy-toodie carried with the billows of mesquite smoke, cotton candy, and cooking oil. Children started chasing the dog through the grounds, yelling his new nickname.

Gloria stepped next to Lacy. "See, what I've always said—the worst is never the worst. What looks like complete disaster is, in fact, an unscripted grand opening for Lavender Lodge."

Noise, chaos, Christopher picking straw from Amy's hair, it was all nuts. A bubble of laughter hovered perilously close to her panic button. "Did Rudy-toodie just steal my show?"

"Yes, dear. He did."

"And there are at least a hundred folks recording this carnival with their cell-phone cameras, right?"

Gloria nodded.

Lacy fell against her friend's side. "Talk about a recipe for disaster."

She laughed, wrapping a motherly arm around Lacy. "I think we can amend that to say the best stories are remembered from handwritten recipes. You've just collected one for the ages."

Chapter Thirty-Three

Luna slept on a pile of sofa cushions tucked against the stone wall, while Lacy rocked in a chair underneath the starlight gleaming from the velvet sky. Lavender Lodge's patio boasted a previously unappreciated view of the Hill Country. Tables, folding chairs, and bars were propped against the ledge, ready for the rental company to collect. But she couldn't move to make sure all the elements had been rounded up. Even thinking about hauling away the trash made her brain hurt, not to mention her back and legs.

Rudy stepped from the sliding door, two bottles of water in his hands. "This is as close as I could find to a nightcap. Sorry, they're room temp. Ice buckets melted down hours ago."

Taking one of the water bottles, she said, "I'm so dehydrated that I'll say thanks, even if it's warm."

He pulled a rocker close to her side and settled into the wicker. Silence stretched between them, but it wasn't stiff or uncomfortable. After the day they'd endured, the stillness felt easy. A raccoon skittered trough the lavender, and a bat dipped and danced in the distance. The night air settled on her shoulders, reminding her the work was done.

"Don Hurt called after seeing the Austin news tonight and regretted he'd missed the festival. Said it look like more fun than where he was. Better food, too."

"I'm sure he'd not want to be associated with our circus."

The series of unfortunate events, ending with bee stings and sunburns, could be collated into a notebook that would scare any novice away from attempting to do something new, but weirdly enough, she was proud of everyone's efforts. From Drue's flowers to Luke's jazz group, everything had been done to a high standard. Even if it did nose-dive, thanks to that dust mop with legs.

"Someone once told me even bad press is good for the brand."

Those words circled back from a day when she thought she understood how to get on top of a spectacular flameout. "Well, that person is an idiot."

Rocking motions competed with cicadas' song, and Lacy could also hear the distant clatter of plates and cutlery being moved around in the catering kitchen, along with the hum of conversation from the last of the volunteers.

"Seriously, Rudy." She reached across the space and laid her hand over his arm. "I'm sorry we roped you into such a disastrous PR fiasco. If it helps, I don't think Stella's will get burned from this exposure. You were great to give the award to the chef from Helotes, even though he will never admit to being in Comfort today after the dog ran away with his trout."

"His second attempt at the trout was even more delicious than the first. He deserved the award." Rudy lifted her hand and let it settle between his fingers. "Everyone will remember the Gray Moss Inn after today. And, to be clear, I'm not worried for Stella's. The restaurant is in good shape and will carry on just fine even if we never post another thing to Twitter."

She looked at their hands joined together, marveling at how wonderful his calluses felt against her skin. "Explain how Amy Marsh's meltdown will turn into something good."

Chuckling, he grinned. "There's no way to spin her hissy fit into anything that reflects well on her. If the cameramen roll that footage, her PR company will have to buy YouTube to keep it from going viral."

"But everyone is going to blame me. *Again.*"

Rudy leaned toward her, pulling her hand against his chest. "She surprised you. She admitted it on TV, and you were nowhere near the tent going down on her head." Rudy kissed her fingers before setting her hand back on the armrest. "I don't buy her claim that the oil ruined her blouse. Someone will have to produce a receipt before I believe that scrap of fabric cost $500."

Sensations from his touch loosened some tension binding her lungs, and his words massaged her heart. He protected her. Regardless of how the event had turned into a hilarious party after the dog ruined the first tasting, Rudy stood with her.

Kali ambled to the patio, a homemade cake balanced in her hands. "Surprise!"

Jake, Luke, and AJ followed, carrying coffee mugs.

"Please say that's not for me."

"It's your birthday," Kali said, leaning to kiss her sister's head. "And though today's party would be impossible to top, we knew we couldn't let the day end without a slice of your favorite strawberry cake."

Rudy helped Kali with the plates and forks. "Strawberry?"

"From a mix and with a box of Jell-O. It's not fancy."

"You went to the trouble to make something during a week that was as busy as any you've endured." Rudy handed Lacy the carving knife. "That makes it the fanci-best-ess, as Luna would say."

They glanced to the child sleeping soundly through the conversation.

"She does have a delightful way of inventing new words." Lacy sure liked that kid. "We'll save her a big slice."

Luke sipped his mug. "You two still have to unpack, don't you? I saw your car at Lavender Hill."

Rudy nodded.

Lacy handed around plates with generous helpings of cake, licking frosting from her fingertips. "Thanks, Kal. You didn't have to do this."

Kali shrugged. "In hindsight, I'm really glad I did. Amy let the news out, and folks have been asking all day if this was a birthday party. Drue read me the riot act for not getting everyone to sign a card"

"The best gift of all would be to forget Amy was ever here." With a fork poised, Lacy sighed. "How strange was it, her showing up on a tour bus?"

Chewing her cake, AJ said, "Very strange."

"But we couldn't have paid for that level of publicity. I had three people request rental information today." Kali settled on the rim of the firepit. "So, not a total fail. And, as far as I can tell, she didn't seem to ding your success, so it was little more than a childish prank."

Rudy lowered his voice and reached for her arm. "She didn't hurt you, did she?"

"Not in the least." Lacy savored his touch, as well as the sweet, gooey flavors of the cake. "Christopher escorted her through the crowds, and I haven't seen him since. Who knows, maybe they'll start talking. He did seem to be a fan."

"You'd be okay with that?" he asked.

"Sure. He's my attorney first, and a friend second. No other attachments."

Rudy relaxed into the chair. "Good. And I'm sorry I didn't know today was your birthday. I would have brought a gift."

His steadying presence and on-going confidence had been the best gift she could have received. The guests laughed along with him as he judged the entries with enough critique to be credible, and a heavy dose of humor to balance the mix. Luna's cooperation had been an added blessing. She and Gloria became buddies, riding on golf carts, serving vendors cold beverages and special snacks supplied by Provence Farm. They'd been nicknamed "the Lavender Ladies."

Conversation buzzed around the other highlights from the day. Too tired to offer comment, Lacy let their words seep into her brain for later consideration. Images from the day flew behind her eyes, reminding her that there had been more positive experiences than negatives for the guests. Though her muscles dictated a week to recover, she'd sleep well tonight knowing they'd done the best they could do for a first-time event.

The most important revelation of the day sat next to her. If she thought she'd loved him before, he was going to be doubly hard to forget after tonight.

AJ yawned. "Luke, take me home. I can't stay upright a minute longer."

Nodding, he set his mug on the firepit. "Your wish is my command. I pulled the golf cart around ten minutes ago."

Turning to Rudy, she asked, "Do you want to let Luna ride home with us and Beans? I hate to wake her, but it might be more tolerable if a dog is involved. Beans is no match for Rudy-toodie, but he's a decent runner-up."

"If that's not too much trouble? I can follow in the car, and we'll get her right to bed."

Jake sighed, leaning against Kali. "Let's go home, Momma. I haven't seen Charlie all day, and I'm going through withdrawals."

"Right." Kali laughed, shucking his weight off her shoulder. "You heard the word 'bed,' and your brain started shutting down. I know you too well."

Struggling to stand on legs that felt wooden, Lacy fetched the plates and mugs. "I'll turn the lights off here, y'all all go home. The rental company is coming tomorrow about two, so we can draw straws to see who lets them into the lodge."

"Drue's grandsons were such a big help, I think everything is stacked here on the patio. So, maybe none of us has to get out of bed tomorrow." Kali grimaced. "Except we'll have Charlie who will want to play."

"You can distract him with the rest of this cake. Thanks for making it. That meant the world to me."

Kali's eyes turned misty. "Love you, baby sister."

"Love you, Kals."

Waving them off, Lacy wandered into the lodge, grateful someone had swept the floor and stacked the garbage bags. A new to-do list was forming, and she wished she could shut her brain down. She jumped, hearing footsteps following her indoors. "I thought you were driving to the farmhouse."

Rudy shook his head. "I'm not leaving you alone. I know it's Comfort, but I'll follow you to your car and make sure you get to town."

Her heartrate shot high, but she didn't think it had anything to do with dark country roads. "I saw AJ's friend, Walter, doing a security check a few minutes ago, so I think we're clear."

"Don't argue," he said, taking the plates from her and stacking them in the sink. "I'm not leaving you alone."

"Who's arguing? I'm too exhausted."

Rudy ran water over the plates, glancing at her with longing. "Tomorrow, we need to talk. A lot has happened in the last few days, and I regret telling you we didn't have a future. But I'll not push it tonight. I want you coherent when we consider what tomorrow might bring."

His voice warmed cells she'd thought hibernated. "You know we don't talk well. We're like puppies stumbling over words."

"Please, don't mention dogs. That mutt you named Rudy has created a legend. Luna cried herself to sleep, worried he'd be put in doggie jail."

Chuckling at how their lives were interconnected, she saw a glimmer of hope where they'd not been one yesterday. To celebrate, she shut off the lights, plunging them into darkness.

Rudy cut the water, reaching for a dishtowel. "So, this is how you want to communicate?"

"Our bodies seem to say what our words twist."

He met her at the doorway, reaching his arms around her waist. "You drive me crazy, do you know that? I can't get you out of my head. Not that I've tried. Not very hard, at least."

"I did try. I've made a conscious effort, but I failed miserably," Lacy confessed. "I didn't want to fall for you, but I can't seem to help myself. You're too delicious to resist."

He nibbled her ear. "Nothing makes sense without you in it."

"Kind of like your secret ingredient?"

He kissed her thoroughly. "You're the most prized ingredient in the entire universe. I never want to cook without you by my side."

Sagging against his chest, she laid her cheek over his heart. "Never is a long time."

"It doesn't sound long enough to me." He rubbed circles into her back. "Promise we'll figure a way to be together? You with your newspaper, me with my restaurant."

"When you hold me like this, anything is possible."

Rudy picked her up and set her on the counter, stepping between her legs. "Love is a recipe worth every effort."

She wound her arms around his neck, her lips hovering near his. "I'll give you five stars if you say nothing so corny ever again."

Laughing, he swooped in for a kiss and ended any more discussions about the merits of trust, respect, and communication for an award-winning dish.

Epilogue

Three Years Later

The freelance writer drove the rental onto the freshly tarred parking lot, searching the surroundings for a sign to confirm she'd reached her destination. Comfort, Texas was not someplace she'd imagined travelling when she accepted this assignment, but at least it wasn't too far off the interstate. About an hour from San Antonio, she felt reasonably sure she'd find her way back to the airport tonight.

Still, there wasn't much to see this far into limestone-carved hills. The town must be in the other direction. Bubba's Bust-A-Gut gas station had been the landmark before she turned onto a paved drive and wound around a hillside, seeing newly staked grapevines and a barn. Thankfully, the building, white stucco with wide, black-framed windows, looked as if it had been designed as a restaurant. The portico welcomed the curious closer with oversized brass lanterns, gigantic, potted flowers and herbs, it also boasted a welcome mat as wide as a carpet. But her notes indicated there was a vineyard and a family house on the property, so she'd tread carefully in case she'd made a wrong turn.

Rising from the car, she gathered her recorder and camera, prepared to spend the afternoon interviewing people. *Bon Appétit* magazine had offered her a hefty fee if she could turn this piece in before their next deadline, and she was determined to succeed.

A mutt of indiscriminate heritage wandered from under rosemary shrubs and investigated her tires.

"Shoo!"

Impervious to commands, he dogged her steps toward the iron-and-glass doors. Pendant lights and chandeliers warmed the room beyond, but hours of operation or a logo were not apparent. She had twenty-four hours to get this article turned in, so it seemed wise to tug the handle and enter, begging forgiveness if this wasn't the right address. When she glanced away from dark wood floors and linen-draped tabletops, she noticed the mutt settled next to her sandals. Frightened to have admitted a stray, she bit her lip, wondering the risks of picking him up and setting him outside. If everything was bigger in Texas, did that include fleas?

"Toodie!"

She whipped around, seeing a tall girl enter the dining room, pushing a stroller.

"Don't mind him," the girl admonished as the mutt wagged his tail. "That's our dog. He comes and goes wherever he likes."

He smelled like bologna. "He belongs to you?"

"He follows Mom-ella around like she's a queen, even though she mostly hates him."

"Mom-ella?"

"That's what I call Lacy 'cause she's not my real mom."

The writer scribbled in her notebook. "Does that mean you're Luna Delgardo?"

Luna bowed, "At your service. I'm in charge of tying ribbons on the birthday presents today and saw you drive up. Are you the reporter?"

For the first time in her career, she handed her business card to a ten-year-old. "Yes, but I wasn't sure if I was at the right location."

Luna spread her arm wide, showing off the interior's modern aesthetic and a collection of string bracelets she'd made in art class. "We don't open until tomorrow."

Distracted by the aromas of onions, garlic, and chicken drifting from the kitchen, she checked her notes. "I thought it was tonight?"

"Today is Mom-ella's birthday. She insisted we never, ever open anything of importance on the same day as her birthday ever again. It was her only request."

"But you're wrapping presents?"

"The newest iPhone is Daddy's surprise. As is Aunt Kali's strawberry cake. Eva and I are giving her a spa day." She squinted toward the wide glass doors at the back. "Everyone is on the patio. Uncle Beau is testing the gas logs. You can go that way if you want to visit my aunts, uncles, and cousins. But avoid Charlie. He's a biter."

Her arm twitched with an uncomfortable muscle memory from first grade. "I didn't realize you had such a big family."

"My Granny Gloria says we have the best type of family because we chose each other. Have you met my sister? She's only a few months old. Her name is Eva. Please don't tell her she's not pretty. We're really surprised she's not beautiful like Aunt AJ's baby. But her baby has lots of curly red hair and has learned to walk and sticks her finger in her nose all the time, but she's so cute no one can tell her that it's wrong. We don't know what color Eva's hair is going to be because she's bald. And fat. Did you know babies can be fat?"

Exhausted from the monologue, the writer gazed into the stroller, seeing two blue eyes peek from behind a frilly blanket. "She's cute."

"You're saying that to be nice. Everyone does. But I love Eva best of all, and she'll always be special. Even if she's never, ever going to be beautiful."

Toodie stood on his hind legs, propping paws on the stroller, and peered over the edge. He yapped his greetings. The baby cooed in response. He happily panted, as if this were an ongoing conversation.

Luna petted the dog, moved the stroller, and motioned for the writer to follow. "I can show you around. Daddy is still in the kitchen with his staff, and Eva and I are not allowed to go there today because we have impressionable young minds." She lowered her voice. "Sometimes the cooks say bad words, but the food is always good."

Writing it word for word, she decided that would be her lead quote. Quickly, she glanced again to the back of the dining room, where wide sliding doors opened onto an expansive porch. A bar was built into a stone wall and tables, chairs, and lounge furniture created a cozy outdoor room. A handful of adults stood staring into a firepit, and she'd assume these were the aforementioned relatives.

"So, if I wanted to meet your father," she asked, looking in the direction of a see-through kitchen, where classic-rock radio almost drowned the sound of pots and pans clattering, "should I walk into the kitchen?"

Luna propped her hands on her hips. "Not yet. Kenny came to help train the new staff, so maybe you should talk to him. Or you could talk to our nanny, Mrs. Lin. She knows absolutely everything. Except how to find Kenny a wife. Are you married? Because Mrs. Lin would want to know."

The writer backed into a table, stunned by an interrogator in braces. "Are you talking about Ken Lin, head chef of Stella's in Austin?"

"You do know him. He's funny." Luna pushed Eva's stroller toward the wide door as the dog trotted behind. "Let's tell Mom-ella you're here. She likes to talk to journalists. She hired three new ones last month."

Jotting details about the décor, she followed the tween guide onto a patio that gave an unrestricted view of a sweeping vineyard and wild hilltops beyond. Beautiful people gathered around a firepit, laughing and enjoying each other's company. A breeze brought a whiff of soil and stone under her nose, and her shoulders suddenly relaxed. This was a space designed to linger.

Before they stepped away from the shade provided by the deep metal roof, a tall blonde turned, lifting an arm in welcome. The notes said Lacy Cavanaugh Delgardo was a former Miss Texas, but, wearing a maxi dress and her hair braided down her spine, she looked more like a person you'd want for a best friend.

"Mom-ella doesn't know about the presents, so don't say anything. Okay?"

She glanced at her hostess, a little envious of the Jonas Brothers T-shirt. "Our secret. But I'm embarrassed to admit, I was never told the name of this restaurant. I didn't see a sign out front and have to know before I interview the chef."

Luna grinned. "Why, it's Stella Luna's, of course."

Friends,

Thank you for spending your reading time with Lacy, Rudy, and the cast who danced through this story (including some familiar faces, if you've read my other Comfort novels.) If Rudy and Lacy's story gave you pleasure, I'd be honored if you left a review at wherever you purchase books. Readers trust other reader's opinions about these things.

For those wondering if there will be another book set in Comfort, the answer is—yes! *Comfort Zone* will debut in 2021. You didn't think I'd leave Anna Weber and her delightful daughters without a story to tell, did you? Wait until you meet the football star who upends their tidy world. He's a handful.

If you want to know Kali and Jake's love story, visit kimberlyfish.com and subscribe to my newsletter—their crazy little escapade is *Emeralds Mark The Spot,* the free e-book download that's a gift to all subscribers. Colette and Beau's story is the plot of *Comfort Plans,* while AJ and Luke meet, though pride almost shreds their potential in the second book, *Comfort Songs.* All my books are for sale through the website at www.kimberlyfish.com

While I'm working on the next novel, feel free to browse through the blog where I've randomly detailed elements from the writing process. For the *extra* curious, there are storyboards on Pinterest at Fish Tales, photos I post to Instagram at fish_writer, or chat with me on Facebook at Kimberly Fish, author. And, last but not least, I'm available by email at kimberly@kimberlyfish.com. Like Lacy Cavanaugh Delgardo, I'm plugged in and happy to stay in touch. All the best!

Kimberly

Recipes from Comfort Foods

Lavender Simple Syrup
(can be used over fruit, waffles, and ice cream, or as floral touch with your favorite beverages.)
1 c. water
3 Tabl. Lavender flowers (fresh or dried)
2 c. white granulated sugar
Bring water and lavender to boil in a saucepan. Reduce heat and stir in sugar until fully dissolved. Simmer for 15 minutes. Remove from the heat and allow to cool and steep for at least one hour. Strain out the lavender. Pour the lavender syrup into a bottle and keep in the refrigerator.

French Toast
3 tabl. Butter
4 eggs
1/3 c milk
1 teas. Vanilla
Dash of salt
Dash of cinnamon
8 slices of thick bread (day old is best)
Powdered sugar, jam, or syrup for topping

In a large sauté pan, melt butter on med/high heat. In a large bowl, whisk 4 eggs, milk, vanilla, add in dash of salt and cinnamon (to taste.) Soak each slice of bread in egg mixture until thoroughly coated on each side. Place in hot, melted butter and cook for 1-2 minutes on each side. Repeat until bread is drenched and cooked. Serve warm with a dusting of powdered sugar and top with jam of choice or syrup.

Steak Diane (courtesy of Guy Fieri)
1 qt. beef stock
Four 6-8oz filet mignons
1 teas salt
1 teas. Pepper
4 tabl. Butter
2 tabl. Extra-virgin olive oil
3 c. thinly slice cremini mushrooms
2 shallots, thinly sliced
4 cloves garlic, minced
½ dry red wine
1 tabl. Dijon mustard
1 tabl. Worcestershire sauce

Add beef stock to a sauce pan, simmer for an hour as it reduces to ½ cup. Sprinkle steaks on both sides with salt and pepper. In a large skillet or cast-iron pan, over medium heat, heat 2 tablespoons of butter and the olive oil. When the butter is melted, add the steaks. Brown the steaks on both sides, 3 minutes per side. Transfer the steaks to a plate and set aside, lightly covered with foil. Add mushrooms and shallots to the pan and cook for 2 minutes, stirring frequently. Add the garlic. When the garlic is lightly colored, wine, mustard, Worcestershire and the reduced beef stock. Simmer for 2-3 minutes. Return the steaks to the pan and finish cooking them to desired temperature, 2-4 minutes

depending on side of the filets. Add remaining butter to the pan.
To serve, place each steak on a plate and cover with a portion of the sauce.

Parmesan Fries (courtesy of Ree Drummond)
5 lbs. russet potatoes
Peanut or canola oil for frying
Salt, pepper and grated, shredded parmesan cheese

Peel and rinse potatoes, then cut them into sticks by cutting potato in 4 or 5 vertical pieces and then cutting each piece into sticks. Place them in a large bowl and cover with cold water. Allow them to soak, 2-3 hours, or overnight.
Drain off water, and lay potatoes on 2 baking sheets lined with paper towels. Blot with paper towels to dry them. Heat a few inches of oil in a heavy pot to 300 degrees F. In 3 or 4 batches, cook the potatoes until soft, 4-5 minutes per batch. They should not brown at this point. Remove each batch and drain on new/dry paper towels. Once all the potatoes have been fried at 300 degrees F, turn up the heat until the oil reaches 400 degree F. When the oil's hot, start frying potatoes in batches again, cooking until the fires are golden and crisp. Remove the potatoes from the oil and drain on new/dry paper towels. Sprinkle immediately with salt, pepper and shredded parmesan cheese.

Made in the USA
Columbia, SC
10 October 2020